# The Colour of the Times

# The Colour of the Times

## Margaret Shippen Arnold and the American Revolution

### A Novel of Treason

## Forrest Bachner

*The Colour of the Times: Margaret Shippen Arnold and the American Revolution—A Novel of Treason*, copyright © 2016 by Forrest Bachner. All rights reserved.

ISBN 978-0-9972897-0-1

*Published by*

Illume Writers & Artists
PO Box 86, Gilbertsville, NY 13776

Printed in the United States of America

Cover: Portrait of Margaret Shippen Arnold, Margaret (Peggy) Shippen Arnold and Child, circa 1783-1789, attributed to Daniel Gardner (1750-1805). Philadelphia History Museum at the Atwater Kent, Philadelphia.

Cover Design by Jane Evelynne Higgins

For David

*"I am sorry you did not get Arnold, for of all the Americans, he is the most enterprising and dangerous."*

Lord Germaine to General John Burgoyne, August 1776

*"...he (Sir Henry Clinton) can concur with you in almost any plan you can advise and in which you will cordially cooperate. Join the army, accept a Command, be Surprized, be cut off-- It is such as these he pledges himself shall be rewarded beyond your warmest Expectations. The Colour of the Times favours them and your Abilities and Firmness justify his hopes of Success."*

Mid-June, 1779, from a letter written to Benedict Arnold by Major John André for Sir Henry Clinton

*"There is seldom any simple truth in treason."*

Carl Van Doren

PROLOGUE

# 1804
## The Great House, Philadelphia, Pennsylvania

*M*y name is Edward Shippen. I am the fourth Edward Shippen, a law-yer, father of five, and member of a well-known and respected family. Since the arrival of my great-great grandfather in 1694, we Shippens have made our homes, prospered, and I believe contributed to the greatest city of my acquain-tance, Penn's masterpiece, Philadelphia. Until the last years preceding the war, we were loyal and happy residents living under the Proprietary Government of Penn-sylvania and, of course, under our sovereign, George III.

Throughout my youth and career, Philadelphia was a haven of prosperi-ty, growth, and tolerance. With thriving agricultural, commercial, and seafaring sectors, the city grew to be the second largest in the British Empire and our ex-ports were in demand from England to the Azores. But more than just numbers and prosperity, Philadelphia, from the time of its founding, was a forward-look-ing, well-intentioned city. Protestants, Jews and Catholics were not only accepted into this Quaker city, but by virtue of the Founder's vision, embraced. Charitable organizations sprang up to care for our poor and disabled, while two newspapers as well as Franklin's subscription library kept the public informed. And to add to all this, the Pennsylvania Hospital and medical school led the colonies in modern approaches to medicine.

As one would expect with such a marvel of a city, a natural aristocracy of educated and concerned citizens flourished before the revolution—people like Ben-jamin Chew, John Dickinson, John Penn, Thomas Wharton, Joseph Galloway and, re-linquishing modesty, I would like to say my father and myself. Of all these good and thoughtful people, none initially wanted to see the Declaration of Independence signed. For some, like members of the Society of Friends, the issue was religious. Independence meant a call to arms, a doctrinal impossibility. For others of us, the *matter was one of heritage. It wasn't that we couldn't see that North was wrong. The laws he supported were indeed punitive and broke the essence of entitlement under the British constitution. But we were sensible men who could see the situation for what it was: mediocre administrators attempting to improve finances. Should we, then, because of a remediable situation, have stepped so easily away from the power and logic of British law or the several centuries required to develop it? Should we then have stepped so easily away from our King? And my God, how people have rushed to forget the form democracy took here in Pennsylvania after the independence was declared. I swear to you, it was little more than formalized mob rule. Where the Founder exalted inclusion and open-mindedness, the new government, headed by a Supreme Executive Council, practiced exclusion and intolerance. When John Adams read our Pennsylvania constitution, he predicted that, within two years, we would be badgering Great Britain to be let back in.*

*It was with this influence that my youngest daughter, Margaret, whom we called Peggy, came to the country's notice in the spring of 1778 shortly before her eighteenth birthday. At that time, we in Philadelphia, at least those of us not in favor of independence, were feeling more secure than we had since the beginning of the conflict. Sir William Howe had brought his army to Philadelphia, forcing Congress, the new government of Pennsylvania, and many of our enemies from the city. It seemed that our problems were at an end. Certainly my daughter Peggy and her friends thought so. The flash of bright red regimentals suddenly filled our parlors, taverns, and greens, while the girls swirled between assemblies, dinners, and receptions. I was happy for Peggy, for after three years of war she was enjoying a glorious moment of youth. Not one of us in the family, not in our wildest imaginations, could have envisioned that soon she would attract the attention of the most heroic and infamous man of our times, Major General Benedict Arnold. And certainly not one of us could have envisioned her future prominence, much less the prominence of the events that would surround her. In the spring of '78, all I saw in Peggy was what stood before me, a young and beautiful girl.*

CHAPTER 1

May 18, 1778

*The Great House, Philadelphia*

"Miss Peggy, time to wake up! Cook's almost got the breakfast ready."

Peggy Shippen pulled the heavy damask bedspread up around her shoulders and turned toward the closed bedroom door. Outside the Great House, on Locust Street, the city was already bustling and noisy with heavy wagons and carriages rumbling by, dogs barking, the poor arriving nearby at the Friends Alms House, tradesmen knocking at back doors hoping to sell their services to the affluent of Society Hill, even Cook out back loudly bargaining with John Roberts, the family's long time miller. From downstairs she'd heard the usual family sounds: her mother calling her father to the parlor; her father's resigned reply; a growled, "Not now!" from brother Edward followed by doors slamming; silly giggling from Sally and Polly, her middle sisters; even a muttered oath from the new Irish maid, Melora, after a reprimand from Jenny, the Shippen's housekeeper. The only household voice she hadn't heard was that of her oldest sister, Betsey, who invariably spent these first hours of the day in her room writing to her fiancé, Neddy Burd, imprisoned on a British warship.

If this were any other day, her voice would have already joined those downstairs, either planning errands with her mother and sisters or with her father in his study. Since starting lessons on the copy book as a determined youngster and continuing through Greek, the classics, finance, and political thought, the study was understood by the family to be their special place. Most recently she and her father had been busy strategizing the sale of a gristmill just outside of town.

Today, however, since opening the shutters at dawn, she had sat propped against the headboard of her four-poster bed in the streaming sunshine pondering the mannequin in the center of the room and the enormity of the day ahead.

She parted the lawn draped around the bed. "Come in. I've been awake for hours."

Dark eyes under a muslin cap peered into the room. "Why, Miss, it's so late. Are you sick or something?"

"No, just..." Peggy hesitated. How to explain that she just needed this time alone? "Melora, don't tell anyone but I am so nervous. So, please, I'd like my tea in bed."

Melora, a small, wiry girl about Peggy's age, leaned against the door and shrugged. With ebony wisps of hair escaping onto her face and neck and black eyes to match, the Shippen girls often commented that she hardly looked or talked like a proper servant. Today was no different. "You might as well. Your father has a large group calling on him. Shall I fetch your mother?"

A large group calling on her father? Since the new Pennsylvania government had taken his position at the admiralty court, almost no one called on him. Peggy shook her head. "Just the tea."

As soon as Melora closed the door, Peggy returned her attention to the middle of the room and the ball gown and petticoat of the Polonaise sort fitted to the cloth statue there. In the soft air and brilliant sunshine of the early May morning, the white silk gown caught the light, gleaming, while a turban and sash made of filmy silver gauze shimmered slightly in the breeze. With long, tapered sleeves and the bodice plunging vee-like above a full, billowing skirt, the ball gown, her first real ball gown, was the most beautiful she had ever seen. And that afternoon she would stand under a flowered arch, wearing this same dress, as one of a very few ladies and gentlemen chosen to take part in the grandest party Philadelphia would ever see: her new friend Major John André's *Meschianza* in honor of Sir William Howe.

Throwing the covers aside, Peggy slipped from the bed and crossed the room to stand in front of the gilded, full-length mirror. Though there had been numerous opportunities to study herself since the British occupation the fall before, she was often still surprised at the girl looking back from the glass. The bow mouth, white-blond hair, and wide-set blue eyes, these she'd had since memory. But the rest? Mrs. Shippen had observed to their cousin Grace Galloway that her youngest had simply burst into bloom, and that was how Peggy felt. Seemingly overnight, gawky young girl features became rounded hips and breasts, dresses from Polly and Sally no longer were routinely handed down, and Edward's friends suddenly quit teasing her. For the Shippen daughter mostly known for her prowess with an account book, this transformation felt at times public and awkward, while at other times, thrilling.

Stepping behind the dress, she held the sleeves out to either side, trying to imagine herself in front of, as André had put it, anyone who was anyone in British-Philadelphia or New York. At least she would have her sisters, Sally and Polly, standing aside her, as well as her friends Becky Franks and Peggy Chew.

André was a genius, an organizational genius, that was what everyone was saying. That only André could have managed the planning and coordination of the medley, which *Meschianza* meant in Italian, of pageant and ball to be held at the Wharton estate on the river. Rumor had it that André and his officers emptied every shop in Philadelphia and New York for fabrics, ribbons, china, food, wine, and candles. She had also heard the artificial-flower arrangements would make a grizzled soldier cry, and that the fireworks would be grander than those for King George's coronation.

She glanced over at the gauze sash and turban. Because the first part of the affair was to be a mock joust set during the Crusades, André landed on the idea that the ladies' costumes should have something to do with harem attire: hence the head piece. She twisted her shoulder-length hair into a knot and studied her profile first from the right and then from the left. For the party, her hair would be piled very high in the latest style from Europe and topped with the turban, just as André sketched her when he was designing the ladies' *Meschianza* costumes. When she seemed surprised that he had chosen her as the model, his answer had astounded her: "Why wouldn't I choose the most beautiful woman in America?"

The clock in the front hall chimed the half hour. Nine-thirty. Where was Melora with her tea? The hairdresser would be here soon. The seamstress was also stopping by, but not until right before the dressing, just in case any tuck or seam needed an extra stitch. And Mother would be walking in any minute because Melora, unable to keep a thing from her mistress, would have mentioned that Peggy was feeling out of sorts. Yet, with the first clutches of nerves rising in her stomach, that was quickly becoming an honest statement.

Hearing a short knock at the door, she dropped the tangle of curls and called for Melora to come in. But it wasn't Melora who came through the door; it was a confused-looking Polly. "Peggy, get dressed. Father wants to see us immediately."

# CHAPTER 2

## The Same Day
### The Great House

*P*eggy, Polly, and Sally stood at the bottom of the stairs as five gentlemen, Quakers, emerged from the parlor followed by Judge Shippen, Mrs. Shippen, and Betsey. The mood was serious, talk subdued, and the visitors' plain black suits and stiff white collars particularly forbidding. Why on earth were they here, Peggy wondered. Turning to Polly and Sally, she saw the same bewilderment on their faces. And what could their father want to talk to them about at this hour of the morning? Surely they hadn't been called downstairs just to say hello. At last, after several polite inquiries concerning family and friends, the men took their hats and canes from Melora, said goodbye to Peggy's parents and Betsey, and without a word to the younger Shippen daughters, left the house.

"Mrs. Shippen, I'll take care of this," the Judge announced, closing the door to the Quaker delegation.

The girls' mother, sweet faced and brunette, a middle aged version of Betsey, nodded. "Yes, my dear. Glancing toward the younger girls with a teary nervousness, she pulled Betsey behind her. For her part, Betsey seemed relieved to be leaving.

"Polly, Sally, Peggy, I need to speak with you. Melora, please find Edward and have him join us." Without waiting for his daughters he turned and walked down the hall.

With shrugs and mystified glances at one another, the sisters followed their father into the study, Polly and Sally taking the small love seat to the left of the Judge's desk, Peggy, her usual chair on the right. All three girls sat bolt upright. Not from breeding but tension. They knew their father well and something had him very, very upset. For his part, the Judge seemed to spend an inordinate amount of time adjusting the hands on the wall clock before pulling out his chair and taking a seat himself. Always a dignified man, this morning was no different, white hair pulled back in a black ribbon, pale gray waistcoat, ivory stock and shirt. Poised in front of floor to ceiling blue, black and brown volumes, hands folded over his desk, he looked every bit the Middle Temple graduate that he was.

"The gentlemen who called this morning were considerate enough, let me rephrase, kind enough, to share with your mother and me the community's reaction to your plans for this evening." The Judge looked at each girl in turn as he spoke. "First, the community is revolted that female members of the Shippen family would appear publicly in clothing suggestive of a harem."

"But Father," Sally broke in, "they don't...look like that."

Polly ran a hand down her own dress. "They're just...gowns."

"Beautifully made gowns," Peggy added quickly, the gleaming silk fresh in her mind.

The Judge held up a hand for silence. "I don't care if you were to be dressed in full Quaker garb, this is what people believe. There is no way to change that."

"What...you want us not to wear the dresses?" Polly asked.

"Just look at them," Sally begged.

Frustration spread across the Judge's face. "Costumes are the least of the community's concern. This event is apparently seen as ostentatious in these difficult times and, most of all, a very partisan and public tribute to Sir William. A tribute, by the way, that none of you will be attending."

Peggy grabbed onto the edge of her father's desk. "But we are partisan. We want reconciliation. And I think there should be tribute. Because of Sir William and the others," she held a hand up, blocking a sudden glare, "we're safe and this horrid war is almost over."

"She's absolutely right," Edward announced from the doorway.

The Judge glanced from Peggy to Edward. At twenty, his son had looks, good manners, little will, and absolutely no judgment. He looked back at Peggy. He might have expected Edward to be blind to circumstances. But Peggy? "Our family is neutral. I took that oath and won't risk being seen as otherwise."

"But," Sally interrupted, "we've gone to dances, dinners, parties all year with the officers. We've entertained them in our house many times.

Why the concern now?"

"Yes, why now, Father?" Edward mocked, propping himself against the mantel.

"Because a Tuesday night dance for bored young people is one thing," the Judge said, trying to tamp down a rising anger at the fools his children seemed to have become, "an affair perceived as lauding Howe is quite another. If the British leave Philadelphia, the Supreme Executive Council will return from Lancaster to take over rule. *And,* our visitors caution, the Council would view our family's involvement in this *Meschianza* very dimly. Perhaps negate my oath." The Judge gazed at his son. "You know the Council is collecting names of those they consider to be British sympathizers. Do you want us to join that list, be exiled from Pennsylvania, stripped of our property, perhaps executed?"

Edward laughed. "That's hysteria and you know it. The British came from New York to occupy Philadelphia. Why in the world would they leave?"

The Judge pulled a map of the colonies from his top desk drawer and shoved it at Edward. "To win the war. They can't do that from here."

"Howe doesn't have to win," Edward countered. "The King's Commission has peace terms for Congress right now."

"France just recognized America, why would Congress take peace terms now?"

Listening to her father and brother banter, Peggy winced at the first rays of a migraine. Her first ball, the gown, fireworks, dances already promised...all suddenly slipping away. "I don't care what those old men said or what you say." She held her temple. "I'm old enough to make my own decisions. And I'm going."

Polly and Sally turned to Peggy in astonishment. No one, not even Edward, had ever spoken to their father like that. With one long sweep of the Judge's hand, books and papers flew from the desk. "Not one of you will leave the house today. Polly, send Melora for André and have him remove those costumes immediately." Taking a deep breath, the Judge stared at Peggy. "And you, who I did think capable of making your own decisions, you'll stay in your room until I say so."

Rising from his chair, the Judge pointed to the door. "Now go, all of you, and try very hard to understand that we are only as safe as our wits allow, and that includes keeping the good opinion of our neighbors such as those old men. Moreover," the Judge paused, his voice turning bitter, "we have no idea when this war will be over."

# CHAPTER 3

## May 21, 1778
### New Haven, Connecticut

Benedict Arnold looked out from the back of his proper-ty over the waterfront. The night was clear, the only sounds light waves breaking against the pilings. After a long carriage ride from the hospital in Albany, the numerous dignitaries waiting to welcome him home, the many speeches praising his heroism from Ticonderoga to Val-cour Island, and the rowdy demands of his sons, this quiet evening back in New Haven should have been comforting. But the quiet, rather than being a solace, only provided more space for his terrible anger.

It was true what his friend Comfort Sage had come to the hospital to tell him. His sister, Hannah, confirmed the news just after the reception. Despite a very public promise from Congress, his family had never received a penny of what he was owed. Not a penny in reimbursement for loaning his personal fortune to support the army. And not a penny of pay for the past three years as a General with the Continental forces blocking British expeditionary forces first in Canada, then with a makeshift Navy on Lake Champlain. *And* he'd been shot twice in the same leg: once in Quebec, the next while leading the American troops fighting Burgoyne at Saratoga to the first major American victory of the war. Instead, the Congress, already in possession of every document, account, and receipt he'd accumulated since the beginning of the war, now believed his situation required further review. This pronouncement from a group of self-serving, deceitful politi-cians who, for the most part, had never fought a day in their lives.

"I wondered where you were, Brother."

Arnold turned to see his sister walking toward him. As children they looked so much alike, tall, with gray eyes and jet-black hair, that people often took them for twins. Now, however, just three years his junior at thirty-three, Hannah had grown prim with sharp features, reminding him sadly of their mother in her later years.

"Where is everyone?" Arnold asked.

Hannah stopped several feet from the edge of the dock. For a child of a sea faring family, she was oddly afraid of water. "Your sons, I hope, are all asleep. They were up at dawn this morning waiting for you."

"And Major Franks?"

"Your aide is in his room as well. I'm not sure if he was tired or simply desperate to get away from the boys. Richard and Benedict insisted that the Major reenact the attack at Danbury when they shot the two horses out from under you. Poor Harry fell asleep on the floor in the parlor, where he is now."

Arnold could well imagine that. The little fellow had barely made it awake through dinner. "I always thought the boys worried more about the horses than their father."

"Oh, you know that's not true." She held out a hand. "Here, walk back with me to the house. In case Harry wakes up and needs me."

With one arm on a crutch and the other on his sister's shoulder, Arnold turned back along the walk toward his house. Hannah had done well in his absence. His property here, perhaps the finest estate in New Haven, was, if not in immaculate, in good condition. Stepping up the wide stairs to the front porch, he saw that Hannah, ever attentive to his needs, had already set out the port decanter on a low stool and poured two glasses. While she took a seat on the broad oak bench and gathered up her knitting, he leaned his crutch against the house and decided the stairs would be just as comfortable a seat as any other and easier to get to.

"Were you very disappointed, Brother?"

"Disappointed?"

Hannah smoothed the piece flat against her lap before beginning another row. "About the young woman in Boston, Miss Blois?"

Arnold wrenched the boot off his bad leg. "Though certainly gay and quite pretty, Miss Blois had parents who dictated her decisions, and," he tried to summon up a smile, "freckles across her nose. My next wife, I hope, will have neither. What about my sons? Were they terribly disappointed I had no new mother for them?"

The clacking of needles slowed. "I don't think so. I believe they, at least Benedict and Richard, still think of their own mama."

Arnold looked back through the broad windows into the parlor and dining room now dimly lit by flickering candelabra. After eight years of growing indifference to him and their three children, his wife, Margaret Mansfield Arnold, had finally become indifferent to life itself. He'd lost her at the age of thirty while leading the army in Canada. Hannah, a confirmed spinster, was left to manage his sons as well as his home. Yet now, because of Congress, he could be in danger of losing that as well. But he wouldn't.

"I'll be leaving soon, Hannah."

She lowered the knitting onto her lap. "What could take you away? You've just returned after all this time."

Arnold reached for the port. "I'm to meet with General Washington at Valley Forge. Possibly receive a new command."

"But your wound!" Hannah rolled the loose yarn about the ball, stuck the needles into it, and placed the entire bundle off to one side.

Arnold held the glass against his face; the thick, heavy scent alone was comforting. He wished that he, like Harry, could simply lie down on the floor and sleep. "I will recover; the surgeons have assured me."

"Benedict," she reached for the second glass, "I've never questioned your judgment. Not when you left me alone, at seventeen, to operate your store while you went trading. And not once in all this time that you have been at war serving our country with such distinction."

He didn't like her tone. "What are you asking, Hannah?"

"I'm asking," she fingered the fringe on her shawl, "how much more investment in the revolt are you willing to make? Particularly..." her voice dropped to a whisper, "with this most recent decision against you by the Congress?"

Somewhere in the distance a ship's bell clanged. Arnold closed his eyes. Between his leg and the clawing fury that had been building since Sage's visit, he was almost afraid to speak. "Hannah," he tried to keep his words even, paced. "General Washington has asked for me. He, unlike the Congress, has only the interests of his country at heart. I have no choice."

She leaned toward him, her hands now clenched about the glass. "Do you realize the hardship your absence is for me, and for your sons without their father?"

Arnold reached for the decanter. First, the Congress. Now, his sister.

"No, Hannah, I don't. A true hardship is having a father like ours who died a drunkard and a beggar. Who lost both standing and a considerable fortune and sent his family into disgrace." He drank quickly, recalling the elder Benedict Arnold's weight and his own humiliation as he tried to raise his leaden father from a chair, from the ground, from his own vomit. Yet that memory paled compared to the day he'd been taken from school and apprenticed to an apothecary.

"Benedict, you can't think I was comparing you to him."

The tears glistening on her cheeks surprised him. But this issue she would understand. "The Congress will never repay me if I leave the army. And I will be repaid. We, all of us, may have to tolerate difficulty, but, by God, we will never tolerate poverty again." Arnold stood and, taking the crutch, pulled Hannah up with him. "Now, I truly am extremely tired."

She reached for the candle but then, in a wholly uncharacteristic gesture, suddenly rested her head against his chest. "I will do better. Just sometimes, I feel so alone. Is that impossible for you to understand, surrounded as you always are by your men?"

Arnold sighed and smoothed her hair. Impossible to understand loneliness? He, who for a short time, had believed that a gay, laughing girl with a scattering of freckles across her nose would be standing here in his arms tonight?

"Shh, Hannah, it's very late."

CHAPTER 4

May 22, 1778

*The Great House*

"Peggy, you have to at least try and understand," Betsey said, her dear, sweet face completely scrunched up in earnestness. "The Quakers were honestly trying to help our family."

Several times since the *Meschianza*, Betsey, seated on the side of Peggy's bed, had attempted to help her sister over her mood. "It was like Father said. Many people didn't see it as just a grand party André dreamt up. They saw it as a monstrous humiliation to honor Howe so publicly, in an occupied American city, especially when there's so much desperation all around."

Peggy lay against the pillows. For two days after the scene in the study, the migraine raged, as always, a cruel, vicious thing. But for the past two days she had felt "somewhat better." Certainly better enough, Betsey noticed, for Becky Franks to visit and describe the *Meschianza* in minute detail. Also, better enough for Peggy to expand and elaborate upon her first-ever quarrel with her father. The only thing she didn't seem capable of was walking downstairs.

"I don't have to try and understand. If Father declares to be neutral, fine. If Neddy, Uncle William, Cousin Tench, are all for the independence, then that's fine too. But I didn't declare independence, and no piece of paper, however beautifully written, will do it for me. And since I want the British to win, why shouldn't I attend an event for General Howe?"

"This isn't about declarations, Peggy. This is about safety—"

"But we are safe! Sir William, thousands of soldiers..."

From outside the bell clanged. Betsey rose from the bed, walked over to the open window, and looked out. The afternoon's expected visitor had arrived.

"Rumors have been swirling since the *Meschianza*. Very serious rumors."

Peggy sat up against the pillows. "About what?"

Betsey walked from the window to a cupboard, pulled out a print dress of tiny roses, and handed it to Peggy. "Major André has come to call. Perhaps he can tell you."

Judge Shippen and André stood from their chairs as Peggy and Betsey entered the sea green and ivory parlor of the Great House. From what Peggy had heard in the hall, their conversation was amiable, unforced. André, as usual, scarcely looked the part of the conquering warrior. At twenty-seven, with soft expressive eyes, long lashes, and thick dark brown hair curling over the collar of his scarlet regimentals, he resembled more nearly the image of an artist or playwright, which in fact he was when time permitted. His pretty boyishness and soft features, however, completely belied his reputation as one of the brightest, best prepared, and most ambitious members of General Howe's staff. Even a Huguenot background had not impeded his career within the chary ranks of the British officer corps.

After a curtsey to André, Peggy turned uneasily to her father and was relieved when the Judge kissed her on the forehead and smiled. "Wonderful to see you looking so well, my dear. Please join us." Then without allowing an opportunity for unpleasantness, he waved the two girls toward the couch across from the chairs where he and André had been seated.

André spoke first. "It's so pleasant to see you both. Miss Shippen, I trust you're over that nasty headache."

Peggy glanced inadvertently at her father. "I think I am, just about—"

"Shippen!" The shriek from outside was hysterical, desperate. "Let me in! Now!"

"That's Cousin Grace," the Judge said, rushing from the room, almost colliding with Melora, also running to the front door. By the time Betsey, Peggy, and André reached the foyer, Grace Galloway was already inside and berating Melora for the time it had taken her to answer her call.

"Couldn't you hear me out there, girl? I'll have to speak with Mrs. Shippen about you."

"But I came as fast as I could. I was in the back of the house helping Cook." By way of proof, the maid held up her hands, spraying flour across the floor.

Betsey hurried over to the older woman and tried to put an arm around her. "Calm down, Cousin Grace. Whatever it is, I'm sure we can help. Melora, bring some ginger tea for Mrs. Galloway, or..." Betsey turned again to her cousin, "something cold?"

Grace pulled off her gloves and shoved them toward Betsey. "The tea, nothing cold."

Betsey sent Melora as pleading a look as she could muster. "We'll be in the parlor."

But Melora, wiping her hands, shook her head, "I'm so slow. Perhaps someone else should fetch it."

Seeing that Grace was getting ready to explode all over again, the older girl gave Peggy a little push down the hall. "Go. Take everyone to the parlor. Come, Melora, I'll help in the kitchen."

The maid, watching as the group retreated toward the parlor, answered in a voice loud enough for all to hear, "You're the only one who would, miss."


"That maid of yours...that's the kind who will be left to judge us." Grace, spilling out of the largest chair in the parlor, spoke directly to Judge Shippen. Even when Betsey arrived with the tea, she took absolutely no notice of anyone else in the room.

"Now, Grace, you're saying that General Howe directed the magistrates to make peace with the rebels. When? When did he do this?"

Grace held a handkerchief to her cheek. "Mr. Galloway said that Sir William met with a group of them last night. The very men he put in power over the city must now make peace with those they've been in charge of." The group in the parlor had grown to include Mrs. Shippen, Polly, and Sally back from their shopping. They sat silently while Grace told her story.

"And why did Howe advise the magistrates to make peace with the rebels now?" The Judge continued to speak slowly and softly, as if any wrong word could send her toppling over some inner precipice.

Grace looked at him in total exasperation. "Edward, he's telling them to make peace out of guilt! Sir William is returning to London, Clinton is in charge, and all of them are quitting the city. Going back to New York. The others, all our enemies, they'll be back. We'll have no one to protect us."

André put his hand to his collar. Since realizing who the woman speaking was and the kind of information her husband was privy to, he'd felt a slow sense of suffocation. Of course she would know what Howe and Clinton were about; her husband was one of Howe's closest advisors. André had heard that the man had a fabulously wealthy wife, but he had never connected the Shippen cousin Grace Galloway with Joseph Galloway's wife.

Slowly all the faces in the room turned to him, including Grace Galloway's. He saw recognition register there. "You're John André, one of Howe's favorites. What I'm saying is no news to you. Your *Meschianza*, that was his farewell, was it not?"

He watched dimly as Grace rose from the armchair, coming to stand in front of him, and grabbed onto his lapels as though he were the British army, navy, King, and Parliament all in one. She leaned so close that he had an insane idea that she might attack, even bite him, and was stupidly relieved when the bitter whining started again. "I hate you. I hate every one of you. You've only played at war all winter, and now you're leaving us for dead!"

Against the silence following Grace's accusations, André stood silent, hearing only the ticking of the great clock in the hall until Peggy, clutching onto her mother, begged, "Say it's not true, John. Please, God, say it's not true."

# CHAPTER 5

## June 6, 1778

*En route to Valley Forge*

Arnold looked out from the coach to the low hills, fields, and woods of the Pennsylvania countryside. Although it was June, the day had the look and feel of late April or early May: crisp air, soft dewy grasses glowing in the sunlight, a radiantly blue sky marked only by a few playful clouds, and the scent of lilac on a light breeze. On Major Franks' orders, the driver held the horses to a fast walk, taking no chances with ruts, fallen limbs, nor Arnold's leg, propped up on the seat facing him. In just moments, according to the outpost, Arnold and Franks should be at their destination, the Continental Army's headquarters at Valley Forge. The sentry, a very thin young man still in his teens, had been very clear that they were to stay on this road until they reached a fieldstone house where they would be given directions to their quarters.

"It certainly doesn't appear to be such a hard place," Franks said as the coach passed a stand of birches. "Yet they say two to three thousand dead, without a musket fired." David Salisbury Franks, urbane and patrician, was not only an aide but also a close confidante to Arnold. Though a relative of the loyalist Franks family of Philadelphia, he was staunchly patriot and, like Arnold, had helped finance the early American campaign in Canada.

Arnold, impatient to be done with the stuffy, cramped coach, reached for his jacket and sword. "Neglect killed those men, Major. The Commander in Chief wrote that for weeks after coming here the army lacked shelter, clothes, blankets, food, even straw to take up some of the damp underneath them. And all the while, farmers and merchants near here were sending their crops and goods to Philadelphia for Sir William's hard currency. I don't know how the General endured it."

Franks brushed a light layer of dust from his otherwise gleaming boots. The Major, it seemed to Arnold, was much calmer since the departure from his sons and Hannah.

"You respect the Commander in Chief a great deal, do you not, sir?"

Arnold paused to buckle his sword. "The best man I have ever met." He motioned out the window. "Look!"

To the right and left on the hills above the coach, rows of rough-hewn log huts sat side by side in clusters forming a line close to a mile and a half long—the outer line of defense. According to the sentry, the huts had been built with few supplies during a particularly severe winter and housed eleven thousand men. The sentry also mentioned that General Washington offered one hundred dollars to the man devising the best idea for roofs. To the far left, close to Valley Creek, blacksmith and wheelwright shops, rough corrals, and laundries formed still another cluster of buildings.

"I see the Commander in Chief chose well," Franks offered. "High ground, water, an easy ride to Howe."

"I agree," Arnold said, sliding on his jacket. "So tell me, am I presentable?"

Franks glanced over. "Certainly, sir. Why do you ask?"

Arnold eased his leg from the seat. "Not many soldiers travel by carriage, Major. General Washington, the men, they may doubt my worth."

The two men fell silent, listening as the coach passed a makeshift parade ground where troops marched and wheeled in neat even rows as three men stood off to one side barking out commands, one after the other, first in German, then French, and then in English. In another part of the field, men drilled in pairs with bayonets. Arnold sat back against the seat. "Good Lord, Franks, they look like real soldiers. And that one giving orders in German...that must be the von Steuben fellow I've heard about."

Franks hooked an arm through the window and studied the road ahead where more encampments rose up on the banks of the Valley Creek to the left before a small wooded area and a dip in the road leading to a broad clearing. A slight buzzing filled the air.

"Sir, you might want to look this way."

Arnold followed Franks' gaze. There, not one hundred yards in front of the coach, hundreds of men lined both sides of the road; some on horseback, some in wagons, some hanging from trees, but most standing three and four deep in the dusty, midday sun lounging against muskets, sticks, and one another. As the coach approached, the buzz grew louder.

Arnold raked his hair back off his forehead. "Stay on the road indeed."

Suddenly, with cries of "Arnold!" and "Arnold is here!" the men surged onto the road, some waving hats, others flourishing greenery and handkerchiefs, while still others ran alongside the coach window trying to clasp Arnold's hand as he leaned out waving back, shouting his greetings and thank you's for the welcome, and signaling to a good number of familiar, esteemed faces.

"I see no doubt about your worth, General," Franks yelled over the roar.

"Such men," Arnold laughed. "Can you believe it?"

The bedlam continued until an officer stepped into the road and held up a hand for quiet. Signaling Arnold's driver, he directed the coach to the front of a handsome two-story fieldstone house framed by huge oak trees in the back and a low split-rail fence in the front. The Schuylkill River glistened in the distance.

"General Arnold," the officer came around to address Arnold through the window, "Lieutenant Colonel Tilghman, at your command. His Excellency asks that you remain as you are. He will join you shortly."

Arnold looked out on the gathering before drawing on his gloves and straightening his sword. "Thank you, Colonel. However, I think not." He reached for the door.

But Tilghman, a man of medium height with narrow, determined eyes, stood firm.

"Please, General, recall whose request this is."

With a quick turn toward the house, the colonel came to attention while the men parted in waves to clear a corridor from the fieldstone house to the coach. Arnold watched as the front door to the house opened and the Commander in Chief and his lady emerged, General Washington as tall as he remembered, solemn and dignified, and Mrs. Washington, tiny, elf-like and with a hook nose, but smiling sweetly. When the couple reached the door of the carriage, Arnold thought he could see the barest flicker of amusement pass over Washington's face.

"Colonel Tilghman: you have your orders."

With the same quiet authority that kept Arnold in his carriage just moments earlier, Washington's aide wheeled back around to face the troops. "Gentlemen! General Arnold is come, an event as happy as our recent alliance with France. To properly welcome the General and ensure that General Howe in Philadelphia learns of his arrival, your Commander in Chief would have you give three very, very loud cheers!" Tilghman raised his sword into the air. "Now, after me!"

Against the deafening hurrahs repeated over and over again, Arnold bent toward Franks and whispered, "As you see, General Washington, the very best of men."

From his vantage point on the couch beside the tea service, Benedict Arnold decided that Kitty Alexander was going to be beautiful in about ten years. Her mother Lady Stirling probably had been beautiful, but that was the best one could say now. And as a duo, their recital just completed left much to be desired. Mrs. Knox, who had the previous year introduced him to Miss Blois, was in good and large form as always, and Miss Nancy Brown was pleasant, but there was no one lady present who caught his attention. He supposed that, among those gathered for the officers' evening's amusement, a sing, Mrs. Greene was what could best be termed the belle of the ball. Although an extremely handsome woman, gracious and accomplished, her primary asset was her knowledge of French language and French literature. The foreign officers hovered around her as a lone oasis of refinement. It was also rumored that she was completely devoted to her husband, General Nathanael Greene.

All in all, Arnold was surprised, actually disappointed, in his first night at headquarters. After the fervor of his entry to camp had died down, the Commander in Chief had allowed that "there was much good news to be shared but all in good time." Arnold and Franks could rest, see the grounds, and then join a small party for dinner and singing this evening. Tomorrow, bright and early, they would get down to business and discuss a position he hoped Arnold would consider.

Yet, despite the Commander in Chief's renowned love of wine and dancing, the dinner so far had been a brutally plain affair. Was this Mrs. Washington's influence on camp deportment? Arnold had also been surprised to find two veterans of Quebec seated at his table, Aaron Burr and Matthew Clarkson. Clarkson, blond and earnest was solid as a rock, and about as enjoyable as one for a dinner companion. On the other hand, Burr, a small, dark young man with a mind for ambition and intrigue, could be counted on for all the latest news and gossip. What one couldn't count on was the truthfulness of anything he said. Nevertheless, Arnold listened intently at dinner while his former comrade dropped background tidbits on almost everyone at Valley Forge. And when the singing commenced, Burr followed Arnold to this couch declaring he'd rather play "Ring Around the Rosey" than join in with that bunch of braying horses.

"Did you know that the Commander in Chief is not from the aristocratic family people think?" Burr asked edging closer to Arnold. "I've heard that his mother was a shrew, mean as well as illiterate, and our illustrious General Washington had to educate himself. It's said he got his manners from a Jesuit pamphlet."

Arnold studied the man beside him whose own father was a much admired teacher and minister. "Not all of us have had your filial good fortune."

Burr grinned. "That's true. But—"

"They should all be hung."

The provocative comment came from just behind the couch where Burr and Arnold were seated. The man talking was medium sized and wore a plain brown vest and coat. Even though his back was to the couch, Arnold was sure he hadn't seen him at dinner. He did know the other two men in the party: the Marquis de Lafayette and another of Washington's aides, Alexander Hamilton.

The speaker, clearly impassioned about his topic, continued. "Anyone who has given aid and comfort to the enemy deserves nothing less. Our committee already has the names of four hundred known sympathizers to be published and prosecuted. Sometimes I think people forget we're at war."

"But," Hamilton began, choosing his words carefully, "suppose a man is for the British and his wife is not, why would you not consider the two separate cases? Or a family declares itself neutral. Should we not give them that option?"

The man shook his head emphatically. "No! We've no time to sort out mixed loyalties. The laws of Pennsylvania are very clear. Those accused must surrender and be tried. If they don't surrender, they will forfeit all their property, and if caught, hung."

The man turned to put his tea cup down, staring directly into Arnold's face. No wonder the voice was familiar. It was Joseph Reed, Washington's secretary in the first years of the war. During the planning for the campaign to Canada, Reed had been a great help, was organized, a good correspondent, and hard working. But, whether in private conversations or meetings of the General's staff, the man's sheen of moral superiority shone much too brightly for Arnold. And why was he here now, talking of hanging anyone, anywhere?

"Why, Mr. Reed," Arnold bowed toward the Congressman, "It's been a very long time. We met in Cambridge when the army was headquartered there." Across the room, David Salisbury Franks launched into a rollicking farmer's tune.

Reed returned Arnold's bow. "Of course, General, and I, along with the country, owe you our thanks." Turning to Burr, Reed bowed again. "Good evening, Colonel Burr."

Burr nodded but didn't rise. "Hello, Congressman. I trust your family is well."

Reed's expression softened slightly. "They are, thank you. I hope that we shall all be reunited soon in Philadelphia."

Arnold had to speak over the music as most of the party had now joined Franks for the chorus. "I've only just arrived from Connecticut so I must apologize to you, Congressman. I was unaware you had joined that august group."

"You sound disdainful."

Arnold nodded. "I am disdainful of those who choose not to pay their debts."

Understanding flashed across Reed's face, "Ah, yes, your pay." Reed smiled, the kind of smile Arnold remembered from the Puritan ministers of his youth. "But, there are many of us who are sacrificing, sir."

Without taking his eyes off Reed, Arnold began tapping the crook of his cane slowly against his open palm.

Reed, his face a brilliant red, sighed deeply. "Forgive me, I spoke quite without thinking."

Arnold rose with Burr's assistance to face Reed. "I have found, Congressman, that politicians often speak without thinking. And if I choose to sacrifice for my person that is one thing, but for the Congress to decide to sacrifice for me and my family, that is quite another."

# CHAPTER 6

## The Next Day
### *Valley Forge*

A fly buzzed around Arnold's face as he strained to hear the history Tench Tilghman was providing for the officers and staff. It was clear that Washington's aide was leading up to the outline of the summer campaign, but he was taking his good time about getting there.

Getting out of bed that morning had been difficult, what with the long carriage trip the day before and the rather late evening. What he needed was a good day's rest and something heartier than the little piece of rabbit served as last night's dinner. At the least he needed some good strong coffee to battle Tilghman's monotone and the whispered commentary of the other officers.

"By all accounts the first half of the year has been remarkable for the United States," Tilghman announced. "Due to our alliance with France we can now expect infusions of men, money, and materiel. In addition, because of the alliance, the King's forces must now consider that they are not simply fighting a localized rebellion, but an enemy more like themselves with far-flung geographical interests and ambitions.

"We also expect the imminent departure of Sir William," Tilghman continued. "Rumors from Philadelphia indicate that he has been called by London to explain his decision not to join General Burgoyne in the north earlier this year."

At the mention of Burgoyne's name, a number of the officers nodded in Arnold's direction. "And, of course, we are not clear what Sir Henry's promotion to Commander in Chief will mean. We have heard that he is more interested in pursuing the Highland forts than General Howe."

Shooing the fly away, Arnold was suddenly struck by a delightful scent

26 FORREST BACHNER

from just outside the window. Looking out into the yard, he spotted bright yellow flowers. Lemon lilies, his mother had called them. They bloomed in early summer, just about the time he and his father generally began their trading trips south to the Caribbean. His mother would sometimes quote the verse from the Bible when the buds would open and the scent was released. "Remember the lilies of the field, they neither..."

"The news is not all good, however." Arnold returned from his memories as Tilghman picked up a third sheet of notes. "Of the 2,600 Americans captured during the Battle for Fort Washington, only 800 have survived imprisonment in New York." Arnold already knew this from Sage Comfort. The men had been stuffed into a building named the Sugar House, inadequately fed, unclothed, and provided with no protection against the elements or disease. Tilghman shook his head. "The news is bound to lead to public outrage."

As if to prove the prediction, several of the officers jumped to their feet, cursing the terrible news. Tilghman motioned for them to sit down and then looked in the direction of Washington, who was listening from a chair in the front row.

"The General will now discuss tentative details of the summer campaign. General."

As Washington stood, all grumbling, fidgeting, coughing, and whispering immediately ceased. In fact, the only sound in the room came from the buzzing of the tenacious little fly who didn't seem to understand that the next phase of the war was about to begin.


Washington walked slowly to the front of the room. In contrast to the previous night he appeared solemn, pensive. "Thank you, Tench," Washington began with a nod to Tilghman. "I would like to add that in all likelihood the French would never have joined us had we not experienced the great victory at Saratoga last fall." Washington paused and Arnold could feel the heat rising about him, eyes turning his way. The quiet, steady voice continued. "We are all grateful for the valiant efforts of those who fought there and certainly to General Arnold who joins us today." Washington paused again as a glimmer of a smile crossed his face. Freed by the gesture, the men broke into wild applause while Arnold, embarrassed, nodded quickly and remained seated.

Once the commotion calmed down, any suggestion of levity left Washington's face. Picking up a baton, he pointed to the map that Hamilton was holding. "As Tench said, we've heard that the British troops in Philadelphia may be returning to New York. Our information is that should the evacuation occur, it will be carried out both by sea and overland.

"Therefore, our immediate plans for the army are as follows: If Howe or Clinton leaves the city we will attempt to engage him as opportunities occur. Philadelphia itself, however, presents a challenge for several reasons. First, we presume that should the British leave, the Congress as well as the Executive Council of Pennsylvania will return as will, very likely, many others of those who fled the occupation. All these groups must be protected.

"We have also been told that the British would be unable to transport numerous articles that our army could use, and we would like to avail ourselves of those supplies as soon as possible.

"Finally, we are aware that there is a sizeable population of Quakers and others who are generally believed to be at least neutral in the city. These citizens could be in considerable danger if the British are no longer there to offer protection." The Commander in Chief looked directly at Reed as he described the situation in Philadelphia. Arnold noted that Reed looked right back. Washington continued, "Therefore, I intend to establish a new command to oversee our interests in Philadelphia and to prevent unnecessary bloodshed in the capital from vengeful elements should the evacuation occur."

Washington paused again before shifting his attention in Arnold's direction. "And I would be deeply indebted to General Arnold if he would consider accepting responsibility for this command and serve as the military governor of Philadelphia."


The midday meal was finished. It was now the hot, quiet time of day at camp. Most men were either in their tents or their residences napping while the remainders used the time to perform necessary little chores, write letters, or pursue various amusements. Arnold, too provoked to consider resting, sat on the grass with Franks watching a game of bowls being played by several of the officers and the Commander in Chief.

"Sir, regarding the General's proposal," Franks began casually, "you should be honored."

"Honored with a peacekeeping post, Franks? You surprise me. Or do you agree I'm so badly impaired as to need this makeshift work?"

Franks pulled at a blade of grass trying to decide exactly how to put his case. Ever since the morning's meeting, the General had done nothing but rant against the post, said it would be "akin to arriving late to a grand party, then forced to stay in the empty ballroom."

"Sir—" Franks began again.

"Go on," Arnold interrupted, gazing absently out onto the playing field. "I have to respond to Washington sometime in the near future."

"All right, I'll be plain. You aren't ready to sit a horse for days on end and follow the British about the countryside. Surely you agree with that much." Franks waited. Nothing. "And if General Washington were to offer you a staff position at headquarters, you'd be consigned to hours of preparing orders, letter writing, requisitioning, and in all probability begging from Congress. I don't believe that would suit you either, sir."

At this Arnold loosened his collar and stock.

"And sir, I see some very positive aspects to this appointment should it actually occur. Your sister and sons could easily come and live with you. The military governor of Philadelphia should, I would think, be well housed and provisioned."

Remembering the tiny bit of dinner from the night before, Arnold nodded slightly.

"Also, from what the General said, there would be a true need for a military presence in the city, to maintain order, to act as a liaison in the capital, but also to ensure that British supplies left in the city are routed properly to our army, who are so desperately in need. And if there are among these British goods, items that are not required by the army, then perhaps there are some opportunities to be had." Franks paused to let this last piece of information have its impact.

Arnold nodded. "Of course, with the British going back to New York, the lines will close, prices for British merchandise will skyrocket. And we would be in control of it all."

"Are you gentlemen discussing the capital?" Arnold and Franks looked up, startled, to see Aaron Burr standing above them. "Did you know I lived there for quite some time?"

Of the two, Arnold gathered his wits first. "No, no I didn't. I haven't been there since '74."

Burr took a seat on the grass and wiped his face with a handkerchief. "I'm wondering about a family in Philadelphia I resided with for some time, the Shippens. They, at least the part of the family I was intimate with, remained loyal to the King, I believe. They're cousins of Tench Tilghman and even closer to Dr. William Shippen, our chief surgeon."

"Yes," Arnold agreed, "I attended meetings in their home during the first Congress."

"I know them too," Franks said. "They've been in business with my cousin there, also David Franks." Franks turned to Arnold. "He's a merchant of considerable influence, although not of our political sentiment, I'm afraid. His daughter, Becky, is close with one of the four Shippen daughters, the youngest—a beauty I've been told."

Burr suddenly sat up and pointed to the far end of the field. "Look, a fascinating scenario."

Franks turned to watch the game while Burr explained. "You see, Clarkson has his ball positioned just alongside His Excellency's. Does he play full out or does he let His Excellency win?" The small man inspected the field like an observer at a chess tournament.

Franks, for the sake of social convention, was just about to offer his solution when Clarkson hit a nice shot which hooked just off to the right. Exultant, Washington took position and whacked his ball cleanly at the jack to win the game.

"What a diplomat!" Burr exclaimed, jumping up from his seat. "We should have sent him to Paris. I must congratulate the General."

Watching Burr run down the field, Franks was struck with the peculiarity of the man. "Such a character. What did you think Clarkson should have done?"

Arnold, completely taken over by the opportunity of a city filled with disowned merchandise, plentiful food, comfortable lodging, and young beauties, was very far away from the game before them as well as Valley Forge.

"Sir, I was asking you, Colonel Burr's question. Should Clarkson have watched how he played against the General, or just gone full out to win?"

Arnold's answer was curt. "Just decide what you want, Major. That determines the rest."

# CHAPTER 7

June 10, 1778

*The Great House*

*H*olding onto the street lamp for support, Peggy stood on tiptoe and waved one last time to John André as he cut through the dust and carriage traffic from Locust onto Fourth. What a good friend. In the midst of all his duties for the evacuation he'd stopped to say goodbye and give her family the latest news. While she'd initially been furious with him for concealing the real reason for the *Meschianza* and the planned British departure, he'd laid out his case in a word. Orders. Sir Henry Clinton simply wanted to keep the army's plans a secret for as long as possible. Also, there had been the bare hope that the peace terms from the King might bring the entire war to an end. Had been. That was André's bleak message today. Picking up her skirts, she raced up the broad steps back into the Great House, the massive oak door slamming behind her. Melora, with dust rag in hand, stood to one side in the foyer.

"My father, Melora, where is he?

"Out back, miss. Been there all afternoon."

She should have known. If the Judge wasn't in his study then he could usually be counted on to be in the garden, even more so now since the beginning of the war and his enforced time at home. Slipping down the hall and past Cook and Jenny in the kitchen carving lamb and potatoes, Peggy let herself out the back door and into the delicate scent of mock orange and the very large garden at the rear of the house. Actually not so much a garden as a complex of gravel paths winding among stands of fruit trees, boxwood hedges, rose beds, trellised wisteria, fenced-in kitchen and strawberry plots, and a wilderness park at the back of the estate. A serene landscape, ordered, calming, and completely at odds with the chaotic picture André had just painted for her of most of Philadelphia. She shaded her eyes, then spotted her father in the herb garden weeding.

"Father!"

The Judge looked up and motioned her over. "You've come to help?"

At another time Peggy would have appreciated the sarcasm. "Major André just left. He said the King authorized the Carlisle Commission to offer everything, and Congress said no." She ticked the concessions off on her fingers, "No military housed in North America without Congressional approval, every freedom for trade, America's debt discharged, a seat in Parliament. Everything anyone ever said they wanted...except independence."

The Judge leaned heavily against his spade. "So the war will go on."

"Exactly. John says hundreds, thousands, are trying to get passage out of the city on British transports. And those not going out on the river are stealing carts, wagons, anything to get out before the evacuation and the Congress and the Council return."

To her surprise the Judge bent to pull an errant calendula from the comfrey.

"So we have to hurry. Find transportation. Pack."

"No, Peggy."

"No, what?"

"We're staying." With terrifying calmness her father began a trough between the parsley and sage, prying soft green leaves from darker lacy ones. "Philadelphia is our home. If we leave we'll be marked as traitors and lose everything to the new government of Pennsylvania. Everything my family has worked generations for. And that would be insupportable. Moreover, we would have nothing to support us in exile. Nothing."

She felt stunned. "But the proclamations? So many people against us."

The Judge hesitated, his eyes sweeping over the back of the house, the layers of greens rippling over the grounds, and finally at Peggy. "There is risk, I admit it. But my neutrality is a matter of record. I've signed all the oaths. Also I believe we will be treated fairly out of respect for my father's and grandfather's service to the city."

Listening to her father, Peggy was struck by the fact that only one week earlier she had lashed out at him in a way she could never have imagined, over attending a ball. How absolutely absurd. Now everything her father had warned of was coming true. And, yet, the family would be staying in Philadelphia.

From the kitchen door, Melora rang the bell for lunch.

"But what if we're not treated fairly? Or your oaths *are* challenged? What would we do?"

The Judge propped his shovel against the fence, then put his arm around his youngest's shoulders. "We would have to find our way. Now come, the others will be waiting."

CHAPTER 8

June 12, 1778

*High Street, Philadelphia*

Walking down High Street, John André tried to control his impatience. With precious time to spare from the evacuation, the invitation from David Franks, Rebecca's father and his good friend Oliver Delancey's uncle, could not be coming at a worse time. Yet declining a meal with the foremost contractor for the British army in the colonies was clearly not an option.

Crossing from High Street onto Front, the city's houses, offices, stores, stands, and spires gave way to wharves and pilings and the open panorama of Philadelphia's harbor, glistening blue and filled with the sails of the Royal Navy. In contrast to many of the boarded and ravaged sections of the city, the wharf businesses—carpenters, coopers, sail and block makers—were lively and bustling. The needs of a navy would always be served, André noted, but especially in these hectic days with the fleet preparing to leave and, as he'd described to Peggy Shippen, somehow accommodate the thousands of Philadelphians clamoring for passage to New York.

The fishy smells of the wharves mixed with the salty wind as André turned into the alley where Mrs. Miller's was located. Spying his host at a corner table, his curiosity was more piqued more than ever. "Mr. Franks, hello."

"Major, it's good of you to see me today." David Franks, dressed in immaculate charcoal gray linen, stood and bowed. The suit, as beautifully cut as any André had ever seen, spoke, like everything about the man, of elegance and wealth. "While the atmosphere here is plain, the food is very, very good. Also an excellent place for a quiet talk."

And that was the point of all this, André realized, pulling out a chair. A quiet, clandestine talk.

"I haven't seen you in some time, sir."

"How could you," Franks smiled, "with your return to New York to attend to, and the *Meschianza* for Sir William before that."

André shook his head. "I hope he was pleased."

"Yes, Sir William," Franks repeated as he withdrew a pipe from his coat pocket. Once before over a pipe, Franks had described his grandfather's and father's travels from Germany, first to London and then to New York, and how he had continued this tradition by moving to Philadelphia as a young man to join an uncle, Nathan Levy, in business. This same, much beloved uncle, Franks continued, had bound the tiny Jewish community to the city forever by purchasing land for a cemetery.

Over a second pipe, Franks described his first acquisitions, stores and ships, the first cautious forays into Philadelphia society through the Library and the Mt. Regale Fishing Companies and, ultimately, through his own marriage to a stalwart member of Christ Church. A marriage that was barely noticed in the wake of his sister Phila's elopement with Oliver DeLancey's father and their mother's threat to sit the traditional days of mourning. Then at the very end of the evening he mentioned, without a shred of irony, how he had joined other leading members of the Philadelphia business community in signing the Articles of Nonimportation against England.

"It is about Sir William that I asked to see you."

André looked up in surprise.

"For some twenty years I've served as the American agent for the firm in London contracted to provide for the British army here in the colonies. More recently, by direction of the Congress, I also, and to a much smaller extent, provide for certain segments of the Continental Army."

"Yes sir, I know that."

"Many people form the networks that make this work possible."

"I can understand that, but—"

"But what does it have to do with you?" Franks asked softly.

André nodded.

Franks sat back in his chair as the serving girl placed two steaming bowls on the table between them. "From what I gather you are a man who can get things done, you have connections."

"You flatter me," André answered quickly.

"I see I must cut through this. I'm in quite a bad way, Major."

André studied Franks; the man looked to be the picture of equanimity. "Why is that, sir?"

Franks looked about the tiny room. "Because I've had to pay suppliers from my own pocket since your loss at Saratoga. The firm's headquarters' contact says the war was never expected to last this long. The upshot is that our bills are not being honored, and I'm owed a great deal of money."

André hesitated, trying to see what Becky's father was asking of him. "But, sir, I have no influence in London. What can I do?"

Franks put another match to his pipe, another moment to arrange his thoughts. "I've been advised to approach your commanders here and I've tried. But to no avail. Oliver mentioned that your family is involved in commerce, first in France and now in London. I thought perhaps you could comprehend my dilemma. Speak to those in New York when you return."

André understood immediately. Most of the officer corps and certainly those at the top, like Howe, Clinton, and Cornwallis, had no notion of how hard cash moved the world. Titles and inheritances precluded that necessity. Franks needed an advocate, someone who could explain the urgency associated with accounts due. Someone like himself...from trade.

"And you trust your advisors in London?"

"My advisors are my brothers Moses and Naphtali. They stand to lose a great deal also."

"Then I'm to understand," André struggled for words, "that there is an immediacy about your situation."

Franks put down his pipe and clasped his hands over the exquisite gray linen. "Tactful words, Captain. What you should understand is that I could be ruined within months. I trust you won't share this with my daughter or nephew."

CHAPTER 9

June 15, 1778

*The Great House, Philadelphia*

*P*eggy lay in her bed, terrified. Someone, or was it some people, were pounding furiously at the front door. Or were they trying to break in? She glanced through the open windows she'd forgotten to close the night before when the heat had become overwhelming in the shut up, stuffy room. Windows her father specifically forbid all the members of the family to open, fearing rocks, musket balls, or whatever instruments a mob might care to use.

Drawing the sheet up over her, she frantically looked about the room for a weapon. Chair, mirror, bed, bedside table...she grabbed the candle stick. Then her eyes fell on the chest. She could block the door with the chest. But wait...she tried to shake off the fretful, half sleep from minutes earlier...when André came to say goodbye he said the British weren't leaving for at least a week or ten days. Trouble, if it came, wouldn't start 'til after that. A door opened. She heard her father's urgent command from the hall, "All of you, stay in your rooms. I'll see to this."

Peggy closed her eyes and tried to remember the words to the General Confession, but found herself instead offering up a rare prayer for help. If not for this day, then for the next, and the day after that, and the day after that when Congress, the Council, and all the thousands of others who fled the city in fear of the British occupation would return. Thousands who might feel justified in taking revenge against British sympathizers of any degree, like the Edward Shippen family. Little wonder friends, acquaintances, and cousins like Grace Galloway's husband and daughter were leaving for New York with Howe. Most felt in mortal danger.

That afternoon, walking home from a shopping trip to Franks' store, she noticed the destruction caused by the occupation as though she had never seen it before. Entire neighborhoods lay black and charred, government buildings gutted, shops vandalized, cemeteries desecrated, and private homes looted and abused by companies of soldiers quartered within. Soldiers, according to news Jenny gleaned at the market, who often shoveled their waste into cellars through holes cut in floors or, when cellars overflowed, into the street. There was even a rumor that the family boxes in several churches had been turned into stalls for the officers' horses. By comparison the area close to her own home was relatively undamaged; the area where so many loyalists lived. Taking a deep breath, she vowed, if she lived through the night, to hide a knife somewhere in the room.

The pounding began again. She heard the door open and the low tones of her father speaking to whoever was there. But then, almost immediately, the conversation ended, the big oak front door slammed shut, and footsteps retreated toward the street. Wide awake now, Peggy slipped out of bed and into the hallway overlooking the foyer. Mrs. Shippen, Edward, Betsey, Sally, and Polly poured out of their rooms to join her.

"Edward," Mrs. Shippen said gripping the banister, "what is it? What's happened?"

Judge Shippen, standing at the bottom of the steps, looked up at his family, and for the first time in days, genuinely smiled.

"Betsey, a message from Neddy! He's been exchanged!"

His eldest daughter stared at him blankly.

"Betsey!" her father called again, waving a piece of paper furiously. "Neddy's coming home!"

# CHAPTER 10

## *Judge Shippen*

*O*n June 18, eight months and twenty-two days after having entered the city, the British occupying forces under the command of Sir Henry Clinton left Philadelphia to return to British headquarters in New York City. Fearing for their lives, five thousand of our citizens also left the city on the three-hundred-vessel British fleet, along with the sick and supplies. The ten thousand troops traveling overland marched with a cavalcade of fifteen hundred wagons that stretched for twelve miles. Howe's grand occupation had accomplished nothing except the destruction of large parts of the city and his own career.

The failure of the exercise to bring the war to an end was odd to many of the participants. The country should have been humbled by the loss of its capital. In fact, traditional European warfare had it that if a capital was taken, then, on a de facto basis, so was the country. But this was not Europe, and Philadelphia was not the capital so much as the city where Congress happened to be when war broke out. There was no particular advantage in headquartering the army or the Congress in one place or another, and the colonials were quite willing to move them about as necessity dictated. As one British observer noted, the strategy from the American side seemed more appropriate for a shell game than for a war.

But I can tell you, as I saw the troops leaving the city, I had no idea whether my decision to keep the family in Philadelphia would be a prudent one. Or, our ruin.

CHAPTER II

June 19, 1778

*Locust Street, Philadelphia*

*T*he heat. The skin under her arms and at her waist stung as the
sweat caught in the tight places of her dress. Squirming to relieve
the irritation, Melora suddenly looked around realizing how foolish she
must appear, wriggling like one with the fits. But there was no one about.
Few people from this part of town were out today. She pushed her hair
back up under the bonnet and, taking a handkerchief from underneath her
sleeve, dabbed at the back of her neck. Glad as she was to be out of the
house, this was a high price for an hour or two of freedom. Mother of God,
she'd never known heat like this in Dunquin.

In her mind's eye, she could see the dark little hut in Ireland with everyone and everything a little gray from the peat smoke. One step outside,
though, and you'd be in a good breeze from the ocean. The village sat directly on the water at the head of the Dingle Peninsula. It was the most
beautiful spot on earth, she thought, with its soft, velvety green peaks and
valleys. The skeligs stood just off shore and the Blasket Islands loomed in
the distance beyond. As children, she and her brothers and sisters roamed
the peninsula from Sleighhead at the outermost point to the ancient burial
mounds back on the hills. However, neither its beauty nor its location at the
foot of holy Mt. Brendan could put enough food on the table of a Dunquin
household. Which was why her mother had arranged passage for herself
and her brother Patrick, as the two eldest, to Cork where they could board
a ship bound for America. "Leave," her mother had said. "Leave while you
can." And they did leave, to endure ten weeks stuffed into two-by-six-feet
bedsteads amidst vomit, dysentery, rot mouth, black water, and food so
infested she still shuddered at the memory. Upon docking in Philadelphia,

she and Patrick knelt and gave thanks for their lives, little knowing it was to be their last time together. Almost immediately, buyers looking to purchase servants came on board examining the newly arrived cargo like they were sheep. As the captain led these people about, pointing at this family here or that lad or lass there, the price he must be reimbursed for the wretched crossing was repeated over and over.

Patrick had been taken almost at once by a wagon builder somewhere in the west. For herself, she felt lucky to have caught the attention of Judge Shippen and Cook. All in all, the arrangement was not a bad one. For five years the family would have her labor, and she in turn would be taught housewifery, reading, writing, and how to figure accounts. She would also be sheltered, clothed, and fed, no small assurances for a child of Dunquin as, even now, two years away from home, she could still remember the hunger.

But want was not a problem here, not for the Shippen household in any event. Even on such an ordinary day as today, a special trip out to the market was deemed necessary just for some spices and fruits. The Master advised that she should look sharp and keep her wits about her. And yes, to please stop by his study on her return. She understood. He, all of the family, wanted to know what was going on in the city. So here she was, in this heat, with the shopping basket on her arm.

Stuffing the handkerchief back under her wrist band, Melora turned onto Third Street and walked in front of the stately red brick town houses. These were grand houses. All the people of her village could probably live in two of them happily. The mayor of Philadelphia, Samuel Powell, resided on this block, as did the simpering Chew girl, another Peggy. How these people used the same name over and over, Peggy, Betsey, Becky, Nancy. Her mother would laugh at that. All these little girls! She thought of them that way, they who did nothing all day but drink tea, take little walks and rides, and look down on others they had no right to. The grand houses were all shut up today, however, with their inhabitants wondering what this day would bring, the first day without Howe and Clinton to shield them.

Melora stopped directly in front of Mayor Powell's house. During the occupation the mayor and his family had been forced to live in a back wing while the British took over the rest of the house. She couldn't stop herself from laughing at the thought. It wasn't that she wished the British a comfort in this world, but she didn't mind seeing some of the proud ones of the city taken down a bit. Jenny, the other girl in the house, had explained to her how things had been before the independence, how such a few people in Pennsylvania, like the Shippens and their friends, had so much and kept all the good jobs in the colony for themselves and their children. No wonder they feared the new government; they might have to do an honest day's work like the rest of the world. Stirred by righteous indignation, Melora wiped the sweat once again from her face and neck and continued up Third.

The quiet of the Shippen's neighborhood gave way to a holiday atmosphere by the time Melora reached the great covered stalls at the intersection of Second and High. Crowds of people lined the street: hundreds, thousands, laughing, some singing, some waving the new flag of the United States. This was not the angry mob she'd heard the Master anticipating. No, these people were joyous, giddy. The mood reminded her of a sunny day in Dunquin after a long spell of the gray, soft misty weather, when people would find ways to stay out all day, whether they had good reason to or not.

Experiencing an unfamiliar sense of abandon, Melora pushed her small frame into the crowd to see for herself what was causing these masses to gather. Arms, backs, soldiers, mothers with children, all blocked her way as she wormed through the mass of bodies. Closer to the street, the gaiety turned to a frenzied exhilaration, the cheering, clapping, and whistling reaching deafening levels. As her abandon slid into a fear of being trampled, Melora gave a final push through the crowd only to trip and land on her hands and knees. Shaken, the breath knocked out of her, she looked up in confusion. Horsemen were proceeding down Second Street, not twenty feet away from her, riding in formation.

Suddenly, large hands grabbed her waist from behind, pulling her up and back from the path of the horses. Astonished, Melora turned to see the owner of the hands but saw only a linen shirt and brass buttons. "Are you all right?" a voice with the barest trace of home floated down to her. Melora looked straight up and saw ruddy skin, dark red hair, smiling eyes, and genuine concern in the face of the very tall man who had just saved her from continued embarrassment, if not injury. Shouting to make herself heard, Melora tried to answer. "I am, thank you. I wanted to see what was happening." Then, standing as high on her toes as possible, she asked,

"Why are they cheering?"

The tall man put one hand on her shoulder as he leaned down to speak directly into her ear. "It's General Arnold; he's come to guard the city. The Commander in Chief..." But at that moment the horsemen passed in front of them to the renewed cheers of the people watching and she couldn't hear him. Acknowledging that fact through gestures and shrugs, her new acquaintance turned to watch the parade.

Melora found out later that the soldiers she'd looked up to see that day were members of the Philadelphia Light Horse enjoying a triumphant return to their city. Massachusetts Continentals assigned to the Philadelphia garrison were next in line, followed by a grand coach with a dark man peering from the windows.

Almost collectively the onlookers craned their necks, stretched, and leaned in an attempt to see the man designated as the city's protector. The crowd's ability to get a good look was precluded, however, by the quick clip of the procession and the mostly drawn red velvet curtains. Surprisingly, it seemed to Melora that the crowds quieted as the coach with its famous cargo passed, although she didn't inform the Master or any of the family of that when they quizzed her about the events of the day. Later, as she thought more about it, she was not sure if the change in mood was out of respect for the man himself or from surprise at the level of comfort in which he traveled.

With the procession at an end, the mass of people began to break into smaller clusters or drift away toward the market. Yet the tall man who had pulled her from the street still stood not a foot away. What could she say? She didn't want him to just leave. "I want to thank you again," she stammered nervously. The man smiled slowly. "And may I ask who is thanking me?" he asked finally, extending a rough sunburned hand.

Shyly, Melora held out her own hand worrying whether this was right. She'd only seen men and women curtsy and bow to one another. "I'm Miss McBride, Melora McBride."

Taking her hand in both of his, he looked around at the throngs of people and pointed to her basket. "Well, Miss McBride," he began, with the emphasis on the "miss," "you came here to buy, didn't you?" Melora nodded. "Then perhaps I could walk with you a bit in case you find yourself on the street again." And before she knew it they were headed toward the stalls, her basket in one hand, the crook of his arm in the other.

That evening, as she recalled the afternoon for the hundredth time, she regretted that the curtains were closed on the General's carriage. Jared had spent a good deal of time speaking about the General. Jared said that after General Washington, General Arnold was the greatest man in the country and that he and most every soldier in the army would follow him to hell and back, twice if he asked. And he should know, because Jared had served under Arnold both in Canada and New York and been selected by the General himself to serve on his staff here in the city. He was actually on duty there at the parade, in case any kind of trouble broke out. Thinking of the parade, Melora remembered the weight of his hand on her shoulder. Jared, he introduced himself. Jared Donovan. A strong name, a beautiful name. A name her mother would like.

# CHAPTER 12

## The Same Day

*The Indian Queen, Fourth Street, Philadelphia*

"This will not do," Arnold said loudly to no one but himself. The room couldn't have been more than eight feet by six feet and its lone piece of furniture was a bed; no table, no chest, no wash basin and no room nearby for even one servant. Not only was it small and prison-plain, but it smelled. Philadelphia's stench as strong in this room as it was in the streets. Moreover, he'd had to climb two flights of stairs to get here. He was hot, filthy, his leg felt on fire, and he had a great deal of work ahead. No, this would not do.

Hobbling to the top of the stairs, Arnold spied the weak-eyed corporal who had escorted him here waiting on the landing. "Get me Franks!" he bellowed down the steps.

"But, sir," the man protested, "I don't know where..."

Fortunately for the cringing corporal, Franks, crisp and at ease in the sweltering heat, chose that moment to stride into the foyer. "General, I see you got my message about the room."

Arnold's relief at seeing his friend and aide paled beside the frustration, exhaustion, and discomfort of the day. He came back down the steps. "This," he said with disgust, pointing up the stairs, "this is where you believe the governor of the capital should reside?"

Without a hint of contrition, Franks gestured to the street outside. "Sir! You must have looked out of your carriage as you rode in. Philadelphia is devastated. Quarters are all but nonexistent. Coming across this place was a stroke of luck itself!"

Arnold had to admit that this was true. The reports to Valley Forge had not prepared him for the ruin in the city, or the smell. He'd had to partially close the curtains on the coach in fear of being publicly ill. Badly needing to put his leg up, he leaned against the wall.

"But," Franks said, tapping the new governor ever so gently on the arm. "I have, I think, hit upon a better idea." Torn between the need to lie down and revulsion with the room, Arnold simply shrugged his shoulders. "As long as it's nearby."

Taking his general by the arm, Franks steered them toward the street. "Back to your carriage then, sir."

Arnold, glad to have the younger man back with him, allowed Franks to help him into the coach and even with situating his leg on the opposite seat. "And did you get the notices up about the stores closing? You had such little time."

"Indeed I did, sir. I rode in just ahead of our troops and just after Howe."

Relief washed over Arnold. "That's good, Franks, very good indeed." He relaxed against the back of the seat and continued. "You and I, we've been like bankers, giving this government money, loaning them money, having them owe us money. It's good we have a chance to make a little back."

Franks nodded in agreement, glad that at least Arnold was unwilling to forget the money he'd loaned the army in Canada. "Make an appointment with the clothier general," Arnold's voice interrupted his thoughts. "We need to speak with him immediately about those British goods, what he's taking. Make it for tomorrow, first thing."

Savoring the escape from the mean little inn, both men were quiet for a few moments as the carriage clopped steadily toward the west. Glancing at the General's closed eyes, Franks thought that Arnold had nodded off until once again the low voice broke the quiet. "You know, Franks, the Commander has given us another hard job. It's not just that he wants us to keep the peace here or even to guard the city in case Clinton decides to come back. There's more."

Franks, surprised by this news, instinctively straightened. "And what's this other work, sir?" he asked, trying to sound eager even though he too was exhausted from the past few days.

"His Excellency believes that a great number of those in Philadelphia who profess neutrality, Quakerism, or even an allegiance to the King might be somewhat undecided and, therefore, may yet be brought to our side."

"Indeed sir," Franks answered, "and how does he propose that?"

Arnold shook his head. "He isn't sure, but he thinks that if we take a lighter touch, show ourselves as rational, then we have a good chance of winning at least a portion of them over. We might as well try since we certainly don't have the men or arms to arrest them all." Franks was about to argue when Arnold slapped the seat beside him and roared. "Good God, Franks, are we going to Baltimore?"

"Just a moment, sir," Franks answered, looking out the coach window. "Ah yes, here we are now."

Grasping the window frame, Arnold pulled himself up to look out onto his headquarters. The view of a completely undamaged, magnificent red brick mansion brought his first pleasant moment of the long day.

"Whose house is it?"

"A grandson of the Founder, sir, away in London now."

Arnold's eyes wandered over the detailing above the windows and doors, the magnificent grill work. "It looks to be in superior condition, Major. I'm surprised the British left it alone."

"Oh, but they didn't, sir."

"They didn't?"

"No, General, Sir William departed only yesterday."

After three years of constant movement, camping, and hospitals, Arnold stared at the regal home as if it were a mirage. Howe's headquarters, and now his own. Without taking his eyes from the mansion, the new military governor of Philadelphia reached out and placed his hand on Franks's arm for assistance and announced quietly, "Yes Major, this will do. This will do very well indeed."

# CHAPTER 13

## Judge Shippen

*O*nce again our family felt ill at ease in our home and in our city. Depending on one's persuasion, the patriots or rebels had barely retaken charge of the city when reports of unrest surfaced in numerous quarters, the jubilation following the British evacuation supplanted by a grim accounting of the ravages on the city and individuals. Most who returned found their houses and businesses burned, looted, or horribly abused, and naturally turned suspicious eyes on those not likewise affected. As citizens cleaned garbage and excrement from houses and alleyways, rumors of who had helped whom over the past nine months filled the city's neighborhoods and public areas. Fingers pointed and eyebrows rose as story after story of duplicity, complicity, and outright treason were repeated along the wharves, in front of locked storefronts, and over public wells and wash stations. The closed stores and scarce supplies further irritated an already raw population.

And where was justice? How would these scores be settled once Congress and the Council were established in the city again? That is, if the citizenry could wait that long. One member of the Council, Charles Willson Peale, the newly appointed Agent for Forfeited Estates, was already back in town with lists of traitors in hand. Why wait for arrests, people asked.

And what was Arnold doing, everyone wanted to know. What job was the new military governor performing as he shuttled around the city in such a fine carriage? Word was he was living well and enjoying the comforts of the Penn Mansion, much as Howe had. The word was also out that he, as military governor, planned to host the Second Anniversary of the Declaration of Independence celebration. But why was he planning parties instead of doing something, anything, to right the scales for those who had suffered so bitterly in support of the glorious cause? Was this his idea of justice?

This was the sort of talk we heard much of in the summer of '78.

CHAPTER 14

Late June, 1778

*The State House, Philadelphia*

"For God's sake! When will we have justice?" Joseph Reed glared around the oak table with near desperation at the eleven members of the Supreme Executive Council of Pennsylvania. "How long do we have to wait?"

Shafts of sunlight fell from the tall, shattered windows lining the second story of the State House. The day was already steaming and the ventilation provided by the broken panes was welcome. The State House, like much of Philadelphia, was ravaged but not destroyed.

"He's right, you know," declared Timothy Matlack, the gaunt, red-faced Secretary of the Council. "Anyone who showed support for the British should pay, and pay dearly. There's no reason we can't arrest those people. That's why I invited Mr. Reed here today, to move this Council from threats to action!"

"Mr. Reed, Mr. Matlack..." Jacob Arndt, a councilman from Northampton County rose from his seat. "...It's not been two weeks since the British left, since we were able to return ourselves. We have many, many matters to consider, and I would suggest that the first should be the northwestern area. Butler is on our doorstep."

At the mention of the British Colonel's name various councilmen shifted nervously. Butler and his Iroquois allies, led by Joseph Brant, had for some months been on a murder and pillage campaign throughout the western settlements of New York. Word was that Butler was traveling south and was even now on the Pennsylvania border. "Surely, we should take up these more immediate matters, even if that means giving the accused an extension." Looking at his fellow councilmen, Arndt opened his hands in a gesture of candor. "These are extraordinary times."

"So they are," Reed agreed, trying to keep an edginess from his voice. "And as such, they call for extraordinary actions." Turning his attention to the group as a whole he continued. "Since this past March three proclamations have been issued notifying those accused that they must turn themselves over within forty days or automatically be considered guilty of treason. If I'm not mistaken, the fortieth day for the first of these proclamations has passed."

"True," Joseph Harts observed from the corner. "And Chief Justice McKean and two other justices are waiting at City Hall all this week to hear the statements of those accused who come forward." Harts, a farmer from Bucks County, was one of the few moderates in the room. While he wanted justice to be served, he also knew that some of the accused from his area were just farmers, never touched by the taxation policies that so bothered the merchants and professionals.

Reed rose from his chair and began to pace. How could he make it clear? The Council hadn't seen the misery he'd seen at Valley Forge. They hadn't been, as he had, at Monmouth Court House to see how valiantly and yes, how well, the Continental forces had fought. How could there be any complaisance toward Tories who had helped the enemy, who had paraded their support of the crown in front of their fellow citizens? Were they to be left to go about their errands as if the past eight months never occurred?

"Gentlemen," he said finally, fully aware that all eyes had been following his little walk around the room. "The way the law reads is perfectly clear. So I ask again, why is no one being arrested?"

Mackay, a representative from Lancaster County, shrugged his shoulders. "You know the cause. General Arnold stopped Peale. Said it was against his orders."

"But that is a wrong reading of our instructions, gentlemen." All eyes turned back to Reed. "Congress and the Commander in Chief instructed the General that he was to protect property and peaceable individuals in the city and, likewise, he was to put down any kind of abuse or persecution of the citizenry or among the citizenry. Why General Arnold expanded on that, why he would protect these lawfully accused people, these Tories, I can only speculate."

"Do sit, Reed," said George Bryan, the Council's president, pointing to his empty chair. "We appreciate your contributions today; clearly your feelings toward the city and the state do you proud. In fact, to listen, one would think you were a member, here, rather than the Congress. But Arnold is not our appointee. So now, on to our next order of business." Looking down at the agenda before him, Bryan pointed the gavel at Reed and smiled. "This will restore your confidence in us. We have the orders prepared for the eviction notifications. I believe the Galloway and Shoemaker properties are first."

As Matlack began to read the report, Reed looked back out the window at the city and all its devastation. He should go home now. As Bryan had pointed out, he was not a member of this group. And Hettie needed him to help get settled. Yes, it was good that the Council was proceeding with the confiscations and evictions. And yes, certainly Joseph Galloway's property should be among the first to be taken. But, as he looked over at the eleven men seated around the table, there was so much more they should be doing to punish traitors, to clean up the city, to help Washington and the army with men and supplies, to become a more active capital of the new country. Feeling his anger rising, Reed walked over to the pegs by the door and quietly gathered his hat and gloves. Then, nodding to Matlack, he exited the chamber to the busy corridor and headed toward the mangled wooden staircase to the ground floor below.

Why hasn't this been fixed? Reed wondered as several gentlemen picked their way up and down the precarious jumble of broken and missing steps. It looked like a comparatively simple repair, and the eleven men he'd just left had it in their power to make the job happen quickly. But, indeed, why would that happen, he thought as he began his descent holding onto the railing for dear life, when the most important repair work in the capital hadn't even begun?

CHAPTER 15

Late June, 1778

*The Great House*

$\mathcal{P}$eggy looked down at the blank stationery sheets, her pen and ink, and the elaborate walnut writing box, a special present from her grandfather on her sixteenth birthday. Usually, just the feel of the wooden box was enough to ensure that her letters got written, but not today. For some time now, she had deliberated listlessly on how she should start the letter. Should she address it to "Dear Nancy," or should she highlight her friend's new title and send it to "Dear Mrs. Paca"? It was hard to get motivated when she had absolutely nothing else to do all morning. What news was there, anyway? Father had forbidden writing on any topic that could possibly be misconstrued by an unintended reader. And that included about everything she could think of: the British evacuation, the Congress's return, their mutual friends who had left for New York, the tension in the city, even the scarcity of supplies. "So," she rationalized as she put down her pen, "I have nothing to write about."

Another long, quiet day staying away from windows stretched out in front of her. No going out, no friends coming in—again, Father's orders. Only the staff were allowed, actually encouraged, to venture out into the city. None, not one of them, could be accused of having loyalist leanings and as such were safe from vengeful patriots. Jenny, Melora, or Cook made the rounds each day for fresh foodstuffs as could be obtained, as well as information.

The only other access to the outside came in the form of Neddy Burd. The very evening of the British evacuation, Neddy appeared at the door, just as he said he would. Running downstairs to greet her cousin, Peggy stopped in shock at the sight of him. Neddy's slightly plump boyish looks were gone. Now the soft physique was painfully thin, and the face beneath the brunette curls was creased and angular. When he hugged each family member, his intensity made Peggy uncomfortable. And, while he did his best to entertain them as he always had, albeit now his jokes focused on nitwit army officers rather than nitwit lawyers, it was clear he was trying too hard. This ridiculous, terrible war. Sometimes Peggy just put her head down and cried. Why couldn't things be as they were before? She had been so convinced that the British would have it all ended by now, a rational truce declared. Everything back to normal.

Poor Neddy. Now he was a victim of this foolishness, too, hurt in a way Peggy knew she couldn't comprehend. The saddest part was the way he looked after Betsey. If she left the room he would noticeably fidget, stare at the door, and be impossible in a conversation until she returned. Father said it was probably nerves from his experience on the prison ship, or maybe from the battle. Time would help, he added, as well as the emotional safety and security that marriage would bring. "If that is true, then December can't come too soon," Peggy declared to her parents. Betsey and Neddy were to be married on Christmas Eve.

It was hard for her to think of her sister and her cousin as a married couple, standing together in church whispering as young couples do, making social calls and entertaining, sharing a house, and a bed. For herself, she'd not met a man with whom she could imagine that prospect. Well, only once, vaguely. Thinking of the unwritten letter to her friend Nancy, she recalled Mr. Paca at the engagement party. She'd been told beforehand that Mr. Paca was quite a bit older than Nancy, was established with a great estate in Maryland, even serving in the Congress. Because of his age, mid-thirties, she had envisioned him as someone of her father's generation. But her vision had been very wrong. Her friend's husband was not only darkly handsome but exuded confidence, worldliness, and something irresistibly strong. Nancy had indeed made quite a match, even if he was against the Crown.

Deciding that anything would be better than writing Nancy Paca a letter, Peggy opened the walnut writing box and carefully put her supplies away. Perhaps she could talk somebody downstairs into a game of chess.

Pausing on the landing, Peggy watched as Melora all but bounced down the steps in a freshly pressed lavender calico dress, a hand-me-down from Sally, no apron, a slightly familiar wide-brimmed straw bonnet, gloves, and a little string purse. All in all, Melora looked little like a serving girl about to run errands but rather some genteel person's daughter.

At the bottom of the staircase, Melora called down the hall toward the kitchen. "Cook, I'm leaving, I need the list." Next, walking to the mahogany mirror hanging in the foyer, she examined her profile, first from the right and then from the left. Apparently pleased with her reflection, she finished by pinching her cheeks and smoothing her hair back under the bonnet. At the first stroke of the hall clock she called out again, but more loudly this time. "Cook, hurry, it's eleven."

For Peggy, all the injustice of the war was suddenly symbolized by Melora's primping in the front hall and the fact that the maid actually got to go outside looking not at all like a servant. Leaning over the banister she called down to the girl in the coldest voice she could muster, "Melora! Stop shouting! Go get whatever list you want from Cook."

Melora looked up from the mirror. "I can't. Cook said nobody was allowed in her kitchen this morning. She's cleaning."

Descending the staircase with an arrogance worthy of Grace Galloway, Peggy stopped at the bottom step, folding her hands at her waist. "Well, at the very least, I believe there's a perfectly good mirror by the rear entrance."

To Peggy's astonishment, Melora turned with great deliberation back to the mirror, smoothed her hair once more against the bonnet, and straightened her collar before finally moving toward the back hall. As Melora passed Peggy, she spoke softly but firmly. "The mirror in back's too high for me, miss."

"I do not understand you, Father. This makes no sense." Peggy looked down at the chess board in frustration. After her disastrous encounter with Melora she'd found Polly making an arrangement of phlox with lilac branches and talked her into a game before lunch. Although a little slow in some areas, Polly was a brilliant and ruthless chess player. So ruthless that Peggy needed to pass on her earlier mood and give the game all her attention—that was, until her father ushered in the rest of the family. He had an announcement to make. So here they all sat, reacting to her father's latest edict while he stood quietly in front of the empty fireplace.

Not two months ago in this very room she'd drunk tea with André and some of the other British officers. But now her father expected each and every member of the family to attend General Arnold's reception honoring the second anniversary of the Declaration of Independence. "You've not let us out of the house since Sir William left. You've said repeatedly that Polly, Sally, and I are looked upon as some of the *Meschianza* ladies. But now you say it's in our best interest to attend an event where there may be danger and where we'll surely be despised." Finishing her little speech Peggy sat back in her chair so hard that the chessboard swayed on its stand. Feeling ridiculous once again, she felt compelled to add, "It's completely hypocritical."

"I agree, completely hypocritical," Edward said lying back against the couch. Edward with tousled hair and bright eyes was ready for a fight. He had taken the forced incarceration quite hard—in fact, too hard. On several mornings lately the rear entrance had been unlocked when Cook or Melora rose to light the oven. The young master would usually sleep through breakfast on those days.

"The Shippen family will attend the reception together. And," the Judge's gaze bore down on Peggy and Edward, "lest any of you forget, whatever your personal beliefs or hopes are concerning the outcome of this conflict, our family is neutral. That means, at the very least, that we will be gracious to all."

In spite of his father's words, Edward was hardly ready to yield. "But we don't want the independence. Why would we celebrate the Declaration?" Suddenly remembering his oldest sister's loyalties, Edward looked in her direction and added quickly, "There's nothing against Neddy in this."

Betsey, apparently unsoothed by her brother's hasty assurance, reached for her mother's hand while Mrs. Shippen, glaring at Edward, slipped beside her daughter. But by now Judge Shippen had had enough. His eyes swept about the group, again lingering on Edward and Peggy. "Listen to me! This very public event is a God-given opportunity to show that we're active and committed citizens of Philadelphia. I don't see how that could be too difficult to understand." With those words Judge Shippen walked to the parlor door. "A word with you, Edward, and Margaret, perhaps you can hurry our meal." The Judge held the door for his wife, while his son remained slouched against the couch. "Edward?" Judge Shippen repeated. "A word, now!" Smiling sullenly at his sisters as though he'd won some secret victory, Edward rose and walked past his father into the study.

———

"Lord, is he in for it," Polly muttered as soon as the girls were alone in the parlor. "Betsey, don't think a thing of what Edward said, and," she shifted to face her youngest sister, "Peggy, you will go to the reception won't you?"

"I don't think I have a great deal of choice," Peggy said walking over to the window she wasn't supposed to go near and looking out on the sunny sparkling June day. Other people were out there walking, meeting friends, going on with their lives. What she wouldn't give just for a stroll. Sometimes, and today was certainly one of them, she wondered why her father would not just declare. They could all go to New York for a while with their friends. Then when the British won, they'd come back to their home, and all would be sane again. At least in New York they could go out, mingle in society, and end this charade of neutrality.

Watching the activity on the sidewalk, Peggy suddenly realized that Melora was one of those meandering up Fourth. And she was with a young man. "Look at this," Peggy said to her sisters.

Collectively ignoring their father's warnings, the three sisters joined Peggy at the window. "There, coming up Fourth, it's Melora and a man."

"Quite a handsome man," Sally said. "Wonder where she met him."

"That's beside the point," Peggy said. "You know Mother's rule, the servants aren't to have visitors except on Sundays."

Betsey frowned at her sister. "They may have just run into each other, or simply be going the same way."

Peggy sighed. "Just ran into each other? Betsey, you're impossible! Didn't you see how she was dressed? And how important the time was? Of course she was going to meet him. I'm going to speak with Mother right now."

Betsey caught her arm. "Oh, don't. She did the marketing. So what if she has a beau? It's nice for her."

"I would like a beau who looked like that," Polly added softly, moving a little back from the window as the couple approached the house.

And clearly, the couple were more than casual acquaintances, Melora's sometimes surly expression gone, replaced with a carefree lightness. For his part, the tall, young man walked a little closer to the girl than a mere friend would, his posture signaling to Peggy a certain protectiveness of her.

Reaching the house, the young man handed Melora her basket, holding her hand for a long moment in the process. Finally, stepping away, he tipped his hat and began walking back the way they had come. Lingering on the street, Melora watched until he turned at the corner and was out of sight. Then, slowly, she too walked out of the sisters' line of vision to the back of the house. "See now, Peggy," Betsey searched her sister's face for agreement, "it's all over, no harm done. Don't tell Mother."

But images of shining black hair against lavender, the obvious interest of the tall man and the spaciousness of the walk in front of the house shut out all of Betsey's pleas for lenience. And how could Betsey understand anything anyway, Peggy thought. She never stops thinking about Neddy.

"No!" Peggy said, marching away from her sisters and toward the door. "Melora is taking advantage of our situation to break the rules. We can't have that." Then, drawing herself up to an irregular height for the second time in the day, Peggy Shippen went in search of her mother.

CHAPTER 16

Late June

Franks General Store, Second Street, Philadelphia

avid Franks was growing exasperated. For the fourth time he inserted the key into the lock. Then, ever so slowly, he turned it to the right, anticipating the tiny bit of resistance that preceded the key's clear sweep in the lock. Nothing. Pulling the heavy oak door more toward him, he tried again. There, finally, the click. The door swung open in his hand and David Franks entered his store.

Outside, the sun was just peaking over the stalls of the covered markets, but inside the cavernous building it was still pitch black. No matter. He could have found his way about the place blindfolded. For almost thirty-five years he had owned this store, at first with his Uncle Nathan. Would that Nathan were still alive, Franks thought as he paused in the threshold. He could use his advice very much right now.

The store owner struck a match and lit the lantern next to the door before taking a seat at the massive walnut secretary. Reaching for his order books and inventory logs, he sighed. What was this business Arnold was about? The news that stores and warehouses would be temporarily closed was completely understandable. There was a war going on and the city was full of abandoned British merchandise that an army could use. The Continentals were only being prudent to avail themselves of this windfall. But how was it that the Clothier General was buying up Tory goods on demand that an army wouldn't want, now while the stores were closed—and asking for receipts to be made out to himself, a second man, and Benedict Arnold?

Actually, Franks could understand very well what was happening. The General was speculating. Franks looked down at his books. He had a substantial quantity of goods, nonessential goods, ordered but abandoned by loyalist customers leaving for New York. What to do? He wasn't a Tory, he wasn't a rebel. As a Jew he couldn't even vote. The British owed him money that he owed to other people. The Executive Council of the state considered him a loyalist and untrustworthy. And now, Arnold, sent here to keep order, was obviously misusing his office at the expense of honest businessmen.

One thing he knew: He couldn't afford to lose any more money. Reaching for his pen, Franks began the process of annotating various entries under the "orders received" heading with backdated delivery times. Stock would be hard enough to come by with the British departure; he wasn't about to allow Arnold or any of his cronies to help themselves here. And besides, Franks thought as he looked up, surprised that sunlight was now flooding the room, speculation was his job, not theirs.

CHAPTER 17

July 4, 1778
City Tavern, Philadelphia

*P*eggy tried to take in the giddy euphoria hanging over center city. All along Second Street, lanterns, streamers, bouquets, and, of course, the new American flag festooned trees, fences, poles, even front doors while carriages and horses decorated with garlands of summer greens and flowers paraded up and down the street alongside drummers, flutists, and impromptu singing groups. Amidst circles of admirers, infantrymen on leave stood proudly turned out in the new Continental uniform of linen shirt and leather breeches, while their officers gave Philadelphians their first long look at the handsome blue and buff uniforms recently prescribed by the Commander in Chief. And surrounding the Shippen family, hundreds of people, maybe thousands, all dressed in holiday garb, waited impatiently in the street, on the porch, and in line to enter the City Tavern. It seemed as if all Philadelphia had turned out for the double celebration—the second anniversary of the Declaration of Independence—and the city being once again in American hands after nine months of British rule. Everywhere she looked, someone was calling out in joy to see a friend or relative returned to the city.

With her parents leading the procession, the Shippens picked their way closer to the City Tavern. Sally, Polly, and Peggy following behind Judge and Mrs. Shippen with Betsey, Neddy, and Edward bringing up the rear. Sensing, or fearing, the attention of those they were passing, Peggy kept her eyes carefully fixed on her father's back. While she had laughed when her father suggested this order, she only wished now they had thought to have Neddy wear his uniform within this maelstrom of patriotic fervor.

All of the family had dressed with particular care that afternoon.

Looking every bit the conservative but successful jurist, Judge Shippen was clothed in his most severe black coat, waistcoat, and breeches. And Mrs. Shippen was surely the successful jurist's wife in a plain but elegant midnight-blue silk. Her daughters, in youthful and frothy contrast, were arrayed in various summer prints and stripes. Despite the association, Peggy had chosen the tiny rose print that she'd last worn on the disastrous morning with Grace Galloway and André; her mother and sisters deeming it the most becoming.

And her hair. Melora had accomplished miracles that morning, not only with her hair but with Polly's and Sally's as well. During one of the long days of isolation Melora asked if she might try doing Polly's hair after watching Miss Martha's technique on several occasions. Eager for a diversion, Polly gave herself completely over to the maid's eager hands and at dinner startled the family with a creation every bit equal to that of the professional's. Melora's new job in the family begun!

Peggy was even the tiniest bit sorry that Melora was not allowed this evening off because she had broken the rules with that young man. The maid had been so efficient this morning, bustling among the three sisters: first curling, next powdering, and finally arranging brunette and blond locks into the towering white coiffures of the *Meschianza*. Much to her sisters's disdain, Betsey opted for nature, saying Neddy preferred it. Sally shared the thought that Betsey might as well already be married.

And although Peggy would never have admitted it to a soul, she was thrilled to be out of the house, even with all the anxiety of their situation. Not only to be out of the house, but to see friends, have on a beautiful dress, and to surrender, just a little, to the unknown possibilities of being eighteen years old and on her way to a party.

Once inside the chalk and dusty blue foyer of the City Tavern, the family hovered together assessing their situation. From where they stood, all the downstairs rooms, the Subscription Room, the Coffee Room, as well as the large dining room were just as jammed as the outside porch had been. Peggy, along with her mother, brother, and sisters peered at Judge Shippen for a sign of what to do. But just as her father waved toward the dining room, a uniformed servant took up position at the bottom of the steps, announcing, "Upstairs, if you please. General Arnold is receiving guests in the Long

Room." With each new group coming in from the outside, the instruction was repeated over and over. "Upstairs, General Arnold is upstairs in the Long Room receiving guests. Upstairs, ..." As the servant droned on, one gentleman observed just loudly enough for the benefit of everyone else present, "I thought we had gotten rid of Howe." Low chuckles rose from the group.

For his part, however, Judge Shippen seemed relieved to have a destination for his little herd. "Of course, we must greet our host. Come children," and offering his arm to Mrs. Shippen he led the family to a landing at the end of the line approaching the ballroom. From the vantage on the steps Peggy, Sally, and Polly studied the groups of guests below.

"I don't know anybody," Sally whispered.

"I don't either," Peggy said. "Where are all our friends?"

Polly put her arms about her sisters' shoulders. "And I only see four ladies using powder, much less jewelry. It's so odd."

"Oh Judge! Mrs. Shippen!" a voice above the girls called. Looking up, the sisters saw Sally Bache, Benjamin Franklin's daughter, standing near the front of the line with her husband Richard and Elizabeth and Henry Drinker. Sally was a small, sweet-looking girl but resembling her famous father just a little too much. As Polly once devilishly observed, "A fur hat could be the ruin of Sally Bache." Today she was looking particularly severe, Peggy observed. Even Franklin's own daughter showing not a trace of powder.

Mrs. Bache leaned over the railing and called down again while holding Henry Drinker's hand high in the air. "Isn't this the happiest of days, for us all to be together again?" Mr. Drinker was only recently back from exile in Virginia.

"Yes, certainly, welcome home," Judge Shippen said, "and congratulations to you also, Elizabeth." While Mr. Drinker waved enthusiastically, Mrs. Drinker's bright expression faded. Nodding almost imperceptibly, she turned her back to the family to bestow her full attention upon Sally Bache.

"Did you see that?" Polly whispered to Peggy and Betsey. Betsey nodded. "Sukey Andrews told us that Elizabeth Drinker was greatly offended by the *Meschianza*."

Sally, generally careful in public, all but hissed, "How can she hold that against us? We didn't even go."

"Girls!" Looking up to see their father's scowl, the daughters stood silently once again and watched the crowd. The line inched tediously forward.

Nearing the top of the staircase, Peggy looked into the small dining rooms off to either side. In the one to the left, she recognized the Drinkers, the Matlacks, the Baches, as well as Joseph and Hettie Reed, newly returned to town since the occupation, she guessed, amidst a throng of beribboned patriots. But like the crowd downstairs, the majority were strangers. Hearing a familiar voice followed by much laughing, Peggy turned to the dining area on the right. Thank heaven, she thought, spotting the cluster of Becky Franks, Becky Redmond, Peg Chew and their families. She would escape into that room just as soon as she'd paid her respects to her host. And how wonderful that Judge Chew was here tonight. Like Mr. Drinker, he'd only recently returned to the city.

Just steps from the entrance to the Long Room, Peggy glanced once again to the left to see the Reeds along with another couple staring and pointing at her family. Inexplicably, Mrs. Peale reached up with a flourish to her hair and the foursome broke out into gales of laughter. Peggy looked at her sisters in bewilderment. Why were they laughing? What had her family done that was so wrong?

Suddenly, all the freedom of the outing, the security of her family, even the pleasure of the rose print dress, were gone. And once again all that she wanted was to be home, to be safe, and to have this nightmare end.

# CHAPTER 18

## The Same Day

### City Tavern

*E*ntering the emerald green and mahogany elegance of the Long Room, the ballroom running the entire length of the Tavern's second floor, Peggy, along with her family, immediately joined the greetings, bows, curtsies, and formalities of the extensive receiving line. Looking down the row of officials charged with welcoming, Peggy recognized several delegates to Congress and a few older members of the Pennsylvania Assembly. But, again, mostly these were faces she had never seen. Faces of the new, independent Philadelphia.

Yet, while most faces were strangers to her, many of the dignitaries greeting the revelers clearly either knew or knew about her family. Chatty, gay repartee turned discernibly cool as the Shippens made their way down the line. After initially introducing individual members of his brood to each person or couple in the line, the rebuff quickly became too awkward and the Judge left the others to their own devices, speaking only for himself and his wife.

Realizing their new situation, Polly, Sally, and Peggy quickly formed a unit, meeting each dignitary first with a curtsey, then with a hello and a smile, and finally, with hands clasped at the waist, a thank you and short bow. After the first five or ten people, Peggy and Polly left the verbal part to Sally, simply curtsying, smiling, and bowing whenever their sister did. Edward moved through the line on his own, silently and stiffly, without an iota of grace or care. Only Neddy and Betsey, the last of the Shippen procession, passing through last, received a sincere welcome. Neddy's loyalties apparently absolving them of the stigma carried by the rest of the family.

You're Margaret Shippen," a voice announced. "I should have guessed."

Crouched in a pro-forma curtsy, Peggy needed a moment to realize that the deep voice was directed at her. Glancing from side to side, she also found she was quite alone with Polly and Sally curtsying to the next person in line, a young man also in uniform.

Peggy rose awkwardly in front of a stranger dressed in a Continental Officer's uniform and leaning on a cane. "Yes, I am."

Amusement played across the soldier's his face. "You don't remember me."

And she didn't. Frantically, she tried to recall something familiar about the stranger. He was tall, maybe ten years older than Neddy, his uniform like that of the other officers, but better cut or made of better cloth...something, gray eyes, thick black hair.

Feeling completely foolish, she dropped back into a quick curtsy. Then, with a nod to the line stalled to her left and the unknown officer still waiting for an answer, she sped away to join her sisters.


"You left me!" Peggy said as she and her sisters entered the small dining room looking for Becky and the others. "There I was, like a complete fool, thinking you were right beside me."

Sally smiled and slipped her arm through Peggy's. "And we thought the same, but you were back with the General."

"What was he saying to you?" Polly broke in.

"Who?" Peggy asked.

"The General," Polly answered. "General Arnold, Benedict Arnold."

Peggy stopped to face her sisters. "I didn't know who he was. He never introduced himself; acted as if we had met."

"You have," Polly said matter-of-factly and then paused as a servant approached the sisters holding a tray of glasses. "He visited in our home during the first Congress."

Peggy sighed. "Well, of course I don't remember him then, it seemed like the entire Congress was in our house." She reached for a glass of citron water." Where are Mother and Father?"

"I don't know," Polly began as shrieks of laughter erupted from the porch side of the room. Spying Edward near a window, Peggy, Polly, and Sally rushed to where he was standing. "What is it?"

Edward pointed toward Becky Franks standing in a small group of those closest to the railing. "Ask Becky, she saw best. Becky," he called over the crowd. "Over here!"

At the sound of her name, Becky Franks fixed on Edward and his three sisters waving her over, and squirmed through the crowd to join them.

"My sisters couldn't see the vision just down in the street," Edward said.

Becky, a vision herself in a pink and white striped challis, nodded. "Ladies, we have been ridiculed. Just now a very plainly dressed negro female was pulled down Second Street in a cart."

"How does that ridicule us?" Peggy asked.

"The lady also wore quite a huge white wig, intended, I believe, to resemble our hairstyles for the *Meschianza*," Becky explained. "And, since the tune being played to accompany the lady was the Traitors March, I believe the insinuation is that we must be traitors to America."

Even before Becky finished speaking, the mystery of Mrs. Peale's gesture toward her hair and the laughter of the two couples as they stared at the Shippen family was solved, albeit miserably. Peggy looked at Becky in dismay, tears filling the wide blue eyes. "Our hair?"

"Some believe it's not patriotic to wear styles from Europe any more. My father says he is seeing it in the store." Becky took her friend by the shoulders. "But, I'm proud of my friends who have the interests of America, if not its independence, at heart. The political zealots who set this up are just narrow-minded. They simply can't grasp a larger stage in this war."

"Excuse me, what larger stage would that be?"

Startled, the group of young people spun around to see Joseph and Hettie Reed walking toward them. "We came in search of punch," Joseph Reed began glibly, holding up an empty glass with one hand while pulling his reluctant wife into the group's circle with the other, "but instead we find an intriguing political discussion concerning political zealots." Head cocked, he looked directly at Peggy, first, and then Becky before asking, "Do you mean here in Philadelphia?"

The room grew still as Reed continued to smile at the two girls and then, one by one, at Edward, Polly, and Sally. The fury behind Reed's smile was terrifyingly evident to Peggy and she assumed, from their sudden silence, to the others also. For once, even Edward was cowed.

"I meant..." Becky began.

"Just a minute, Rebecca," her father crossed the room to join the group. Positioning himself in front of his daughter, David Franks faced Reed. "I, too, am fascinated by the issue of...the larger stage."

"Meaning," Reed interrupted, "in the wartime context as your daughter mentioned?"

Franks grinned a father's wry grin. "Of course, I can't speak for Rebecca, but I expect she was referring to the various scenarios that could occur from this war, given the interested parties."

"I'm sorry sir," Reed interrupted again, "but I thought we were only two here at war. And as for various scenarios, I believe we need only concern ourselves with one. America's uncontested independence." Then, glancing briefly at his wife as if to reassure her, he effectively threw down the glove. "Do you see others?"

"I do," Franks answered evenly.

At this Reed's smile disappeared altogether. "By all means, inform us."

"What if America wins, where do we turn for help if someday France or Spain decide to attack us? We've always depended on the British for that. Or what if Britain wins? Will we continue as sovereign colonies? Will the crown maintain our previous liberties? Or we will be treated as a vanquished nation?"

Reed stared, incredulous. "These issues were discussed, debated, and votes taken. I think you are no great friend of America to speak like this, today of all days, the second anniversary of our independence." Hettie Reed, who until now stood motionless, nodded slowly in agreement with her husband. She had been heard to say that the fragility of the new country terrified her.

"Excuse me."

Peggy turned and saw that the voice behind her belonged to Judge Benjamin Chew.

"I must beg your pardon, sir. Some debated, some voted, but very many could not. Mr. Franks and I were two of the latter."

At this Joseph Reed looked around the room at the primarily loyalist and Quaker guests and exploded. "I wonder why most of you are even here tonight. I also wonder if you would not be much more comfortable in your homes, or, Mr. Franks, Mr. Chew, even in New York, with your children and," he paused to look around the room, "your children's friends." Taking his wife's hand, Reed added, "As a congressman and a fervent supporter of this nation, I must say you are not welcome here tonight." With that pronouncement, the couple moved aside, distancing themselves from the others.

David Franks moved quickly, putting his arm around his daughter's shoulder. "It's late. I think you misunderstand, Congressman. But perhaps it's best to say good night. Come Becky,"

"No! In no way is it time to say goodnight."

Peggy turned to see Benedict Arnold limping into the room.

"What's this talk? The party's just beginning."


Once again, it seemed to Peggy, the atmosphere swung around as the General made his way across the room, stopping here and there to greet scattered guests. She was surprised by how smoothly and quickly he moved given the limp and the cane. Then he was standing across from her once again. She even saw the same flash of amusement as he welcomed her along with everyone else in their group. When he came to the Reeds, Arnold bowed as best he could. "Mrs. Reed, Mr. Reed, thank you for looking after my guests. My absence was inexcusable." Turning away from the couple, he bowed again, but this time in the general direction of David Franks and Benjamin Chew. "I want to welcome everyone in this tavern to our celebration tonight. We are so pleased you made the effort to come."

As the two men returned the gesture, Joseph Reed made a point of returning to the circle. "Just one moment, General Arnold. We welcomed you as a military envoy sent here to guard the capital, but Congress is here, as well as the duly elected government of Pennsylvania. We are well equipped to manage the affairs of the city."

Arnold nodded. "I'm certain you are, but, as you pointed out, we are in a wartime situation. And the Commander in Chief appointed me military governor with orders to show cordiality to all."

Reed cut in quickly, "I cannot believe that is what our Commander intended."

Arnold answered coldly and unequivocally. "Then, sir, perhaps you should take this up with General Washington himself. But until then, I have my orders and I intend to follow them."

"Even if that means consorting with those not clearly supportive to our cause?" Reed challenged.

Arnold answered quietly. "Sir, I will consort with any of Philadelphia's residents that I choose. And, Mr. Reed," Peggy felt the General's eyes brush over her as he finished his sentence, "they will all be under my protection."

# CHAPTER 19

## July, 1778

*Outside British Headquarters*

*Archibald Kennedy Mansion, One Broadway, New York City*

The Union Jack that was supposed to hang majestically over the front of One Broadway had lost its battle with the wind again. Rather than doing its job and proclaiming the might of the British Empire, it was wound all around the flag pole like a dust mop. John André, returning from a quick trip to the shoemakers, wondered if the flag's predicament wasn't symbolic of the British command structure. Amidst top officers coming and going, the word from London was that British strategy in America was being seriously rethought. Meanwhile, inside the building, activity was fierce, if largely unproductive. Staff officers hurried back and forth, preparing letters, examining reports, issuing directives, establishing Clinton's command by wiping out any trace of Howe's previous tenure. And the letter he held in his hand from David Franks was just another indication of the muddle at the top.

Franks' situation was rapidly growing more desperate. Now, it looked like both London and New York bureaucracies were passing his bills for reimbursement back and forth. Could André speak to Sir Henry for him? André crumpled the letter angrily. For an army stationed far from home to treat a reliable agent like this was such a colossal blunder. But, no, he couldn't speak to the General for him. While he had tried to take on the matter before Howe's departure, his relationship with Sir Henry was much too new for him to question anything.

"Pardon me, sir." John André looked down from the flagpole to see a young man about his own age standing before him. A little boy, probably no more than two or three years old, held onto the man's trousers. Both the father and the son had a pinched, underfed look. From his accent, the man was surely an American and from his dress and hands, André guessed he was not too long from a farm. The young father was also obviously nervous, barely able to look up from the ground.

"Yes, what is it?" As much as he didn't want to go back to the paperwork on his desk, neither did he relish dealing with indigents.

"I wondered if you might know of some work, sir." The man's voice had a begging tone to it. "I thought with the army being back, there might be some need. I have a wife, children."

He really didn't need to continue. New York was packed with hungry people looking for work. André had known their situation before the man ever opened his mouth. "I'm sorry, I don't. But why don't you ask inside? Ask for Major Winslow and..." he paused to take a few coins from his pocket, "for the boy."

Whisking the child up into his arms, the young man bowed quickly. "God be with you, sir. Thank you."

André watched the father and son make their way across the street to the white brick mansion and disappear inside. This was another reason to delay returning to the office. There was no work. But why be the one to carry out the difficult job of saying so? However, André acknowledged, the poor wretch had been right. There would be more employment opportunities in New York in certain quarters, now that the army had returned. In all probability that young man's wife would end up supporting the family, on her back, one redcoat or green-coated Hessian at a time.

The brothels were full of girls and women whose families had sought a safe haven in New York. What they also found, however, was overcrowding, little work, and a disdainful superiority on the part of the British military. Some of these families were loyalists and supported the King. To others, however, the British simply seemed a better bet if one had to pick a side. And very often that was the case. Now, another wave of loyalists was joining the refugee ranks in New York, the five thousand from Philadelphia. For those with money or connections, the move was probably smart and only a little inconvenient. There would be no question in British minds of their allegiance at the end of the war. But for those without means or connections, New York was largely a miserable place to be.

And here he was, too, André thought, as the guard outside the headquarters entrance batted at the flag attempting to straighten it. Eleven years it had been since he was abruptly taken out of school in Geneva and put to work in the family business, a counting house. His father was ill and there was a large family to support. Overnight, the pursuit of academics and social graces was replaced with bills of lading.

Within a year, life brought two more shocks. His father died and he'd fallen in love with Honora Sneyd. Honora: lovely, poetic, and delicately consumptive. Peggy Shippen bore a slight physical resemblance to Honora; that was why he had sketched her over and over, even using her for the *Meschianza* designs. But fortunately or unfortunately, there was none of the heartbreaking longing for Peggy that ruled his affair with Honora.

He could still hear Honora's father now, quietly, evenly, calling off the engagement. And why? He'd never known. Maybe his family's French background didn't rest well with the Sneyds, perhaps his prospects weren't grand enough. Neither Mr. Sneyd nor Honora had ever seen fit to explain.

But if he couldn't have Honora then at least he was free to try another profession. Offering travel, the possibility of prominence, and escape from memories, the military was the one socially acceptable employment that interested him. So at age twenty, he left the mind-numbing inventories behind and purchased a commission as a Second Lieutenant with the Royal Welsh Fusiliers. His mother was neither pleased nor optimistic with the move.

He'd risen quickly, however, until this recent change in command. Now, at twenty-eight, he was starting over again with a provisional commission on Clinton's staff. This was probably going to be his last and best chance to gain a high rank, free himself from the counting houses and Father Sneyds of the world, and completely and solidly raise himself in British society. He had to excel in a huge way.

But it would not be easy. Clinton was peevish, difficult, and surprisingly vain for a round, tubby man with little hair and black shaggy eyebrows. Most of the staff disliked working for him although they were, by and large, his handpicked choices. Personality aside, the man was unable to make or keep to a plan. Moreover, meetings would generally devolve into his rantings over policy and how the war was being fought. Assigned to America since the revolt started in Boston, he had disagreed bitterly with the occupation of Philadelphia and laid the loss at Saratoga on Howe's doorstep. More than that, Clinton believed he knew America best, having spent ten years as a boy in New York with his father, the Royal Governor. Many times Clinton had stated he should be the one to bring the conflict to an end.

André suddenly stood erect. There was the Commander in Chief now, emerging from One Broadway with several other officers, no doubt for the afternoon's activities. Lately, Clinton would rise from his papers not long after lunch and announce that a little outing would be animating for the staff—clear the mind, maintain the body. Then, with winks and grunts of agreement, the afternoon would be dedicated to handball, billiards, bowling, brothels, and, with any luck, mad rides about the country. While some of the older officers looked down their noses as the group tromped out of the building, he just felt lucky to be included.

"André!" a voice yelled. "Come along!" André pushed his hair back from his eyes. The Commander in Chief was calling! The day before he'd taken a chance and beaten Clinton in handball, an ongoing sports competition being as good a way as any to catch a man's attention. Straightening his jacket, André hurried across the street to join the group on the way to the stable. The flag might not be heading in the right direction today but, God willing, he just might be.

CHAPTER 20

July 11, 1778

*Robert Morris's Home, Philadelphia*

One week after the July Fourth reception, the Shippens were pleased to receive an unexpected invitation to tea from their friend, Mary "Molly" White Morris. The invitation was not unexpected because of the family's political stance; their friend would never tolerate any awkwardness over that. The invitation was unexpected only in that entertaining on the American side had been viewed as not only impractical but also frivolous, practically since the independence was signed. But now Philadelphia was beginning to open up again, albeit uncertainly for the Shippens, and shed some of its wartime prohibitions.

The General had maintained quiet in the city with none of the feared mob retribution, at least none yet. And as the Council got down to the business of ordering evictions and the appropriations of loyalist properties, Arnold did arrest some of those whose names appeared on the proclamations. Most of those named, however, chose either to flee or to turn themselves in voluntarily. Moreover, Chief Justice McCain was said to lack the zeal of Reed, Matlack, Peale and the others for prosecution, preferring Washington's policy of conciliation. Still, Judge Shippen asked his family to continue being mindful around windows and to limit their appearances in shops and on the streets to the bare minimum.

Besides being a good friend, Molly was married to Robert Morris, a patriot, and a business partner with a cousin of the Shippens, Thomas Willing, in an enormously successful mercantile firm. While both men were vehemently in favor of American economic freedom from Britain, both experienced their own doubts about the need for total independence. Even though Robert Morris eventually signed the Declaration of Independence, friends said he refused the honor initially due to his hopes for a reconciliation. And Thomas Willing, the Shippen's cousin, maintained connections on both sides. In fact, General Howe contacted Willing to pass the word among Philadelphians that they should remain in their homes for safety's sake during Cornwallis's arrival with the army.

Surveying the interior of the Morris's home, Peggy felt like she was going back to the time when she regularly visited her friends and relatives in this sort of elegance. Even the refreshments reminded her of days gone by, with a lavish assortment of smoked hams, sausages, quail, duck, sturgeon, oysters, vegetables swimming in butter, cheeses, puddings and pasties. But when she considered the other guests milling about the Morris's, she was jolted right back to the present by the absence of so many old friends removed to New York or England. Even now her parents were next door trying to comfort Grace Galloway. With Joseph Galloway in New York, the Council had turned its eyes on his wife and ordered her to submit an inventory of their personal belongings. Although Ben Chew believed it would never come to Grace actually being turned out of her home, Judge Shippen was not so sure.

Glancing through the glass doors to the formal gardens in the rear of the house, Peggy spied Betsey and Neddy sitting with a small group among the roses. Just recently Neddy had been appointed prothonotary to the Supreme Court of Pennsylvania, and the family was very proud of him. While her cousin was losing a bit of the terrible thinness that so alarmed the family upon his return, he still resisted letting Betsey out of his sight. Currently, he was living just around the corner from the Edward Shippens in Dr. William Shippen's house while the doctor was off attending to his duties with the Continental Army. However, should trouble come back to Philadelphia in a violent way, all of the family members intended to escape to her Grandfather's house in the country. Her grandfather...how she missed him, and how lonely he must be since his wife Mary's death.

Seeing no one in the parlor she was much interested in talking to, Peggy decided to join Betsey and Neddy. Picking up a glass of punch, she started for the door when her hostess came fluttering toward her. A renowned brunette beauty in her day, Molly Morris was now some twenty years past her bloom but obviously glorying in her role as wife, mother, and hostess. Sometimes a little too much, Mrs. Shippen whispered to her daughters from time to time.

"Peggy, my dear, just one moment!" Concerned over what could possibly have so overtaken Molly, Peggy took her friend's hand. "Is everything all right? Shall I find Mr. Morris?"

"Oh, no, my dear." She linked arms with Peggy, steering her toward the library. "It's simply that you've been asked for."

Peggy sighed. It was always the elderly ladies who just had to see you, knowing they could have you practically chained to their side since there were no husbands or children to call you conveniently away.

"But I need to take Betsey some punch. She's terribly thirsty."

Molly waved to the Negro behind the punch table and pointed to the rose garden. "Take this punch to the young lady in the red striped dress." Then she turned to Peggy, "Now, please hurry. The Harrisons have just arrived; I need to speak with them also."

Wondering what Betsey would do when the punch arrived, Peggy dutifully followed Molly Morris out of the crowded parlor, down the hall, and into an almost empty library. There in front of the mantel, Robert Morris stood deep in conversation with General Arnold. David Salisbury Franks, whom she now knew was one of the General's primary aides as well as a relative of Becky's, stood slightly apart but obviously in attendance.

"Look, General! Look who I've found," Molly said in much too loud a voice. When the gentlemen turned and bowed, Peggy thought that she might faint. What could Molly be thinking?

Dropping to a half curtsey, she managed a muted "Good afternoon, Gentlemen," before Molly Morris burst into conversation again.

"You see, Peggy, we were badgering the General, our guest of honor, for all sorts of details surrounding his transfer to our city. How does he find it? Is his residence sufficient? Has he met any charming people?"

"And can you imagine our surprise when he mentioned that he had found one of Edward Shippen's daughters particularly charming," her husband interrupted. "From there it was only a matter of seconds before we determined the Shippen daughter to whom he was referring."

Peggy thought she'd never seen anyone who looked quite so pleased with himself as Mr. Morris did at that moment. A brilliant man with money, Robert Morris's physical attributions were somewhat less remarkable. He was a short, round man with many chins and tiny hands. He was also, however, kindness itself.

Feeling all eyes upon her, Peggy struggled for something to say. "We were all pleased to welcome the General."

"Indeed we were," Molly Morris said. "And now, Peggy, Mr. Morris and I must see to the Harrisons. Please be a wonderful friend and see if you can arrange some refreshments for the General and Major Franks." Then, speaking in the voice of a conspirator she explained, "The General would like to relax a moment quietly before the rest of our guests find out he's here." Turning to her husband, she gestured toward the door. "Come, my dear."

Robert Morris, obviously accustomed to following his wife's instructions, bowed, saying, "Consider our home your own, sir." And just as hastily as his wife had swept Peggy into the library, she swept her husband out.

"So, Miss Shippen, do you mind if I sit?" At the sound of the deep voice, Peggy suddenly felt timid. This was all terribly awkward. Forcing a smile, she pulled herself together as best she could. "Please, do." She turned to Major Franks. "Major, have a seat also. What shall I have brought to you?"

"Franks, perhaps you could attend to that. You know what I like. And," the General continued matter-of-factly, "I wish to speak with Miss Shippen for a moment before the others return."

Franks bowed to Peggy. "Of course. Excuse me, Miss Shippen," and left the room. Peggy, not at all sure of what was happening, wanted to run after him and beg him to stay.

While Peggy stood in quiet panic, the General grasped both arms of a large wing chair, lowered himself into it, and then proceeded with the business of arranging his wounded leg onto an embroidered ottoman. As she watched all this, the realization came to her that though the one leg was damaged, he was an exceptionally fit man. Much more than her brother Edward, and infinitely more so than Neddy. Suddenly the accounts she'd read or heard of the march to Quebec, the battle for Valcour Island, and the heroic ride at Freeman's Farm came alive in the wounds and musculature of the man—of the general—before her.

"Won't you also take a seat, Miss Shippen?" Arnold asked, rubbing the back of his neck and glancing at the sofa beside him. "I find it a little hard to chat with standing people."

Chagrined at the oversight, Peggy sat, immediately blurting out the first convention that came to mind. "I take it you are otherwise in good health?" Even as the words left her mouth, she wondered if he could possibly guess at her thoughts.

"Indeed, I am otherwise in good health," Arnold answered evenly. "The surgeon assures me that the leg will mend entirely and that quite soon I will enjoy perfect health." Then to Peggy's continued consternation, he stared directly at her and added, "But I can see that you already enjoy perfect health, Miss Shippen."

She felt a wave of heat wash over her. Not another headache now, she begged silently. Just one week earlier she had experienced a headache so violent that she had no memory of anything for three days except pain. From her mother's account, she had accused Cook of poisoning her and Polly of scalding her forehead with hot irons. "I hope my parents have the pleasure of speaking with you this afternoon, General."

"They're here also?"

"They will be shortly. They're next door with our cousin, Grace Galloway."

"Mrs. Galloway is a relative of yours?"

Peggy paused, realizing she had stumbled onto dangerous ground. In all likelihood the General would not think highly of the Galloways. "Yes. Her husband and daughter are in New York, waiting to leave for London. But she's staying here."

Arnold pushed a shock of heavy, black hair back from his forehead. "That's a bad business," he said slowly, "that the state may choose to put a woman out of her home. I can't agree with that."

His remark caught her off guard. He didn't agree with the new state government? Not knowing how to answer, Peggy tried to turn the conversation once more. "And how are you finding Philadelphia, General?"

As he considered the question, Arnold's gaze wandered to the rows and rows of volumes forming Robert Morris's library. "I find Philadelphia to be quite pleasant," he began matter-of-factly. "Most of the Philadelphians I've met have been nothing but welcoming and hospitable, like your good friends, the Morrises. There are, of course, some components of the population who are easier with my appointment than others. Mr. Reed and his colleagues, for example, would like very much to see me gone."

"See you gone?" she repeated stupidly.

"Yes, gone!" The country's most famous hero suddenly shrugged his shoulders and winked. "Absolutely."

The wink was her undoing. She looked out into the garden at Betsey and Neddy talking with the Morrises, her parents walking toward them. But, friends, family, and certainly hosts might as well have been across the Atlantic. She leaned toward Arnold, flushed again but not from any headache. "Then, General, it seems we have something in common. I suspect that Mr. Reed and his colleagues would very much like to see me gone as well."

Arnold, fidgeting with a jacket button, turned to face her. "My sincere wish, Miss Shippen, is that we'll have many things in common."

CHAPTER 21

August 10, 1778

*The Great House*

*M*elora stood back from the highboy and smiled. There was a bit of good work. She'd spent the past half an hour rubbing the wood and herself into a good shine, even livening up the brass with a bit of salted vinegar. At first, the chest of drawers set up on thin wooden legs looked absurd to her, like some piece of dancing furniture. But over time she'd come to appreciate the workmanship involved in making such an item—indeed, in many of the items in the Great House. This room, the main parlor, was her favorite room in the house and, as opposed to some of her chores, she loved taking care of it.

The room was large, fifteen by thirty feet, with three windows extending from the ceiling to the level of the chair rail. Beneath the windows, paneled seats had been built with doors below that opened like cabinets for extra storage. And while the color scheme of the room, sea green and ivory, seemed odd at first, she'd gradually gotten used to that, too. Colors like this must exist in Ireland, she thought. But she'd never been in a house there grand enough to have more than whitewash. Perhaps, now that she and the mistress were back on good terms after the Independence Day business, Mrs. Shippen would tell her how these colors were made. According to Jenny, it'd all been Miss Peggy's doing anyway, making such an issue of her walking with Jared and getting the holiday taken away. Miss Peggy! What a spoiled, temperamental girl that one was! And now, the General singling her out.

Marveling at the unfairness of the world, Melora gathered up her wax and rag and tried to decide which piece of furniture to take on next: the bombé bas secretary? The low curly maple chest of drawers? Or the camel-backed sofa and two arm chairs covered in creweled blue and lavender flowers against a pale green background? The only other piece of furniture in the parlor was a cherry side table where the Shippens' tea service was placed. The tea kettle—could one call this a mere kettle?—was a mass of scrolls, initials, and shells with the spout being a duck's open beak! As she studied the ornate, funny tea kettle, she thought as she had many times before how much she wished Jared could see this room and how beautifully she kept it.

Perhaps if he saw it, he would speak about his grandfather's house in Maine and how it was for him growing up. All he'd told her was that his grandfather had come to Boston from Cork, settling there until all the Irish in Massachusetts were warned to leave the colony in 1720. So his grandfather moved to a place named York on the ocean in Maine, where both Jared and his father were born. That was how he'd gotten to Canada. General Arnold had gathered all the seamen he could find from the militias massing in Cambridge for the trip north to stop the British. But it was rare for Jared to speak of his family. They were all dead now, his father dying in Jared's arms on the march to Quebec.

But maybe, if he saw this room and what a good housekeeper she was, he would start to think about a house and a family for himself. And maybe, one day, if they worked very hard, she could see them in a shop, examining a low chest, like the curly maple...

A loud knock brought her back to the curly maple at hand. Wondering, as she had many times, why no one else in the family seemed capable of answering a door, she hurried to the foyer and pulled the heavy wooden door open. There was Jared. Jared, looking like he came to the Shippen front door everyday.

"What are you doing here? The mistress will be furious."

Jared just stared at her, obviously amused. "You should see yourself."

"And why's that?" she said, angry that he would put her in such a position.

"Because you hardly look like the girl I take for walks on Sunday." And with that he reached over and touched her cheek.

Appalled, Melora saw brown wax on his fingers. "Well, what do you think I do here? And if you don't get away I won't be doing anything here much longer," she added, glaring up at him.

The lanky Irishman smiled, studying her as he often did. Then, slowly and awkwardly, he reached into his bag with his clean hand and withdrew a white envelope. "Did you really think I'd be so foolish?" He handed her the envelope. "An invitation for Miss Shippen. The General apologizes that he's unable to deliver it himself."

Understanding washed over her. He was here as an aide to the General, not as her special friend. "I'm such a fool."

The young man nodded in agreement. "Yes, you are." And then, holding up his hand he asked, "A cloth, please?"

Pocketing the letter, Melora sighed deeply and held out her apron. As Jared leaned toward her and the dark red head came closer to hers, a now familiar weakness passed over her. "Forgive me?"

"Perhaps. We'll see on Sunday." He touched her cheek once again, but very softly and slowly this time.

As she watched him gather the reins of his horse, mount, and trot away from the house she thought again what a fool she'd been, and how utterly in love she was.


Peggy pulled one dress after another out of Sally's cupboard. "You have to have something I can wear. The General has seen each of mine already this summer." She held up a soft pink crepe. "Maybe this one."

"Excuse me, miss."

Both girls looked up from the delicate afternoon dress to see Melora at the door.

"A letter for Miss Peggy."

Peggy held out her hand for the envelope. "Who's it from?"

"The General's man. Came while I was cleaning the parlor."

Looking up from the invitation, Peggy surveyed Melora's waxed and sweaty state. "You answered the door? Like you are now?" While Melora nodded icily, another thought occurred to Peggy. "Was the General in the carriage? Did he see you?"

The question hung there in the space between them.

"Well, did he?" Peggy asked again.

Melora pushed back her kerchief. "Not certain. Perhaps in the future you'll want to see to the door yourself." Then, without waiting to be dismissed, the maid turned and walked quickly down the hall.

Astounded, the two sisters listened to Melora's footsteps descending the stairs. "Imagine," Sally said, "going to the door like that!" Peggy took a seat on the bed, staring at the closed door. "I wish Mother would just let her go."

Sally shrugged. "She can't. Melora has a contract. Besides, Mother thinks she's too hard a worker, and she does do our hair very well." Then, sitting down beside her sister she pointed to the letter. "Why don't you open it?"

Peggy removed the small card from the envelope and held it up between the two of them. In small, neat script the invitation read:

*General Benedict Arnold requests the pleasure of the company of Miss Peggy Shippen at 6:00 in the evening on August 25th, 1778 at 190 High Street for a ball to honor the birthday of His Highness, Louis XVI of France. The favor of a reply is requested.*

And scrawled across the bottom of the card, in bold handwriting she'd come to recognize, was a postscript: "*With best wishes for your health, Your obedient servant, B. Arnold*"

Sally took the card from her sister. "A ball! This means the entire French legation will attend. Perhaps even the Commander in Chief! And he signed the card himself! He signed it, B. Arnold." She took her sister by the shoulders. "The General is pressing very hard. Are you sure this is what you want?"

Peggy looked down at the white parchment and felt a thrill of pride. "I believe I do, Sally, I truly believe I do."

CHAPTER 22

*Judge Shippen*

The afternoon at the Morrises was just the first in a succession of teas, dinners, and receptions that summer where the General either very obviously sought Peggy out or had arranged beforehand to have her seated conspicuously at his side. When asked by Betsey how the romance began, Peggy was at a loss for an answer, offering only that "The General was decided, from the start."

At first their conversation was stilted, difficult for two strangers eighteen years apart in age and from different regions of the country. Gradually, however, topics came more easily. She thrilled to the stories of his trading in the Caribbean, the innuendo of smuggling and daring, and the business plans he had for the future. Riding in his carriage, accompanied by uniformed drivers and footmen, she was reminded not only of better times in the Shippen family but also of the sublime pleasures of safety and security. At the dinner marking the arrival of France's ambassador to Philadelphia, Arnold's open admiration, reflected in the expressions of the French, the Congress, and the collected aristocracy of Philadelphia, filled Peggy with a heady sense of entitlement and rank.

Also, and more to the point, in those summer days while I figured the household accounts, Edward did nothing, and Neddy began a law practice, the General was the General. He commanded armies, worked with the French, and made crucial decisions with Washington, Schuyler, and Greene. None of this escaped Peggy, who I think was searching for a strong male in those turbulent times. Once I even heard her say that Arnold bore a strong resemblance to my father: decisive, dynamic, and strong. They were cut from the same cloth, she said, and expressed a wish that her grandfather and Arnold could meet soon. That wish was never fulfilled. Perhaps if it had been, she would have understood the difference.

Anyone could see she was captivated by Arnold's relentless—what shall I call it—will? force? power? Especially when it was directed in pursuit of her. It was like winning a contest over and over, being singled out for extraordinary attention, and having friends and strangers alike envious of your situation. Arnold's attention was overwhelming, enveloping, wholly masculine, and causing other men, myself included, to appear pale and insipid in comparison.

Little by little, however, Peggy found that she, too, had power. Except for his sister Hannah, the General was unaccustomed to a woman who understood money and trade. Peggy could not only keep up with him in business conversation, but his successes as a merchant and trader fit in with well with the mores and expectations of our family. Moreover, on the subject of politics and my neutrality, they agreed to disagree and she saw that he respected her for it.

And somewhere in that summer, she also learned that there was enormous power to be gained in other ways—for example, by touching the General's arm ever so lightly to point out an approaching dignitary, pushing her curls slowly from her neck on a humid day, or placing an earnest hand to her bosom in conversation. Children believe their parents are blind to such things. I think they see us as asexual beings with no history or experience ourselves. But of course we do see, with crystalline clarity, what is happening and, more so than the young ones, understand it very well. Just as I also understood that Arnold would not be content with mere coquetry for very long.

# CHAPTER 23

August 15, 1778

*Grace Galloway's Home, Philadelphia*

G azing about the Galloway's city home, Peggy decided that it was, if anything, even more splendid than the Morris's, and certainly one of the finest in Philadelphia. Perhaps this was the real reason the Council was so determined to have it. While Mrs. Shippen, Betsey, and Peggy drank tea in the dining room of the Galloway's house, their beleaguered hostess sat stolidly at the table, relating details of the siege being waged technically against her escaped husband, but in actuality against herself.

Two months had passed since the day the Shippen family feared that Grace Galloway would physically attack John André in their parlor. That day, Peggy observed a wide-eyed hysteric and was embarrassed to call her "cousin." Considering Grace's current predicament, as well as the general atmosphere in Philadelphia, she could now only think of that earlier behavior as prescient. It seemed that every day there was a new eviction, jailing, or accusation against so-called Tories by the Executive Council. Just yesterday Edward announced at luncheon that Joseph Reed had been formally requested by the Council to relinquish his Congressional seat and join the Pennsylvania government. "Why would the Council make such an extraordinary request?" her brother asked for dramatic effect. "Because they need Reed to prosecute all our friends."

Returning her attention to the conversation at the table, Peggy fought the revulsion she felt at the sight of her relative. Approximately the same age as Mrs. Shippen, Grace now looked a good twenty years older. Today her hair was mostly fallen out of a torn lace cap onto the shoulders of a stained satin evening dress. Worst of all, her breath was disgusting. But it was the glimmer of a new expression that scared Peggy the most. From time to time during the afternoon, her cousin would pause after some comment, close her eyes, and then smile as though she were privy to something unavailable to the other three. The habit was highly disconcerting and Peggy longed to be away from it.

"Ben Chew? What does he advise?" her mother asked, knowing that Grace relied heavily upon the former judge.

"He says very little, only that I must stay here. Occupy the premises," Grace said. "Chew has no time for me. He scarcely steps outside since his return."

"Well, Mr. Galloway then," Mrs. Shippen continued, "what are his thoughts?"

"Mr. Galloway thinks that I should get a friend to buy the house for me. That is the best he can imagine." With shaking hands, Grace gripped her cup as she continued. "You see he can't be bothered from planning his trip to London. He still expects to be saved by Howe and that gang of traitors."

"Perhaps you know someone who would do that for you," Betsey offered. "Have you spoken with anyone?"

"It's no use," Grace answered, smiling one of her crooked smiles. "The Council has made other plans. First, Peale informed me that I must pay them 300 pounds a year to stay in my house. Pay them, the Council, to stay in my own home."

"But isn't that good news?" Mrs. Shippen interrupted, reaching out to steady her cousin's arm.

Without acknowledging the woman's question or gesture, Grace continued, "Then President Bryan arrives a few days later and informs me that I may not even do that. He swears I have to leave, even though this is my house, given to me by my father. The Council has confiscated it for Mr. Galloway's lifetime. That is the law, he said, and that is all there is to it."

Grace paused for a sip of tea, but even with two hands and Mrs. Shippen's support, most of the tea fell into her lap or onto the table. Placing the empty cup in front of her, she resumed her story, still speaking in the same flat voice. "Since Bryan's visit, they have come and made lists of all my possessions to sell at auction. The government will rob me of this house, as they are robbing me of all my homes, and then they will put me in the street. And who," here she changed to a queer, almost amused tone before asking the question that was at the back of all their minds, "who will take me in? The four women sat in embarrassed silence while Grace peered first at Mrs. Shippen, then Betsey, then Peggy, and finally back to Mrs. Shippen.

Who indeed would take Grace Galloway in, Peggy wondered, full to bursting with gratitude that this was not her problem. Grace was difficult at best and a spoiled and willful woman at worst. But it would not be her character alone that would discourage would-be hosts. Sane people would fear the Council's vindictive nature. Who knew what troubles might enter the door along with the wife of a known loyalist? Staring at her cousin, Peggy was suddenly struck with the personal implications of the situation. If they would turn a lone older woman like Grace out of her house, they would turn anyone out, including her family. And what if we couldn't get to Grandfather's? Then, just as it had occurred to Grace months before, the next obvious thought slipped into her mind. And who would take us in?

As Peggy sat contemplating this newest terror, Mrs. Shippen began speaking, murmuring, "Grace, dear..." only to be interrupted by yelling and banging in the foyer. The women stared at the dining room door, transfixed, as three men barged into the room unannounced, followed by Mary, the Galloway's housekeeper. Mary, who was at least in her sixties, looked to be in a perfect muddle.

"Mum," she said, gesturing to the men with her apron, "I couldn't keep them out!" For their part, the men stood in a trio just inside the door. Peggy recognized Charles Peale and Timothy Matlack at once, but the third man was a stranger. As a group, the three men appeared to be caught off guard, perhaps not expecting to find Grace accompanied.

"Mrs. Galloway!" Peale shouted. "You must go out of this house. We have our orders."

"Leave my house immediately," Grace answered, glaring back at the men. "You have no authority here."

"But we do have authority, Mrs. Galloway," Matlack interrupted, "the authority of the Executive Council of Pennsylvania, and it will be you who will get out of this house." Looking around at the Shippen women, he added a bit more softly, "We don't want to use force."

"Well, you'll have to if I'm to leave," Grace answered as she sat heavily back in her chair. Then, smiling her odd smile again, she added primly, "But today I am very, very sick. Just about to retire to my room. You may speak with my lawyer, Benjamin Chew."

All eyes fixed on Matlack, who appeared to have warmed considerably to the job at hand. "As I said, we have no desire to use force. But," and here he pointed to Grace as one would to a child, "this is for you to fix, madam."

The three men's arrogance was too much for Peggy. Rising from the table, she was amazed to hear herself ask, "And what if I decide to stop you?"

Matlack's answer was chillingly calm. "Miss, you would be hung."

Once again the women heard knocking at the front door, then slow uneven steps preceded by a tap.

Peggy recognized the sound, crying out in relief as Benedict Arnold entered the room.

# CHAPTER 24

August 17, 1778

*Grounds of the Great House*

"The General ordered me to call a guard to the Galloway house," said Jared. "He said he couldn't leave a woman unprotected."

"He wanted to protect that witch?" Melora asked in surprise. Jared's description of Arnold's intervention the day before baffled her.

"I believe he felt he had to."

"And Peale, Matlack, what did they do?"

"Left in a fury," Jared answered as he tore a piece of bread from the loaf, "to talk to the Council."

Exasperated, Melora searched Jared's face for some sign that he, too, was bothered by the General's actions. But the clear steady eyes, the slight smile, revealed nothing.

The day was surprisingly cool for August and, on this distant corner of the Shippen estate, wonderfully quiet. Secluded amidst soft grasses and bushes, Melora and Jared sat in comfortable privacy, partaking of their Sunday picnic. As hungry as she always was from hours of physical labor, Melora ate sparingly, leaving most of the basket's contents for Jared. While food was always sufficient at the Great House, meals at the General's residence were spotty—like the allowances from Congress, according to David Salisbury Franks. Jared reported that Franks blamed Congress for the constant lack of funds for the mansion, in front of whomever happened to be listening at the time—footmen, cooks, soldiers, or congressional visitors. Clearly, however, Franks's rantings made little difference. Every Sunday afternoon Jared ate the Shippens' food like a man starved.

Every Sunday afternoon. Melora dreamt her way through each week in anticipation of these outings. In fact, they organized her week. Sunday night was a bittersweet time when she could still feel his hand holding hers as she lay alone in bed. Monday was terrible, all of the chores ahead and an entire six days of waiting. Tuesday, wash day, was just a horrid day in and of itself. At night, she could barely climb to the attic after an entire day of hauling water, scrubbing, hauling more water for the rinse, and finally hanging the clothes out to dry and folding. Ironing day on Wednesday was almost as bad. Dawn to dusk she stood hovered over a hot iron. Then on Thursday she, Cook, and Jenny spent the day with their skirts hitched into their belts for some small relief from the heat and as a slight protection against catching themselves on fire as they endured baking day. At least they were all three together. By Friday, at last, the very worst of the week was over. She had only to clean the steps and downstairs floors at her own pace and in her own way. And on Saturday, her second favorite day of the week, she would actually allow herself to consider clothes for Sunday while shopping at the market. In fact, Saturday barely even counted. A slow day, all anticipation preparing for the Sabbath, preparing for Jared. Then, after six long days, it would be Sunday again.

On Sundays the family and staff rose early, the Shippens heading to Christ Church while she made her way to St. Joseph's for Mass. The master, going against custom, did not insist that she join the family, and for that she was grateful. In addition to being able to avoid the discomfort of being in an Anglican church, the time on her own made the day even more special. Returning home having fulfilled the obligation, she would join in the flurry of heating and serving the midday meal, most of which would have been prepared the day before. This was done partly in observance of the Sabbath, but also so that the family might sit down to what was always a major meal as soon as possible after the three-hour service. Once the Shippens were done, the staff enjoyed their primary feast of the week, as well. That is, all except for her.

About a month after Jared's and her first Sunday outing, Cook mentioned the extra in the Shippen kitchen. Wouldn't Melora like to take a few things with her? From that Sunday afternoon on, she could expect to find a basket by the back door neatly packed with a full meal by the time Jared arrived for her at two o'clock. Today Cook had been good enough to put aside cold chicken, bread, and some plum cobbler. Cook was indeed her angel in America.

Melora put down a half-eaten drumstick and sighed in frustration.

"Why should the General help the Galloways? Joseph Galloway is with General Howe in New York, waiting to sail to London."

"But Grace Galloway is not," Jared answered. "She's just a woman and she's not helping the British." Then, posing his own question, he continued, "And why should a group of men want so much to get a woman out of her house? Have they nothing better to do?"

Melora had to admit he had a point. She'd overheard more than a few conversations in the markets concerning the Council's zealous pursuit of accused traitors. The consensus in the market and the Shippen's kitchen seemed to be that there were more pressing matters needing attention.

"Wait," she held up her hand. "I'm asking about the General, not the Council. What right does he have to stand in the way of Pennsylvania's government?"

"But he's not," Jared replied, reaching again for the bread. "He didn't try to revoke the eviction notice. He just refused to have a lone woman forced onto the street with nowhere to go."

"But the Council passed the law last year, traitors would have their property taken and..."

"Melora," Jared interrupted, "the General is under orders from Washington, not the Council of Pennsylvania. And Washington ordered him to guard the residents and keep the peace."

Melora looked down at the pale blue blouse and dark gingham skirt she had ironed so carefully the night before. Did he notice? She'd even ironed the black silk ribbons on her bonnet. Jared's logic was a bit too straightforward for her. The whole thing was more complicated than that. Rummaging around in the basket, she decided to raise another question also discussed frequently at the market. "Some people say it's odd how the General lives so well, with carriages and servants when, as you've said, the Congress won't give him any money."

Having said this in as conversational a tone as she could manage, Melora busied herself cutting the cobbler very deliberately into two pieces, one quite large and the other a sliver. But before she could transfer the pie to a smaller plate, he caught her wrist, the tough reddish brown of his skin dark against the pale blue sleeve. "And what else do people say?" Still staring at the two pieces of pie she considered the question carefully before answering in a soft voice. "People say it's odd, those people whom he seems to favor."

"Those people?" Jared repeated, raising her chin with his hand, forcing her to look at him.

Realizing she'd gone too far to stop now, Melora put the knife down. "People like the Shippens, the Galloways, the Franks."

Jared frowned. He too had heard the innuendo, the gossip, but he, unlike the others, knew the man for the leader he was—on and off the field. "Melora, the General's not like other men. You weren't there on the trip to Quebec when only his spirit got us through seven weeks of marching through land I wouldn't wish on Cornwallis. Sometimes the snow was so deep and cold even those of us from Maine thought we would die. At first men prayed, and I was one of them. But I can tell you," he paused, then looked away.

"Go on," she said.

He took a deep breath. "I can tell you that God was no more on that march than he's been in any part of this war. And if Montgomery's men hadn't given up, the General would have won, taken the city. There's no man alive who is more of a patriot! These people, the Galloways and those, he's not favoring them. He's just carrying out orders."

Still far from convinced, Melora lashed out with what, to her anyway, was the crux of the matter. "Is choosing Peggy Shippen to be your lady, just 'carrying out orders'?"

Jared released her hand, methodically packed the food, then closed the basket. What was he doing? Had she made him so mad that he was going to leave? Sitting back against the tree, Jared seemed deep in thought until she realized that he was struggling not to laugh. "So, this is all about Miss Peggy, is it?" He pulled her to him and took hold of the ribbons beneath her chin. "Not a particular favorite of yours."

"That's true," Melora said, relieved beyond measure. "But, even you, Jared Donovan, have to agree..." she paused as he removed the hat and placed it on the picnic basket.

"I have to agree with what?" the young man asked playfully. He lowered himself to lie on one side, head propped up in the palm of his hand.

Melora sat up in triumph. "You have to agree that there are many ladies in Philadelphia whose politics are much closer to the General's than Peggy Shippen's."

With a lazy sigh, Jared reached up to catch the tendrils suddenly loose and long. Winding the dark curls around his fingers, he leaned over and whispered into her ear. "And is that why I picked you up off the street that day? Because of your politics?"

As Jared pulled her down onto the grass beside him, Melora felt a little shock at the simplicity of it all. She and Jared, the General and Peggy Shippen.

CHAPTER 25

Late September, 1778

*190 High Street*

She had not said no. Benedict Arnold leaned back in his chair and savored the memory of the night before. On the way home from the Southwark Theatre, he had finally taken Peggy in his arms and explained that he must have her, that she must be his, that age, politics, and war be damned, they must marry. And she had not said no.

Covered in some creamy silken creation that glowed softly in the darkness of the carriage, Peggy had allowed him to kiss her mouth, throat, ears, and neck, even brushing the width of her bodice with a gloved hand as he did so. At first she had sat still as he made his advances, a soft quiet doll. But slowly one hand and then another crept around his neck as she lifted her mouth to his. Never in one moment with his first wife, neither before nor after the consummation of their vows, had he felt the raw desire he'd experienced the previous evening.

Arnold sat up and pushed aside the report he was preparing for Congress on the state of Philadelphia's defenses. He would have her.

Dipping the quill in the inkwell, he began to make a list of personal holdings and assets. While he was still a man of means, this was a hard time to prove it. The New Haven store had long ago run out of goods for sale, and besides, Hannah and the boys were in the process of moving to Philadelphia. Moreover, like the store, the wharves and fleet in New Haven had been effectively shut down by the ongoing British naval presence. The house in New Haven would show at least some of his wealth, but, unfortunately, no Shippen had seen it. And the little money he'd derived from the store closings had gone to support the kitchen and staff of the residence on High Street. That was typical of those fools in Congress, to imagine he could perform his duties as governor with no money.

He did, however, have prospects. Hannah's investments had done very well and a particularly bright spot on his financial horizon was the ship's cargo he'd purchased a half interest in. He just needed to arrange some horses and wagons to convey the load to a local merchant. Not too onerous a task for the military governor of Philadelphia. There was also a possibility in New York. Philip Schuyler and Gouveneur Morris were trying to put a package together in New York as a thank you for his help against the British there earlier in the war. They wanted him to see some property there, two estates abandoned by Loyalists. He might start a settlement at one of the properties; recruit some of his men and their families to join him there.

Putting the pen aside, Arnold rose from the desk and began walking slowly about the lavishly furnished study of the residence. Here, in the privacy of his rooms, he was working very hard to make his limp less noticeable, not only to Peggy but to her father. He needed to impress that father, yet he had to admit that if he were Judge Shippen, neither his recuperation nor the list he'd just compiled would inspire great confidence. It was a terrible irony, that at this point in his life, he needed to prove himself physically, and even more so financially. His ability to provide had never, ever been in doubt, since a very young age.

As a boy, spring meant that soon he would travel with his father on summer voyages across the sound, down the coast, and into the Caribbean. Even as a youngster, escaping the confines of Norwich, with its rigid customs and near suffocating preoccupation with the hereafter, was complete exhilaration. He was the Captain's son both at home and on deck, and he reveled in the position. Meanwhile, Captain Arnold boasted of his son's nautical abilities and innate understanding of trading and cargoes to anyone who would listen.

But when the ships came to sit idly, a result of his father's faltering business, he'd sought a new vessel and converted the local boys into a land-based crew. While his father slid into drinking and poverty, the son gained a reputation for raw, if outrageous, courage, directing his men on increasingly perilous voyages over barn ridgepoles and onto millwheel blades, maintaining the family's prominence in the only way he knew how.

At last, however, his mother could not even afford the tuition for Dr. Cogswell's school. He'd been withdrawn and, like any common laborer, gone to work at an early age. But while serving as an apprentice to the apothecary, Dr. Daniel Lathrop, the sea and commerce still called. Convincing Dr. Lathrop that his talents lay more in the import-export segment of his business than in the shop sorting, grinding, and measuring, he was allowed to travel to Canada, the West Indies, and London, procuring the fruits, fabrics, and wines that made his master's apothecary unique.

In 1762, turning 21, the apprenticeship was over. His mother and father were dead and Hannah was seventeen. Even though Dr. Lathrop presented him with 500 pounds and an offer to collaborate in business, he opted instead to open his own store in New Haven, some forty miles away. Expanding on his mentor's idea, he added to the apothecary's usual inventory cosmetics, jewelry, prints, maps, stationery, surgical supplies, and books for the students at nearby Yale College. Soon he was traveling to London to procure for himself, leaving Hannah to run the day-to-day affairs of the store.

Five years later he owned three ships in addition to the apothecary. With his trade routes expanding from London to familiar ports in the Caribbean and Canada, he was becoming a very wealthy man. But just as he was coming into his own as a merchant, Parliament began to get serious about the colonies contributing to the cost of government. Laws designed to raise cash, such as the Sugar Act in 1764 and the Stamp Act in 1765, were disastrous for the largely barter-based economy and infuriated any right-thinking colonial. Also, for him and so many others, the new laws cut directly into the ubiquitous and very profitable smuggling trade. Although the Stamp Act was repealed in 1766, the equally inflammatory Townsend Acts were passed just a year later. Now married to Margaret Mansfield and soon to be father of three, he became a visible and vocal leader in the New Haven Sons of Liberty, and, in 1774, the men elected him Captain of the New Haven militia. Yet, even as his reputation as a leader in the rebellion spread, his fortune declined.

Arnold's eyes wandered to the report to Congress. Of course there was what the army owed him, but that would never support Peggy's accustomed level of comfort, nor his own, for that matter. But she was his fate, he was sure of that. Now to convince her father.

A little tired by the exertion, Arnold seated himself in one of the magnificent wing chairs in front of the empty fireplace. To be worn out by four turns around the room seemed impossible. But he would not be thwarted by wounds anymore than he'd be stopped by finances. He just needed to be more alert to the opportunities. With Philadelphia settling down, that was exactly what he planned to do. Too much of his attention had been demanded in playing politics here, especially by that damned Council.

Thinking of the Council reminded him of the horrific scene in the Galloway parlor: Peggy, terrified and threatened by that monster Matlack simply for trying to protect her older, clearly-ill cousin. The Congress might be filled with self-serving fools. But these newly elected rulers of Pennsylvania—Peale, Matlack, and the others—these men were evil.

# CHAPTER 26

## *Judge Shippen*

T he fall and early winter of 1778 were uneasy times for our family. Despite the fact that we were all joyously anticipating Betsey's wedding, the tense atmosphere that clung to Philadelphia could not be avoided. The fourth proclamation was issued at the end of October, containing fifty-seven new names. Those I knew on the list, however, were long since gone to New York.

Finally bending to the inevitable, Grace left her home to move in with Molly Craig who, although married to an ardent Whig, was herself (to use Grace's terms), "a violent Tory." Meanwhile, Joseph and Betsey Galloway reached London and placed great faith in Howe's ability to get them set up correctly. In retrospect, I believe Grace should have joined them, as her bitterness alarmed us even then.

Joseph Reed must have taken the Council's request to heart, as he did in fact resign his seat in Congress to take a position on the Supreme Executive Council. The rumor was that he complied only on the promise that he would be elected the Council's next president at the December elections. And, only a short time into the job, the man brought such great sadness to the city. But I will discuss that in great-er detail in just a moment.

On the broader front the war seemed to be... well, no one was quite sure. In July of 1778, John Butler struck terror in the most valiant of hearts as his Tory and Indian force of from 500 to 1000 (the reports varied widely) attacked settlements throughout Pennsylvania's Wyoming Valley. Having traveled from Ft. Niagara in Oriscany, New York to Forty Fort, barely 100 miles from Philadelphia, Butler's men were responsible for taking 227 scalps and only five prisoners. Moreover, a thou-sand buildings were burned, eight forts destroyed, and huge numbers of cattle, sheep, and pigs killed or driven off. The Wyoming Valley Massacre, as it came to be called, proved, according to the rebels, the barbarity the British were capable of.

Elsewhere, a French-American operation poised to strike the British at New-

*port was abandoned as a deadly late summer storm descended on the French fleet under d'Estaing. The long-awaited involvement of the French was then, once again, maddeningly postponed while the fleet sailed to Boston first for repairs and subsequently to winter in the West Indies. And late that summer, Washington spread the Continental Army from the Hudson over to Connecticut expecting, I assume, that Clinton was still interested in the Hudson or perhaps in attacking the French in Boston. But the great one sat apparently idle as British strategy, obviously unbeknownst to Washington, was being rewritten. London had decided to shift focus and take advantage of what was believed to be strong Loyalist sentiment in the south. That is one drawback in fighting a defensive war: The defenders are never sure where the war will be.*

*In November, Walter Butler, the inexperienced son of John Butler, and the notorious Joseph Brant led a late-season raid on Cherry Valley in New York, completely destroying the village. The Butlers' image was not improved as thirty women and children lay among the dead, more than a few of them members of Loyalist families. Some said the raid was purely offensive while others recalled Unadilla and Oquaga, towns in Brant's territory, burned just a month earlier by Continentals and militia out of Schoharie. The fighting season closed with Washington setting up winter headquarters in Middlebrook, New Jersey, and Clinton in New York directing what was to be the first thrust of the southern strategy. News also reached us in November that William Franklin, Benjamin Franklin's illegitimate but highly regarded son, had at last been freed by the rebels from prison in Litchfield, New Jersey. Such a good man, a moderate by nature, but unfortunately the times were against moderation. Even his father, the mighty Franklin, could not persuade him to go against British law.*

*And yes, early that fall the General finally approached me on the matter of Peggy's hand. I should have been more prepared. It was already family lore that he had gone so far as to refer to her "heavenly bosom" in a love letter. The man was mad for her, that was plain, but who wouldn't have been? In addition to being a great beauty, over the summer she'd become a confident and somewhat aware young woman. I say "somewhat" because I have yet to meet the eighteen-year old who is very wise in the ways of the world.*

*The General sent his man Jared to ask for a special meeting, which of course I granted. At the appointed time the General burst into my study, prepared for battle I guess, plans and budgets blazing. And with almost none of the conventional conversational niceties, Arnold informed me that it was his deepest wish to love and care for my Peggy, to become a member of our family, and a son to me in particu-*

lar. A son? The man was only twelve years my junior, and six to my wife. But that was not the real issue I had with Arnold. And no, it wasn't his allegiance either. In fact, at times the notion of having a famous patriot hero in the house seemed like protection sent from heaven.

The real issue was the haze of impropriety that seemed to follow him about, for example, the over-zealousness of his early political activity, and the allegations of financial irregularities during the Canadian campaign. There were even stories floating about Philadelphia that he was currently misusing his office for financial gain. Of course Arnold assured me it was all politics, the Council jockeying for state power over Washington and Congress. And, as he reminded me, he had been cleared years ago of all wrongdoing in Canada. On a pettier note, I also found the man to be brash. He filled his space too much. At the same time, I will concede that perhaps this is a useful trait for a battlefield commander, and as a lawyer, I obviously have no experience of such things.

Finally, and on a very practical level, Arnold was a cripple with three sons, a maiden sister, and a nearly defunct business. That was quite a bit for the plate of any young bride. So I asked him to be patient as I considered the subject. I also pointed out that he and Peggy had really not known each other for very long. While none of this was what the man wanted to hear, I have to admit he handled the situation with the utmost grace. Peggy, on the other hand, was not nearly so obliging when I shared these same thoughts with her. She stormed out of my study, then pouted for a week.

My attitude toward Arnold improved later that fall during the terrible business with Reed. Two of those attainted for high treason in the second proclamation were Abraham Carlisle and our family's miller, John Roberts. Although both men, elderly Quakers, turned themselves over to authorities within the specified time, they were still charged with providing services to the British. While Roberts and Carlisle were probably guilty as charged, the case was not simple. This was because both men were also cited as having performed many humane acts toward American prisoners of war. In addition, and from a legal standpoint more pertinent, many of those included on the proclamations had done much worse and received far lighter sentences.

One thousand people from all political and religious walks of life signed petitions asking for mercy for the two men. Robert's wife and ten children fell to their knees begging before the court, but Reed, the prosecutor, would not be moved. Justice must be served, he demanded, and the power of the Supreme Executive Council was never in doubt. Four thousand accompanied the two men on their way to the gallows.

But what of Arnold? The night before the executions Arnold held a grand reception at the City Tavern inviting numerous known Loyalists and Quakers. His action reassured many of us that we were not totally in the hands of Matlack, Peale, and Reed. And on the day of the executions, after the two condemned men were forced to walk through the city with nooses about their necks, Arnold had his men stand at attention while the two unfortunates climbed the stairs to die. Against the uncertainty that once again threatened to consume Philadelphia, the brave nobility of those gestures touched me. How could my opinion not have improved?

CHAPTER 27

Mid-December 1778
*British Headquarters*

"André!"

At the sight of Sir Henry filling his doorway, John André dropped the attendance log he had been reviewing and jumped to attention. "Yes, sir!"

Clinton gazed about the tiny office piled high with the surfeit of useless reporting required by the British Empire. With this amount of kindling, he thought, a poorly aimed match could level the entire lower end of Manhattan within hours. "Captain, sit, please."

As André looked uncomfortably over the cluttered office, Sir Henry dropped into the vacant chair opposite André's desk. "You didn't join us for the hunt today. In fact, I haven't seen you out of the office this week."

"Trying to catch up, sir," André motioned to the stacks of papers on his desk. "I made a promise to myself to get this all cleared out by the new year."

"A worthy goal," murmured Sir Henry. "I wish a few of your colleagues might make a similar vow."

"They probably don't need to."

Clinton shook his head. "I doubt that very seriously, Major. I've noticed your work. You're organized, you're clear, you have good ideas, and you seem to work well with others. Another trait I would like to see more of on the staff."

Taken aback by his superior's praise, André groped for an appropriate response. "It's my job, sir."

Clinton looked the young man over. "Is that all the military is to you, André, a job? Be frank."

André twisted nervously in his seat. Of all the times he had imagined having an intimate chat with Sir Henry, he had never foreseen the cliff he felt looming in front of him with that one instruction. "Be frank." He could get himself sacked in a moment. Taking a deep breath and hoping that the saint of honesty, if there was one, was watching, he reached into his desk drawer and pulled out a sheaf of drawings. "If you'll bear with me, sir." He rifled through the papers, pulling out several and arraying them on the desk facing Sir Henry.

"This first drawing, this is a seascape I made during my crossing from London in '74. The second here is of a group of red men we encountered in Canada, along with some of the local wildlife." André paused, recalling a long night wrapped in bearskins in the Canadian wilderness. "This next one depicts General Grey's victory at Paoli. It was my closest experience with bloodshed and the first in which I wondered if I might die." Pointing to the fourth sketch of officers on horseback, he laughed. "You should recognize this one, sir. It was done after one of our rides to Long Island. And this one," he pointed to a pen and ink of a young woman in a turban, "is Miss Peggy Shippen of Philadelphia."

Clinton picked up a picture, noting the clarity with which André had drawn his fellow officers, including himself. "You have talent, that's undeniable, but I'm afraid I miss your point."

"Please see this last one, sir, and then I'll explain." He handed Clinton a small sketch of four women and a man. "My family, my mother, my sisters Mary, Anne, and Louisa, and my brother William."

"Your sisters are not married?"

André smiled. "Would that they were, sir. Would that they were."

Clinton leaned back in his seat. "I understand. I have two sisters-in-law that are dependent on me for every mouthful. Although, to be fair, in my case they also earn their keep. My wife died some years ago; they care for my children while I'm away."

"I'm very sorry, sir."

Clinton shrugged impatiently. "These are nice, but, again, your point."

Using his pen as a pointer, André began. "Yes, the military is a job... well, actually, a profession, but it is a profession where one might find all this." He touched quickly on the seascape and the scenes from Canada, "Please understand, sir, that my alternative opportunity for advancement is a seat behind a desk for all my life in our family's firm. As a member of

His Majesty's army I'm allowed to travel and see the world.

"This one," the sketch showed a British soldier bayoneting a Continental in a tent, "the battle at Paoli, shows that by virtue of being an officer in His Majesty's army I am allowed to serve my country, earn my place as an Englishman, as one of the King's devoted subjects. And this girl here," he tapped the turbaned image, "one of many new acquaintances here in the colonies."

André looked up at Clinton hesitantly, unsure if the Commander in Chief saw all this as so much drivel, before plunging on. "This one of the ride illustrates the society of men I've been allowed to join, the comradery, the esprit de corps. Men I respect. Finally, sir," he held up the picture of his family, "they need my support, my material support, now more than ever."

Clinton looked at André quizzically.

"I'm afraid that much of our family's income was derived from holdings in Grenada. Holdings that, due to the recent French conquest there, we no longer have access to."

"Your brother is not a help in this?"

"William? I'm embarrassed that he is not. Thus far, in fact, he lives above the means that I am able to provide for him."

"I see. Is there anything else?"

André paused for a moment. "Yes, yes, there is. There is the hope for personal glory. I hope you see nothing wrong with that, sir."

Silence filled the room as Sir Henry picked up each drawing again, seeming to see them in a new light from moments before. "You've given voice to many of my own thoughts about our profession," he said finally. "I wonder if you could not only give voice but direction to certain other ideas I have."

André held his breath. "Now I do not understand, sir."

Clinton leaned against the desk. "If you're in search in glory, then you're no different from most of the soldiers in most of the world. I think that's worthy. But more important, when General Grey recommended you to my service he said that he had never known a more accomplished young man, with a great knowledge of his profession and the best disposition in the world. I am coming to share his assessment."

"You pay me a great compliment, sir."

"Compliments are all well and good, but I think we must put you to better use than screening letters and promotion lists. Have you had your supper yet, Major?"

"No, sir, I told my man, Peter, not to expect me."

"Well, then, stack up your papers and get your jacket. Usually I dine alone, but tonight you will join me. We can talk about sisters and sisters-in-law, how you must organize your work better and rejoin the hunt, and," Clinton stood and walked toward the door, "how I have every premonition that we might do each other good."

# CHAPTER 28

## Late December, 1778
### The Great House

Despite the new dress made from Coffin and Anderson's most elegant pale blue satin, the heirloom veil from Belgium, the hundred twinkling candles about the house, and the scent of pine boughs wrapped down the banister and over the mantel, despite all these outward signs of a joyous Christmas wedding, Betsey entered the parlor on her father's arm looking like a trapped and desperate animal.

Peggy felt a soft punch to her side but didn't dare face her cousin Elizabeth, standing beside her. One raised eyebrow from Elizabeth had been enough to send them both into a fit of smothered giggles just moments earlier, and her mother was not amused. All of the group gathered in the parlor, some twelve cousins, several aunts and uncles, plus Sally, Polly, Edward, and herself were privy to the story now. And if one of them succumbed again, she knew they all would.

That very morning Peggy and her cousin Elizabeth Tilghman had, after hearing sobbing from Betsey's room, demanded that she open the door. But it was only after Peggy's threat to return with her father that the two girls received a tremulous, "Come in." There under the covers they found the bride-to-be cowering against the white pillow.

"What is it?" Peggy begged, stroking her sister's hair. "Please, you've got to tell us."

And little by little Betsey did tell them, albeit through many more tears and much quivering. Inching up against the headboard and clutching the blankets to her chin, the stricken woman told the following story. It turned out that earlier that morning, on the morning of her marriage to Neddy, Judge Shippen called her into the library for a little talk. At first everything was pleasant. They sipped tea and spoke of times past, the Judge telling her how much he would miss her and what a pleasure she had been as a daughter. Then, lowering his voice, he went on to say that most importantly he wanted to remind her of a married woman's duties. Not only must she remember the honor of her family at all times and assume responsibility for the management of the home, but first and foremostly she was honor-bound to please her husband. "Please my husband," she whimpered. "You know what he means."

"But Betsey," Elizabeth whispered, "you know that is part of the married life, for the procreation of children." Covering her eyes with her hands, Betsey shook her head. "I know, but I can't...I love Neddy, I do, but why can't we just not do...that?"

Suddenly Betsey sat up and, taking both Peggy's and Elizabeth's hands, pulled them to sit beside her on the bed. "Promise me that you will never marry. I can't bear to think that the two of you will ever have to experience this fear as I am."

When neither Peggy nor Elizabeth answered, Betsey squeezed their hands fiercely. "Promise me! It's the only consolation I can think of."

Therefore, with faces as straight as they could manage, the two cousins dutifully promised Betsey they would never marry. Then, as Peggy hurried off to find her mother and some possible relief for her sister, Elizabeth ran downstairs to tell the story to anyone who would listen.

But from the looks of Betsey tonight, her face white and drawn as Neddy took her hand to stand in front of the minister, Mrs. Shippen had done no more good than the promise forced upon herself and Elizabeth. Over her giggles now, Peggy speculated ruefully that Neddy would need every bit of compassion and persuasion he possessed to calm his bride tonight.

Glancing around at the mass of family about her, Peggy regretted that she hadn't been able to persuade her parents into inviting the General. The decision was to include family members only, and he was not family... yet. But he would be. The General's assistance to Grace as well as the way he handled the Roberts and Carlisle affair had impressed her father deeply. Moreover, with the General getting along so often without a cane, the wounds were scarcely an issue. And finally, the Judge's concern for her own health was a huge factor. He knew how easily the headaches set in when she was worried or unhappy.

Peggy looked back at Betsey and Neddy and thought how different her own wedding would be. Rather than a sweet, simple boy, Arnold was one of the greatest men of the country and the century. And, unlike Betsey, she was excited and intrigued when the General looked at her in that special way and somehow maneuvered to have her in his arms, kissing her, and whispering of the full expression of love between a man and a woman, whispering that they must be married soon, as his desire for her was almost beyond restraint.

Neddy was placing the ring on Betsey's finger now, and Peggy could see her sister's hand shaking from across the room. She could also see, in her mind's eye, how the General would look when he placed the ring on her own hand and led her, his wife, from this house and away to his own. In fact, she had thought of little else for the past few days even amidst all the comings and goings of her sister's wedding. She had thought of little else since her father, after swearing her to silence as this was Betsey's time, had quietly and gravely, one week earlier, given her permission to marry Major General Benedict Arnold.

## CHAPTER 29

## January, 1779

## Outside the Third Presbyterian Church, Philadelphia

The day was bone chillingly cold as the congregation spilled out of the Third Presbyterian Church and onto Pine Street. After thanking the minister for the fine sermon on Moses' descent from the mountain, Joseph Reed tightened the blanket about the baby in his arms and nodded to Hettie to come along. He wanted to get her home where she could rest a bit while he helped with the children. The baby Dennis, at eight months, put particular strains on her limited energy. Moreover, as the new President's wife, she had acquired her own official duties. Just the week before, General Washington asked if she could organize a ladies' assistance campaign to help clothe the army.

How wrong he had been to assume that he might be more of a help to her by being back in Philadelphia. His new workload was more demanding than ever. Somehow, all the problems of the country were condensed here in Philadelphia: the currency depreciation, shortages, the needs of the army, and fights in Congress. The Commander in Chief upon his recent visit commented on the pettiness of the Congress and the luxury in which its members lived. "Where had all the good men gone?" he asked. Reed felt the same way. To get anything accomplished required tedious fawning and flattery. Spying several gentlemen with whom he badly needed to confer, Reed felt even now a twinge of regret for the Sabbath prohibitions on work. Otherwise, quite a bit could be accomplished right here in front of the church.

"Mr. President, do you have a moment?" Reed turned to see Timothy Matlack pushing his way through the crowd toward him. He also noticed Hettie stepping away. His wife could not understand the alliance he had formed with Matlack. She considered him to be crude and ungentlemanly.

"Good day, Mr. Matlack."

"Mr. President, an urgent matter has arisen."

Reed, accustomed to Matlack's urgent matters, put a hand on his colleague's shoulder. "It's the Sabbath, Timothy. Are you sure?"

Matlack's ruddy face grew even redder with the wind and his agitation. "I'm..." he began, but then, looking around at the many churchgoers still surrounding them, nodded down the street. "Perhaps we might walk a moment, sir."

Smiling graciously but with a resignation only her husband recognized, Hettie Reed took the baby and, beckoning to the other children, started up Fourth Street. The President and Secretary of the Supreme Executive Council followed a few paces behind.

"So, Timothy, what thoughts have such a hold on you this morning?"

"It's the General, sir," Matlack answered anxiously. "I've been told he's planning to leave Philadelphia...very soon."

Reed stopped, his generally placid features giving way to astonishment. Just one week previously the Council had voted unanimously to prosecute Arnold for misuse of office. "Who told you this?"

"A friend of my son's—a member of the militia still posted to the General's guard—he heard the General and Major Franks speaking of it."

"But where is he going? Another command?"

Sure of Reed's attention, Matlack grew more businesslike. "No, they say Philip Schuyler and some of those from the north want to reward him for keeping the British out of their lands back in '75. He's to get property or an estate of one of those gone over to the King."

Passing by Willings Alley, Reed struggled to maintain a normal expression in front of the St. Joseph parishioners also emerging onto Fourth. As he smiled and made small talk, the full implication of Matlack's news became stunningly apparent. Arnold was ahead of him. And if Arnold reached New York, how might the government of Pennsylvania prosecute him there?

Arnold. Reed could see the man's sneer as though he stood before him—as he had seen it so often that year—through the General's constant misuse of office for personal gain, through complete lack of respect for the elected government of Pennsylvania or its laws, and, perhaps worst, through audacious display of favoritism toward the Tories in town, even taking one as his lady. This criminal motivated only by self-promotion and greed was simply going to walk away to be rewarded with spoils of war, lands and an estate? Never.

"Timothy," Reed said as soon as the two were alone again, "did your son's friend say when this might happen?"

Matlack nodded. "He's to travel to New York in February, meet Schuyler then."

The men walked in silence as carriages and wagons rumbled by. From time to time Hettie would look back, hoping, Reed was sure, to see him walking alone. But that was not possible, not just yet.

"I need some time, Tim," Reed announced at last, "to prepare our case against Arnold. In the meanwhile could you write again to The *Packet*? Perhaps you could work in the charges brought against him after the Canadian campaign."

As a familiar carriage rolled by and turned onto Locust, Matlack hesitated, rubbing his beard nervously. "But Mr. President, begging your pardon, those charges were dropped."

Reed paused and then walked Matlack back to the corner of Fourth and Locust. "We have a responsibility to the electorate, Timothy. Many Congressmen have described how hard it was to gather evidence in those days. So, please, look into the case again. And, Tim," he continued, pointing in the direction of the Shippen's home, "remember the circles in which our General has chosen to place himself. Consider how he lives."

The conversation was clearly at an end. The gaunt man, now calm and purposeful, touched the edge of his red stocking cap. "Yes, Your Excellency." As the President moved to join his family, Matlack took one last look at Arnold emerging from the carriage and murmured thanks for gifts both seen and unseen. Then, with the paragraphs already forming in his mind, he turned eagerly toward home.

## CHAPTER 30

## Late January, 1779
### The Great House

*M*elora balanced the tray of cookies against her hip and knocked on the parlor door. When there was no answer she pushed the door open and entered.

"Melora!" Polly hissed, "Against the wall!"

All but dropping the cookies onto the tea table, Melora darted to the side of the gleaming highboy as Polly, Becky, Peg, Sally, and Betsey grouped themselves behind the tea cart. Once again the doors opened, this time with Peggy standing in the doorway.

Peggy looked stupidly at Sally. "You said Mother wanted to see me."

"I lied to you, silly," Sally said laughing out loud. "This is an engagement party. Now take a seat and we'll have some tea. Melora," Sally pointed to the cart, "pass the tea around and then check on the biscuits Cook has heating for us."

Stung by her earlier reception, Melora fought the impulse to walk out of the room and leave the young ladies to the arduous task of pouring tea. And check on the biscuits? Just who did Miss Sally Shippen think had mixed and rolled them out? Sometimes she had no idea how she could serve out the remaining three years of her indenture. Not if it had to be around the likes of these. The good news of this engagement was that Miss Peggy would soon be gone.

"So, Peggy Shippen, or should I say Arnold," Becky took the cup of tea from Melora, "you kept your friends waiting long enough. We've all been wild for news."

"She kept us all waiting," Betsey added.

"How can you accuse me of that?" Peggy said. "You made me faithfully promise never to marry."

The very happy new bride stared down at her tea cup. "I suppose I had it wrong."

As the laughter died down, Becky resumed her questioning. "When will the wedding be, and what made your father change his mind?"

Peggy looked around the room at her friends and sisters. "I think Father changed his mind when he saw that the General would make a full recovery. That was always his primary concern."

"I think Father couldn't tolerate you ranting and raving around the house and taking to your bed every other day," Sally offered, picking up the cookies to send around again. "Melora, the biscuits."

"But Peggy," Peg asked earnestly as Melora nodded to Sally and turned toward the door. "Are you a rebel now?"

"Of course she is," Becky taunted. "She'll be out working side by side with Hettie Reed to clothe the army. Or perhaps you'll take up sewing, like Mrs. Reed's family did in England."

"Becky, you're terrible. That woman has done nothing to you."

Becky took a cookie from the tray. "No, but her husband has. I think he has us watched all the time. And he's making it very difficult for my father to do business in New York. They're treating him like a spy when he's only trying to collect money that's rightfully his. Sometimes I think we should just give up and go to New York."

"You'd leave Philadelphia?" Polly asked.

Becky sat up very straight in her chair. "Why not? Most of our friends from here are already in New York. And think of André, and all the others who are posted there." Then, with a wink at Peggy, she added dryly, "With the exception of Mrs. Arnold here, most of us have been bored to tears since the British left. They're probably all up there having a grand time."

"I don't know if they are having a grand time," said Peg. "But they miss us very much and inquire frequently about our health."

"How do you know that?" Sally said, astonished.

"We, my sister, myself, and some of the officers formed a little birthday club. We drink to each other's health on our special days and send our best wishes."

"But," Sally continued, clearly shocked by Peg's news, "how do you get their messages?"

"Don't be silly, Sally," Becky chided. "Sometimes Peggy's General gives people passes. But there are hundreds of other people going back and forth across the lines constantly."

"She's right," Peg piped up. "It's not hard. We know a china and glass merchant who delivers our messages for us. Sometimes we even ask him to place some orders for us, for things we can't buy here. I don't know how it proceeds after that, but we always get our letters as well as our parcels."

"Aren't you taking a terrible risk?" Betsey asked.

Becky shook her head. "It's harmless, just a few hello's and some pins and ribbons. Surely they can't jail us for that? But," Becky turned a wicked eye to Peggy Shippen, "enough of our secret ways. I want to talk about our friend's marriage. And I want Peggy to tell us how she can be so sure that the General is recovered...in every way."

Standing behind the parlor door, Melora hugged the empty tray to her chest. She could not believe her ears. Bored? Sending birthday good wishes to the enemy? Placing orders for hair ribbons? Those silly, ridiculous little idiots. Did they think this war was all a game? And the General giving out passes. Perhaps Jared would listen now.

CHAPTER 31

February 9, 1779

The Hungry Hound Tavern,
En route to Middlebrook, New Jersey

Benedict Arnold sat back against the stiff wooden chair. He relished the comforting warmth of the fire and the cognac as it spread through his body, aching from the four-day ride in the freezing coach. How in God's name would he make it to Poughkeepsie? And where the devil was Franks?

Despite the pleasure of leaving the coach and the cold for this tight, warm tavern, he was anxious to be on his way. With only a four-week furlough, he had many miles to cover and much to accomplish. The first item on the itinerary was a visit with Washington at the winter headquarters in Middlebrook. Besides the issues of military business to attend to, he wanted to discuss the New York possibility with his commander, a great landholder himself. Then, all being well, he would continue on to meet with Schuyler and the New York legislature to work out the details. As he'd written to Peggy, the property at Skenesboro particularly excited him. There were great possibilities for iron works and mills there. He'd seen it all on the way back and forth to Canada, and now it might be his. His thought was to found a settlement there, populated with soldiers who had served under him. New York would, in turn, be better protected by having another strong presence on its frontier. Of course, the settlement and development would be a huge undertaking and not one that he was sure he could afford.

But now this plea from Franks to stop, and meet him here on a matter of the greatest importance. Please to God it had nothing to do with Peggy. This was Arnold's last thought before dozing off in the warm glow of the fire.

"Wake up, sir!"

Arnold looked at the dripping young man standing before him. Why was Franks so wet, and why was he waving a newspaper?

Slowly, the events of the day returned to the exhausted General, and he recalled the reason for his being propped up in front of a fire in this strange tavern: Franks' urgent request to meet him here. Arnold sat up abruptly. "David, is Miss Shippen well?"

"I've heard nothing otherwise, sir." The young officer shivered as he spoke.

"Take off those wet things," Arnold ordered, signaling the serving girl at the same time. "Hot cider for the Major. And one for me as well."

Franks removed a soaking muffler, coat, gloves, and boots while Arnold looked around the room. The tavern was small, only five tables with another ten or so chairs spread around. And besides his own man and driver, only one of the other tables was occupied. That was good. One never knew who might be listening.

"So, the matter of greatest importance?"

Placing his tankard to one side, Franks reached for the copy of The *Pennsylvania Pacquet* and spread it on the table in front of Arnold. "They're bringing eight charges against you for misuse of office. They say they'll pay none of the army's costs, nor will they call out the militia while you're in command. And they've sent the charges to Washington, the Congress, and the states, besides printing them here."

"Who are they?" asked Arnold tersely. He pulled the paper closer to him.

"The very group you'd imagine, sir. The State of Pennsylvania."

Arnold read down the list of the charges: granting illegal passes, benefiting personally from the shop closures in Philadelphia, use of public wagons for transporting private property, showing favor to Tories, and on and on. Lies, slander, malicious presentations of innocent facts written by some of the most despicable people to set foot on earth. And it had gone out to all the states, the Congress, and to one of the few men whose opinion he truly cared about in this world, the Commander in Chief. Even to Peggy.

"It's all false. You know that, I trust."

"Of course," Franks answered, barely stifling a yawn. "But what will you do now? Continue, or return to the capital to deal with this matter?

"How does one deal with tyrants? Tyrants who hide behind their own laws? The King at least fights honestly!" Signaling to the coachman that their repast was over, he accepted Franks' arm and pulled himself out of the chair. "We'll go to Middlebrook. General Washington will want to help."

CHAPTER 32

February, 1779

*Middlebrook, New Jersey*

*Winter Headquarters of General George Washington*

Washington read the charges once, twice, and then a third time before removing his spectacles and settling back in his chair. Arnold, impatient and angry, wondered why a page of trumped up lies deserved such attention. Had he not just given the rational explanation to each of the eight charges?

The afternoon was quiet, chores and drills were over for the day, and outside it was snowing in great, heavy swirls. Inside the house, which John Wallace had graciously offered for the Commander in Chief's use, most of the staff were resting or attending to personal needs in the short period before dinner. Although the coach had made good time, arriving on schedule before breakfast, the Commander had been unable to meet with Arnold until now. And Mrs. Washington had yet to greet him.

"You say you purchased nothing while the stores were closed?" Washington asked.

"Nothing but what was needed to outfit the residence for official service."

"The wagons?"

"It's all in the Quartermaster's Report submitted to the Council. Every cent repaid for the men's time, as well as for the forage and water costs for the horses."

"And you say this pass to New York was to deliver a letter to Sir Henry?"

"Yes. A merchant's request for payment. A simple business transaction."

The Commander in Chief stood and crossed the room to warm his hands in front of the fire. As always, Washington's quickness was surprising. Outside, a series of short commands signaled the changing of the guard around the mansion. "So, General," Washington asked in a low voice, "how can I be of service to you?"

Taken aback, Arnold looked up into the impassive face. "I thought a letter of unqualified support, perhaps a demand for the charges to be withdrawn..."

Washington leaned against the mantel; one more issue to be strategized, one more plan gone wrong. "My demand would be just that, a demand. It wouldn't be enforceable and my support won't clear your name. I wasn't there, I don't have any evidence. These are formal charges. They must be dealt with formally."

"But, sir," objected Arnold, "I would never be heard honestly. Unfettered power in the state is all that they want, and they see me as an obstacle to that. For the same people to judge me as have accused me is insanity."

"Your point is well taken. If all is as you say, then these men have done you an egregious injury, one that should be put right at the nearest opportunity. Ask for a court martial or that the Congress look into the matter first. Make the Council prove their case. Even if the Congress agrees with any of the charges, they should be dealt with in a court of your fellow officers."

Arnold rose from his seat, frantically trying to think through the scenario that Washington was painting. Being tried for these ridiculous trifles had never occurred to him. The thought of politicians once again pawing through his life, those who did nothing but whisper and point fingers, made him close to physically ill.

"I fear politicians, sir—their treachery, their church-house sanctimony."

As the two men stood silently looking into the blazing fire, Washington recalled his own recent thoughts on politicians. He'd written a very long letter just a few weeks earlier to Benjamin Harrison deploring the state of Congress and the very low quality of men he saw there. Indeed, he passed many a worried night wondering if all the congressional triumph of '75 and '76 would simply be undone by the pettiness and pursuit of personal fortune so rampant now within that chamber. But what alternative was there to the government he was sworn to defend?

With his face still toward the fire, Washington gave the only advice that was practical. "I would return as soon as possible and demand a hearing. This is our government, and we must trust to it. Again, General Arnold, if all is as you say, you will certainly prevail."

# CHAPTER 33

February 28, 1779

*The Great House*

"*W*hat does one do with this?"

The *Pennsylvania Packet* lay open on the card table before Peggy and Benedict. There, prominently inserted at the top of the page, was the most recent of the printed barrage of attacks against Arnold by Matlack.

"When I meet your carriage in the streets, and think of the splendor in which you live and revel, of the settlement which it is said you have proposed in a certain case, and of the decent frugality necessarily used by other officers of the army, it is impossible to avoid the question: "From whence have these riches flowed if you did not plunder Montreal?"

"When he meets my carriage? The splendor in which I live and revel? How can he write such things? Besides the fact that Congress dismissed all those ridiculous charges years ago, and he knows that, how am I supposed to live? Shall I receive the French delegation and members of Congress in a tent? Truly," Arnold repeated without looking up from the paper, "what does one do?"

For once wishing she was wiser if not older, Peggy sat back against the love seat. She couldn't bear to see the pain in those dark eyes, the weary set of his mouth and shoulders. The raw maleness she found so irresistible was uneasy, wounded.

Since his return from the aborted New York trip, he had asked her advice on several occasions. This new openness both pleased and frightened her. Pleased because she did have ideas and thoughts, and frightened because as a major general and military governor of Philadelphia, he shouldn't need them.

"People know Secretary Matlack and the others for who they are,"

Peggy answered softly while taking one of Arnold's hands. "They're despicable people."

"But," he countered, "they have such power. Look at what they are doing to me, these charges, my reputation."

She moved closer toward him and tried again. "The Congress went against them. Not one state except Pennsylvania voted in favor of your suspension. And you have the Commander in Chief's support."

Arnold sighed. The evening in Middlebrook was one of the very few things he had not shared completely with his fiancée. Washington was helpful, but not supportive. That conversation alone, never mind the state of his finances, ensured many, many turns about the residence in the tiny hours.

He looked again at the paper. "Congress may not have voted for suspension, but they have sent the charges to committee. And even if the chairman is married to a friend of yours, I'm not certain my case will be dealt with fairly."

Peggy recalled the jealousy she'd felt over her friend Nancy's great catch. "But I've met him. Mr. Paca is truly a gentleman. He won't believe those lies."

"But others will, or they'll trade some political favor for a vote. The Commander in Chief shares my opinion on this, that our politicians are for the most part a wretched, self-serving lot. I think my leg wasn't enough of a sacrifice, they want all of me—bleeding and injured."

Arnold stood suddenly, pacing in little rows, reminding Peggy of a cat caught indoors. "And they'll probably use this as another excuse not to pay me." Seeing Peggy's puzzled expression he elaborated, "They've never paid me, not for one day of more than three years of service as a commissioned officer in the Continental Army, or for any of my expenses. And now I can't take another command with this unresolved, and I can't leave to see to my business as I have to be on hand as a witness for myself. How am I supposed to live?"

Peggy pulled Arnold back to the couch. "My grandfather always says that the heart of good business is dealing with people one can trust."

"I agree," he lifted an arm about her shoulder. "In truth, I think I trust the King and Parliament more than our Congress. At least they do what they said they will do." Then, he added with a shrug, "For good or bad."

"And His Majesty's forces have the very good sense to recognize your stature," Peggy added, referring to a recent series of highly complementary articles about Arnold that had come out of Tory newspapers in New York. In one, the *Royal Gazette,* he was described as "more distinguished for valour and perseverance" than any other American commander. She settled against him. "Do you really think they want to recruit you?"

Arnold nuzzled her hair. "It only makes sense. While certain of our politicians may think me expendable, the boys would be devastated if I were to change sides. I'm sure a great many would even follow me."

"Perhaps you should see that each member of Mr. Paca's committee receives copies of the Gazette then," she laughed.

At the thought of the Paca Committee reading the Crown's view of his record, Arnold's mood finally cracked. Glancing out into the hall and seeing no one, Arnold leaned down and kissed Peggy's neck.

"Benedict!" Peggy pushed herself away. "Not now!"

Staring into the wide blue eyes, Arnold wondered how he could wait the six more weeks until the marriage. Six more weeks until she would be his at any time of day or night. But first he must pull himself out of this malaise. Then he'd devise a strategy to convince the Paca Committee of his innocence. And after that, he resolved, pulling her to him again, he would never, ever allow anyone to interfere in his life again.

# CHAPTER 34

## *Judge Shippen*

$\mathcal{A}$ fter the commotion and bustle of Betsey's wedding and Peggy's engagement, a brief period of calm entered our home. The war, the part being fought anyway, was now in the south. Three thousand British troops under Campbell were sent to take Savannah and, by taking advantage of the large Loyalist populace located in the region, to achieve territorial dominance. Whether the southerners were not as loyal as supposed or simply not too active remained a question. While several battles were fought in early '79, clear dominance had not been established.

Locally, no new proclamations had been issued since the previous fall. While never completely at ease, we didn't have to search lists for our own names or those of friends and relations, and that was a relief.

Our poor Grace did, however, receive two blows—neither fatal, but both surely trying. First, she received a letter from her daughter in London saying that she was very lonely. Betsey was not being received after all; in fact, some of those who had enjoyed the Galloway's hospitality in Philadelphia were snubbing her outright. In short, she longed to return to her mother.

The second blow added insult to the injury of her eviction. By an Act of Assembly, the lovely house on Sixth and High was set aside for the exclusive use of the President of the Executive Council of Pennsylvania. Reed, the author of so much of her agony, was to reside in the comfort of her home, with her furnishings, utensils, and even her chariot. Fortunately, one of the female Quaker ministers developed a great interest in Grace and was said to be providing a solace that no others could.

But, Grace's situation aside, I enjoyed our personal little hiatus from worry for the month of January and even a bit into February. Then, in the snowy grayness of winter, anxiety reentered my study.

When our children are small, we pray only for their health. As they grow, our concerns expand to lessons, morals, manners, and obligations. This is our work, our role as parents to protect the little ones from disease as well as indolence and bad character. But the motivating force in all this work and anxiety is our fear that they will somehow be endangered or terribly unhappy, and that this will be due to some neglect on our part. Therefore, after many years of protection, protection, protection, we're bewildered by our inability to stop our adult children's bad decisions, decisions that can affect their health and happiness much more than any of the petty fears that preoccupied us for so long. Bewildered, frozen, impotent—these were all sensations I felt that spring.

My reservations about the General had returned, and I'm not exactly sure why. The urgency of the trip to New York, which was now suddenly a poor idea. His murky involvement with enemy goods and disputed ships. The daily letters attacking him in the paper. The proceedings of the Council. Even if he had done nothing objectively wrong, the man certainly had a knack for agitating those around him. I was reminded of my own son Edward as a little boy at birthday parties...What am I saying? I am reminded of Edward now.

Of course, the General hurried to explain his innocence on each and every charge published in the paper to his papa. (Me! His Papa!) And while his explanations appeared entirely logical, my legal instincts were not convinced. But what could I say? I had no evidence to the contrary. And, after his appearance before the Paca Committee, all but two minor charges were dropped, and those referred to a court martial. Arnold, naturally ebullient, invited the entire family to dine at the residence in celebration.

Moreover, he had made a sumptuous gesture in purchasing one of the handsomest country estates in the area, Mount Pleasant, for Peggy. Truly for Peggy, placing the deed in her name. John Adams thought Mount Pleasant to be "the most elegant seat in Pennsylvania," and I must agree. Suddenly feeling like the poor relations, we wondered what it would be like to visit her there.

Screwing up my courage, I asked how such a purchase was possible on an officer's pay. The General smiled with outright glee and explained that he only needed to make the down payment. The house was leased to the Spanish mission, therefore the mortgage payments would be covered for as long as needed. Yes, the sumptuous gesture. I'm afraid all of this made my poor Peggy a little grander still, and clearly less likely to listen to such a stodgy old character as myself.

Calling her into my study, I begged and pleaded that she postpone the wedding. As reasons, I used the General's uncertain future, her own youth, the outcome of the conflict, even more time to accrue a trousseau. But my Peggy, my favorite, knew much more than I.

# CHAPTER 35

## Mid-March, 1779
### The Great House

At Cook's summons, Melora glanced up from the ironing to see her prayer for the day answered. There, propped up against the frame of the open back door, was Jared, sunlight surrounding him like a painting at church. She glanced at Cook for permission to go outside and was rewarded with a finger pointed at two chickens lying on the large kitchen table in front of the fire. "Take those to the stoop, you can clean them there." Beaming a smile of appreciation, Melora grabbed up the chickens, a bag, and her cloak before following Jared out the door where they seated themselves awkwardly on the narrow step.

"I hoped you'd come by today," Melora said, plucking the feathers without looking down. "I thought of you in the garden this morning, and thought maybe you would." Suddenly her voice sounded shrill against Jared's stillness, and she knew that he had something unpleasant to tell her. "What is it? What's wrong?"

"There'll be a change in my orders."

She looked at him blankly, gathering that she was supposed to know what that meant.

"I have to leave Philadelphia," he explained. "The General's resigned his Command here as military governor and I'm to be reassigned."

Melora continued plucking the chicken, but now slowly, very slowly, as her fingers couldn't find their previous rhythm. "But why do you have to leave? Where will you go?"

Jared sighed. "I could be sent to the south with Lincoln, but I've put in to join Colonel John Lamb at West Point. The General will recommend me. Colonel Lamb was with us on the march to Canada and in my mind he is one of the best officers in the army."

Melora struggled to place the name, her immigrant's geography lacking. "And where is West Point?" she whispered. "I've not heard of that before."

Jared took the chicken from her lap and, placing it to one side, folded her in his arms. This was hard news, hard for him but harder for her. At least he'd be with comrades and closer to home. "It's in the northern highlands, a three or four day ride from here. It's a very important place. The British could divide the country if they took it."

"Divide the country?" she asked incredulously.

"There's a river there that joins New England to the Atlantic. If they take West Point, they take the river."

Tears crept out the corners of Melora's eyes and onto the rough suede of Jared's jacket. She fought to put the parts of this calamity together. "I see, I suppose. But the General? How can he resign?"

"He's got no choice. They keep writing rubbish about how he stole and looted in Canada and done more here, and it's all a lie. I know because I was in Canada and I've not seen it here. These people just won't let him alone." Jared paused to take his handkerchief and pat her face. "And now, Joseph Reed, Timothy Matlack, the Council have had the Paca report thrown out. They've said Pennsylvania won't support the army unless Congress investigates the General again on their charges, with a new committee. So Congress has to do it. The General found out yesterday. He's telling the Shippens now."

Melora looked miserably out beyond Jared's coat to the garden just steps away. Charges? The Paca report? How could these matters be taking Jared away?

"But isn't there work for you here? Or at least close to here?"

"I have to be where I can do the most good. We've fought too long and lost too much not to."

Burrowing her face deeper into Jared's shoulder, Melora allowed herself to cry as she had not cried since her time on the ship. What did she and Jared have to do with the Paca report, the Council, even the General? Perhaps he hadn't done anything wrong in Canada, but she believed, even if Jared didn't, that there had to be something to the talk here in Philadelphia. And now they had to suffer because of the General's problems? Perhaps Miss Peggy Shippen should suffer, but why should they?

---

Reaching into the cupboard for bonnet and gloves, Peggy willed herself to be strong. The General was downstairs waiting in the carriage; she had to pull herself together from the extraordinary news of his resignation.

She'd always believed that the General would prevail over anyone and everyone. But he had not prevailed. Reed had. And now she saw so clearly not only the power of the rogues governing Pennsylvania, but also, to use the General's term, the absolute fickleness of Congress. There was even the tiniest possibility that the General could be charged. Her future, their future, all terribly at risk.

Smoothing her hair, she felt a great surge of protectiveness toward the man she loved so much. A valiant man. A great man. Would to God that he had chosen for the King.

## CHAPTER 36

### The Same Day
### Benedict Arnold's Coach, Philadelphia

The General sat silently beside Peggy as the carriage rumbled through the city streets. With her parents he had been philosophical, even stoic about his situation. Now he was edgy, taut, the full mouth set in a line, his eyes fixed in concentration. The black hair, usually pulled tightly back, fallen forward so that he was constantly pushing some of the shorter strands back from his face. An outlet, she realized, from the heaviness of his thoughts. She looked over at him and found he was studying her.

"Yes, Benedict?"

"I won't hold you to the engagement."

"But why not?"

Arnold sighed, anger and frustration welling up together. "Because I seem to have enemies bent on my harassment, if not my destruction..." he placed his hand on his knee, "and also, I have this."

Peggy pushed the black hair back from his eyes, then wound her arms about his neck. "And you have me. You'll always have me." Then, unable to stop herself, she asked the question. "But why must you stay with them?"

"Them?"

She whispered directly into his ear. "Those who are jealous of you, who are persecuting you, the Council, the Congress."

"What are you saying?" Arnold asked, glancing toward the carriage window.

Now that she was into it, the words poured out. "If you were to join His Majesty's forces, you would be out of the clutches of these petty, power-mad people. You would be safe at the end of the war, we would be assured a place in society for ourselves and our children—"

His arms tightened about her. "But...all that we've fought for."

Pressing her check against his, she struggled to make her point. "Did you fight for repeal of the laws or did you fight so that Reed and those in Congress could rule over us?"

He answered slowly, "I fought so I could be free to operate my ships and my business as I wanted." Suddenly, she felt him tense again. "Has someone put you up to this?"

Peggy shook her head. "Of course not. I think it was the article in the *Gazette*. I thought about how all of our troubles have come from your support of the rebel side. And I have very good friends in New York. Very good friends."

Arnold stared at her in bewilderment. "Your thinking terrifies me. We could be shot."

Taking his face in her palms, she tried again. "Promise me you'll consider the possibility. It would solve all of our problems. And don't hate me for these thoughts. We're about to be married; I only want what's best for us."

Then, as if Peggy had summoned a conjurer, all of his late-night demons rose before him: the empty warehouses in New Haven, Reed, Congress, Hannah and the boys, the hospital in Albany, the loathsome cane. Turning, he buried his face into the silky softness of Peggy's throat. He could never hate her, she was the only good thing in so long. The only good thing.

CHAPTER 37

April 8, 1779

*The Great House*

With a conflicted heart, Melora placed the last twig of forsythia into the arrangement over the mantel. Forsythia, pussy willow, and quince, lovely flowers of spring. Backing up to assess the overall effect, she had to admit the room looked beautiful. Many hours of polishing, waxing, and dusting had gone into the parlor as well as the entire downstairs in the past few days. And while she and Jenny grumbled about with brooms and rags, Cook had taken her responsibilities as a sacred trust, scarcely shaking the flour from her hands for days. The result was a truly outstanding panoply of culinary delights for the newlyweds and all the well-wishers expected to call upon them.

In addition to the cleaning and decorating, it had also fallen to Melora to iron the wedding dress that morning. Mrs. Shippen said that Melora was the only one she could trust with the job, the only one with a light enough hand. The dress itself was, surprisingly, an old one of Miss Peggy's, an iridescent silk that the General was said to particularly admire. While not as ornate as the unworn *Meschianza* dress, Melora believed that she preferred this one—had she the choice, if this was her day. She almost laughed at the foolishness of her thoughts.

As the clock struck four, Melora made one last adjustment to a quince branch, then hurried over to the door and closed off the room. The guests would be arriving soon, and she might be needed to help Jenny get the rest of the female family members dressed and downstairs. With all the housework to be done, she'd not been asked to do the ladies' hair as well, thank heaven. Miss Martha was upstairs attending to that now. And she prayed that she would not be called upon to help the bride dress. She could iron, she could clean, and could even help cook for the occasion, but to be forced to join in the cooing and fussing over Miss Peggy as she prepared for her husband, that she could not endure.


An hour later, Melora stood in the hallway with the rest of the staff, hearing but not seeing the wedding of Miss Peggy Shippen to Major General Benedict Arnold. At four-thirty the General had arrived with his three sons, sister Hannah, and an aide to form the Arnold faction of the wedding party. Hannah Arnold was a small, peevish-looking woman, while the three boys were quiet and somewhat shy. Melora hadn't really put the sister and sons into her thoughts on Miss Peggy's marriage yet, but from the looks of them, she wouldn't envy that. And while there was to her, as always, something off-putting in the General's air, she had to admit that he was indeed quite a figure of a man, even leaning, as he was, on his aide for support.

The Shippen and Francis relations were clearly caught up in having a hero in their midst. They watched him more than they did Miss Peggy as she floated down the stairs, all lace and silk, on her father's arm looking only toward Arnold. There could be no doubt that this was a match of true love.

Although the General was never reticent about showing his feelings toward Miss Peggy, they'd seemed even closer in recent days. She, less like a young bride-to-be and more a woman already married, in full confidence of her position.

What a puzzle life was! Melora reflected. That some should be given so much while others were given so little. What rule of heaven allowed Miss Peggy to receive wealth, family, beauty, and a man she truly loved? Was it the same rule that permitted herself, Jenny, and Cook to labor fourteen or sixteen hours daily, often going to bed aching and exhausted so that this family might live in ease and elegance? And why should the General be here enjoying his wedding while Jared was now far away in New York? The General, Miss Peggy, most of the people in the house tonight...such good fortune.

Then, thinking of those left at home, Melora felt a wave of guilt, and she prayed quickly to be freed from the sin of covetousness. Silently repeating twelve Hail Mary's, the Father's usual penance, she tried to turn her attention to the words of the Reverend William White and the vaguely familiar Anglican wedding ceremony.

# CHAPTER 38

## April, 1779

*190 High Street*

M elora walked toward the door and, balancing the tray on one hip, knocked loudly. "Your tea." After a momentary silence, she heard Peggy's girlish giggle and the low tones of the General. She'd already been up for two hours and, newlyweds or not, she had little patience for this. Had they no shame?

"Just a moment, Melora," the General called. She waited. Then: "All right, come in."

Melora entered the room and stopped, trying not to look in the direction of the large walnut four-poster. "Where would you like your tea?"

Again, the silvery giggle. "Here, in bed. We're being terribly lazy today." Although she'd brought early tea for days now, she was still as embarrassed as the first day. One morning the General didn't even bother with a night shirt. He'd just pulled the covers up to his neck.

Trying to look no higher than the dust ruffle, Melora crossed the room as quickly as possible and placed the tray at the foot of the bed. Then, with no further conversation and equal speed, she fled to the hall. As she reached the back stairs to the kitchen, she could hear their laughter. Oh, they might laugh now, and they might be desperately in love, but she knew that all was not exactly fine.

For the three days following the General and Miss Peggy's wedding, well wishers had filled the Great House from all walks of Philadelphia: distant Shippen and Francis relations, friends of the family (those who were not in New York or England), rank and file soldiers who had served with Arnold on and off since Canada, congressmen, and clients of the Judge. Cook, Melora, and Jenny were kept running from early morning until late at night when they again had to ready the house and food for the next day's onslaught.

With her adoring General by her side, Miss Peggy had reveled in her new state, wearing one new satin, brocade, or gauze dress after another. The staff had gossiped that each item in her trousseau was getting a performance. But at least she would be leaving for good very soon, and so all this silliness was worth it. But on the fourth day, just hours after packing the General's carriage with Miss Peggy's things and waving the couple good-by, the Judge and Mrs. Shippen called Melora into the parlor. She was terrified. It could only be bad news from Ireland, or Patrick, or Jared!

Doing as she was told, she waited for the inevitable blow. But instead, the Judge began talking about Peggy's new situation. Given the General's position in the country, he began, it was essential that Peggy should be properly dressed and coiffed at all times. And although Peggy could avail herself of Hannah Arnold's maid, he and Mrs. Shippen felt that Peggy needed someone of her own and that they should furnish this person, a sort of wedding present, as there had been enough talk about the size of the General's staff. This person? Did they want to know if she knew such a lady's maid?

Next she heard Mrs. Shippen saying that the family could do without her for a time, since two daughters were on their own now. When Peggy was completely settled, and the General's affairs were more stable, then she could come back. Dimly, Melora realized that she was to be the wedding present. She was to leave the Great House, leave Cook, Jenny and the garden, even her regular duties like the high boy and the marketing, and become Miss Peggy's personal servant. Even in the relief that no loved one was gravely ill, dead, or dying, she couldn't control herself in front of the Shippens. Pulling her apron over her face, Melora burst into tears.


"Why should I have to go?" she moaned later in the kitchen with Cook and Jenny. "Miss Peggy doesn't even like me."

For the only time that Melora could remember, Cook stopped her work and took a seat. Jenny, who knew Miss Peggy best, was the first with an answer. "I don't think it has anything to do with you, it's just about what you can do. You're the best with an iron and comb."

Cook nodded in agreement. "She doesn't need a cook. She doesn't need anyone to clean that house. But she does need a maid to make her look beautiful."

"But I'm not that!"

"You're the closest thing in this house," Cook admonished. "And look at you, going on when you're about to see some more of the world and have less work. It'll be an adventure."

"She's right," Jenny agreed, "you should make the best of it." With a little shrug, she added, "Particularly, since there's nothing you can do about it. You go as they tell you or you go to prison."

Melora sighed. There it was. Until she'd fulfilled the terms of her contract, she was as much the Shippen's property as the highboy in the parlor.

That was how she'd come to be rambling around in this castle with very little work to do. Her only responsibilities were for Miss Peggy's hair, helping her dress in the morning, putting the clothes away at night, her mending, laundry, ironing, and the orderliness of her closet in general. Of course she also prepared her bath and brushed her hair in the evening. She supposed that if Miss Peggy were to travel, she would be called on to prepare her wardrobe. But that was the extent of her work. Miss Hannah was quite clear that she had the rest of the staff assigned exactly as she wanted and that she was not about to yield her authority on household management to the young girl who'd married her brother. Not that she'd seen Miss Peggy involving herself too strenuously with the day-to-day work of the mansion, much less with the care of the General's youngest son, Harry, still at home. Rather, Peggy's day consisted of meals, the morning hours in the study with the General discussing plans and accounts, and afternoons, if the General was away, taking one or another of her friends for a ride in the carriage or returning to the Great House for a visit.

These few duties gave Melora plenty of time to talk with the rest of the staff, walk about the city, and investigate the house. She'd thought the Shippen's house was grand but Cook had been right. There was more to the world. And that was how she'd come on her surprising discovery, the tiny crack in the otherwise blissful new marriage. The Arnolds were worried about money.

---

She hadn't meant to snoop, but one particularly rainy, depressing day while the General and Peggy were out visiting her family, she'd wandered into the General's handsome study to see the portraits there. The staff said a grand family used to live in the mansion—descendants of the Founder—now off in England. While studying one of the female Penn's portraits, little Harry had burst into the room, grabbing for books and paper weights on the dark mahogany desk, and scattering papers high and low. Then with eyes round and wide, he'd held a finger to his lips, pointed to the stairs and what she assumed must be his aunt in pursuit, before sliding behind the heavy velvet curtains.

Retrieving the General's work, she saw mixed in among maps of New York and letters to various officers, pages and pages of calculations, many edited with Peggy's tiny script. One page seemed to be about payments from the army, another, about properties in Connecticut, and others with entries about the three boys' education, money for Miss Peggy, and staff expenses. Given the rumors about the General's business affairs, she was intrigued. When Miss Hannah, quick on her nephew's trail, ran into the study and pulled Harry by the ear from behind the curtains, Melora's explanation of the disturbed desk brought only an exasperated sigh.

She probably wouldn't have given the calculations much more thought (what newlyweds wouldn't be planning their finances?), but one night while waiting to brush Miss Peggy's hair, she'd heard the General and Peggy in the study, apparently in the midst of a terrible argument.

"Why won't you at least contact my friends? Find out what they might offer."

"The court martial's in ten days. I'll be cleared as I was before."

"How can you know?"

Arnold sounded anguished. "Because the boys believe in me. The Commander in Chief believes in me. Congress knows that. Some want to dismiss the charges now, forego the whole business."

"But what if Reed wins again?" Peggy's voice had taken on a pleading tone. "How would we live? My friends, we may need them."

Quiet followed. Was Peggy crying in the General's arms? Finally, just when Melora thought the conversation was over, she'd heard Arnold speak in a soft voice she'd never heard before. "I promise, I swear, if that day should come..." But then the sound trailed off and she could hear no more.

Assuming Peggy wouldn't be wanting her services on this particular night, Melora slipped up the steps toward the attic. Did the General need money? With her own eyes, she saw that he had expenses enough. Was that what the newlyweds were arguing about? The General hesitating to take help from Peggy's friends? Cook and Jenny often talked about the Shippens' powerful friends, how they helped each other with money, properties, and work. Melora opened the door to the maids' quarters and was hit by the stale odor from four women sleeping in a close, cramped room. What a miracle it would be to have friends with such great gifts to give.

# CHAPTER 39

## April, 1779

### City Tavern

*J*oseph Reed stood in front of the City Tavern and wondered if he really wanted to go in. Everyday pleasures, such as a hot cup of coffee or a glass of port, were simply not worth the effort when accompanied by the barrage of complaints and suggestions that he was sure to hear inside. Nearly every soul on the street had an idea for working with the rampant price inflation in Philadelphia. And if they didn't have an idea, then they certainly had a complaint. But who could blame them, with prices increasing by fifteen percent or more a month, and the Continental currency worth one thirtieth its original value? A quick check of his pocket watch showed that he was already fifteen minutes late for his appointment with Timothy Matlack. Once again, there was an urgent matter to attend to. Reed drew a deep breath, assumed his public face, and climbed the stairs to the tavern.

As expected, someone at nearly every table needed a word as he made his way to the corner of the Coffee Room where Matlack was seated. This man couldn't feed his family, another couldn't clothe his mother, yet another was afraid of a summer Indian strike destined for Philadelphia. However illogical the threat, Cherry Valley seemed fixed in people's minds. Reed spotted the merchant David Franks and wondered what his thoughts were this morning. A rumor was sweeping the city that all those suspected of disaffection for the United States were about to be rounded up and sent to New York. Would that the rumor were true.

Motioning for Matlack to keep his seat, Reed pulled up a chair and removed his hat and gloves. At least with Tim, he didn't have to feign interest where there was none.

"Hello, Tim."

"Hello, sir. How are Mrs. Reed and the children today?" Matlack picked up the tumbler in front of him and signaled to the girl for another. A beer bottler by profession, he seemed personally set on raising demand as much as possible.

"Happy for the sunshine, Tim. They've had a hard winter, as you know. It's been particularly hard on my wife." The children seemed well enough, but Hettie was not strong and it worried him constantly. The whole family had caught colds in February, but she had yet to totally throw hers off.

"It must have piqued your wife that General Arnold married Miss Shippen, a girl half his age." Both men paused as Matlack's second beer arrived.

"It's true. However, there is not much about the man, as we know, that strikes us as appropriate."

Matlack nodded. "I know, but public opinion seems to be against us. I've been told that the Congress is leaning toward dismissing the charges against him after all. He has such popular support from the army."

So this was the reason Timothy had asked for the meeting, Reed realized. He could have saved a great deal of time by just dropping in at his office. Reed leaned over the table. "I've heard that also, Tim. And that is why I paid a visit on the President of the Congress yesterday. The charges will not be dismissed. There will be a court martial. And it will be on all eight charges."

"What changed their minds?"

Reed smiled. "I made it very plain that Pennsylvania is not fighting a war for independence only to trade Parliament and the King for the Congress or the army."

"That was enough?"

"Not quite." Reed stood, annoyed by the unnecessary trip. "The Congress and General Washington know that Pennsylvania's support is critical if they are to proceed with this war. They just need to be reminded of that fact from time to time. Now if you'll excuse me, I should be off."

Matlack smiled a contented smile of confidence as Reed stood and once again wound his way through the crowded tavern. For all his gentlemanly ways, Joseph Reed was once again proving his mettle. In fact, Matlack thought, it would be a very cold day before he would choose to go up against him. Not against a man who would threaten not only the Congress but also the Commander in Chief.

# CHAPTER 40

## April, 1779

*190 High Street*

The carriage crunched to a halt in the street below. The General was home, finally. Peggy rose from the secretary and the correspondence she'd barely touched, pinched her cheeks, and hoped she looked as happy and enthusiastic as she wished she felt. The summons for him to meet with a small group of congressional delegates today was completely unexpected. They could only speculate that Congress had changed its mind and there would be no court martial.

Crossing the foyer, Peggy pulled the massive oaken door open just as Arnold reached the stoop. One look told her, however, that the news was not good. "What happened?" she asked quietly.

He handed her his hat and gloves and nodded up the stairs. "Not here. In the study."

Peggy sat quietly in the armchair in front of the desk, waiting for Arnold to speak. How many times had she sat in a chair in front of her father's desk? But here she was a wife, a partner, a helpmate, and whatever concerned him now concerned her as well.

"Benedict?"

Arnold, folded into the corner of his chair, stared dully down at the desktop before him. "It's starting all over again, every bit of it."

"What is?"

Looking up from the desk, his eyes met hers. "The court martial will be held. Once again, strangers and voyeurs intend to review my affairs. What I've asked to be paid, what I've asked to be reimbursed, what they've paid me. Receipts, bills, estimates, everything I've prepared, explained, gone over and over many times. And now there's not even a date for the trial. An indefinite postponement."

"But why?" Peggy demanded as a telltale circle of light surrounded her husband.

"You know they owe me a great deal of money. By going through it all again, they can just debate and delay endlessly. I have enemies there. And I'm sure Reed is very much in this too. They could keep me bound up for years."

Peggy was not at all sure what the postponement meant, only that Reed had clearly won again. The light was now almost blinding. She slumped back in her chair. "Benedict...a migraine."

Arnold looked up dully. "What?"

Never having witnessed one of Peggy's headaches, it took him a moment to understand that something was terribly wrong. Before, when Mrs. Shippen tried to describe her daughter's episodes, he'd mentally dismissed them to the veiled range of female ailments. But he'd never seen her like this, the stillness, the silent crying. He started for the hall. "I'll get Hannah."

"No!" Peggy gasped as she lowered herself to the floor. "Get my mother, get Melora, but not Hannah!" Then with her hand covering her face, she whispered very slowly, "Now? Will you contact New York now?"


Three days later Peggy woke from a long sleep. With vague memories of her mother, Melora, and the surgeon flittering around the darkened bedroom, she looked up to see the General in the chair beside her, unshaven, haggard, and with paper and pen in hand.

"Benedict?"

In an instant she was in his arms. She heard him speaking of his love for her, of how terribly afraid he'd been when nothing seemed to make her better, that she not worry about anything, ever again. Then, just before slipping back into sleep, she heard him swear to keep his promise, that the bastards could be dammed, and that nothing, *nothing*, was more important than their future together.

CHAPTER 41

May 10, 1779

*British Headquarters, One Broadway, New York*

The atmosphere in the office was tense and heady as John André
studied the four men before him. Jonathan Odell to his right, a mis-
sionary and physician, was also one of the most prominent and hard-work-
ing supporters of the Crown in New York City. Because of him, huge numbers of loyalists had been put to work under arms, as spies, or simply as
suppliers to the British army. And there was Odell's companion, Philip
Stansbury, whom André had known since the occupation of Philadelphia
where his songs and poetry delighted the entire officer corps. After the
evacuation, Stansbury had remained in the capital, taking the oath of allegiance to the United States and continuing his mercantile activities in
china and glass. He was also one of the seventy-odd secret agents that the
British left behind in the city. His two aides, Captains Patrick Ferguson and
George Beckwith, rounded out the foursome. Good men, dependable men,
their faces impassive, as André hoped his was.

Struggling to order his thoughts, André wondered if the Commander
in Chief should be brought into the conversation, but then immediately
rejected the idea. Since that first late-night conversation and dinner, their
relationship had grown beyond his wildest expectations. The two men
were now, surprisingly, each other's closest confidant. Besides being in and
out of one another's office several times a day, they also enjoyed a close
relationship outside of work, on the hunt and in the taverns.

But this was his job. Sir Henry placed him in this position as a mark of
confidence and trust, over the heads of many older and more seasoned officers. He could not disappoint his mentor by appearing indecisive or out of his
depth. He must simply quiet his mind and look for the right questions to ask.

The news Odell and Stansbury brought was just too stunning. He doubted the headquarters staff would even believe it. In fact he could already imagine the sniping and second guessing. They'd say he manufactured the communication to justify his surprising promotion to head of the secret service. Or, that it was an elaborate hoax designed to penetrate the workings of British intelligence.

But what if their news was true? That the most revered field commander in America now believed that the break with England had been a terrible error. That he wanted to offer his services, either outright or in some concealed manner, to Sir Henry Clinton and the King. That Major General Benedict Arnold, the new husband of his little Philadelphia friend, Peggy Shippen, wanted to talk.

CHAPTER 42

*Judge Shippen*

After Peggy's wedding our household settled down once again for a period of months, indeed until the spring of the next year. But while we settled down, the city heated up. Grain prices were absurd and the people demanded controls and lower rates. To make matters worse, those with grain far preferred to sell it to the French fleet for their gold rather than to the city folk paying in continental currency. Mobs gathered and rioting broke out—all the bad effects of a hot and hungry populace.

I did not envy Joseph Reed his job at that time, not that I ever had. During what has come to be called the Fort Wilson riot, Reed was called from his sick bed and physically stood between the opposing sides to stop the bloodshed. Arnold was involved in that too, a leader of the conservatives holding out against the mobs. Later he asked Congress for protection for himself and his family, but the Congress refused.

The fortunes of our friend and business associate David Franks continued to decline. After selling off numerous personal effects to raise funds, he was imprisoned for writing to the enemy. Once again he had just been trying to collect on old accounts. Although judged to be not guilty of providing intelligence to the enemy, his situation grew steadily more intolerable.

And our ever-suffering Grace suffered more. But this time the culprit was neither the Council nor the Whigs. It was Grace herself. She became even more self-obsessed, petty, and indifferent to all but her own troubles. The constant vacillations between wanting to join her family in England and her determination to protect Betsey's inheritance in the city grated on all of us who listened. She also lost the good will of many of our friends by her constant harping against the English army and leadership. Grace truly believed, and would say to anyone, that if Howe and the others had been more resolved at the time of the occupation, all would have been very different. While it sounded like ranting and raving at the time, I now agree *with that assessment completely.*

*On the war front, the events were a scrappy jumble that summer of '79. First the British marched north and took the very strategic crossing at Verplanck's Point on the Hudson. But just as soon as Clinton moved out of view, Anthony Wayne took it back along with the works at Stony Point for the Continentals. Dismayed, Clinton stopped all campaigning for several months. Only in December did the British become active again, with Clinton and André leading a huge expedition to lay siege to Charleston in early 1780.*

*While Clinton traveled south, Washington endured much at the winter headquarters in Morristown, New Jersey. Scarce generals retired, the three-year enlistees neared their termination with no replacements, military pay depreciated further, and the French sailed not against New York but for the West Indies. Moreover, the misery of camp life was said to rival even that of Valley Forge. Twenty-six snow storms in the area that winter, desperately cold temperatures, the Hudson frozen eighteen feet deep in places, few shelters, and ridiculously inadequate provisions punished the men and many simply left. With the sentence for desertion being one-hundred lashes to the bare back, I can only imagine how wretched the poor fools must have been to risk it. Washington finally appealed to the civilians of New Jersey for help, and I think it is fair to say their effort saved the army that winter.*

*During this time, from the spring of '79 through the spring of '80, Peggy and the General called on us regularly. A little over two months into her marriage, Peggy announced that we were to achieve a new status, grandparents. While Mrs. Shippen and I wished that the new couple had given themselves a bit more time, we kept silent with our opinions. Peggy seemed very happy, and at the time I thought that was enough.*

CHAPTER 43

April 1, 1780

*190 High Street*

The little eyes stared up from the crook in her arm. Blue and steady, they were like panels reflecting the workings underneath. There was some serious thinking going on, now a smile, and just a second ago, anger. But then the tiny face screwed up and the cry for food began in earnest along with the sudden fullness within her breasts. Now there were two beings in the world who could lay claim to her body. One with the slightest touch or even a gesture and the other with just one good howl.

Pushing the flap of her robe aside, Peggy lifted the baby to her and settled against the pillows. Even after the months of pregnancy, of the kicks and turns of the live being inside her, and after an extremely difficult labor, it was still something of a surprise that this baby was here, that he was hers. She honestly hadn't given the baby or motherhood much thought during the nine months prior to his birth. It was a peripheral issue to their plans and the newness of marriage. So, when Edward Shippen Arnold was first put into her arms, she was shocked by the ferocity of her feelings for the child. Baby Neddy, perfect little baby Neddy, tiny, helpless, and just as caught up in the tyranny of the war as she was.

For a time last summer she'd believed it might all be over by now. The General would defect, the army would follow him, and the United States would be but a memory. What a delicious dream it had been. Shifting the baby as he suckled and tugged at her breast, a familiar melancholy came over her. What was her baby's future now? Or her own?

When she and the General had made the decision last summer to have Stansbury contact Clinton in New York, she had been so reassured. Indeed, it looked as if providence was smiling on their decision when she learned they were to deal with her very good friend John André. While the negotiations had been harrowing—invisible ink, code books, aliases ("Mr. and Mrs. Moore" for herself and the General), hiding this great secret from her family and friends—at least there was action, a plan. Then it all stalled. Clinton let them know he wanted bold action, troops, a fort, more than just the acquisition of a famous American defector. But that was not what the General had envisioned; he began to rethink the decision. Besides, André seemed unable or unwilling to become definite on the financial terms. Finally, near the end of the summer, frustrated and fearful of the risk, she and the General had broken off communications with New York altogether. Pursuit of the General's innocence and military career within the Continental Army appeared to be a more prudent course.

Since then it had all turned around again. After a long, tedious fall, the court martial was called in December, and just a few weeks ago the General received the verdict: cleared once again except for two minor charges. The recommendation was for Washington to issue a formal reprimand. Benedict had been so sure of the exoneration that he'd had the findings reprinted for public distribution at his own expense. Moreover, he expected a new command at any time. Even now Philip Schuyler was speaking on his behalf to the Commander in Chief about an important new position.

But while the trial had gone in the General's favor, his enemies remained. So weren't they in just as much danger now as they had been last summer?

She didn't even know what she wanted any more, particularly since Neddy's arrival. During those last weeks of the pregnancy her mother and sisters, and her friends Peg and Becky, visited every day, keeping her company and helping her sew and knit the baby's things. What would she do without them now if Benedict joined the British? Who would she visit on Sundays in New York? Who would come to Neddy's first birthday party? When would she get to introduce her grandfather to her husband and son? It was all too complicated.

The baby was beginning to get full now, a drowsy, satiated look spreading over his face. For so long she had wanted only her own safety, and now she only wanted his. Baby Neddy, perfect little Baby Neddy.

———————

Melora opened the door a crack, peaking in. They were a vision those two, mother and child sleeping together, blond curls against the snowy linens. Easing the door shut, Melora turned and tiptoed into the study. Her orders were to stay within earshot in case Miss Peggy needed anything.

The study was much different since the baby's arrival. To make room for the crib, chest, and rocking chair in the master bedroom, Peggy's desk, writing box, books and sewing materials had been transferred to the study, now a sort of storage facility. The General and Peggy rarely used the room any more. Whatever had caused their frenzy the summer before—money, she'd always thought—must have taken care of itself. There had been no more late-night arguments in quite some time.

Seating herself at Peggy's desk, Melora contemplated Peggy's writing box sitting directly in front of her. The intricate walnut box had always been a marvel to her, another example of how the wealthy could surround themselves with so much beauty. What would it be like to compose a letter to Jared in such luxury? To tell him about the new baby, the flood of congratulations, the presents and visitors that poured into the house. She wished she could write to her mother, too. Surely, having a child had never been an occasion to stop one's work and be waited on for more than a day or two in Dunquin. No, the mothers at home with six or seven little ones in the cottages would most likely hand the new one to an older brother or sister and get on with their chores. Hand over those that lived anyway.

Suddenly, writing a letter to Jared seemed like the most wonderful idea in the world to Melora. He was posted now to West Point, the place he'd described to her on the Shippen's back porch over the half-plucked chicken. But her paper and pen were upstairs in the attic room. What if Miss Peggy rang? She lifted the lid of the writing box halfway. Neatly arranged against a green felt lining, the contents of the box lay before her—three pens, paper, a seal, blotter, and a stack of letters tied together with a blue silk ribbon. Recognizing the handwriting on the letters, she held the bundle to her nose and identified the source of the faint rosy scent wafting from the box. Who would have thought the General capable of such a romantic touch?

And what was this? A fold of paper peeked out from behind the felt lining of the lid. Why would Miss Peggy hide a letter from herself? A secret? A secret lover? Despite the thought that she could be sent to jail for less, Melora slid the note the rest of the way from its hiding place.

The letter was dated last August, August 1779. Was this a source of those early quarrels? But the letter could not have been more mundane, except that it was from Headquarters in New York. The author wrote *"that it would make me very happy to become useful to you here."* Then he continued by offering to get her anything she needed in the millinery department, and closed by sending his respects to all the Shippen and Chew females. So, she thought, the sleeping princess must have availed herself of the same shopping opportunities the girls at the tea had spoken of. Melora scanned to the bottom of the page. The letter was signed *"your most obedient and most humble servant, John André."* It must be the same John André who had visited the Great House so often during the occupation. Certainly, there were not two John Andrés at the headquarters in New York. And certainly, she glanced nervously toward the closed door to the bedroom, Jared Donovan would not be receiving a letter from this lovely box today.

Spoiled, foolish, idiot girl, Melora fumed as she carefully tucked the letter back behind the felt. The wife of Benedict Arnold risking the public's good opinion or worse, for some "capwire, needles, and gauze."

The Commander in Chief really had no time to be reading protracted court proceedings. For reasons he did not understand, the records of Major General Arnold's court-martial had just arrived from Congress, two and a half months after the verdict. Terrible timing. In addition to the innumerable letters and reports that usually took his evening hours, he desperately needed time to think. LaFayette's last letter indicated that the French court was prepared to send a second fleet. While good news, the need for planning and developing resources for such an operation was critical. Moreover, the battle in South Carolina was going badly. The British looked invincible; the entire strategy must be revisited.

Washington picked up the stack of papers. Once again all charges against Arnold had been dropped except two minor ones. Yet Tench, solid and steady as always, reiterated that the verdict called for him to issue a reprimand. And when he had suggested that the matter just be dropped, Tench, a little pale and asking his indulgence, explained that this was a hard position for him to be in, since his family and the Shippens were related. But he believed, as the Commander in Chief had impressed upon his men time and again, that the military must be the most chaste of all the professions. So, mentally putting aside the French fleet and South Carolina, the Commander in Chief began to read.

CHAPTER 44

April 10, 1780

*Philadelphia Market*

The market was crowded. Arnold wove through the bodies on his way to the china shop. He felt good, optimistic, and energetic, as he always did once a course of action was decided on. And unlike the previous summer, he was very clear on the current course of action.

Making his way through the carriages, wagons, and pedestrians, two or three friendly faces called out to say good morning. But for the most part, people simply went about their business. Or appeared to. Had they discussed his case over breakfast? Were they recalling the copy of the Commander in Chief's reprimand so prominently positioned in The *Packet* just two days before? Did they, like Washington, also find his conduct "peculiarly reprehensible"? Washington, his friend, who by this reprimand had savaged him to all his countrymen.

Spying the sign he had been looking for, PHILIP STANSBURY, CHINA AND GLASS, Arnold turned into the shop, pausing for a moment as his eyes adjusted to the darker interior.

"General," Stansbury called out over the head of two very well-dressed female customers, "what a pleasant surprise. I'll be with you in just a moment."

"Take your time," Arnold answered. "I want to pick out a present for my wife." That was true, he did want to get a present for Peggy, some little something that would mark their first year together, as well as the birth of Neddy. But he didn't need this shop for that.

She had been so tired this morning after their very late conversation the night before. Peggy was the one who was now unsure, mostly because of the baby. There had been much crying, fears over leaving her family, doubts that the Commander in Chief could have turned on them so cruelly. Hadn't he sent the nicest note congratulating them on Neddy's birth?

As Arnold paused in front of a hanging shelf displaying china dogs, cats, and ladies in bonnets and parasols, he felt the eyes of his fellow customers upon him. Turning, he saw that the older woman, the mother he presumed, was staring at him. "Were you fancying something from this shelf?" he asked affably.

"Oh, no," the woman said quickly, then caught herself. "Well, possibly."

"Do come and make sure," Arnold demanded moving to one side. "Perhaps the statue of the lady with the dog?"

Arnold bowed as the two ladies crossed the room to pretend to admire the whimsical statue and wondered if he should charge Stansbury a commission. Turning his attention to a cabinet filled with elaborate glass bottles and vases, he picked up a particularly graceful bud vase he felt Peggy might like. As he ran his fingers over the fluted rim, he also thought of the reprimand and the personal letter he had received from the Commander in Chief concerning it.

After a gratuitous beginning he wrote, "*Our profession is the chastest of all. Even the shadow of a fault tarnishes our finest achievements.*" The Commander in Chief then, in a backhanded sort of way, offered to help him. If he (Arnold) would "*exhibit anew those noble qualities which have placed you on the list of our most valued commanders. I will myself furnish you, as far as it may be in my power, with opportunities of regaining the esteem of your country.*"

But did he care for the esteem of the two busybodies standing in front of the china cats and dogs? Did he care for the esteem of all those Philadelphians busily buying or selling in the market today while attacking the rights of others to earn a living? And did he care about the esteem of Congress, who in all its wisdom had finally concluded that he was owed nothing for his considerable expenses feeding the army in Canada, but instead owed them? Congress, who had yet to pay him for over four years of service as a General! And the Commander in Chief. Did he care about the esteem of Washington? No. No, he did not. The very awful reprimand coming on the heels of what he thought was his vindication by the court martial had finished all that. He saw now that Washington was no real friend, that his opinion could be bought and sold like any other politician to appease those in power. And even if Reed, and now Washington, had not utterly slandered his name and reputation to the entire country, the finding by Congress forced his hand utterly. He had given the country five years of service, his health, and his fortune. But now the foolish days were over. No more indecision. No more hesitancy.

Deciding for the bud vase, Arnold saw that the two ladies were leaving without making a purchase. Stansbury's loss. Surely, however, the British would pay him well when they received word Arnold not only wanted to reopen negotiations but could meet their demands, that is if they could meet his. And indeed they should, because Philip Schuyler had all but assured him he would be named Commander of the Highland District. And that meant that within a very few months, control of West Point, Clinton's long sought objective, would be his.

# CHAPTER 45

## Early June, 1780
## British Headquarters

*M*ajor John André strode into his office to the cheers of George Beckwith and Patrick Ferguson. "Well done!" Beckwith slapped André on the back.

"The conqueror returns," Ferguson added.

"Well, at least one of them," André answered, pulling out his chair and taking a seat. "I must tell you it is good to be back in New York—the heat down there is deadly. My man Peter threatened to desert me by noon every day. Take a chair, gentlemen."

As the two young men settled themselves, André glanced about the office. It was good to be back. Although a towering success, the expedition to Charleston had been a grueling, overwhelming job for André as the acting Adjutant General. Not only was André in charge of directing Clinton's entire staff but, alongside his good friend Oliver DeLancey, was head of intelligence for the effort. Far from their *Meschianza* revelries, the two spent their days meeting with loyalists and runaway slaves as Clinton lay siege to the city. Finally, after six weeks of grinding British assault, their efforts were rewarded. Some five-thousand Continentals, militia, and armed citizens led by General Benjamin Lincoln, surrendered to Sir Henry's superior forces. The south was very nearly entirely theirs.

"Don't you want to hear how we've kept the home fires burning?" Beckwith asked, winking at Ferguson. "You did leave me with your job."

While Ferguson launched into a monotonous account of what their primary spies had been doing, the state of the Associated Loyalists under William Franklin, and the plan for Knyphausen, now in the field on his way to New Jersey, André's thoughts drifted from Ferguson, the piles of requests, requisitions, inventories, and official correspondence stacked on his desk, and the office in general. What he hadn't mentioned to his colleagues was that now, owing to the Charleston success, the Commander in Chief wanted him to prepare a strategy for achieving complete victory in both the south and the north. Sir Henry was also considering raising him to Adjutant General, the highest office in America below Clinton himself. He would be in line for a permanent commission and a solid financial future. Indeed, a job well done.

"André, you don't seem to be giving your full attention to Captain Ferguson," Beckwith said.

André looked up from the pile of documents and grinned. "I don't have to. Sounds like the same report I heard the day before I left for the south. I wish you gentlemen had some real news."

Beckwith turned to Ferguson. "Didn't we have some real news?"

"I believe so," Ferguson answered slowly," fairly important news as I recall."

Realizing the two men were having a good laugh at his expense, André glanced between them. "What?"

"We had an unexpected message," Beckwith said matter-of-factly.

André willed himself to play their game. "And the message was from?"

"Mr. Moore. He can deliver what we want. There's a memorandum on it."

For a moment André was confused. There were so many names to keep up with. "Mr. Moore?"

"Good God, Ferguson, it must have been hot down there," Beckwith exclaimed. "His brain has rotted. Mr. Moore, André. Think!"

Suddenly the connection clicked. He jumped to his feet, feeling like a small child on Christmas morning.

"It's Arnold! He's got West Point!"


Arnold was not asking so much: 5,000 pounds for his personal property and fortune, 5,000 more for the debt owed to him from his military service, and command of a new battalion. But André could see one sticking point. While West Point was worth at least 20,000 pounds, the Crown would never promise to pay unless there were results. Surely Arnold would understand that. The last thing that Arnold wanted was a face to face meeting with a high ranking officer to work out the details. Arnold even suggested him, André, as a possibility.

Sitting back in his chair, the acting Adjutant General gave into the implications embedded in Beckwith's memorandum. Just hours before, his ambitions stopped with commissions and finances. But now? To be the man to secure Arnold, and therefore West Point, and therefore, in all likelihood, the end of the war...the possibilities were breathtaking! He could see himself in London already, receiving the thanks of the King, with his mother and sisters looking on. He had to be that man.

## CHAPTER 46

## September 7, 1780
## *The Great House*

"And didn't I say you'd be seeing a bit more of the world?" Cook's expression was positively gleeful as she hunched over the bread board, slapping and kneading a huge mound of dough.

"Yes, you did," Jenny agreed, taking cups and saucers from the cabinet, "just as I said she should make the best of things."

From her seat at the table, Melora smiled at her two friends. "You both did, and you were both right. When I leave for West Point tomorrow I'll be sending up many prayers, and I'll ask that you be remembered, too."

The kitchen was warm as always, but outside the blue and gold Indian summer afternoon was warm as well, with no hint of fall. So odd to think that in New York she'd need warmer clothes almost immediately, at least according to Jared, and that there might even be snow in the Highlands before the end of October. The Highlands. Snow. Jared. All very soon.

This day was an unexpected holiday, with Miss Peggy wanting to spend the last afternoon before the trip with her family, and agreeing that Melora could come to say goodbye to Cook and Jenny also. The past few weeks had been exhausting. Not only were there the trip preparations to be made, but also the bulk of Miss Peggy's and the General's possessions at the residence to be packed, moved, and stored temporarily at the Great House. The Arnolds were long overdue moving from the mansion on Market, and Hannah Arnold had taken a much smaller house for herself and Harry. As Miss Peggy explained, who knew where she and the General might end up after this current command in the Highlands.

"But Melora, are you scared at all," Jenny said as she paused from arranging biscuits and cookies on small plates, "traveling so far from home?"

"Me? No, but I crossed the ocean in what felt to be little more than a curagh. I think Miss Peggy is, though." Melora held the oven door open for Cook.

"Why?" Cook's words came floating over her shoulder, "because she'll have the little one with her?"

Melora shrugged. "I don't know. Ever since the General left for West Point she's been a needle to all of us—me, Miss Hannah, everyone at the residence. And since the General sent for her to come, she's been all but intolerable."

"Well," Jenny announced as she rose to take the tea tray into the family, "it's important that she be with her husband. Not many men have as important a job as the General at West Point."

Nodding in agreement, Melora took an apron from the peg beside the fire and, seating herself at the kitchen table, began separating twigs and leaves from a pail of blueberries. She understood that West Point was a very important garrison for the American forces. More to the point, it was a very important place to her. Jared was there, under the direction of General Arnold, who she hoped was as excellent a commander as Jared believed him to be. Her Jared, whom she would see within the week, all because she'd been forced to take the job as personal maid to the very spoiled and self-important Miss Peggy Shippen Arnold.


Peggy took the tea cup from Jenny. It was incredible how her family could be so completely oblivious: Her mother and Betsey discussing Hettie Reed's ongoing maladies following the recent birth of a son, another George Washington namesake; Judge Shippen listening with folded hands and tight lips to Edward explaining why he'd brought one of the horses home lame the night before; and Baby Neddy cooing and chirping happily on Polly's lap while Sally hovered overhead waiting for her turn to hold him. No one in the room had the slightest clue about the enormity of the trip she would begin tomorrow to West Point. No one anywhere did, except Benedict.

Since his departure, she'd endured day after day of terrible waiting and uncertainty, all the while having to join in the usual round of parties, receptions, and visits with friends. She'd never imagined such loneliness. And even though Benedict now had the prize within his grasp, he'd been stymied by new logistics, communicating with André and Clinton from

West Point. In fact, she had routed some of his letters from West Point to New York City herself. It was terrifying. During the day she could set the fear aside sometimes through busyness, but during the night her body literally hurt with the anxiety of it all.

And now she was to leave to join him tomorrow and to... Her imagination stopped there. When the British took the garrison, would she be across the river in the mansion Benedict was occupying? Would she go ahead to New York? Would the war be over so quickly that she would indeed be home in a few weeks, as she had told her parents? Time was so uncertain. Even with most of the details agreed to, Benedict had yet to arrange the meeting with Sir Henry's envoy.

"My dear," Judge Shippen turned to her, unable to tolerate more of Edward's wild talk. "You say Major Franks will escort you to West Point?"

Peggy smiled at her father. He not only knew that Benedict had sent Major Franks to Philadelphia for the sole purpose of accompanying her on the trip north, he knew the exact itinerary that she was to follow, the number of trunks and parcels she was taking, and probably the names of the horses that would pull the coach. If only she could tell him what she was really about, perhaps the terrible anxiety might subside.

"Yes, Father, it's Major Franks, our friend and a good soldier, as you know."

Judge Shippen sighed. "You have to forgive me. I'm just an old man concerned over his daughter roaming about the countryside."

Afraid to speak, Peggy nodded in agreement, tears welling up in her eyes.

"Peggy?" Concern filled the Judge's face.

She willed the tears back. "I'm just tired...with the packing and the baby. And I'll miss all of you while I'm gone."

"Is Melora not taking good care of you?"

"Shhh!" Peggy whispered quickly. "She's in the kitchen with Cook. Melora's very helpful. Not particularly good humored, but very helpful."

The Judge looked thoughtful. "I'm still surprised that she agreed to go so readily."

"She has her reasons, Father. Remember her young man, Jared? He's posted there. In fact, he's one of nine who row the General's barge up and down the river."

"Peggy," Sally interrupted from across the room, "is Miss Arnold going to West Point also?"

"No," Peggy answered, managing a weak grin. "She says the Hudson is a dark, dreary place that she wouldn't enjoy, and that I won't either."

"I think she's rather dark and dreary herself!" Polly shot back, still staring down at the baby.

Judge Shippen raised an eyebrow at Polly. "Don't listen to Miss Arnold. It should be a beautiful trip."

"You'll be right in the middle of Indian country," Edward noted with a quick glance toward his father.

From Judge Shippen's tone Peggy understood immediately that this was the main concern he must have voiced to the family. Her poor father. She had been so neglectful of him in the past year, unable to give him the attention he deserved in the whirlwind of her courtship and marriage. And here on the eve of this momentous thing she couldn't even say goodbye honestly or properly.

"If you wish to stay with us, Edward," the Judge's expression was unequivocal, "then you will watch yourself." Then, taking Peggy's hand, he softened. "You know how your brother likes to stir up trouble. You also know that the General would never let you come if he thought there was any chance of danger. You'll be perfectly fine and back before we know it."

As hard as she tried for the rest of the afternoon, Peggy could not quite pull herself together. Everyone, even the house itself, seemed to be conspiring to enfold her in the embrace of home and family: Cook preparing her favorite stew for dinner, the breeze in the garden rising just enough to keep them all laughing and joking on a late afternoon stroll, and the conversation at the table focused on ways to force Grandfather into town for Christmas. Where would she be? The thought brought on a new episode of crying.

First, her mother took her aside to ask if all was happy between herself and the General. A little later Betsey wondered if Benedict's very public political issues might not have taken their toll. Even Edward apologized for his comments on the Indian Country. Sally and Polly did their part by taking Baby Neddy on very long walks. Finally, her father asked if she might be pregnant again.

To each she answered the same: She was just very tired, perhaps a headache was coming on. At last, however, the long ordeal was over and the coach arrived for herself, the baby, and Melora. After many goodbyes and kisses, she climbed onto the high seat and, waving a last farewell, sank finally into silence. Holding Neddy to her chest, she recalled the pain in her father's eyes as he tried to get to the bottom of her sadness. But he had not and would spend, she was sure, a worried night trying to solve the mystery. Clearly it was a good thing for his health and his nerves that she had never confided in him, and that he had no idea of the actual journey his daughter was about to make.

But soon the conflict would be over! Friends would return from New York and London. Her grandparents Shippen and Francis, her thirteen sets of aunts and uncles, and cousins too numerous to count, would be reunited, gathering again for birthday parties, dinners, lawn games, holidays, weddings, and christenings. Her father would be restored to his position. Her future, the General's, and Baby Neddy's—all would be secure.

The coach was stopping now, one last night at the residence. And then the end of the conflict...very soon.

CHAPTER 47

September 11, 1780

*Belmont on the Hudson*

*A*rnold handed his sword and pistol to the waiting servant and collapsed into one of the huge rocking chairs on Squire Smith's front porch. Far below, the Hudson spread out blue and serene against the densely wooded hills and mountains of the majestic Highlands. Above, hawks rode wind currents searching for their next meal. The only sound outside of his own labored breathing was the late afternoon wind softly rustling the pines about the house. A bucolic setting if there ever was one, despite the fact that he'd almost been killed on the river just hours before. And why was Peggy not already here to greet him? According to the express sent by Franks, the group should have arrived here at Joshua Hett Smith's country house by midday. Would to God that nothing had gone wrong with that plan, too.

The front door opened, and the black man who'd taken his weapons stuck his head out tentatively. "Something to drink, General?" Arnold eyed him in annoyance, not bothering to answer. His treatment of the man wasn't called for, he knew that, but at the moment he was still too frustrated with today's plan gone so wrong. Plans and more plans. He was sick to death of it, he wanted action. For the two months he'd been in command of West Point and the surrounding military outposts; that was all he'd done. Plans to get communications through the lines to Clinton and André, plans to shift men away from West Point before the British attack, and plans to appear above reproach to all parties.

Yet, for all his efforts, he knew that some at the garrison were perplexed by several of his orders. Especially difficult were comrades from the Canadian campaign and Saratoga, like John Lamb and Richard Varick, who felt they had the right to question his authority. He could see the confusion in their eyes.

This house, Belmont, was about the only place where he could really escape from the demands and curiosity of his subordinates. Smith and his wife were eager hosts, deeply interested in ingratiating themselves to the new commander of the Highland District. And the house was so perfectly situated for his needs, Arnold thought, again looking out over the water. Fifteen miles to the north lay West Point, the military complex designed to control all navigation passing through the upper Hudson. And to the south, fifteen miles on the river would put one not quite in Clinton's Headquarters in Manhattan, but fairly close at Dobbs Ferry where he'd spent the afternoon hiding.

"Where the hell had André been? For two months he'd tried to set up a meeting with the man to nail down the terms of his defection. Through double agents and coded messages, he'd proposed that André cross the lines in the guise of a secret agent. Suspicious militia would have accepted that. But then not a week ago he'd received word from André, cloaked in the language of a merchant needing to discuss orders, that he would meet Arnold on the shore of the Hudson at Dobbs Ferry today to ostensibly talk about mercantile matters. But just as Arnold's bateau approached Dobbs Ferry, a British gunboat came about and opened fire, very nearly scoring a direct hit. Rowing furiously, he and his men barely escaped to an American blockhouse on the far side of the river. They were all now, with his blessing, ensconced in a tavern in Haverstraw drinking away the shock to their nerves. But he would have to start all over again. In fact, he should be preparing a message for André right now.

"General! You're finally here!" the very southern voice of Mrs. Smith called from behind him.

Arnold rose awkwardly and bowed to the auburn-haired South Carolina beauty that Smith somehow enticed into marrying him. "Good afternoon. I hope you don't mind that I'm making myself at home here on your porch."

"Of course not." Mrs. Smith motioned to his seat. "Please sit down."

Where the lady before him was quick with a natural charm, Smith, an attorney, was more slow-witted and overly eager to please. He did have, however, besides his house, another attribute that made him potentially very important to Arnold. Not only did he know everyone on both sides in this part of the world, but he was also the brother of William Smith, a loyalist and the Chief Justice of New York, an association that might be useful to Arnold in the future but which was an anathema to his staff at West Point.

"We waited for your wife's arrival earlier, and I'm sorry to say that Joshua's now run out for a small errand. Can I get you a cup of tea, or something stronger?"

Arnold lowered himself into the chair once again, grimacing slightly. "No, thank you. I also wonder at her whereabouts."

"My poor General," Mrs. Smith cried, "did no one tell you? A rider came at noontime. They were simply late making their start this morning. She should be here any moment."

Arnold sighed in relief. "I was concerned."

Mrs. Smith patted his arm in sympathy. "Of course you were. But I see this delay as a good thing."

"How is that, Mrs. Smith?"

His hostess smiled. "Because now you certainly can't expect Mrs. Arnold to travel the rest of the way to West Point after such a long day. You and your wife will have to spend the night here at Belmont with us. A little rest will do you both good."

Glancing around at the large porch and the view, the pleasantness of the surroundings crept into Arnold's edgy, weary body. Mrs. Smith was right, he shouldn't ask Peggy to make the rest of the trip to headquarters tonight. She would be tired, too. With that thought a sense of Peggy assailed him. He had missed her these two months, but now, in just a few hours... Arnold allowed a moment of silence to pass between himself and his eager hostess. Yes, if he stayed here it would be much easier to get another message to André, to make this meeting happen. And if he stayed here he would be alone with his wife just that much sooner.

Peggy awoke abruptly as the coach halted in front of a large white manor house. Groggy from a deep sleep that blessedly descended after another headache, she wondered where they were and why were they stopping. After nine days of rocking and bumping along uneven and sometimes washed out roads, the swaying of the coach felt more natural than this sudden halt.

The baby must have preferred the motion also, as all at once he broke into a piercing wail.

"Poor little man," Peggy crooned, leaning over to kiss him as he squirmed in his new nurse's arms. "You're ready for this trip to be over, too."

"I believe we all are," Melora said, pulling a small mirror from her bag. Pinching her cheeks she added, "I feel as if I've grown to this seat."

"But where are we?" Peggy asked, still dazed from her nap.

"Belmont, Mrs. Arnold," said Major Franks from outside the coach. "Belmont on the Hudson, and a prettier place you will not find."

As Franks busied himself removing luggage from atop the coach and placing the stairs for the ladies' descent, Peggy's nerves faltered once again. It was a pleasant enough looking place, but why was she here? Why wasn't she sitting in the parlor of the Great House with her family all around? Or at Becky's having tea with her friends?

"It certainly is a grand place," Melora observed fluffing out the ribbons on her bonnet. Dressed in the lavender calico from so many months ago, Melora looked as fresh and eager as Peggy felt wrinkled and scared.

"Go help Major Franks with the boxes."

"Why, miss? The men attend to that."

Melora's puzzled expression only annoyed her more. She knew what the girl was up to. She was primping for her young man. "Do as I asked, and try to remember why you are here."

While Melora lowered herself slowly from the coach, the front door of the manor swung open. Arnold, followed by a man of medium build and fair hair cut above his collar, rushed out. Behind him, a petite woman followed with a servant.

"Peggy, come here!" Arnold held up both hands to help her down. She wasn't sure her feet even touched the ground before he pulled her to him and, despite the presence of the Smiths, Major Franks, and the servants, kissed her as he might have in a more private moment. Releasing her at last, he turned to the Smiths. "Meet Mrs. Arnold, whom I have just embarrassed into all eternity. Isn't she all that I described?"


A few hours later Arnold released her again and, turning to his side of the bed, quickly settled into the slow rhythmic breathing of sleep. Though also tired, Peggy stared up at the ceiling, wide awake from the uneven sleep of the headache, the unfamiliarity of Belmont, and the behavior of her husband. While the General was always forceful and direct in his lovemaking, he never failed to make her feel admired and prized. But tonight he'd been a stranger, reaching for her fiercely, almost cloddishly, kneading and prying into her body.

Lifting the blanket to cover her husband's naked shoulders, she sat up and searched through the covers for her shift. He had been desperate for her tonight, or so she'd thought. Pleading a long day, he'd risen from the dinner table and excused himself from port and cigars. He'd even come around the table to take her hand, leaving no possibility that she would remain downstairs to socialize with the Smiths. Once upstairs, however, he insisted on writing a lengthy letter as Melora brushed her hair and put out her clothes for the next day, rendering any real conversation impossible. And when he'd finally come to bed, talk was very far from his mind.

Pulling her shawl around her, Peggy slipped out of bed and wandered to the window. Outside the night was pitch black, silent except for the sounds of the wind, an owl, and the howling she supposed was that of a wolf. Hannah Arnold was right. This was a dark and dreary place. And she didn't like it.

She also didn't like the Smiths, found them country-ish, prattling, and wondered how Benedict could think them enjoyable. Perhaps, however, she'd find anyone in this wilderness country-ish and prattling right now. Tomorrow they would travel to the headquarters at Robinson House, a mansion across the river from West Point previously owned by a loyalist of that name. This Robinson, Beverley Robinson, was a fine man, Smith said, a friend of George Washington's since the French and Indian War, but driven from his land and home, and now serving under Clinton aboard the Vulture, a British war sloop stationed on the Hudson. But even with such a previous owner, she couldn't imagine that Robinson House would be anything but another lonely structure. Another lonely structure far, far from the comfort of Philadelphia's noises, lights, and bustle.

Glancing over at Arnold, she felt the current that had bound them almost from the beginning coil through her. She longed for him to awaken and gather her to him in his usual way. And there in that warmth, she would have him give her all the details of his communications with the British, explain exactly what was happening in their lives, and assure her that in his heart he still believed the defection to be the best course. Then, finally, as husband and lover, he would make her forget all this madness for a while.

CHAPTER 48

The Same Night

*Belmont on the Hudson*

*M*elora knelt down, struck the tinder box quickly several times, then blew softly on the pile of grass and twigs until a flame ignited under two sturdy oak logs. With the fire crackling to life and burning off the chilly edges of the room, she sat back on her heels, consumed with gratitude and anticipation. In her wildest dreams she would never have imagined having a place, a tiny house, actually, to herself for the night. And never would she have imagined having a tiny house all to herself and Jared. Wishing there was a mirror of some kind about, she straightened her dress for the tenth time and pinched her cheeks. The fire and the candle were lit. He should come soon.

She had been such a jumble of nerves and excitement when the coach pulled into Belmont. Would Jared be there? He could be accompanying the General, or be at West Point on another duty, or, she supposed, he could even have been reassigned since his last letter. Clambering out of the coach to help Major Franks and the driver with the trunks and parcels, she had willed him to emerge from the house to help her. But only the General, the Smiths, and some servants had come out to meet them. Almost immediately after the introductions, Mrs. Smith swept the Arnolds inside for tea and the rest of them to their rooms. Major Franks, the baby, and Anne, the baby's new nurse, were to stay in the big house near Peggy and the General, while Melora and driver were placed in separate servants' cottages to the rear of the kitchen. Mrs. Smith seemed apologetic, but Melora was thrilled. Even if Jared did not come to meet her, the idea of a night in total privacy was a solace. The cottage even reminded her of many homes in Dunquin. A bed, a chair for the father, a table, small fireplace, and low ceiling. No adornments of any kind except a blue blanket on the bed and some muslin curtains dyed black. Noting the single candle holder on the tiny table, she decided that tonight, when her work was finished, she must write a letter home all about this trip to the north.

Her next surprise came when Peggy called her in to announce that Anne was working too hard and must relax. Melora should take the baby until after dinner. Was this another slight like the boxes? Was Peggy genuinely concerned for Anne? Melora had not an inkling, but the result was the same. While Major Franks and the Arnolds enjoyed a lazy evening with the Smiths, and the servants shared their own dinner in the kitchen, Melora was left to keep the young master quiet. And this was no small task. Perhaps the trip had taken its toll on the child, perhaps he was coming down with something, but clearly little Neddy was in a state, alternating only between whimpering and full-fledged wailing. Finally, after receiving permission from the General, she'd taken the baby outside to see if the fresh air might not brighten his spirits.

That was where he found her. As she sat on the hill overlooking the river, she felt the odd sensation of being watched and knew he was there. She looked back toward the house and saw him walking toward her—his tall angular body, his wry smile, his orange-red hair gleaming in the late afternoon sun.

Without a word, Jared dropped to the ground beside her and the crying baby, reached into his pocket, and took out a rabbit's foot. Touching the soft fur to Neddy's pale pink cheeks, the cries subsided and the child grabbed the charm for himself. Then Jared took her hand, slowly raised it to his cheek, and kissed the palm.

He had changed in the sixteen months since she'd seen him. He was leaner, more hardened. And there were the beginnings of lines at the outer corners of his eyes and mouth. "I thought you weren't here," she whispered.

Jared kissed her hand again, this time the red hair tumbling over his forehead in the way she remembered. "When the General decided to stay overnight, I thought it meant you weren't coming until tomorrow. I've been in town with the crew."

"But you came back?" she said as Neddy began whimpering again, the rabbit foot having fallen from his grasp.

"Yes, just in case," Jared answered, placing the toy in the tiny fingers again. "Who is this noisy fellow? You haven't kept anything from me?"

"This," Melora answered dryly, "is Master Edward Shippen Arnold, who I don't believe likes me. I think he wants his nurse or his mother."

"And when will he have one or another?"

Melora looked down at the little one. "I have to care for him until his nurse has had her dinner."

"And then?"

"I don't know if Miss Peggy will need me or not," she answered wistfully. "She's been quite the mistress on this trip, scarcely able to tie her own cape."

"I have to see you," Jared said softly.

Melora shrugged, "I don't know how. As soon as I'm finished with one or the other, I'm sure they'll expect me to go directly to the..." she felt weak, "...the cottage."

The pressure on her hand increased. "Where?"

The words came out in a rush, "I'm staying in one of the little cottages behind the kitchen, alone. The driver, Thomas, is in the other. I could light a candle when I'm done for the night."

Jared held her hand to his cheek once more. "Good."


"Melora!" The whisper was so low that she might have missed it for the wind had she not been listening. Lifting the latch, she opened the door just enough for Jared and a blast of cold air to slide into the room.

"You must be freezing," she said, stung by the sudden drop in temperature from the afternoon.

Jared, with no coat, hat, or gloves just shook his head. "You become used to it."

Now that he was here, she felt shy and awkward in the little cabin. "Please sit down." She patted the chair. They had never been seated in a room together before. They'd sat on the ground in the park, on the stoop, on benches in the city, but never in a house together, not even in the Great House. While Cook adored him, a young man's place was not in the kitchen.

Perching more than sitting, Jared tried to fit his long frame onto the tiny wooden ladder back while Melora leaned against the side of the narrow bed.

"Your trip was fine?" Jared finally asked.

"It was. I've never seen country like this, so wild."

Jared glanced toward the window and then back at her. "Do you like it?"

How to explain the thoughts she'd had in the coach when they'd reached the pine-covered cliffs and soft valleys of the Highlands? She answered softly, "It seems noble in a way."

"Noble?" He grinned. "I'll have to think about that." He reached into his pocket. "I have something for you."

Puzzled, Melora leaned forward.

"No, I think you'll have to come closer to see," Jared announced and placed a knotted handkerchief on the table beside them. As Melora moved the step or two toward the table, he caught her hand and pulled her onto his lap, wrapping both arms around her waist.

Feeling more awkward than ever, Melora turned her attention to the cloth, needing some moments to loosen the knotted fabric. Inside, no bigger than a thumbnail, was a silver locket with the initials DM carved in an ornate scroll. She turned to Jared in bewilderment. "This is for me?" The times she'd received presents in her life could be counted on one hand, and never more valuable than a piece of candy.

Jared nodded, obviously proud of his surprise.

"But where did you get it?" she asked picking up the piece of jewelry. "And who is DM?"

"I won it in a card game and I have no clue who DM is," Jared explained, adding slowly, "but I thought it could be for us, Donovan and McBride."

His words seemed to hang in the air against the faint popping and rustling of the fire. "Why don't you put it on?"

"I don't have a chain," Melora answered, fingering the filigree work around the edges of the heart.

"Perhaps you could use this," he countered, untying the purple ribbon she had so carefully arranged in her hair that morning.

Melora guided the satin ribbon through the delicate loop at the top edge of the locket while Jared gathered the loose mass of black hair with one hand so that she could see. Then, as she shivered in spite of herself, he began to trace D and M on the bare skin at the top of her dress with the other. She dropped the locket twice before finally pulling it to the center of the ribbon and handing the necklace back to him. "You should do this."

Taking the locket, he swept her hair over one shoulder and tied the ribbon at the base of her neck. Then, as she was praying for him to do, he kissed her in the same spot before turning her slightly to face him. Nuzzling along her throat, he finally kissed her fully and slowly on the mouth, ending with a kiss between her breasts where the locket lay.

"I love you, Melora," he murmured as his hands felt for the tiny wooden circles fastening the front of her dress. And as the row of buttons gave way, Jared followed, kissing the hollow of her throat, her shoulders, and finally the bare whiteness of her breasts.

Helpless to stop him, not wanting to stop him, Melora made her mother's protest: "But we're not married....a sin."

Pausing for just a moment to push the calico bodice aside, Jared whispered against her shoulder, "We will be married, Melora, and this is no sin."

The General's slight moan startled Peggy from her reverie at the window. She should sleep herself, tomorrow would come soon enough. As she reached to close the curtain, a light glimmered from inside one of the little cabins below her window. In the next moment the door opened and a tall man emerged followed by Melora, wrapped in some dark cover. Peggy watched as her maid caught the man's arm and pulled him back to her. While the couple embraced in the open doorway, the blanket around the maid fell, revealing bare shoulders, back, and arms. Gathering the blanket back around Melora's shoulders, the young man, Jared Donovan she was sure, kissed her one last time before walking away. Peggy remained at the window watching as Melora closed the door and the cabin grew dark once again.

Closing the curtain, Peggy glanced over at her sleeping husband. She wanted to wake him, insist that Melora be sent home. The girl had been bad business all along, never knowing her place, stubborn, and now giving herself to men. But if Melora was sent away who would arrange her hair and look after her clothes? What if she was sent into New York? She couldn't be presented to Sir Henry without help.

Stepping back into bed, she reflected on what a horrid day it had been. And what a horrid day it would be tomorrow with the tiresome Smiths, the trip to West Point, and Benedict strange and on edge. She needed to sleep. She had to sleep. But at each hint of slumber the image of the lovers in the doorway rose unbidden. Over and over she saw them, over and over she felt that need, until the tears that had been waiting to fall all evening, finally ran down her cheeks and onto the pillow.

CHAPTER 49

September 17, 1780
*Robinson House*

"Promise me," Arnold demanded, "should anything go wrong, today or anytime in the future, you know nothing." His arms tightened about her. "Promise me."

Peggy looked out through the open front door to where a servant held the General's impatient mare. "I promise. Of course I do. I just wish you didn't have to leave."

"But," his manner turned businesslike, "you know I must. And you also know that all of this may be over very soon."

"Do you really think..." she began.

"Shh!" he whispered in her ear. "No talk of that. Now, give me a kiss before I'm off."

Peggy stood on tiptoe for the perfunctory going-away kiss. She knew that mentally he had already left her, his thoughts on the possibility of events down river. Following him out of the house and into the afternoon sun, she stood nearby as he took the reins from the servant and mounted. "Wave to me from the river."

Arnold smiled and nodded to the guards accompanying him. "I will. Kiss the baby for me." And with that, the group of men trotted lightly off in the direction of the path leading down the steep hillside to the Hudson.

Standing there alone, she thought how much she really did wish he didn't have to leave, not just now. The last night at Belmont they'd finally talked, really talked, Benedict apologizing for his gruffness and she for her frustration. Then they'd made love, just as she'd wanted, and he had held her long into the night. She could almost feel his arms about her now, here in the sunshine on this lovely day.

After a brief debate with herself as to whether she should tell the Smiths where she was going, Peggy headed toward the cliff. They could be unattended for a little while. She had not been happy when Arnold extended their stay at Belmont for four additional days, and was even less pleased when, as they were leaving, he had invited the Smiths to come to Robinson House the next day for a visit, even if their stop at Robinson House was a necessary part of Arnold's most recent plan to talk with the British.

The idea, the General explained, was for Mrs. Smith, after a stopover with them at Robinson House, to continue on to relatives farther north. Then, during her absence, Joshua Smith, as well as Belmont, could be put to use for the meeting with Clinton's envoy. Now, however, Benedict had been unexpectedly summoned by General Washington, so it would fall to her to entertain the couple for the rest of the afternoon and evening. Given Mr. Smiths' usual level of babble, that would be a daunting enough assignment for any day. But today, a day where her entire future might be decided, she was close to overwhelmed by the prospect.

Peggy crossed the road in front of the house and made her way through a large clearing to the cliff overlooking the Hudson River. Even though she'd only been at Robinson House for two days, she'd already made this trip to the cliff several times. Sometimes she wanted to watch her husband go back and forth, and sometimes she just needed to relieve the boredom of residing in a forest.

From the vantage point of the cliff, she could look directly across to the western shore of the river and to West Point, the collection of forts, one of them named for Benedict, redoubts, and batteries that Sir Henry Clinton was so eager to obtain. And if she looked below her to the eastern shore, as she was now, she could see her husband's barge sitting at anchor with the omnipresent oarsmen lying lazily on the ground nearby. Melora's man, Jared Donovan, was one of the oarsmen on duty today, the only one of the men she knew.

But when the General and his guards rode into view and dismounted, these same men came alive, jumping to their feet and assuming their positions on the boat. Within seconds, it seemed, the craft was taking off for the short trip across the river. She wondered when her husband would tell any of the men about the true nature of their trip today. Would they be as astonished as he had been upon receiving Washington's message? And imagine their astonishment if Washington and his entire party were captured this evening, as was very possible.

Peggy closed her eyes and tilted her face up toward the mid-after-noon sun. After the excruciating days at Belmont, she, the General, Melora, Anne, and the baby had climbed into the same barge that she was watching now, proceeding upriver and passing the outposts at Verplanck's Point and Stony Point before stopping for a visit at West Point. As accustomed as she was to being the center of attention, she was still unprepared for the welcome by many of the just over three thousand soldiers under her husband's authority. Although they compared dismally to the crisp elegance of the British regulars, she was completely disarmed by the men's enthusiasm in greeting their commander's wife, especially since, as Benedict had impressed upon her, most of them were dispirited, eager for the war to be over one way or another, and quite unsure of their leaders.

Although Benedict had spoken repeatedly about the Brave Boys, she'd never put faces into her mental image of West Point being overtaken. In her mind, she had seen Sir Henry or dear André taking West Point by simply changing the flag over a piece of land, or something like that. But now she was worried. Would these men resist? Later that night, when she tried to discuss the issue with Benedict, he'd grown cold, pulling into himself, saying only that he believed it would be an orderly transition and that overall, lives would be saved. But, at close to three o'clock in the morning, distraught and anxious, he awakened her, thrusting a single piece of paper under the candle.

The letter was from General Washington. He would be passing near West Point on the way to speak with Rochambeau at Hartford on the following Sunday, two days hence. Benedict was to meet him with a force of men, as he would not be accompanied by his regular guard. On the return trip, the Commander in Chief would make an inspection of West Point itself. "If Clinton could be contacted in time," Arnold whispered hoarsely, "the entire party could be taken, the war ended in a single action."

"Take the Commander in Chief?" she asked through a half fog of sleep.

"Of course," he answered brusquely, and then to her horror added, "he is the enemy."

Determined to get a note off as early as possible in the morning, he'd left her alone to work at his desk. She spent the rest of the night thinking of the Commander in Chief's visits to the Great House, his letter at Neddy's birth.

Peggy opened her eyes, forcing herself from the sunny sojourn. The little boat was just about at West Point now. She wondered if the General had in fact waved, knowing in her heart that he hadn't. He had a great deal on his mind, a great deal that could unfold in just the next few hours. Indeed, if Sir Henry had received Arnold's early morning message, General Washington might already be taken. Putting a hand to her forehead she breathed deeply, trying to dislodge the tiny hammer there. She must not succumb. And she should not be standing here, either. At the very least, she should give Melora instructions to organize the baby's things and her own. They should be ready for travel at a moment's notice. And Melora! That was another issue she had yet to attend to.

# CHAPTER 50

The Same Day
*Robinson House Kitchen*

"You would not believe your eyes," the woman who had introduced herself as Sarah announced softly to Melora. "The General has had wagons and wagons of food brought over here from West Point. He brings it over here and then he sells it. I heard him tell Major Franks it was because of all the money the army owes him."

Melora tried not to show too much surprise at what the woman was saying. Along with her regular duties for Miss Peggy, she'd been helping Mary and Sarah in the kitchen at Robinson House. After a brief warming up period of only an hour or so, the two women showed themselves for what they were: good cooks and inveterate gossips. For most of the afternoon, they related one story after another about the various occupants of Robinson House since their master's forced departure. Employees of the house since Beverley Robinson arrived as a newlywed, they appeared to know where all the bodies were buried.

"They say the General also has all kinds of businesses in New York—that's why he's always getting letters from there," Mary put in.

"Melora!"

Wheeling from the chopping board, Melora saw Peggy at the kitchen entrance. Could she have been listening to the kitchen talk? "Yes, miss?"

"I need your help upstairs," Peggy ordered, nodding to the two other women in the kitchen.

"But, miss, I've promised to make my mother's stew."

Peggy glanced at the carrots, potatoes, and thick cubes of beef. "I'm sure that one of these other ladies can make their own very fine stew. I need you upstairs." And with that, she left the room.

Feeling like an errant child, Melora put the paring knife down, wiping her hands on her apron. "I'm sorry," she murmured to the other women. "I don't know what this is about."

"Not to worry," Sarah answered. "We'll make your stew another day."

Melora shrugged. "I'll try to be quick all the same."


Inside the upstairs bedroom, Melora found Peggy kneeling by her trunk, sorting the contents into piles. "You need to go through every item, check to make certain everything is cleaned, dried, and ironed by tomorrow morning. Neddy's things also."

"But why, miss? And why by tomorrow? We've barely just arrived."

Peggy looked up from the clothing. "I'm giving you an instruction. Just do it."

"But, I'll be up all night!"

Peggy stood up from the trunk slowly, careful not to upset any of the stacks piled around her. Clasping her hands, she studied her maid. "I don't think a lack of sleep will bother you."

Melora shook her head. "What are you saying?"

"I'm saying that you didn't seem bothered by lack of sleep at Belmont."

At first Melora could only stare at Peggy in confusion, wondering what in heaven's name she was referring to. Then, as understanding crept coldly throughout her being, she could only stand mute, the cruel words reverberating in her head.

"I should have spoken to you sooner. I saw that you had company at Belmont the first night we were there, and then on each of the other nights."

Nausea rose in Melora's throat. "We're to be married."

"To be married and married are not the same."

"Miss, you don't understand," Melora said, feeling like she was drowning. "We meant to wait. Please, it's just that I have three more years on my contract. I can't marry until then."

Peggy sat down on the bed. "Nevertheless, I'll have to write to my father to ask what actions should be taken."

"What kind of actions?"

"I don't know, but I'm sure your contract must include something about immoral behavior."

"Immoral behavior!" Melora whispered as she made her way to the other side of the bed from Peggy. "I love him, surely you can understand that."

Peggy bent over the trunk, taking out more clothes. "What I understand is that either you are unable or unwilling to restrain yourself."

Images of the Shippen house on Peggy's wedding day, of Peggy floating down the stairs on Judge Shippen's arm, of the dress that would have fed her family for years, of the General and Peggy in bed, all crowded into Melora's mind. "How can you understand? You've never had to wait for anything in your life. You have everything."

"No one has everything," Peggy shot back.

Melora picked up a particularly fragile shift from one of the piles on the bed and waved the mass of lace and ribbons between them. "But you come very close!"

Snatching the garment, Peggy jumped to her feet and stormed to the door. "I forbid you to see that man until I can talk with my father. And don't mention this to the General, he has enough on his mind without worrying about a harlot in the house."

As Peggy's footsteps echoed down the hall, Melora sank to the floor. She had been so happy, everything was so perfect. Now what? Would she be punished? Might she be sent to jail?

From downstairs she heard the familiar bang of pots and Anne cooing to Neddy. She should rise, begin the work, and figure out some way to placate Miss Peggy. But try as she might, her only desire was to close her eyes, curl up tightly, and imagine Jared coming to take her away.

CHAPTER 51

September 18, 1780
*British Headquarters, Manhattan*

"Sir, we have it!"

Henry Clinton put down the report from Cornwallis as his young aide, also his newly named adjutant general, rushed breathlessly into the office. "Another letter from Arnold?"

André nodded. "With your permission, sir." Standing at attention, he held up several small pieces of paper. "Three messages from General Arnold via Colonel Robinson on the *Vulture*."

"Well, for God's sake," Clinton answered, "don't read them, just tell me what our General is thinking today. And sit. My neck aches from this constant craning."

Bowing to his Commander, André flipped the tails of his uniform and sat stiffly on the closest seat, the stool Sir Henry used to have his boots removed. "The first is a response to Robinson's letter, a cover for the other two included within its pages. The second is a copy of one we've already received." André peered over the paper at Sir Henry. "General Arnold must think we've missed some of his notes. We certainly didn't receive the news of Washington's travels in a timely fashion."

"It might be just as well," Clinton replied, removing a flask from his desk drawer. "Let the French explain how little they can do for his cause. And the third?"

André's face brightened. "General Arnold seems to have aborted the plan you disagreed with, that we should go behind the lines. In fact, what he proposes is quite in line with your thoughts for the meeting."

Clinton raised his flask in a mock toast and clinked the inkwell before refreshing himself. "Good man, perhaps we can work together."

"Perhaps, sir?" André asked, instantly alert to his superior's notorious waffling.

"I mean," Clinton answered, pushing the brandy across to André, "if he is who he says he is, and if he can provide what he says he can provide."

André helped himself to the liqueur and nodded. "The very reason for our parley. His plan is to send Hett Smith to the *Vulture* on Wednesday night with a boat and passes to pick up your representative."

"Day after tomorrow?"

"Yes. He also asks that the *Vulture* remain where she is until that time."

Quiet filled the room. Sir Henry sat motionless in his chair. Outside, carriages rattled by, people called to one another, and, just inches away, colleagues walked heavily down the hall. The two men had spent many hours this way, André presenting reports, updates from the field, and strategies for advancement, with the commander slowly absorbing the detail and more slowly committing to action.

This, however, was not a new plan. This scenario had been discussed on countless occasions. Finally, unable to bear the suspense another moment, André went against the most rudimentary military etiquette. "Sir?"

The older man sighed. "André, my dear boy, this mission concerns me. It is of vital importance to the Crown, but I'm concerned."

"Why, sir?"

"Whoever attends this meeting will be taking great risks. I'm not sure it should be you."

"But, sir, it's my duty, and my pleasure, to you and to the Crown."

"It's also," Clinton leaned forward wagging his finger in the young man's face, "your best chance to impress London."

"That's very true, sir. I've never said otherwise."

"But this meeting, it's difficult. You, my dear friend, could be arrested as an agent, a spy."

André laughed and bent over Clinton's desk. "No, I could not, because, as you've explained many times, for that to happen I would have to go behind enemy lines, conceal my identity, or perhaps have something on my person showing illegal business." He paused to take another drink of the brandy, "But, I will do none of those things."

Clinton hesitated. "We don't know this man, his motivations, his heart. We do know he's fearless and has been a great fighter for the colonies."

"What we do know, however, is that I would meet with General Arnold on neutral ground. We would talk, discuss terms. Then I would return to the *Vulture* and speedily make my way back here. If all is as we expect it to be with Arnold, you can send Sir Rodney up the Hudson with his armada and we will have West Point...and, most likely, the end of our time here in America."

"And if it is not as we expect?"

"Then, sir, as you have so aptly taught me, we will re-evaluate our position at that time."

Clinton stood to study the well-worn map of North America pinned to the wall behind his desk. "Indeed, I can't imagine the rebels hanging on if they lose West Point." Pointing to South Carolina, Clinton turned to his young aide. "They say there were four thousand under Gates at Camden. A worse rout than Charleston. According to Cornwallis, the south is subdued, just a few scattered fragments here and there to be excised. He's moving through the Carolinas as we speak."

André joined Clinton at the map, pointing to the group of pins representing the French troops in Rhode Island. "Then, when we move against Washington, the French will have no partner left. Your victory will be complete."

"Yes, my victory," Clinton nodded. Turning from the map, he placed a hand on André's shoulder. "But Arnold, West Point, this will be your victory. Board the *Vulture* on Wednesday. You have your orders."

André bowed. "You have my most sincere thank you, sir, and I—"

"Not now," Clinton interrupted, reaching for his crop and gloves, "we must get ourselves to the stables." The hard work of the day was accomplished and he was determined to put off any vestiges of worry or concern. Besides, he might not have many rides left with André, or in this godforsaken continent at all.

# CHAPTER 52

September 20, 1780
*Robinson House*

*P*eggy lowered the candle to see Neddy fast asleep on his stomach, his entire body rising and falling in regular breaths. "What is it, miss?" Anne rose sluggishly from the blankets.

"I thought I heard the baby. Go back to sleep."

Feeling foolish and relieved, Peggy tucked the blanket around Neddy as Anne dropped immediately back under the covers. She bent down to kiss the tiny cheek, then blew out her candle and tiptoed across the hall.

"The baby?" Benedict's whisper surprised her as she entered the bedroom.

"I thought I heard him crying." She lifted the quilt and slipped into bed. "You shouldn't be awake, you have to rise so early."

He pulled her to him. "I can't sleep. Are you feeling better?"

"Somewhat."

Arnold ran his fingers down her arm. "You scared me at dinner. What happened?"

"I was crying because of the cobbler." She forced herself not to take his hand away.

"Was it so bad?"

"Don't laugh at me. I hate it here. The cobbler was so much like the one Cook makes and I thought of home. Will it be like this in New York, with you always away...while I'm alone?"

Arnold hesitated, his hand moving up her back. "You must be rational," he said finally. "For the time being, I am a soldier."

"I thought when you joined His Majesty's forces it would be simple, you would just leave. But...it's become so difficult—West Point, the people here."

"I know, I know," he murmured, making her feel even more ridiculous. "But think of us in six months, in a year, when we have the thanks of the people and the King. And try to put your mind on something else. You have a great deal of work to do before General Washington's arrival. Everything must appear perfect. Have Melora help."

Trying to discourage Arnold's obvious intentions, she turned on her side. The General's visit was the last thing she could think of. "I doubt she will."

"Of course she will. She's your servant."

"I made her angry. She was sleeping with Jared Donovan at Belmont, and I forbade her to see him again."

Arnold tensed against her. "We can't have enemies in the house now. There's too much at stake. Make up to her."

"Benedict, are you sure we're doing the right thing?"

"It's the only way. Besides," he added, "the Continentals can never win now. The losses at Charleston and Camden were just too high."

Peggy rose on one elbow. "Then let me go with you tomorrow. Let me be there when you talk to André."

"My dear," he kissed her shoulder, "you know that's impossible."

"A wife can't travel with her husband?"

Arnold shook his head. "Not on this errand. Joshua Smith believes that André is a secret agent for the Americans by the name of John Anderson. That's why he agreed to go to the *Vulture*, to bring André ashore to meet me. What would Smith think if you were to arrive also?"

Determined to make him understand, Peggy took his face in her hands. "I don't care what Smith thinks. I can't stay here!"

"But you must." His body was hard and insistent beside her. "Our future depends on this meeting. Possibly even our lives."


The three men stood in quiet attention scanning the silky black waters of the Hudson. To the west lay Haverstraw Bay, and to the east, Teller's Point. Lights twinkled on both sides of the shore, the river lapped gently about the sloop, and a crescent moon rose in the crisp fall night. But that was all. Behind them the crew attended to their chores, whispered complaints and jokes, and speculated as to why the three officers remained on deck in the middle of the night with the *Vulture* riding at anchor. The three officers were speculating as well.

Having arrived by sailboat from Manhattan, André was welcomed on board around seven in the evening by Beverley Robinson and Captain Southerland, the Commander of the *Vulture*. Repairing to the Captain's quarters, drinks and dinner were served almost immediately. Dinner conversation was light, with Robinson and André excusing themselves soon after to strategize the coming conversation with Arnold. Then, they'd begun to wait.

Now, four hours later and with the moon almost directly over head, Southerland asked leave to go below. Mornings aboard ship began very early. A few moments later, Robinson, shrugging his shoulders, also said goodnight. Obviously, the plan had gone awry. Again. Perhaps Arnold was playing them for fools.

Perhaps, André thought, watching the older man make his way along the deck to the hatch leading below. Perhaps Arnold had set up an elaborate ruse using Peggy for authenticity and battle information agreed to by Washington. Clinton thought perhaps, now Robinson thought perhaps as well. Why was he the only one so sure of Arnold's intent?

André turned back to look for the small boat that could assure his future and wondered if that was indeed the point. Without a secure place to return to after the war, he was the only one unwilling to think "perhaps."

A few hours later, a loud "HALT" from one of the Robinson House sentries woke Arnold. He turned and reached for his watch while an indiscernible exchange followed, then silence. Beside him, Peggy lay motionless.

Four o'clock. If he left now, he could meet André in time for breakfast. He stepped out of bed and hurried downstairs to find his man. The British were arrogant enough, he wouldn't be seen unshaven. He opened the front door and called to the guard who sat huddled in the front yard. "Johnson, fetch Sam for me. And have someone prepare my horse."

Johnson, a recent recruit whom Arnold had singled out for his shooting ability, rose awkwardly to attention. "Yes, sir! Sir?"

Arnold looked back over his shoulder at the boy. "What is it? I'm in a great hurry."

"A message just came for you, sir."

Arnold shivered in the pre-dawn chill. "Well, who was it from?"

"A Mr. Smith sent it, but a man by the name of Cahoon delivered it, just minutes ago."

Arnold nodded. The halt that had awakened him. "What did he want?"

"Said to tell you he couldn't get the boat for the errand. Major Kiers didn't have one."

Couldn't get the boat! Arnold's entire musculature constricted. Smith needed the longboat from Kiers to pick up André. Then where in God's name would André be now? He had to get to Belmont.

Arnold looked angrily at Johnson. If he'd had his crop he would have used it. "Why are you standing there? Go, get my horse, have someone alert the boat crew, and don't you ever keep a message from your Commander again!"

As the guard ran toward the stables, Arnold's rage turned to disgust. How could it be that time after time after time in this war he was so completely surrounded by incompetence. After a last curse at Johnson, he raced up the stairs to rouse Peggy. He'd need help dressing for the long, cold trip.

# CHAPTER 53

## September 21, 1780
### *Belmont*

"Smith! Where are you?" Arnold strode into the foyer of Belmont, the door banging behind him. Outside, the morning was brilliantly clear, crisp, and blue, a perfect fall morning in the Highlands of New York.

"I'm here, General." Arnold looked up as Joshua Hett Smith ran down the stairs, his brown curls bobbing like a small child's while his heels clicked against the polished maple.

"You got my message about the boat, I assume," Smith continued. "I didn't know what to do."

Arnold studied the man before him, glad that he'd had the time during the trip from Robinson House to gather his temper.

"You're alone here?"

Smith pointed toward the parlor. "Of course, as we planned. Do take a seat. I have water heating for tea."

Although tea was perhaps the last thing on Arnold's mind, he headed into the parlor as Smith hurried off toward the back of the house. Seating himself on a large velvet settee, Arnold studied the room as though it were his first visit. One of Smith's latest revelations was that his brother William, not himself, was the actual owner of the house. He should have known that the house was on a grander scale than Smith could manage.

"Here, General. This should warm you." Smith joined him on the couch, carrying two steaming cups as well as a leather bag under one arm. "And this came for you, from the *Vulture* just moments ago, under a flag."

Arnold ignored the tea and all but grabbed the bag from Smith. Removing the contents, he saw that there were two letters. One was sealed with the stamp of the *Vulture,* the second, a plain note card.

He broke the seal from the *Vulture* packet first, scanning the paper quickly, murmuring the contents half aloud to himself. Then, after reading the note card in equal haste, he handed both letters to Smith. "Thank God, Anderson's still aboard."

Smith looked up at Arnold from the first letter. "I see nothing regarding John Anderson. Only that this Captain Southerland believes one of his boats was fired upon illegally yesterday."

Arnold reached for one of the cups of tea. "The letter from Southerland, it's written in Anderson's hand. It's just a mechanism to let us know he's on the ship. Also, the second note. They expect you tonight."

"But I still have no boat, and the men I asked to row refused."

Arnold stared at the splendor of William Smith's house and didn't know whether to laugh or cry. Peggy was right. These people were bumpkins. "Smith! You will have a boat! Who do you think I am?"

But later, after an entire day spent in finding a boat, and now the need to cajole some farmers into rowing it, Arnold was ready to doubt his own authority. Immediately after receiving Southerland's and Robinson's letters, he'd left Belmont in search of a boat himself under the guise of an inspection tour around Verplanck's Point. Approaching Major Kiers at Stony Point, he found that there was still nothing available. All of Kiers' boats were in use. Next he'd called on Colonel Livingston, the commandant of Fort LaFayette, across the river. Not only did Livingston not have a boat, but the young firebrand bent his ear for more than twenty minutes on the insult of having the *Vulture* in its current proximity to the American positions. Finally, in sheer frustration he sent his barge back to West Point to have a boat delivered to him. If that were not enough, returning to Belmont he'd found that Smith had once again failed to find someone to man the boat down river to the Vulture. The only possibilities Smith assured him were two of his tenants, the brothers Samuel and Joseph Cahoon, Samuel being the same Cahoon who had delivered Smith's message to Robinson House earlier that same morning.

"Smith, what do you mean they won't go with you? They're your tenants. Make them."

Smith sat down on a chaise opposite the writing table where Arnold was working. "I got to them just as they were going for the cows. Samuel says he's much too tired after traveling to Robinson House last night. And his brother, well, I believe he is just afraid. Perhaps if you speak with them."

Although at that moment he could have leapt across the parlor to claw through Smith's throat, Arnold, for the third time that day, marshaled his inner resources. Soothing himself with the thought that this should certainly be the last occasion that he would have to solicit the indolent man before him, Arnold breathed deeply and smiled amiably at his host. Then, after adjusting his coat and stock, Major General Benedict Arnold asked Smith in his most cordial and collegial voice to please show the Messrs Cahoon into the parlor.

"But, sir, it's like I told Squire Smith, my brother and I've no mind to go," Samuel Cahoon whined from his place beside Joseph on the crushed velvet couch. Looking from his brother to Arnold he added, "And now my wife says that I can't go, she won't have it."

"Think of your country. It's your duty!"

"General, sir, I was up all last night bringing you your message. I need my sleep.

"You will sleep again, man, but this is a mission of great urgency," Arnold lowered his voice to a conspiratorial whisper, "and great secrecy."

Samuel Cahoon rubbed his hands on his pants leg nervously. "Anything but this, General. My wife says going to the British ship is a bad business, guards all along the river."

Arnold walked over to the window and looked out over the dark countryside. According to Jared Donovan, a boat had been found tied up at Colonel Hayes' landing on the Misceongo Creek nearby. These two should be leaving now!

He tried again. "Fifty pounds of flour. I'll see that each of you receive fifty pounds of flour for this short night's work."

The Cahoons looked to one another for advice, and although Arnold saw not a wink or a nod pass between them, neither brother spoke. Exasperated, Arnold stormed out of the parlor to a smaller sitting room where Smith was waiting, sipping port.

"Surely there must be someone else who can take you on the river tonight."

Smith shrugged. "Everyone is away, as we planned."

Arnold swore. "Then they must go."

Picking up the decanter, Smith rose from his chair. "If I might sug-

189 THE COLOUR OF THE TIMES

gest, let me share a dram or so with the men. Perhaps they'll become more amenable to your plans."

"Yes," Arnold agreed wearily, "go work on them and I'll think of something."

Smith chuckled, "You could always arrest them."

As Smith left with the port and two glasses, the downstairs clock chimed ten o'clock, and Arnold wished he had gotten a bit of the wine for himself. It had already been a very long day, and if this damnable situation could not be resolved it would get much, much longer. He could wait, but would André?

Two hours later, a small boat pulled up alongside the massive body of the *Vulture*. Amidst jeers and curses from the crew, Joshua Hett Smith grabbed for the small rope ladder thrown over the railing and pulled himself up and aboard the British warship. Below, Samuel and Joseph Cahoon sat—tired, terrified, and cold on the hard wooden planks that served as their seats. For nearly an hour they waited, sitting close to each other as they had as boys, both for warmth and as a mental barrier to the taunts from above. At last, Smith emerged and climbed back into the boat. A few moments later a second man, a younger man covered in a blue-caped coat, also descended the ladder and took a seat beside Smith at the tiller. With a nod from their landlord, the Cahoons once again took up the oars for the six-mile trip back up and across the Hudson. The rowing would have been faster but for the sheepskins covering their oars, sheepskins that the General had commanded them to use to muffle the sound of the boat on the water. And who were they to go against Major General Benedict Arnold, who not only had the authority to send Squire Smith on this secret mission, but also to arrest them and perhaps more if they did not consent to row the boat onto the river tonight? Samuel was of the opinion, and Joseph agreed, that it would have saved everyone a good amount of time if the General had made that fact plain a bit earlier in the conversation. Even the Missus would have understood.

CHAPTER 54

September 22, 1780 1:00 AM
*Foot of Long Clove Mountain*
*West Bank of the Hudson River*

"*O*ver there, that's where we're headed." Smith pointed to the black shoreline some one-hundred yards away. With the strong tide, cloudy night, and no lights on shore to use as markers, André wanted to ask Smith just how he could be so sure of their position. But, whether dubious or not, Smith's news was more than welcome. After the expanse and comfort of the *Vulture*, he felt like he was riding on little more than a raft, vulnerable and unprotected against the depths of the Hudson.

"We seem to have done well against the tide," André answered with more cheer than he felt. For the Cahoons' benefit, he added, "Your oarsmen are to be commended."

"Yes, they are, Mr. Anderson," Smith said nobly, sitting a bit taller in his seat. "Good men in service to their country."

Blowing on his hands for warmth, André studied the approaching shoreline. Arnold was somewhere out there waiting for him, waiting for a very explicit talk on money and terms. God help me if it isn't Arnold, André thought, adjusting the cloak over his regimentals, and God help me if it is. Benedict Arnold, determined, brilliant, larger than life, and next to Washington, the most potent figure of the colonial revolt. And he, John André, Adjutant General of the British army in America, about to put himself entirely within Arnold's power.

Smith leapt onto the beach as the boat's hull grated along the rocky shore. "Wait here," he called to André, "I'll be right back." Crossing over a rough trail that led down to the water's edge, Smith scrambled up the wooded hillside and out of sight of the others. Meanwhile, André and the Cahoons pulled the boat up onto the desolate beach, silent except for the waves washing against the sand, and horses whinnying somewhere in the forest above them. Waiting idly on the sandy beach, the Cahoons began grumbling about the length of the trip and strong tide. André, watching one wave form after another, moved off by himself. Within moments, however, Smith edged back down the hill, calling his name.

"He's there." Smith looked back in the direction he'd come from. "You're to meet with him alone. We'll wait for you here."

Murmuring a low "Gentlemen" to Smith and the Cahoons, André started cautiously up the embankment. The climb was steeper than it appeared; twice he tripped on roots. Whatever awaited him in those trees, there should be no quibbling about his right to a permanent commission now. At the top of a low ridge he stopped, searching the darkness for some sign of his host. Seeing nothing, he was about to continue up the hill when he heard a muffled, "André?"

He froze. He was supposed to be John Anderson.

"André?" the voice called again. This time André could just make out a dark figure some ten feet away. He took a deep breath and answered, "John Anderson at your service."

"Anderson. Right. Come then."

André walked to a mostly protected spot below the ridge where a small campfire had been laid. André noted there were also two blankets and a flask. Clearly, their session was to be substantial. As the other man knelt to light the fire, André fought an impulse to stare. Was this the man who had almost taken Quebec, confronted Carleton and the British navy on Lake Champlain, and urged his men to victory over Burgoyne from between the lines at Saratoga?

"And you are, sir?" André asked hesitantly.

"You know very well who I am: Mr. Moore, Monk, Gustavus—all the names we've used for this past year and a half. By the way, my wife sends her regards."

Arnold sat back on his heels, while a wisp of smoke curled upward from the fire. As the flames rose, André got his first good look at the man. Arnold was not only shorter than he'd expected, but also older. He must be quite a bit older than Peggy. There was also an arrogant set to the eyes and mouth.

"You're authorized to speak for Sir Henry?"

André nodded.

"And you know my terms. The garrison, its artillery and stores, and three-thousand soldiers for 20,000 pounds." Arnold's voice was cold, businesslike. It seemed to André they could be discussing barrels of sugar or bolts of cloth. "Ten thousand if the effort fails."

André winced. He'd hoped to have some other pieces in place before the financials arose. "Sir Henry has only authorized me to pledge a sum of 6000 pounds should, as you say, the effort fail."

Arnold swore and picked up the flask. He took a long drink and then another before turning again to André. "You bastards. My needs have been very clear. You or Sir Henry assured me I should not be left to suffer."

"Yes, we did write that you should not suffer," André answered, wishing he had his complete correspondence with Arnold here with him now. "However, I also wrote that we could never absolutely promise an indemnification of 10000 pounds. I am quite positive of that, sir."

Arnold looked at André coldly. "But you've never actually promised anything for an indemnification. Now, on the eve of this thing, you come up with six thousand. How do you know the value of the houses and property I'll lose? The investments I can never recoup? Or my unpaid wages as a major general in the Continental Army? And do you have any idea of the risk I've run? That I run every day?"

"But, sir," André interrupted, only to be silenced by a searing glance from Arnold.

"And what sort of risk have you put yourself in, Major André, you or Sir Henry? I imagine that, if our plans are successful, you'll both be rewarded handsomely." He turned to face the fire again. "I've a mind to stop this business right now."

The two men sat in silence as André berated himself for having come alone. Arnold was slipping away, he could feel it. Taking a moment to collect himself, he decided to take the monetary issue head on, again heeding Robinson's advice.

"General, I must tell you that Sir Henry is a fair man. While impossible to assign a quantity to risk, I give you my word that if you can prove the degree to which you stand to suffer financially by this undertaking, he will support your claim."

Finishing his speech, André sighed, his mind a blank. He had no other ideas to offer, no other schemes to consider. Just this paltry promise of Sir Henry's fairness. For God's sake, why hadn't they anticipated this more fully?

Arnold picked up a twig and threw it into the fire, then rose and walked slowly into the woods without a word. Away from the campfire, he was almost immediately indistinguishable from the trees and shadows. André wanted to shout, to command, but at the same instant saw the folly in it. If anyone was in command here, it was Arnold.

He began to shiver violently. Whether it was the shock of Arnold's departure or the dampness that had worked its way right through his clothes, he had no idea. Taking one of the blankets, he wrapped himself in it and walked a little way until he could see over the ridge to where Smith and the Cahoons sat ensconced about a fire of their own. Would they be surprised to see him again so quickly? He'd barely left them. Not twenty minutes and he'd lost Arnold. The magnitude of his blunder was almost inconceivable. He was a fool, an arrogant, impossibly stupid fool.

Peering up through the thick fir trees, André could see a star or two, and realized that the clouds must have cleared. They would have to be especially careful on the return trip to the *Vulture,* as now visibility would be much greater on the river. And what would he tell Robinson and Sir Henry? There was no way to make this right.

"You truly believe that?" André turned to see Arnold standing by the fire holding a saddle bag.

"Believe what?"

"That Sir Henry would see that I receive the full 10,000 pounds if I can prove my estate."

André walked back to the fire and dropped the blanket. He felt weak and ridiculous beside the handicapped man who appeared so completely unfazed by the elements or the tension. "I certainly do, General, and I pledge myself to helping you in any way that I can to make the argument to Sir Henry."

"Then," Arnold pointed to the ground before taking a group of papers out of the saddlebag, "take your blanket again, Major, and gather more wood. There are many things that you and I need to discuss tonight."

As André gathered sticks and broke off more branches for the fire, he felt as though he'd awakened from a terrible dream. He would be more cautious than ever now, he vowed, looking over at Arnold reviewing his notes and turning down page corners here and there. This meeting must proceed exactly according to Arnold's wishes, or hope for a speedy end to the conflict might be dashed once more. Yet, taking a seat by the fire, his shivering now under control, André was again reminded of commerce when the American general cocked his head and asked if Sir Henry had decided on a plan of attack yet...or if he might take the liberty of proposing some suggestions?

The early morning sky was still jet black when André heard footsteps coming up the hill. A moment later, Joshua Smith looked down from the top of the ridge and called to them. "Gentlemen, I must have a word."

Scowling as the man approached, Arnold quickly stashed the papers he had been explaining into the saddle bag, while André took the opportunity to stand and stretch. Every fiber of his body ached, and he was sure that he had already forgotten at least half of what he and Arnold had discussed.

"Pardon me, General," Smith began as he half walked, half slid down the bank to Arnold's and André's camp. The usually kempt Smith looked and sounded the worse for his night in the open, just as André was sure he and Arnold did. "There's just time to get Mr. Anderson back to the vessel before dawn, but the Cahoons, they say they won't go."

"And why not?" Arnold asked.

"Because they are too fatigued. Samuel says that he has been up two nights now in our service."

"But, gentlemen," André said, shaken by Smith's news. "I must return this morning. I have urgent matters to attend to."

"Smith, go and speak to them again," Arnold ordered. "We'll finish here."

Smith shook his head. "I'm telling you they won't do it. Remember how it was with them before? They say they'll go tonight."

The decisiveness with which Smith spoke made André wonder if it was in fact Smith who was not eager to repeat the long trip back on the river."

"Well then, Smith, have the men take the boat back to Colonel Hayes' landing. We'll meet you at Belmont." Arnold spoke with a lightheartedness that struck André as cavalier. Why had Arnold not made more binding arrangements for his speedy return? While elated by Arnold's verbal agreements, he was also exhausted, overwhelmed by talk, and wanting nothing more than to be out of these woods and back on board.

As soon as the attorney was out of sight, Arnold turned to André. "It might not be so bad if you wait until tonight to return. We'll ride to Mr. Smith's house, refresh ourselves, and discuss some last details. My servant is holding an extra horse."

André fumbled for words. "Except I have Sir Henry's instructions. He expects news of our meeting today."

"But," the arrogance was once again written all over Arnold's face, "as you've heard, your return must wait until tonight. Sir Henry is a man of experience. He'll understand a slight shift in plans."

While Arnold kicked dirt on the fire and stamped out stray embers, André looked out over the shoreline and the river. Figuring it to be about five o'clock, he knew that Southerland and Robinson on board the *Vulture* must have watched for him throughout the night. Even now they would be on deck awaiting his return.

"Major, come." André looked up to see Arnold holding the saddlebag. "It's time."

Picking up the blankets, André fell in uneasily behind Arnold as they started up the mountain. Now Arnold had the High Command's plans. He wondered if that was what his companion had really come for. But after only about fifteen minutes of walking, the tiny trail opened into a broad clearing at the side of a clear, flowing stream. There, standing as though he had been expecting them throughout the night, stood a negro with three horses. Indeed, André realized, the man must have been there all night.

After both men had washed in the cold, mountain water, Arnold directed the negro to ride to King's Ferry and alert his barge to expect him by mid-morning. Then, with the black man's help, he mounted an impatient chestnut and waited as his servant untied the reins of a small mare and handed them to André. Refusing the offer of a leg up, André swung his weary body into the saddle and, following Arnold, walked the creature slowly through the dense brush until they emerged onto a well-worn trail. Assuming a slow trot, the two riders headed north in the direction, André supposed, of Joshua Hett Smith's house.

Rallied by the wash and the tip of sun edging over the eastern shore, André's gloom receded to a manageable resolve. The wait wouldn't be so long. Tonight he would be safely back among his comrades and en route to Sir Henry with very good news. The mare, sensing either her rider's lighter mood or a familiar route to the stable, pricked up her ears and quickened the pace. With Arnold's chestnut following suit, both men, sportsmen at heart, urged their mounts to greater and greater speeds. They slowed only when the guard at the American line stepped out of the early morning mist and called for the party to halt.

# CHAPTER 55

## Morning, The Same Day
### Robinson House

"Mrs. Arnold, you know that there is no one we hold in higher esteem than your husband." Colonel Varick's voice floated smoothly from the Robinson House parlor to the hallway where Melora stood nervously.

"And because he is one of the greatest men of this country, we felt it absolutely necessary to speak with you," Major Franks added.

Melora was mortified. Earlier, Peggy stopped by the laundry saying that she wanted to speak with her the minute the washing was done. She would wait for her in the parlor. And here she was, but the two gentlemen were inside. What to do?

Knocking tentatively at the doorframe, she saw the two officers and Peggy seated around the fire. "Miss, I'm here."

"Take a seat outside," Peggy answered, "I'll call you when I'm ready."

Grateful for a chance to get off her feet but too nervous to truly relax, Melora sat primly on a small side chair by the door. Since the terrible afternoon in Peggy's room, no more had been said about the accusation—or the threat of some form of punishment. Could Peggy have gotten a letter to her father? Would she have changed her mind and told the General? Melora felt sick.

Rather than think about the probable reason for Peggy's summons, Melora tried to concentrate on her surroundings. This house, while not nearly so grand as the Great House, was still another miracle to her. It troubled her deeply that these owners were forced from this house, from this perfect place, even if they were for the Crown. Maybe after the war she and Jared could find their perfect place in this north country and—

"Madam!" the daydream was cut short by Colonel Varick's voice. "I urge you to stop your husband from associating with Joshua Smith." It sounded to Melora like he was pacing as he talked. "The General's reputation could suffer. Indeed, it may have already."

Melora smiled at the naiveté of Colonel Varick. Associating with Tories was nothing new for the General. Major Franks, at least, was well aware of that.

"But Colonel," Peggy sounded genuinely surprised, "surely the General has proved his support for this country time after time."

"Of course," Varick answered. "It's just that this man, who many of us believe is of a double mind, and who very often speaks pejoratively of America, also has a brother who is very high in the government in New York. How can it look?"

"No one would suspect my husband of duplicity. It's impossible."

"Mrs. Arnold," now Franks was speaking, "it is all a matter of perception. We're no longer in Philadelphia. We're in a remote corner with thousands of men looking on from West Point and the forts down river. I have to agree with the Colonel. Can't you please speak with General Arnold?"

Surprised that Peggy would allow this criticism of the General, Melora strained to hear what was sure to be a quick send-off for these gentlemen. Then it would be her turn.

"Colonel Varick, Major Franks," Peggy's voice was soft now, demure, her afternoon tea voice, Melora thought. "Although it's painful to hear that some might think my husband less than he is, you've pointed out a situation that I will certainly bring to the General's attention. You have my thanks, as I am sure you will have his. I trust we will see you at dinner this evening."

Melora could hear the chairs scraping as the two men stood to take their leave. "We are so fortunate that you've come here to join your husband." Seconds later, the two officers left the room, smiling and laughing about some matter as they climbed the stairs to the offices on the second floor. Scarcely believing what she had heard, Melora tried to recall Peggy ever having been so acquiescent. And she sounded so sincere!

"Melora, you may come in now."

Standing slowly, Melora smoothed her apron and cap and walked with as much grace as she could muster into the parlor. She might not be a lady, but neither was she a whore.

"Melora, please sit." Peggy picked up the embroidery hoop at her side. "This is difficult."

Please sit? Sit to be sent back to Philadelphia? To be sent to jail? Taking the small stool beside Peggy, Melora felt her face going into the rebellious expression she'd so perfected as a child, and remembered Jared's caution. "You must not fault Miss Peggy. If you do, then both the General and her father, no matter the merit of our case, will be finished with you." Our case. With those two words he banished the fear that Peggy had raised, that he might have thought her an easy, immoral woman.

When he'd slipped up from the boat landing to see her the day after the incident, she'd fallen apart in his arms. Of course she'd disobeyed the order against seeing him. What did anything matter if he could think that of her? But, as she related the incident in the bedroom, she'd never seen him so angry. That Miss Peggy could have caused her to doubt what their love meant to him.

"I think we should make a fresh start," Peggy continued.

"Miss?" Melora held tightly to the arms of her chair. This was nothing she'd expected.

Peggy stared down at the embroidery. "I shouldn't have accused you of anything. It wasn't my place."

"I don't understand."

"I want to apologize."

"But, begging your pardon, miss..." Melora wished she could see Peggy's face, but she was bent over her embroidery. This was all too strange. "...what made you change your mind?"

"It's very lonely for me here." Peggy began slowly, lifting her needle and thread. "I really didn't want to come. I think that's why I got so angry. Then, the other evening, I was thinking about what I said to you and remembered how we're taught to 'Judge not that we might not be judged,' and I saw how wrong I was."

The two women sat in silence, Peggy placing tiny stitches in the floral design and Melora trying to sort out what she had just heard. Miss Peggy was lonely. She supposed that was to be expected with no family and friends to keep her company in the General's long absences. But the other, now that was not to be expected. She'd never thought of Miss Peggy as a religious woman, and not just because she was Protestant.

"You'll not tell your father then?"

"No, I don't believe he would see it as his business, either."

Now she was completely mystified, as she was certain the master would see it as his business. Could this enforced solitude be having a good effect on her mistress?

"And I'm sure you'll be wanting to see your young man soon."

What would she do next? Invite her for a cup of tea? Astonished, Melora could manage nothing more than "Thank you, miss."

"So, will you accept my apology? Can we make a fresh start?"

Melora nodded stupidly.

"And there is something else."

Here it was. Something else. The real purpose of the chat. Melora took a deep breath.

Peggy put down her handwork and handed Melora a piece of paper from her pocket. From a quick glance, Melora saw only routine household tasks, no contract, no anything that was terrible. She looked up in confusion.

"We're about to be honored by a visit from the Commander in Chief and some of his aides. Day after tomorrow. So the house must sparkle and a proper menu laid out, but no one seems to have given the house sufficient care in years." Melora was surprised by the worried, almost grim mood that overcame Peggy. "I've never been in charge of anything like this. I need your help. I don't know if I can count on the others."

"General Washington is coming here?" Melora asked clasping her hands in excitement. It might be blasphemy, but she thought higher of the General than the Holy Father.

"Yes, General Washington, the Marquis de Lafayette, a young Colonel named Alexander Hamilton, and, I believe General Knox.

Melora felt giddy. "What do you want me to do, miss? I'll do anything!"

"I don't really know. I've written down the jobs I can think of. But as you know, I've never managed a house before or arranged a dinner party by myself."

"Oh, miss, I know just what to do. Your mother taught me so much." Melora could already see the table gleaming with every bit of silver that she could force onto it. She could use the exquisite crystal she'd noticed in the hutch just the day before. Perhaps she could even serve General Washington herself.

"So you're up to this, I can rely on you?"

"Yes, of course." Melora barely heard Peggy's words. She was too busy thinking up her own list of things to be done, starting immediately with an inventory of the flatware.

Suddenly the front door banged, and the heavy steps of the General echoed in the foyer. "Peggy, where are you?"

"Here, General, I'm in the parlor with Melora."

Peggy reached over and patted Melora's knee. "I am more grateful than you could know. You've taken a tremendous burden taken from my mind. Thank you."

Melora rose quickly, there was so much to do! Scurrying past the General, she heard Peggy ask how his work had gone and his answer, that they should both be very happy today. His work had gone very well. In fact, it was all that he could have asked for.

Not until somewhere in the middle of cleaning the soup spoons, when the rhythmical motion of applying the polish and rubbing it off had tempered the bursts of excitement, did she return to Peggy's startling change of attitude. Could Peggy's sincerity be just a ploy so she would work her heart out before General Washington's visit? Or could Peggy actually be afraid of being judged herself?

At that thought Melora almost laughed at herself. What had she done but judge Miss Peggy since their first meeting? Reaching for the small tin of polish, she saw the face of her priest at home. How many times had he admonished her in confession to give up the sin of pride, to judge not, because who knew what lay in the hearts of others? But she had never understood, really understood his words until just this moment. One didn't know what was in the hearts of others. This was a lesson she should remember and carry with her.

Attacking the spoons with renewed vigor, Melora felt aglow with her life now, and her life to come. She looked out the window and wondered when Jared would be up to the house. With the General's return, she could expect him at any time. At any time now, he would walk in the kitchen door and she could tell him that they, like the General and Peggy, should both be very happy today.

CHAPTER 56

Late Afternoon, The Same Day
*Belmont on the Hudson*

At the sound of the light knock, André flinched, a combination of fear and exhaustion. His mind was playing havoc with him, flashing scenes of Continental soldiers sneaking up the stairs toward this bedroom, servants confiding in guards near Haverstraw, Arnold returning with a company of men. Turning warily from his window seat overlooking the Hudson, he answered, "Come in."

"Mr. Anderson, you're awake." Smith strode into the room carrying an odd claret-colored coat and beaver hat. "I thought you might be resting."

André wanted to laugh. For almost ten hours he'd been watching and waiting for movement on the river, watching and waiting for the *Vulture* to return. Now it was nearly sunset and still no sign. "No, Mr. Smith," he said wearily, "I've not been resting."

"Well, sir," Smith began, "there's no sign of your ship; it may have been hit during the shelling this morning. I think we should return you by the overland option, as General Arnold suggested."

André, looking back out the window, studied the Hudson below. "It may be that the Captain has decided to wait until nightfall, thinking we would return at the same time as we left."

"Possibly," Smith conceded, "but you must understand that I can't house you here any longer. Because..." he paused searching for the right words, "...because of the special nature of your visit. And my family is expecting me to collect them in Fishkill tomorrow. So you see, if we take you the other way around on horseback, I can return by there and save a great deal of time."

André sighed. Smith's family, Fishkill. Why should Smith's family have anything to do with his return to New York? But looking back at his host, he knew that Smith must be just as tired as he was, tired and ready to have this work done. And what choice did he have? Arnold had left him in this man's hands either to return to the *Vulture* or go overland to reach British lines. He was completely dependent on Smith, whatever the route. "All right, Mr. Smith. I am in your debt."

Smith bowed slightly in response and then held up the coat and hat. "I suggest you leave your jacket behind, Mr. Anderson. These will do nicely for our trip."

André paled. Of course, to take the overland route he'd need civilian clothes while in the American territory. While Smith had inexplicably ignored his regimentals until now, the several sentries between Belmont and the British lines would certainly not. It was only incredible luck that the guard hadn't noticed his uniform beneath the cloak earlier.

"I'll leave you," Smith said, laying the clothes across the bed. "Downstairs in fifteen minutes," he added before backing out of the room.

André took another long look at the river and then rose to see about his new attire. Examining the coat, he shuddered. The coat, certainly the hat, were clearly someone's cast offs. Not only were they very much the worse for wear, they were also gaudy, ungentlemanly, and certainly unfit clothing for the Adjutant General of the British army, or for that matter, any member of the British army at all. He looked longingly out the window again. Here he was, not John André, Adjutant General, but John Anderson, merchant, and—at least to Joshua Smith—double agent.

André stripped off his own jacket and cursed in disgust. How had he gotten into this position? Crossing enemy lines, these clothes, and, he rued, glancing at the pages Arnold had forced upon him for Sir Henry, carrying intelligence. But he knew how he had gotten into this position. Arnold, his prize, had utterly failed to think through his return to the *Vulture*.

From the time the guard called out at the American line that morning, he'd felt heartsick at his own ineptitude and helplessness. And his luck only plummeted from there. Not moments after arriving at Belmont, sounds of cannon fire erupted from the river. Rushing upstairs for the best view, he and Arnold saw the *Vulture* still lying off Teller's Point, receiving heavy fire from American cannon. "Livingston!" Arnold had bellowed, explaining that the young Commander of Fort LaFayette must have taken it upon himself to force the ship from its current anchorage so near to American soil.

Within moments, the *Vulture*'s sails were raised and the British ship was fleeing from the enemy fire, downriver and out of range for the Cahoons and their tiny boat. His escape closed, he was stranded.

Turning to Arnold, he'd been surprised to see the General recovered, composed. "Sir?"

"Don't be alarmed, Major, I'll leave passes. If the *Vulture* doesn't return you can travel overland to your lines at White Plains."

"White Plains. But how, General?" André looked over at the densely wooded eastern shore of the Hudson. "I don't know this country."

"Smith will escort you if it comes to that. The two of you can decide your route later in the day."

"And you, sir, where will you be?"

"Me? Back at Headquarters, of course. I have work to do."

And although they dined shortly thereafter with Smith joining them, Arnold's good humor and apparent lack of concern were cold comfort for André's uneasiness. Even if events passed as smoothly as General Arnold predicted, Sir Henry would have to learn the specifics of his departure. And he would not be pleased.

Donning Smith's jacket, André had to admit that he certainly didn't look like a high-ranking British officer. With the ridiculous beaver hat plopped atop his head, he could never be taken for a high-ranking anything. And Arnold's papers hidden beneath the window cushion: What to do with them? He could follow Sir Henry's instructions on at least this one thing and throw them into the fire downstairs. But, as he well knew, the numbers on those pages would be vital to the Commander in Chief's strategy.

Sitting down on the bed, André pulled off his boots and stockings. Arnold had advised, actually ordered him, to carry the papers between his stocking and his foot, to take no chance of the information finding its way into the wrong hands. He'd been right the night before, he thought, folding the sheaves as flatly as possible. There was only one Commander here, and that was Arnold.

# CHAPTER 57

## September 23, 1780
### *En route from Belmont to Manhattan*

Bright sunlight streamed in through the room's one rough window, and for a second André wondered where he was. A single snore from his bedfellow, however, reminded him that he was in the home of the Andreas Miller family—and damnably lucky to be there. Sliding as far away from Smith as possible, he said a silent prayer of thanks for his safe journey thus far, and asked for continued protection on the ride ahead. Although not a particularly religious man, it was clear to André that some guardian spirit had surely been working on his behalf the night before.

Leaving Belmont with Smith, they'd first run into a Major John Burroughs of the New Jersey line on the way to King's Ferry. An acquaintance of Smith's, the two chatted at length until Burroughs mercifully turned off the main road. Next, arriving at the ferry, Smith decided to take up with the boatmen there, drinking, taunting, and carousing until André feared the crew would be too drunk to take them across the river. As he waited by the water's edge for the men to complete their libations, he thought he would burst with hatred for Smith's unyielding sociability.

Once on the other side, the torment only increased when his escort insisted that it would not do unless respects were paid to the Commander at Fort Lafayette. And while André supposed that Smith knew best, he could hardly think that the yard outside an American fort was the best place for a disguised member of His Majesty's army to tarry. But after more than an hour, Smith finally did emerge from the fort, and once again they were on their way. The last great scare of the evening occurred just after they'd reached Peekskill and turned east onto the Crompond Road. From out of nowhere, militia with muskets suddenly surrounded them while Smith frantically screamed "Friends! Friends!" Had they not had Arnold's pass, he was sure the overzealous captain of the group would have detained them on suspicion alone. Two men traveling so late at night without an escort was reason enough. By the time they'd reached this place, where Mr. Miller kindly offered them a bed, his nerves were shot.

Taking in his situation here, the tiny room, Smith, his own feet, as he'd had to sleep in his boots to keep the papers concealed, André felt a frenzied need to leave. Both the gaucheness of his circumstances and the insidious fear felt like filth clinging to his body. On top of it all, he was famished, as the good Mr. Miller's hospitality had not included anything to eat.

In this part of the country, in and around the neutral ground between the British lines at White Plains and the American outposts near the Hudson, bandits raided at their leisure, taking food and livestock, burning crops and houses, and worse. And that was exactly what had happened to most of Mr. Miller's pantry just the day before. Cowboys, as the bandits with Tory leanings were known, descended on the property and all but wiped him out. These Cowboys and their pro-colonial counterparts, the Skinners, were a wartime scourge causing incalculable misery and ruin. Mr. Miller had voiced concerns over his and Smith's unescorted travel.

"Mr. Smith!" André shook his bed partner. "It's morning. We should be off."

His bed mate grunted. "I've barely slept a bit. You're a nervous one, moving all about."

"You'll have to accept my apologies," André answered with as much amiability as he could muster. "This is hardly my ideal venue for a good night's sleep. Nor, I suppose, is it yours."

"No, it's not," Smith said, pulling the blanket aside. "Mine, my good fellow," he added, winking repeatedly, "would include Mrs. Smith."

Reaching for the detestable coat, a bright thought occurred to André. One way or another, he'd soon see the last of this relentlessly chatty man.

Seven miles later, André, seated on the back stairs of Sarah Underhill's house, peered up at Smith from the pan of corn mush, also known as suppon, before him. Suppon. He'd used the word in a poem as a descriptive "suppon eaters," to characterize the lowly state of the colonials. But on this morning it was his breakfast, the only breakfast this kind woman could offer as the Cowboys had struck her home shortly before Andreas Miller's.

"You're clear on the direction?" Smith asked, his horse prancing beneath him.

"I am, and I have your map." André spoke softly, unable to put the latest scare behind him. In the very little time between their leaving the Millers' and their arrival here, he'd passed a man who by all rights should have called him down as Major John André and either shot him or taken him post-haste to the nearest military authority. Samuel Blachley Webb. He'd known him in New York as a prisoner of war. But for reasons impossible to conceive, the man had, with a nod of good morning, passed him on the road and gone on about his business. André's hands were still shaking.

"Well then, I'm off. You understand, I hope, my decision to leave you now," Smith said. "You're just a short ride, fifteen miles I think, from your destination."

André did understand. If his fear was the Blachley Webbs of the road then Smith's was obviously the Cowboys. He'd been talking of nothing else for most of the morning. Leaving the dish of half-eaten mush on the stair behind him, André walked over to the man and extended his hand. "I do understand. Good travels."

As soon as Smith urged his horse into a slow trot, André threw the rest of the suppon behind a tree, hoping Mrs. Underhill wasn't watching. Grateful as he was for food, he just couldn't stomach any more of the stuff. He'd be in Manhattan soon enough. He'd wait and eat there.

André rode the two miles to the Croton River quickly, checking behind himself frequently in case someone was following. According to Smith, once he crossed the bridge there, Pine's Bridge, he would be out of range of American military patrols. And as he had no reason to fear the Cowboys, his time of difficulty was very nearly over.

But at Pine's Bridge the mare balked. Certain that other riders would appear at any moment, he jumped from the saddle, and flinging Smith's jacket over the horse's head, led her across the creaking wooden rails. Although the mare fought against him the entire distance, they reached the opposite shore with, to his great surprise, no one in sight. Shaking, he removed the jacket and tried his best to calm the terrified animal. He needed to calm down too. He had become much too hysterical at this latest delay, his thinking frenzied. For an instant he considered the soothing, cleansing effect of a quick dip into the Croton. But, as Sir Henry was waiting, the bath would have to also. Swinging himself up into the saddle, he continued south.

As Pine's Bridge receded into the distance, the great weight he'd felt since departing the *Vulture* receded also, and he began to notice the soft, lush countryside filled with golden rod and purple asters. Humbled by this artistry of nature, he tried to fix the colors in his mind for the next opportunity at the easel. This was a lovely country with genial inhabitants, he thought, as he picked up the pace toward New York. And because of him their peace would soon be restored. The job was done, Arnold was theirs, the meeting a success. After West Point was taken, his role in the matter would become public, the accolades would begin, and his place in society secured. Perhaps, it occurred to him, he should formalize the entire undertaking in a serialized account for the *Gentleman's Magazine*. Between laying out the magazine article and rehearsing a briefing for Sir Henry, he scarcely noticed the shuttered houses and burned farms and fields of the neutral ground. He stopped three times, once to ask directions of a young boy, Jesse Thorne, a second time at the farm of Sylvanus Brundage to water the mare, and a third time at Staats Hammond's to get water for himself and to ask again about directions. At each stop he was greeted with politeness and cordiality.

Coming upon a small stream, André pulled in on the reins, trying to remember whether or not this was one of Smith's landmarks. While the horse nibbled a tuft of roadside grass, he withdrew the crumpled diagram from his pocket and saw that he was right. Tarrytown and the British lines were at most a few miles away. He could easily join Sir Henry for dinner.

Confident and eager, he refolded the map for the last time and commanded the mare to walk on. But the little horse would not. Instead, she whinnied nervously, then bolted sharply to the right. Grabbing the pommel, André struggled to right himself as three rough-looking men with muskets walked out of the brush toward him. Cowboys.

"Gentlemen, I hope you belong to our party."

"What party?" one of the three, a sallow-faced man, asked.

"The lower, the King's party," André said, insulted by the men's raised guns. "I'm an officer in His Majesty's service. Let me pass." Then, just to confirm that he was a man of consequence, André drew out his gold watch and held it up for the ruffians to see.

The men looked between themselves but didn't budge. Then, the oldest-appearing of the three, a huge man dressed in a Hessian's soiled green and red jacket, motioned with his gun for André to get down. "We're not in your party." He turned to the man who had first spoken, "Van Wart, get his horse."

As Van Wart reached for the mare's halter, a terrible realization took hold of André. These men were not Cowboys. They were Americans. God help him.

Summoning up his many hours of acting, André grinned and slapped his leg as though he'd just heard the best joke of his life. "Gentlemen, I am a fool. We are of the same party. I pretended, thinking you were for the Crown." Dismounting, he frantically fumbled in his pocket for the pass Smith had given him. "I'm on business for General Arnold. Here, look at this."

The Hessian imposter grabbed the piece of paper from André and handed it to the third member of the band, a boyish fellow with shaggy eyebrows. "Here, Williams, you read it."

"It says he's on official business," Williams announced, "and it's signed by General Arnold."

"But he said he was a British officer, and you saw that watch. He must have money," Van Wart countered, running his hands over the saddle. "He could have it anywhere."

Deciding to take another tact, André grabbed for the pass. "You must let me go. The General won't go easily with you if I'm detained."

Williams caught André's arm. "I'll keep the pass." Then, turning to the leader in the green coat said, "It looks real, Paulding. I don't want Arnold after us."

Van Wart scowled. "To hell with Arnold. We'll say we thought he was British."

While the three men argued among themselves, André got one foot in the stirrup before Paulding jerked him back down. "Damn his pass. Let's see what he's got."

Van Wart snatched the reins from André. "He's right, boy. You both go on. I'll be lookout."

As Van Wart tied the mare to a tree, Paulding jammed his musket into André's back and with Williams following along, forced the prisoner through a gated pasture and into a stand of trees a few yards away. Then, after laughing at a crude remark yelled by Van Wart, the huge hulking man leveled his musket at André's chest and ordered him to strip.

# CHAPTER 58

## The Same Day (Afternoon)
### Robinson House

At the tinkling of the dinner bell, Peggy closed the door to the baby's room and descended the stairs. Maybe it was the cooler air, or the fresher air of the Highlands, but Neddy had not had one fretful instant since that first night at Belmont. Even on this warm afternoon he'd gone down for his afternoon nap with barely five minutes of rocking. He was such a good baby. Anne was hardly needed.

At the entrance to the dining room, she greeted Colonel Lamb, Colonel Varick, and Major Franks. Colonel Lamb answered her in his pleasantly gruff voice while Varick and Franks were polite but distant.

"I wonder where the General might be," she asked.

Varick answered coolly, "With Mr. Smith, in the parlor."

Mr. Smith. The reason for the distance. She had to warn the General.

"Could you please ask Melora to set another seat? And please excuse me for just a moment."

Hurrying into the hall, she met Arnold and Smith en route to the dinner table. "Mr. Smith, I'm sorry I wasn't here to greet you."

Arnold wrapped an arm around her shoulder and explained, "He's only just arrived. He's on his way to collect Mrs. Smith, but will have a bite with us beforehand." With Smith a step or so ahead, Arnold pulled her closer and whispered, "André is safely behind the lines. That's what Smith came to tell me."

Peggy looked up into her husband's face and felt the tiny throb at her temple. "I have to talk to you."

"Yes, of course." He kissed her forehead. "Just as soon as we've eaten our dinner."

The tension at the table was unmistakable, at least to Peggy. Smith, having no idea of the sentiments of Varick and Franks, monopolized the conversation with a series of boastful exploits accomplished by himself and his brother as children.

"Your brother, the one in New York?" Varick asked dangerously.

"The same," Smith answered. "As children we were always together. Always seeing things alike."

"And do you and your brother, our enemy, still see things alike?" Franks asked.

"Gentlemen," Arnold set down his glass. "I won't have this at my house. Mr. Smith is a guest."

Franks shook his head. "Everyone knows this man is most probably a spy. You should arrest him, not dine with him."

Arnold held up a cautionary hand. "You may advise me, sir, but I'll be damned if you'll dictate to me."

Peggy pressed her temples. She had to stop this. "Benedict! Colonel Varick, Major Franks, I beg of you."

The dinner party fell into silence. Arnold picked up his wine while Smith continued eating. Franks made a great study of cutting his fish, while Varick folded his napkin, slid his chair back, and stood. "You're right, Mrs. Arnold," he said, "please accept my apologies. I should leave."

"And," Franks said quietly, crossing his fork and knife on the plate, "I should join him."

After the two men left the room, Peggy tried to pay attention to her food, the fish and potatoes now in a halo of light. Arnold apologized over and over for the behavior of his aides, while Smith managed to consume an enormous amount of food. After all, he explained, when your brother stood as high with the enemy as his happened to, you expected people to wonder.

Arnold closed the door behind him to see Peggy lying across their bed, a towel covering her forehead. "Is Mr. Smith gone?"

"Yes." He hurried across the room. "Do you want the curtains closed?" Over the course of their short marriage, he had turned from a frantic husband into an able nurse. He reminded her of her father that way, always solicitous of her health.

"Benedict, come here," she said, catching his arm and pulling him down beside him. "I should have told you. Colonel Varick and Major Franks spoke to me about Mr. Smith, just yesterday. They wanted me to talk to you. They worry about your association with him."

"So that was it," he smoothed the hair away from her face. "But even if they acted out of concern for me, they showed a shocking disrespect for a guest at my table."

"But I should have told you," she tried to sit up. "It's just that we were talking about so many things. And I had no idea Smith would come back so soon and upset them."

"How could you? " Arnold sat down on the bed beside her. "Is the pain very bad?"

"Not so much. I may have caught it early on." Looking into the anxious face of her husband, a wave of feeling washed over her for this great, great man who loved her so totally. She held his hand against her cheek. "Go downstairs and apologize to Colonel Varick and Major Franks. What if one of them were to say something to General Washington or a member of his staff?"

"Of course you're right."

"Don't take this lightly, Benedict. Go now and make amends. That will make me feel the best of all. You know how I worry."

Arnold smiled down at her. "I do, and I'll speak with Varick and Franks. But with André back in Manhattan, the time for worry is almost over." He drew the sheet up around her and blew out the candle. "You try to sleep and dream of our new lives."

# CHAPTER 59

## The Same Day (Night)
### En route from North Castle to Robinson House

"How much further, Lieutenant?" one of the guards called out.
"About ten miles from the turn to Peekskill."

His hands tied behind him, André bumped along awkwardly, determined to think rationally about his situation. Ahead of him, Lieutenant Solomon Allen held the mare's reins while four militiamen rode at his side and rear. Unlike the earnest Allen, these four were gay and talkative, hatching plans for meeting with friends at West Point after they carried out their orders and delivered him to General Arnold. And God willing, Arnold would be there.

Even though it was dark, André recognized parts of the road he'd traveled down that morning, now almost fifteen hours ago. Since Pine's Bridge they'd retraced his route exactly, only this time the mare made the crossing as easily as she might have trotted around a paddock. And this morning he'd been a free man anticipating an imminent celebratory reunion with his commander.

Ignoring the menacing expression of the guard to his right, he twisted from side to side in the saddle in a useless attempt to relieve the terrible stiffness in his neck and shoulders. He'd been trussed up like this since North Castle, a military outpost some ten miles to the south where the brigands had taken him after finding the papers in his boot. He grimaced. If only he'd had more money on him. That's what they wanted. He'd almost convinced the militiamen, as they'd called themselves, to ask for a ransom, but in the end the big man Paulding had said no. The British might ride out to arrest them just as well as to give them money. So, lacking other options, they'd done their duty and taken him to the military authorities at North

Castle. God, his back hurt, and he needed to think.

"Lieutenant?" André wasn't sure if he had been heard. "Lieutenant?" he called again, this time rewarded by Allen looking back over his shoulder. "Could we stop? A call of nature." Without any acknowledgment, Allen walked on another half mile or so before giving the signal to halt near a stand of trees beside the road. "Dismount, five minutes."

Needles shot through his back and shoulders as one of the guards untied the bindings. He slid off his horse and onto the ground. Accepting the outstretched hand of Lieutenant Allen, André stood, wobbling in the effort. "Perhaps you should sit a moment, Mr. Anderson," Allen said tersely. "General Arnold isn't expecting us; we can delay another moment or two."

"Thank you, Lieutenant," André answered, not moving until he felt sure enough of himself to actually sit. Leaning back against a tree, he knew he had to buck up. After all, he was in an unfortunate but not a catastrophic predicament. After being taunted and harassed, even paraded through taverns by Paulding and his mob, and after admitting out loud that he would have preferred being shot on the road rather than be subjected to this humiliation, his luck finally turned in the person of Colonel John Jameson, the commander at North Castle. After a quick examination of the passes and Arnold's documents, the colonel decided that the matter was of such gravity that it should be turned over to his Commanding Officer, Major General Arnold. Mr. Anderson was to be escorted forthwith to the General at Robinson House.

Astonished, André could have wept in relief. The all-important chain-of-command, his salvation. It was the first moment since David Williams cried, "This man is a spy" after reading Arnold's documents that he had not been completely certain of his own ruin. This American officer was just as terrified of lodging a complaint against a superior as any of the British officers in André's acquaintance. How Arnold would explain away the papers to Jameson, he had not a clue. But that was not his problem. The General would get him out of this, because in many ways Arnold had more at stake than he did, and he, André, would put his faith in that. He had to.

While Allen stood beside his horse, hands wrapped around the reins, André rose and walked back into the trees unescorted. A second comforting decision by his American captors. A moment or so later he emerged from the woods and walked over to the mare where the guard holding the tortuous rope motioned for him to put his hands behind his back again. "Is that really necessary? I won't try to escape. You have my word as a gentleman." The guard looked at Allen, who did not hesitate for a moment. "I'm sorry, sir, but we have our orders."

As the procession started up again, André, again bound and aching, felt lighter all the same. This march was very nearly at an end. According to Allen, they would be at Robinson House within the hour. Arnold held total power in this part of the country, he would find a way.

Half an hour later, outside the village of Cortlandville, a rider galloped up behind them. "Lieutenant! Jeremiah Cole here, Colonel Jameson sent me to find you." Cole tried to catch his breath as he withdrew some papers from his satchel and handed them to Allen. "You're to go directly to South Salem." André shifted warily in the saddle, icy apprehension spreading through him for the second time that day.

"Why?" Allen asked, rifling through the papers.

The courier shrugged. "I think it was Major Tallmadge. He came in and spent a long time with Colonel Jameson. I heard him say that he didn't believe it was wise to take the prisoner to General Arnold." André noticed that the courier kept sneaking peeks at him as he spoke.

"But what about the letter Colonel Jameson wrote to General Arnold explaining the matter, what do I do with that?" Allen asked, a hint of annoyance in the question.

"After you take the prisoner to South Salem you're to return and give it to General Arnold."

André exhaled. Arnold would still be informed of his capture. He would just have to get him released from another post. Then, as another buoy to his spirits, the four guards about him began to protest the change in orders. The one who had ridden to his right for the long slow hours complained the loudest. "Lieutenant Allen, we're tired. If we turn back we'll be traveling all night."

Allen seemed to agree as he handed the papers back to the young man. "At least I could take the letter to the General now, as we're so close, and then continue to South Salem."

Jeremiah Cole shook his head. "Colonel Jameson said for you to turn around where I found you."

"Lieutenant," another guard interrupted, giving the courier a knowing look, "we could keep this meeting to ourselves."

André watched as the Lieutenant looked wistfully at the road ahead.

Compliance with the countermand meant two long trips ahead for Allen rather than a tankard of ale and a warm bed in less than an hour. André closed his eyes, whether in prayer or not he wasn't sure. Adherence to the chain of command had saved him once today. Would insubordination help him now?

But as Allen swung his horse around to face the group, André saw only the face of duty. He announced his decision just as he had to André shortly before, and just as André should have known he would. "Gentlemen, we have our orders. To South Salem."

While the guards around him grumbled and bickered with the messenger, André wearily nudged his confused horse back in the direction they'd come. Another setback, he repeated to himself; difficult, very difficult, but not yet a catastrophe. Following along behind Allen, he tried to estimate how many hours it would be before Arnold would be told of his capture and could effect a rescue. He had to concentrate on that.

Feeling a chill in Smith's thin silk coat, André was about to ask if he could put a blanket or something about him when Cole called out again. "Lieutenant, one more thing. The documents the prisoner was carrying,"

The documents, the only thing not to have gone wrong so far.

"I'm to take them directly to General Washington."

André slumped in the saddle. Washington would see the descriptions of the forts, the troop strengths, all of it, and he would certainly recognize Arnold's large distinctive handwriting. This, he had to admit, was not a setback. This was a catastrophe.

CHAPTER 60

September 24, 1780

*Robinson House*

*M*elora screamed as two arms slipped about her waist, pulling her backward from the cutting board and chicken carcass destined for the evening's stew.

"Have any time for me now?" Jared asked, folding her against him.

"You fool," she answered holding up a carving knife. "I could have hurt you, sneaking up on me like that."

He kissed the top of her head. "No, you wouldn't. I was careful."

She turned around in his arms. "Can you stay for a bit? Talk to me while I work?"

"Surely...if I get a kiss first."

Standing on her toes, she pulled his face down to meet hers. She hadn't seen him since Friday and that was only for a moment. Just long enough to relate the amazing conversation with Peggy and give him the glorious news that she would be in charge of preparing for General Washington's visit. Then she made him leave, as there was much too much to do.

"Where is everyone?" Jared whispered against her cheek.

"Mary and Sarah are taking a nap before beginning dinner. They've been working very hard."

"Are we really alone then?" he asked, his hands playing about her back and shoulders.

"Only until someone comes in. You better let me go."

"But I don't want to. That's not at all what I want to do." And he kissed her again.

"Begging your pardon." Arnold walked into the kitchen, amused.

"General," Melora mumbled hoping her apron was on straight, "is there something we can do for you?"

"Sir," Jared added.

"I don't believe Donovan can, but please take some tea up to Mrs. Arnold. She's still unwell."

"Yes, of course, sir."

"And Colonel Varick has come down with a fever. He might like some tea also. It seems we're becoming an infirmary. I don't imagine either of them will join us for dinner tonight."

A frightening thought suddenly occurred to Melora. "Excuse me, sir, but will Miss Peggy be well enough to greet General Washington tomorrow?"

"I don't know. She's having a great deal of trouble sleeping. You may be on your own." He gestured toward the fire and pantry. "Is everything set? Mrs. Arnold mentioned that she asked you to manage things."

"I think so, sir." She thought of the breads, pies, and roasts that she, Sarah, and Mary had waiting in the kitchen. "Just a few last chores."

"And you have everything you need?"

"Yes, sir, I do," Melora answered, thinking how like a man to ask such a question just hours before the event.

"My wife has put her faith in you, therefore so will I." Picking up several slices of the chicken, he continued, "And if everything is almost ready, you and Donovan might enjoy a walk in the out-of-doors for a bit, perhaps by the stream." Then, to their chagrin he added, "I can't imagine anyone else will be walking there this afternoon."

Melora and Jared watched in silence as Arnold left the kitchen.

"Well, what do you make of that?" Melora asked, falling onto one of the kitchen stools.

"What?" Jared said, pulling up another stool beside hers. "He came to ask you to take his wife some tea."

"Yes, he did," Melora mused, "but he also just came very close to flattery."

He smiled. "Yes, all officers do that. They assure you to make you brave, to motivate you."

"But Jared..." how could she make him understand? "I've been living under the same roof as those two for over a year. Never has there been a word of thanks or praise or anything. Now, both of them in one week. It's so odd."

"Perhaps there's been a change in you." He pulled her onto his lap. "That you never had much use for either one of them has always been very plain."

"I don't think so," she answered, remembering the last time they shared a chair together. "Do you think they could both be truly sorry for Miss Peggy going after me as she did, about you?"

"If they aren't, they should be. But what are we doing? Fix the tea. The General had a grand idea. Let's take a walk."

Melora turned up her lower lip, trying her best to look pitiful. "Don't be angry. I think I should stay here."

He frowned. "You said there were only a few small chores left."

"Jared!" Why didn't he understand this? "General Washington will be here tomorrow! In this house!"

"And you will be in this house all day waiting on him while I will be on barge duty on the river and," his hand crept up the bodice of her blouse, "I want us to be alone."

Determined to ignore the familiar waves of weakness just looking at Jared could provoke, much less what his hands and lips were up to now, Melora jumped off his lap and pulled him toward the back door. "Jared Donovan, I have a great responsibility tomorrow. I need a clear head and time to think." Placing her hands on his chest she leaned up and kissed him. "We will be alone again, and soon. I promise."

"And how will we do that with you living up here and me in a barracks across the river?" he asked, pinioning her against him.

"I'll sneak away." Then she giggled. "And we'll take a very, very long walk."

"You promise?"

"Yes, I promise, as soon as possible, just after tomorrow." Then she wriggled free and pushed him out the door.

Thirty miles away, John André sat at the small desk in the room he was sharing with Dr. Isaac Bronson. The guards outside had finally stopped their taunting and the very likable Dr. Bronson was attending a meeting with Lieutenant King, the commander here in South Salem, and his recently assigned escort, Major Benjamin Tallmadge, another eminently personable man. King, Bronson, and Tallmadge, all men with whom he could pass many pleasant hours. Tallmadge even had a scholarly bent, admitting to having studied Greek, Latin, and Hebrew at Yale College. Unfortunately, the three were now, in every likelihood, discussing his future.

There really was no use in pretending any longer, he thought, opening the writing box Bronson had loaned him. Besides, he was almost ill from being thought of as the merchant John Anderson in a shabby coat and beaver hat. For his own serenity, if for no other reason, he needed to reclaim his identity and explain the conditions leading to his capture. Following that, events would take their course.

Smoothing out the paper before him, the prisoner dipped the pen in the ink slowly and deliberately, as this would surely be the most important piece of writing in his life. Then, hoping he was using the proper salutation, Major John André began his letter to the Commander in Chief of the American Army, General George Washington.

CHAPTER 61

September 25, 1780
*Robinson House*

*M*elora held up her candle and nudged Mary slightly on the arm
before turning to Sarah. "Time to get up." Although the room
they shared with the other servants was still pitch black, she knew it was
close to dawn by the sounds of the sentries changing outside. She gave each
of the women one more shake before slipping out of the room and into the
hall; the fire in the kitchen should be lit so the room would warm before
Mary set the dough out to rise.

Feeling her way down the enclosed back stairs to the kitchen, Melora
screamed as she collided with something hard, a person. She barely caught
the handrail before coming down hard on one knee. "Who's there?"

"Melora?" Arnold asked.

She stood with difficulty, managing a tight "yes." How many other servants with Irish accents were working in the house?

"Thank God, I was coming to find you. Are you hurt?"

"No, sir," she said, reaching down to rub the aching joint.

"Good. It's Mrs. Arnold. Her headache is very bad. Could you make
something for her?"

Melora took a deep breath. There were many tasks she needed to get to
this morning, and nursing Miss Peggy was not one of them. However, saying "no" was not a possibility for a lady's maid, even one assigned recently
to far greater service. "Of course, General, I just need to light the fire first."

Taking hold of the railing with both hands, she placed her weight gin-
gerly on the banged up knee and thought, what a horrid beginning for this
particular day.

Melora placed the tea, a cup, and hot towels on the table by Peggy's bed as quietly as possible. Peggy herself lay stone still against the sheets in the flimsy shift they had argued about that terrible afternoon. Her hair was wild and tangled on the pillow and she was pale, very pale. "Miss Peggy?" she whispered, "Are you awake?"

Peggy's response was barely a nod.

"Do you want some tea or just the tonic? I brought some hot towels too."

This time Peggy opened her eyes and pressed her palms against her temples. "Melora, I am so sick. I can't eat. I can't sleep. I just lie here hour after hour."

"It's a headache, isn't it?"

"Yes, but an evil one."

Sitting down on the bed, Melora took a bottle out of her apron pocket and poured brown liquid into the cup. "Mary from the kitchen sent a tonic. Maybe it will let you sleep."

"But General Washington, I wanted to see him."

Melora held Peggy's head as she drank from the cup. "It's very early, you can sleep for two or three hours before he's expected. Maybe you'll feel better then."

Peggy closed her eyes and forced a wan smile as Melora placed a hot towel on her forehead. "The General so wants me to come down."

Easing herself up off the bed, Melora straightened the blankets around Peggy before leaving the room. Those two, always trying to please each other. Sometimes it seemed like no one else existed in the house for Peggy and the General except each other—and the baby, of course. But this time, no matter what the General wanted, she couldn't imagine Peggy leaving the room for a long while.

Light was just beginning to dawn as she returned to the kitchen where Mary and Sarah were hard at work, kneading flour and chopping apples. With all that needed to be done in the kitchen, Melora knew that she should get something to eat before the opportunity slipped away. But first she withdrew the bottle from her apron again and took a drink herself. The knee was killing her.

A little after nine, Major Franks hurried into the kitchen where Melora stood holding the apple crisp fresh from the oven. Initially chilly and condescending, Franks' attitude had warmed toward her during the months at the residence in Philadelphia and again here at Robinson House.

"Melora, the General wants you to put breakfast out now, but only for four."

"Only four?" She looked around at the loaves of fresh baked bread and platters of ham, bacon, hominy, fish, and eggs. "Why?"

"General Washington's party has been detained. Colonel Hamilton and Major McHenry rode ahead to tell us that breakfast should go on without the rest. So the General and Dr. Eustice will join those two gentlemen to make four."

"But General Washington...All this food..."

Franks smiled. He knew how excited she had been about the opportunity to prepare for the Commander in Chief. "You'll still have stories for your grandchildren. General Washington and his staff now plan to spend the night."

Melora's shocked silence was his reply. "Don't worry. Most of them will have their own servants. But, at this moment," he added in a falsely gruff voice, "General Arnold wants breakfast on the table."

"Tea?" Melora tipped the copper tea kettle as Colonel Hamilton held up his cup to be refilled. She couldn't help noticing what a good-looking man he was, although there was something a bit feminine about his mouth. From his air, the way he spoke, she wondered if he wasn't a man of some means.

"So the French offered nothing new?" Arnold asked.

Hamilton reached for another roll. "Not that I heard. I'm afraid General Washington left Hartford disheartened. He needs some good news. We all do."

"Might there be any coffee?" the other young man, McHenry, asked.

"Some for me as well, Melora," Arnold said, pushing his plate away.

Of course, sir," she answered, impatient with herself that their cups were low. She must pay better attention. And must figure out how to transform all the leftover breakfast into lunch.

As she reached for the coffee pot, angry voices, one of them Major

Franks', clashed in the front hall.

"Melora," Arnold stood, "I'll pour. You see what the fuss is about."

Before she could put the pot down, Major Franks walked in escorting a very dirty and either sick or exhausted young officer.

"Pardon me, General, this is Lieutenant Solomon Allen with a letter from Colonel Jameson. His orders are to deliver it only to you."

Arnold nodded. "You look as if you've come a very long way, Lieutenant Allen."

Allen shook his head, looking like he could fall exactly where he stood. Reaching into his coat pocket, he pulled out a sealed envelope and handed it to Arnold. "Not such a long way, sir, just back and forth a great deal."

"Thank you, Lieutenant; have some breakfast while I read this." Arnold reached for a butter knife to break the seal. "We've got enough, don't we, Melora?"

She smiled wryly.

"And can you look in again on Mrs. Arnold? We'll be fine here."


Afraid that Peggy might be asleep, Melora let herself into the darkened room. Closing the door behind her, she felt depressed. The sick room shuttered and dark against the hustle and bustle of downstairs, the tea and towels she'd brought earlier untouched.

"Melora?"

"Yes, miss." Peggy looked as though she hadn't moved in the three hours since Melora's last visit. Neither did she seem any better. "The tonic didn't help?"

A tear trickled down Peggy's cheek. "No, I...."

The door swung open, Arnold was in the room, jerking open the armoire, clothes flying to the floor. "Peggy, sit up. Your promise, remember your promise!"

"Sir!"

Arnold wheeled around surprised to see her.

"Leave! No wait—find Franks, tell him to get my horse saddled immediately."

"I'm here, sir." Melora looked behind her to see Franks standing in the doorway.

"Well, you heard me then," Arnold said pulling on a waistcoat. "I'll need you to ride with me to the river. I have urgent business."

Franks smoothed his stock, a nervous gesture Melora had seen many times. "But, sir, General Washington's servant has just arrived. The General will be here in moments."

Arnold dismissed him with a wave. "I'll have to meet him at West Point. Now, both of you, go!"

The two fled the room as fast as they could, Franks tearing down the stairs while Melora ran into Neddy's room to get hold of herself. The room was quiet, Anne nowhere in sight, and the baby playing quietly with Jared's rabbit's foot. Sitting down in the rocking chair beside Neddy's crib, Melora tried to make sense of what had just happened. The General could be an emotional man, but she'd never seen him violent before. Something enormous must have occurred. Against the soft cooing of Neddy, she prayed that some horrible event had not gone against America in the war.

Heavy footsteps clattered down the hallway. Suddenly the General strode into the nursery, fully dressed, with two holsters belted around his waist. Without saying a word to her, he picked up Neddy, saying over and over what a good baby he was and how much his papa loved him. Setting the child back in the crib, he turned to her. "Mrs. Arnold will need you today. Please help her." Then, heading for the back staircase he rushed out of the room.

# CHAPTER 62

## The Same Day
### Robinson House

"Melora!" Anne ran into the room. "Look out front."

Melora was furious. This was the girl's only job. "Where have you been? The baby was by himself."

Anne snorted, "Not for long. Anyway he was asleep." She pulled the curtain back and pointed. "I've been watching for General Washington, and here he is. Melora, come see!"

Slowly, Melora rose from her seat. Too much was happening this morning. Through the window, she saw a great procession of men riding up the road. Maybe a hundred, maybe a hundred and fifty, there were too many to tell. Then she saw him. Anne was right. General Washington sitting as tall and proudly as any king she could imagine, his great gray cloak puffed out in waves around the enormous white stallion trotting up to the front door. She had seen him in several parades in Philadelphia and it thrilled her to think that this was real; the Commander in Chief going about the war, leading the troops, and fighting royalty, for people like herself and Jared.

And there was Colonel Varick, sick as he was, going out to pay respects. She saw him salute General Washington and several of the other officers. Then the General spoke, apparently asking questions, for next Varick motioned toward West Point. At this, General Washington must have given an order, because suddenly a good half of the procession, General Washington near the head, wheeled around and at a slow trot rode back in the direction they'd just come. She couldn't fathom what was happening. Racing down the steps, she tried one room after another to locate Colonel Varick, finally finding him curled back upon his cot. Major Franks must have been looking for Varick too, as he came rushing in behind Melora.

"Varick, where did General Washington go? I just got back with General Arnold's horse."

Colonel Varick stared up at them dully. "He's gone over to West Point to inspect the forts and find General Arnold."

Franks sat down on one of the other cots. "General Arnold didn't go to West Point. He went down river."

Varick sat up. "But you said he was off to West Point."

"I know," Franks said, "but the barge headed down river with the General yelling like a madman for the crew to hurry."

Varick looked between Franks and Melora. "I misled the Commander in Chief."

"You probably gave him your influenza, too," Melora said primly. "Do you know when he's coming back? What meal to fix next?"

"He said they'll be back in three or four hours for an early dinner. I've already told Sarah and Mary."

Melora leaned against the wall. Three or four hours, not a great deal of time.

"Why would he go down river today?" Varick asked through the muffle of the blanket, "with General Washington being here?"

Franks rose and began to pace around the room. "I'm not sure, but I've heard a rumor."

"Franks," Varick looked in Melora's direction.

"It's all right, she was in Mrs. Arnold's room when the General made such a scene this morning. Melora, you can't mention any of this to anyone."

"Of course not, sir." Did he think she never heard a thing or two when the General and Miss Peggy were talking?

"One of the riders with Lieutenant Allen told me that a man named Anderson was picked up trying to cross the lines. A spy."

It took Melora a moment to piece the comments together. "You think that's where he's gone? To see to that business?"

Franks nodded. "I think that was the news Lieutenant Allen brought. Whether he's gone as the area commander or something else, I'm not sure."

Varick sighed. "He's a good man, Franks, we have more than enough evidence of that."

Franks shrugged. "I'm sure you're right. Perhaps it's just the coincidences."

As Melora mulled over Franks' news wondering what the "or something else" could be about, Colonel Varick unfolded another blanket from the bottom of the cot. "I'm sure I should be more interested, but spy or no spy you'll have to excuse me." Pulling the wool around himself, he lay back down with his face to the wall. With that unsubtle gesture for incentive, Melora and Franks left the room and got back to work.

An hour or so later, just as the ham was all cut for the hash, she recalled Jared's whereabouts. He had duty today on the General's barge so he would know all the details about the spy. Reaching for the onions, it occurred to her with a thrill that he might even get to see the spy himself.

Three hours later Melora sat down. The rooms for Washington and his staff were ready, the beds aired and made, pillows plumped, and chamber pots installed. Dinner was also ready, although "assembled" might have been the better word, as the ham and bacon had gone into hash and the fish mixed with potatoes and carrots for soup. Most of the hominy and eggs had been taken as a second breakfast by the staff, with the remains going to the horses. And the bread? It would just have to be a little hard.

With a start she remembered Miss Peggy. In all the excitement she'd forgotten to speak with Anne. Where was her mind? After pouring some tea and wrapping a few biscuits in a napkin, she hurried up the stairs.

"Anne?" she said through the nursery door. "Have you seen Miss Peggy?"

"No," the girl whispered, nodding toward the sleeping baby, "but I thought I smelled something burning." And of course she'd never think of going to see what it might be, Melora fumed, continuing down the hallway. Things would be very different if she were mistress.

Melora opened the door slowly to Peggy's room. To her surprise, the curtains were open and Peggy was sitting up in bed.

"May I come in, miss? I brought you tea and biscuits."

"Yes, come in."

As Melora crossed the room to place the food on the bedside table, she noticed that the room had been picked up. The General's clothes from the flurry earlier were nowhere in sight, and it did appear as though there had been a fire in the fireplace. Charred remnants of papers littered the hearth. There was no improvement in Peggy's looks, however. Her hair was still wild and her color very poor.

"You've been up doing things; you must be feeling better,"

Melora suggested.

"No," Peggy murmured, "not at all better."

"Would you like me to help you dress or brush your hair? The Commander in Chief should be here very soon if you want to see him."

Peggy squinted up at her. "Where is he now?"

"At West Point; he's gone to find General Arnold."

"I see."

While Melora stood awkwardly, wondering what to do with herself, Peggy toyed quietly with the ribbons on her shift.

"You can do two things for me, Melora," Peggy answered at last.

"Of course, miss."

"Go and fetch Colonel Varick, and then bring Neddy as well."

"But Colonel Varick is very sick, miss, and,.." Melora focused on Peggy's attire and the unmade bed, "..and your room."

Peggy's voice grew hard. This was a voice Melora had heard before, many times. "I want you to bring him here."

"At least let me get you a wrap." Melora took a thick woolen shawl from the chest and laid it on the bed before leaving the room. "You're not yourself, miss."


After rousing a bewildered Colonel Varick, Melora darted into the kitchen to check on Sarah's and Mary's progress, only to find the two women sitting at the kitchen table and chatting casually with a young stranger. Pulling Sarah aside, she learned that the man was Jeremiah Cole, and he'd been chasing General Washington all over Connecticut and New York with a very important packet. So "naturally" Sarah and Mary invited him in for a bite while he waited for the General's return. But unless that boy is very strong, Melora thought as she climbed the stairs again to get Neddy, they'll have that message out of him before his soup is finished.

Once again finding no Anne in the nursery, Melora was debating whether or not to wake the child when she heard Peggy scream. Snatching Neddy from the crib, she folded him into a blanket and ran into the General's and Peggy's bedroom. There was Peggy, dressed in only her shift, kneeling in front of Colonel Varick with tears streaming down her cheeks. At Melora's arrival, she pointed to the baby sobbing, "Colonel, did you order my child be killed?"

"Madam!"

Melora watched as the horrified Varick tried to reason with the frenzied woman, pulling her to her feet only to have her collapse time after time and beg him not to kill her child.

"Help me, someone help me," Varick cried, and for the first time Melora realized there were a number of people behind her: Franks, Dr. Eustice, and one of the young men from breakfast, Hamilton. The party was back from West Point.

As Franks and Dr. Eustice rushed forward to help Varick, Peggy began to scream for Neddy, scream that there were hot irons clamped on her head, and scream that when General Washington returned he was going to help Varick kill her child. It took the three of them to get her into bed. Once under the covers, she asked for Neddy again, then broke into another bout of hysteria and babbling. Pointing to the ceiling, she wailed that her husband was gone forever, that there would be no one to protect her child when General Washington came to kill him, and that she herself would die if General Washington didn't take the hot irons off her head.

Leaving Varick to deal with Peggy, Franks pulled Dr. Eustice to the back of the room where the others stood. "Doctor, can't you do something, give her something?"

Eustice shook his head vehemently. "She's mad! I have nothing for that! Where is her husband?"

Franks looked at Melora uneasily. "He may be gone."

"In that case," Eustice said, "General Washington should talk to her."

"You're right. I'll go and get him." Franks reached for Melora's arm and pulled her along with him. "You come also. You can explain what happened before I arrived."

Melora felt faint for the first time in her life running down the corridor toward the rooms set aside for General Washington. She could imagine herself serving the Commander in Chief, but she was not at all sure that she could speak to him.

The guard outside the suite seemed at first determined that no one should see General Washington. He was in the midst of a conference with General Knox and General Lafayette, and under no circumstances was he to allow any other visitors in. But at the mention of Mrs. Arnold's collapse and the suggestion of Dr. Eustice, the guard relented and ushered them into an anteroom off the General's bedroom.

From the anteroom, actually more of a hallway, Melora saw General Washington and two other officers seated around a table in the bedroom. As she watched, the young man from the kitchen, Jeremiah Cole, handed General Washington a group of papers, then moved silently to one side. The General's eyes scanned down the pages, until he paused, and went back to the first page, his hand trembling slightly. Finally, after a very long time it seemed to Melora, he looked up in a dull, vacant way at the officers seated around him. "A man named Anderson has been caught near the lines with damaging passes and papers." Then, in a voice more sad than any Melora would ever hear in her life, Washington said the unthinkable: "Arnold has betrayed me. Whom can we trust now?"

# CHAPTER 63

## The Same Day
### The Hudson River

*A*rnold stared down at the saddle on the deck beside his feet and tried to remember. Why had he brought the saddle? He didn't even recall taking it off the horse. And what had he said to the crew in those first moments? Something about urgent business on board the *Vulture*. The oars splashing rhythmically into the water were at odds with the haphazard jumble of his thoughts. The men were never this quiet. He knew they were uneasy, possibly suspicious. Running his hands over his face, he knew that he had to settle down and think through the details.

All rowing stopped. "General?"

Arnold looked up at Jared Donovan, the coxswain, motioning toward Stony Point on their right.

"Stony Point, General?"

A chill passed over Arnold. Stony Point, King's Ferry. He never came down the river on the barge without stopping there. "Not today, row on for the *Vulture*."

"You're sure, sir?"

Jared's steady eyes met his. Through all their years together, Arnold had never heard a doubt uttered by Donovan. "You have your orders," he answered, his hand sliding slowly toward his pistol butt until the veteran seaman reluctantly signaled the men to drop their oars again.

Ignoring the glances being exchanged among the crew, Arnold took a white kerchief from his pocket, reached up, and tied it tightly to the flag-staff. Damn Donovan and damn the crew, he thought as the white cloth fluttered in the wind. He had to signal Southerland that his approach was peaceful.

With the shoreline sliding by, he looked back toward West Point. No boats in chase—yet. They were in good position. And the men were rowing flat out, motivated mightily by the two gallons of rum he'd promised them for a speedy trip. Probably no one could catch them, but he couldn't stop himself from turning to check. By land or by water, they would come. Washington would see to that.

Washington. One of the few men whose respect he had truly wished for. It was really Washington's fault that he was fleeing down the river now to the British, away from his men, away from the child, and away from the most perfect angel heaven had ever bestowed on man. If Washington had only stood up for him...with the Gates inquiry, with the Philadelphia court martial, and with the self-styled government now trying to take his money away. But he had not. Washington, Gates, Reed—all petty, little people playing with power. Arnold closed his eyes and for a moment simply let the fresh, cold breeze do its work, calming his nerves, helping him think.

The outline of the *Vulture*, hovering off Tellers Point, loomed ahead. Would Robinson receive them? He would probably think André was returning. The young man's delicate features rose before him. How the hell had that played out? The boy was green, probably better in an office than a battlefield. But he had given the man more credit than to get himself caught.

As the barge bore down close hauled on the *Vulture*, Arnold tried to imagine himself explaining this blunder in New York. Sir Henry would be doubly upset, upset at the loss of West Point and upset at his adjutant's capture. And what about the ten thousand pounds André promised, forts or no forts? That money would be his life. He could see faces on the sloop now, excited British crew hastily throwing out ladders and ropes while several officers observed them coolly from the bridge. As Donovan gave the order for the sails to be lowered, visions of other British officers across a distance suddenly swept over Arnold. Ticonderoga, Valcour, Quebec, Saratoga, Danberry, the Mohawk Valley. Good God, what had he done?

# CHAPTER 64

## *Judge Shippen*

$\mathcal{F}$rom later accounts by officers and crew members, no protest was made and no shots were fired when Arnold's barge nosed alongside the Vulture. Arnold boarded the sloop and was immediately conducted to the Captain's quarters. In response to Beverley Robinson's first question regarding the whereabouts of Major John André, Arnold answered directly and unequivocally, "Sir, I am sorry. Although he carried the protection of my passes, still, somehow, they have him." Once Arnold shared the details of the meeting and the capture, as little as he knew, the two men asked for a moment and departed. Alone in the Captain's quarters, Arnold wrote two letters: one to General Washington and one to his wife.

When Robinson and Southerland returned, they announced that Sir Henry would be most violently affected by Major André's capture, as of course were they. Their only thoughts were for a quick meeting with Sir Henry and the construction of a strategy that might offer Major André the most hope and protection. Arnold agreed wholeheartedly, only first he must deal with his crew.

Returning to the deck, Arnold called down to his bargemen as they prepared to raise sails and return up river to West Point. "Attention! I have important news!" By the way he addressed his remarks, however, some of those listening felt he might be speaking more to the crew of the Vulture than to his own men. But all agreed as to what came next. First, he declared that his love for his country was unequaled, that the bloodshed and agony his countrymen were suffering was abhorrent, and the fault for this, he believed, lay in the villainy of the American government. His voice rising, he continued by announcing that he could not and would not accept a partnership with France, the natural enemy of freedom-loving Protestant people everywhere. And why, he cried, should the war continue when the Crown was willing to give more than the colonies had ever wanted? Then, taking a deep breath, he announced his appointment as a General to the Crown and his intention of raising and leading a Loyalist brigade to end the treachery. "Come with me," he shouted."

I will raise you all in rank. There will be no more deprivation, and you will be the victors!" Met with a forbidding silence and no volunteers, Arnold beckoned to Captain Southerland and had the entire crew arrested.

What kind of man, I ask you, is capable of such breath-taking decisiveness? And as her father, the ancillary issue is there as well. What kind of woman is capable of loving such a man? I have thought on these questions for many years.

CHAPTER 65

September 27, 1780

*Headquarters of the Continental Army, Tappan, New York*

The column of one hundred dragoons turned off the tree-lined road and into Tappan just as the sun set over the western hills. All were weary from the long trip down from West Point, the horses dragging, and their riders ready to stretch and enjoy a hot meal. But first the prisoner must be escorted to safety through the crowds that had been arriving steadily throughout the day.

Pausing at the sentry's post, Benjamin Tallmadge asked exactly where the prisoner was to be housed. "Casparus Mabie's Inn, sir," the guard answered, "and you're to show special care. There are many angry people about."

Tallmadge thanked the sentry and directed his second in command to take the lead while he rode back into the formation of soldiers that surrounded John André on all sides. André, previously conspicuous in the claret coat and beaver hat, was now wrapped in a cloak of the dragoons. Tallmadge's idea. A deterrent to any violence from the curious people lining the roads, hoping to see the spy for themselves.

The procession wound slowly into the old Dutch town, passing a mill, a schoolhouse, the great red brick Dutch Church of Tappan, and the village green filled with hissing, mocking onlookers. In the center of town they pulled up in front of the low, two-story, solid brick building known as Mabie's Inn. Slipping quickly from his horse, Tallmadge hustled André in through the front entrance accompanied by a dozen of his men.

"Major Tallmadge!"

Tallmadge looked up to see Colonel Hamilton standing in the hallway.

"Yes, Colonel."

"Can I have a word? The guards will see Major André to his room."

"Of course," Tallmadge answered as a wretched André was led down a corridor.

Following Hamilton into the barroom, Tallmadge took a seat at an empty table while the Colonel called for drinks. For forty-eight hours now he had been on the move with the prisoner or guarding him "very narrowly" according to Washington's order. First, he transported the prisoner from South Salem to Robinson House, where they arrived in the midst of a torrential rain storm. A general apprehension added to the misery of the weather: everyone on high alert, aware that the British might strike at any time. Troops had been transferred from Connecticut, Massachusetts, and New Jersey, a prudent action by Washington to protect the Highland Forts, but one that also added to the pervasive sense of alarm. Then today, rising at dawn, they'd first traveled by barge from West Point to Stony Point, followed by the long ride from Stony Point to Tappan. He'd spent days now waiting for the British to attack. He was exhausted.

"How is Major André?" Hamilton asked. "General Washington would like to know his state of mind."

Tallmadge studied Hamilton. He had made the same trip from West Point to Tappan, but with the Commander in Chief. Unlike himself, Hamilton appeared fresh, his aristocratic features all curiosity and eagerness. Hamilton's overt sense of superiority was a constant irritant to Tallmadge.

"I find him to be amazingly candid. And he has been since the very moment he admitted his identity to us in South Salem."

"How so?"

Tallmadge thought for a moment. "He sees no guilt in any of it. He believes he was on a mission for Sir Henry, was caught, and took certain actions out of necessity to escape."

"You sound as though you've become quite intimate since making his acquaintance," Hamilton said dryly.

"We have," Tallmadge said. "I admit I enjoy his company. He's an erudite officer and an accomplished gentleman. I can understand how he rose so quickly."

"And what does he say about his partners, Arnold and Smith?"

Tallmadge hesitated, unsure whether he should be repeating André's remarks. "That's one of the reasons I admire him. He says nothing and asks that he not be questioned about anyone but himself."

"That does speak well of him. Smith, on the other hand, says it was all Arnold's doing. He will be tried after Major André."

"Would that we had Arnold."

"Perhaps we will." Delighted by Tallmadge's shocked expression, Hamilton leaned over and whispered, "Letters are going back and forth between the Commander in Chief and New York. Clinton, Robinson, and even Arnold have written in very forceful tones that André was under Arnold's protection at all times. That he arrived under a flag of truce and was to return with Arnold's passes. They argue that he must be returned. We, however, are arguing for Arnold."

Tallmadge laughed. "Don't be foolish. Sir Henry will never agree to an exchange. The Crown could never hope for another agent within the empire if they gave up Arnold."

"Maybe not, but your André should better hope that they will."

"Why?"

"Because..." Hamilton began. Tallmadge leaned in—he could barely hear Hamilton for the din in the barroom. "...the Commander in Chief is convinced he acted as a spy, although an extraordinarily worthy and naive one. The clothes, the papers, crossing lines. For General Washington there really is no question, although he instructed the tribunal to act impartially."

"So André's only hope is for Sir Henry to provide some remarkable proof of his argument," Tallmadge mused.

"Or," Hamilton interrupted, slapping his gloves on the table for effect, "for Sir Henry to provide us Arnold."


After a quick dinner, blessedly without the companionship of Hamilton, Tallmadge crossed the hall to André's room, waved the guard away, and knocked. Inside, he found André sitting at a small lady's desk, sketching.

"Have you had your supper?"

André nodded. "I was told my dinner was sent from General Washington's own table."

"It would be like him," Tallmadge said. "What are you drawing?"

The prisoner spread several pieces of paper on the table. "Some pictures from my..." he hesitated, deliberating on the right word before smiling up at Tallmadge, "...my journey. Here is the innkeeper's wife who took my dinner away. There I am being rowed to meet General Arnold. And this," André looked up at Tallmadge with a slightly twisted smile, "is how I looked as my four captors escorted me to Colonel Jameson."

Tallmadge shuffled through the pages. The man had an undeniable talent as well as a curiously observant ability, given his predicament. Certainly such a talented man could not be strung up like a common criminal.

"Major André, may I ask you a question?"

"Certainly." André pulled out another blank sheet.

"During the time that you were behind our lines, because of your mission with General Arnold, did you never consider yourself protected by him, by his flag?"

André stared down at the boats and furniture filling the page. "No, of course not." Then he laughed. "I wouldn't have the pleasure of your acquaintance if I had been."

He doesn't know, Tallmadge realized. Clearly, New York was sending one defense while André had concocted another.

"Now, Major Tallmadge," André put his pen down, "since you ask odd questions, I shall also ask one of you."

"Of course."

André stood and walked over to the window. The lights from the crowds out front flickered in the darkness. "I would like to know your opinion of how my journey will end."

Recalling Hamilton's remarks, Tallmadge struggled for a reply. "A military tribunal will question you and give General Washington an opinion. The trial will begin day after tomorrow, and I've heard that Sir Henry is making appeals on your behalf."

André turned slowly to face him and smiled. "But that was not my question, Major Tallmadge. Please. A full and honest answer. I believe we have developed that degree of regard for one another."

Tallmadge sighed, sorry for the modest room, sorry for the guard at the door, and sorry for the answer he was now obliged to give.

"Do you know of Nathan Hale?" he asked.

"The spy ordered hung by Sir William?"

"Yes. Nathan was a school fellow of mine at Yale College as well as a good friend."

André again turned his back to Tallmadge. "I'm sorry. Do you consider our situations to be similar?"

"Precisely similar," Tallmadge answered with a steadiness he didn't feel, "as I believe your fates must be."

Silence filled the room as André continued to look out the window. From time to time a jeer could be heard from the crowd outside, then suddenly a great roar. Crossing the room to see what the mob was up to, Tallmadge found himself shaking at the scene before him and at the composure of his companion. A parade of sorts was circling directly in front of the inn: men, women, and children taking turns carrying two long wooden coffins. After some moments of watching the macabre dance, André at last broke the quiet. "I see, Major, you're not alone in your opinion."

CHAPTER 66

September 28, 1780

*En route from Robinson House to Philadelphia*

"Drive on," Franks yelled to the driver before climbing back into the coach, dripping wet. Melora looked out through the rain at the small farmhouse where the Major had just asked permission to water the horses. By his quick return the answer was obvious. The family huddled in front of the windows looked out at them as if they were animals on display. "They wouldn't even open the door," he said in a low voice.

Melora thought of the pleasant meal of roast chicken and potatoes the family served them on the way north. "And not three weeks ago they asked us to share their dinner," she muttered. The daughter had been particularly star struck with Peggy, asking if she might touch her dress.

"Major Franks, where are we?" Anne whispered over the head of a whimpering Neddy.

"Fairly close to Paramus. We're staying there tonight with Theodosia Prevost."

"Are you sure she'll let us?" Anne whispered again with a sideways look at Peggy, asleep on the seat beside her. "So many on this trip have been so cruel."

"Yes, but Mrs. Prevost will welcome us," he said, adding dryly, "you see her loyalties lie with London."

"I would sleep at Buckingham Palace right now," Anne said as she bounced the baby gently, "if it were dry."

Franks smiled. "You'll be glad of a stop, too, won't you, Melora?"

Melora glanced up at her seat mate. Dear Major Franks, such a rock over the last three days. "Yes, I suppose." But how could he imagine that she could be glad of anything with Jared in some horrible British prison somewhere. Colonel Hamilton knew only that the entire barge crew had been arrested and taken to New York by orders of the General. And now she was driving farther and farther away from him.

For three days now she'd thought of little except Jared in chains, Jared being mistreated, or Jared...some function of the mind stopped her there. Jared, who had trusted the General so completely. The people on the road were right. Why should anyone help the family and household of such a monster? They probably believe we were involved, she thought. General Washington was certainly suspicious, keeping them isolated and in separate rooms for two days until everyone could be questioned. Only Sarah and Mary believed her, swearing that they would remain her friend and that she could count on them like sisters.

The coach lurched over a hole, shaking the passengers against one another. "What is it? What happened?" Peggy shrieked grabbing onto Anne.

"Nothing, Mrs. Arnold, just a bad place in the road," Franks assured her. "You should rest."

Melora, Franks, and Anne sat in silence as Peggy snuggled back into a corner, pulling a blanket around her. Within minutes and to everyone's relief, she was once again sound asleep. And her sleep was a blessing, as she had been crying or babbling practically since their departure from Robinson House the day before.

"Poor thing, he's a devil for what he did to her," Anne clucked.

"Indeed he is," Franks agreed. "Her life has been damaged. Perhaps irrevocably."

Many lives have been damaged, Melora thought as she closed the curtain of the coach. The dreariness of the rain and mud outside added to her despair. Looking at Peggy, she tried to feel pity. Asleep, Peggy looked much younger than her twenty years, more like an innocent girl ready for an ice-skating party than a wife and mother. Washington, Hamilton, Lafayette, all those gentlemen who paid calls repeatedly to Peggy's bedroom at Robinson House kept saying that: "The poor young innocent." And in truth, she had been violated in a very profound way. The same as poor Neddy and Arnold's other sons with Hannah. "What do you think will happen to her?"

"I believe she's chosen to make her life with the family in Philadelphia," Franks answered. "In the letter that Colonel Hamilton brought back to her from the General he said she might come to him in New York or go to her family in Philadelphia. General Washington also said the choice was hers, and you see the direction the coach is heading."

"And the General?" Anne asked.

"I assume he'll take some high role under Clinton," Franks said, then added wryly, "perhaps take over for the one Washington holds captive now."

"Do you mean Anderson, the man they brought to Robinson House?" Anne asked. "The one caught with the General's papers? My, but he was fine-looking. Didn't you think so, Melora?"

"I never saw him. I was kept in a room alone most of the time except when," she motioned toward Peggy, "she needed something from the kitchen."

"Well, they couldn't keep me pinned up," Anne said, bouncing Neddy. "I had to take care of the babe. I saw most of the comings and goings. I saw both of them, both Smith and that poor fool, Anderson, several times."

"His name is not Anderson, and he is definitely not a poor fool," Franks interrupted. "Colonel Hamilton told me that he's the Adjutant General of the British army and was the General's contact in New York. He came through the lines to negotiate the surrender of West Point and a fee for the General's services. His real name is André, John André."

The words crept through the fog of Melora's misery. They'd talked so little on this trip, what with attending to Peggy and the shock of the past three days. Even at Robinson House, no one really talked because of all the suspicion surrounding the General's going over. She had heard nothing about how it happened. But John André, she knew that name. Slowly, a vision came to mind of the Shippen's parlor where she was serving biscuits. Yes, he was one of the young officers who used to visit with Peggy and her ridiculous friends. And he'd come for the *Meschianza* dress as well. Also on the day they'd learned Howe was leaving Philadelphia. She turned to Franks. "John André is the one they took with them yesterday? To Army headquarters?"

"Yes, he's to be tried there by a military court."

This was too much. The war couldn't be this close. "And he was the General's contact in New York? How strange. He visited many times at the Great House during the occupation."

Anne sat up, visibly excited. "He came to the Great House?"

Melora tried to remember his face. Never feeling comfortable when the British officers were around, she'd kept to the corners as much as possible. "As I said, he came many times until the British left; then we never saw him again."

"I wonder how that piece of news will affect Mrs. Arnold," Franks said with a frown. "What a remarkable coincidence."

Melora was about to agree when the puzzle pieces came flying together. John André, Peggy, the General. It was no coincidence that the General found Major André, and it would be no news to Peggy. Peggy was corresponding with André through the lines well after the British returned to New York. The letter in the writing box from those months ago was proof of that.

Melora's heart began to race as the logic of the thing kept unfurling. Of course. Peggy and her family never supported the American cause, and the General would never do anything without telling her. The late night arguments at the residence, the calculations over money—it could even have been her idea. They must have been planning this for months. With a jolt she remembered Peggy's sudden change of heart toward her. That too must have had something to do with the treachery. "Judge not," her mistress had said, and she had believed her.

Melora felt like the revelation must be emblazoned across her forehead. Should she tell Major Franks? No. He was a complete idiot for Peggy. Anne? What was Anne but a simple baby's nurse? She looked across at Peggy. A curl now dangled over the beautiful forehead and cheek. Peggy and the General, two people with every gift nature could bestow, had tried to sell the country for a fee. And now Jared, her beloved Jared, was locked in a British prison because of...them.

Suddenly Melora clawed at the window and, opening it just in time, became violently ill.

CHAPTER 67

September 29, 1780

*Dutch Reformed Church, Tappan, New York*

John Laurance, the advocate general for the tribunal, tapped lightly on the lectern." So, Major André, to summarize: It is your position that you were a prisoner of war and as such were entitled to take any steps necessary to effect your escape?"

André studied the fourteen generals seated on the hard, dark wood pews before him, their faces revealing only interest and dignity. Some he knew, like Greene, Lafayette, Steuben, St. Clair, Clinton, and Knox. The others were unfamiliar. Their job, as it had been explained to him, was to consider the evidence and provide General Washington with an opinion as to guilt or innocence. The final decision would be Washington's alone.

He rose. "Yes. As you see in my letter to General Washington, and as I described in my written statement to you, I considered myself a prisoner of war." André could hear his voice. It was reasonable, non-defensive, and without hesitation. In some other-worldly way, this was not so very different from a briefing for Sir Henry. Except, in this instance, his life hung in the balance, and his argument was not a very good one.

"While on a mission for Sir Henry Clinton, I was taken ashore to meet General Arnold." Throughout that long day at South Salem he'd debated his best strategy, and this was what he had come up with. "Later, I was told that, as I could not be returned to the Vulture until the following night, I would be concealed in a place of safety until that time. While being conducted to this place of safety we crossed your lines, an action I was totally unaware of until a sentry hailed General Arnold."

"And later," Laurance interrupted, scribbling on his notes, "you attempted to return to New York overland, crossing our posts at Stony Point, dressed as you are now and carrying General Arnold's papers concealed on your person."

André looked down at Smith's coat. He'd asked Major Tallmadge if he might request a set of regimentals from New York, but Tallmadge had yet to provide an answer. "Gentlemen, this clothing is not to my liking. As I explained earlier, since the opportunity of returning to the Vulture as I left it was denied, there was no choice but to return by the overland route. I concealed my uniform in fear for my life."

Still scribbling, Laurance bowed. "Thank you, Major. Perhaps while we confer among ourselves you might consider whether there are any points that you would like to clarify or review with us."

As the generals, half major generals and half brigadier generals, stood to meet with Laurance, André was struck again by the cordiality and objectivity of the court. At every turn he had been given opportunities to amend his written and oral statements, as well as question the charges and evidence laid against him. These colonials had surprised him once again. There was not a man in the room he would not be proud to call a friend and a gentleman.

The generals returned to their seats. "There is one last question, Major," Laurance said.

"Yes, sir."

Laurance put down his papers and spoke very slowly. "Did you at any time believe that when you came ashore you were protected by a flag of truce from General Arnold, from our government?"

André shook his head, perplexed. First Tallmadge now Laurance asking the same question. "How could I, sir? If I had come by a flag, I should have returned by a flag."

In the silence that followed, Laurance addressed the tribunal. "Are there any additional questions for Major André?" With nothing said, he turned back to André. "And you, sir, do you have any remarks to add before we consider the evidence brought to us today and the arguments sent by your superiors?"

André sat quietly for a moment before rising. "Thank you but I have nothing to add. I trust that the evidence will speak for me."

Laurance signaled for Tallmadge to come forward. "Major André, this court also thanks you. We are impressed with your candor, your firmness, and a very becoming sensibility. Now you are free to return to your quarters with Major Tallmadge. We will advise you of our decision."

As the two men walked out of the church and into the sunshine, several guards immediately arrayed themselves about André. While the crowds had lessened, the mood of those remaining had not. Unable to speak, Tallmadge smiled nervously at his charge, who by all appearances was enjoying his brief reprieve in the out-of-doors. André winked and called to his room guards, Captain John Hughes and Ensign Samuel Bowman, for a song to march by. Hughes, having discovered a fellow tease in André, immediately questioned the Major's ability to march and sing at the same time. But within moments the solemn cavalcade was delighting most of Tappan with a spirited rendition of "Am I a Soldier of the Cross."

As the party stepped onto the porch of Mabie's Inn, André paused for just an instant to clasp Tallmadge's shoulder. "I am prepared for my fate, Colonel, whatever it may be. The court gave me every mark of indulgence. I could never feel prejudice against Americans again." Then, whistling the hymn, he stepped into the foyer and turned down the hall toward his room.

Tallmadge leaned against the porch railing, stunned. Never in his life had he met a man with such equanimity, such impossible self possession. Should he have intervened? Whispered the right words for André to say? Given André a wisp of a prayer? But he had not, and now this very fine man, with his own words, had just condemned himself to death.

A few hours later, in the fading sunlight, André stood once again before the court to hear its unanimous decision. In low tones, Laurance read the verdict as it was to be sent to the Commander in Chief, "that Major André, Adjutant General to the British army, ought to be considered as a spy from the enemy; and that agreeable to the law and usage of nations, it is our opinion he ought to suffer death." The prisoner, though paling noticeably, hurried to thank the court for its civility and effort on his behalf.

The next morning, Saturday, exactly one week after André's capture, Washington announced his agreement with the court's decision. He also ordered that verdict be transmitted to Sir Henry as soon as possible. Finally, the Commander in Chief announced that following receipt of Sir Henry's reply, the execution would be carried out immediately.

# CHAPTER 68

## September 30, 1780

*British Headquarters in New York*

Sir Henry Clinton leaned forward, his head in his hands. "By God, we have to stop this." Against the flickering candles in the massive conference room, the generally robust British commander looked haggard and drained.

Benedict Arnold, at Clinton's right, sat impatiently among the circle of councilors around the table. He and the seven other men—Chief Justice William Smith; Lt. General James Robertson, royal governor of New York; Lt. Governor Andrew Elliot; Attorney General John Tabor Kempe; Governor William Franklin; Chief Justice Frederick Smyth of New Jersey; and William Phillips, Clinton's closest confidant—had been called practically from their beds to strategize an immediate obstacle to André's execution. For over an hour now they'd discussed the merits of André's case, dissecting the technicalities. While certainly an august group, most of them appeared old and timid to Arnold, afraid to take the problem head on.

"And this arrived unsolicited?" Smith asked as Washington's letter to Clinton announcing the court's decision was handed around the table.

Clinton nodded. "A Captain Ogden delivered it to Paulus Hook, where it was transferred over here immediately."

"I must say," William Franklin said, handing the letter to Robertson, "I still think the evidence appears rather strong."

Clinton sat up, livid. "No, it's false! André was under General Arnold's flag the entire time." Turning to Arnold he commanded, "Tell them!"

Arnold felt his face tighten at the effrontery of the order. Ever since his arrival in New York, Sir Henry had done nothing but badger him for details about his meeting with André. That, and have him write a lengthy letter to

Washington explaining the entire affair. Clinton's agony over his subordinate's situation was so apparent that Arnold could imagine the rumors of their relationship might very well be true. "Indeed, Major André was under my protection," he said coolly, "and as the commanding officer in the area, it was my right to extend the flag."

"But," Franklin frowned, adding to the furrows from his time in prison, "bear with me Sir Henry, General Arnold. How can he be innocent if he crossed lines in disguise, carried papers, and if André himself said that he cannot have imagined himself to have come ashore under the sanction of a flag?"

Sir Henry glared at Franklin. "Governor Franklin, why can you not understand? Chief Justice Smith, please explain."

Smith tried to recall the exact words he used with Clinton just two days earlier when the General put that exact question to him. Could André's actions place him in the category of a spy? While he tended to agree with Franklin, particularly now after Washington's letter, he had not been man enough to add to Sir Henry's despair. "I believe, since André did not set off on a spy's errand, that even with those items you mention, Governor Franklin, he cannot be considered a spy. It is a matter of intent."

"But he was under a flag," Arnold shouted, ready to form his own brigade and attack Tappan himself, "whether he knew it or not!"

"Gentlemen! Gentlemen!" General Robertson rapped on the table. "We have no time for this talk. I suggest we write a letter to General Washington explaining both these points. At the very least we might be able to postpone the..." Robertson hesitated, "...the verdict."

Sir Henry nodded, worn out, desperate. "Yes, and a party of you can deliver the letter to General Washington tomorrow. I'll have the *Greyhound* alerted to carry you as soon as the wind and tide permit." Folding his hands in an almost prayer-like position, Clinton added, "Surely Washington will hear us out."

"Yes, surely," Robertson agreed.

Arnold stared at the doddery old man. "I would recommend another strategy."

As all heads shifted in his direction, Arnold felt some measure of power returning. At least he had an audience. For five days now, no one had cared to listen to his plans for anything as headquarters sat paralyzed by this André affair.

"Haven't I heard that you have forty prisoners from the Charleston campaign in your custody, Sir Henry?"

Clinton eyed him warily. "Yes."

"Then I would write in no uncertain terms that the lives of those forty would be forfeit if André were to be executed. That torrents of blood will flow if André is injured and that humanity will be revolted."

Clinton shrank back in his chair, appalled. "As supreme commander, I cannot stoop to that level of negotiation."

"But I can," Arnold said.

As the group began to debate the idea, an aide stepped into the room and saluted. "Pardon me, Sir Henry, there's an urgent message regarding Major André."

Clinton waved him over, buoyed by the possibility of good news. "Well, come in, come in."

"Captain Miller, sir." The officer glanced in Arnold's direction and motioned to the hallway. "Sir Henry, I think you should hear this in private."

Clinton shook his head vehemently. "Captain, I haven't the time. If this concerns Major André then these gentlemen need to know it as well as I do. Tell us."

Looking decidedly uncomfortable, Miller began. "The captain who brought General Washington's letter is staying at Paulus Hook tonight, because of his late arrival. In conversation with the post commander there he brought up a proposal."

"And?" Clinton prompted.

Miller glanced down uneasily for a second time at Arnold. "He says the Americans will give up André immediately...for General Arnold."

A collective gasp escaped from the council members, followed by Clinton's weary dismissal of the young man. "That proposal was not worth your trip, Captain. You may leave us now." He turned to Arnold and shrugged. "I am sorry for that, General. I'm amazed the idea was even put forward."

Arnold shrugged. "I'm amazed you haven't been approached with the idea before now. Washington probably set this up, had his man arrive late so he could stay and talk. That's what I'd have done."

As Smythe tried to move the conversation back to Arnold's idea, Clinton raised a hand and called for silence. "Excuse me, but I'm very tired and, I'm sure, not thinking well. I believe just a little rest in my office will revive me. In my absence, General Robertson, will you prepare a letter as you mentioned? And General Arnold will you also prepare a letter as you mentioned? I'll meet all of you back here in one hour to review them." Surprised, the eight remaining men stood awkwardly as the Commander in Chief left the room.

While Robertson sat down to begin his draft and the rest of the Council walked outside for some air, Arnold decided to work in the space that had been prepared for him outside Sir Henry's office. He needed some privacy to organize his thoughts, to hit the right note in his writing. Just as he believed Washington capable of carrying out this plan of trading him for André, he must ensure that Washington would believe his own threat about the forty. And Arnold was prepared to do it because André was fast becoming a millstone around his neck.

Sitting down at his desk, Arnold was surprised to hear muted voices coming from Sir Henry's office, Sir Henry speaking to someone named Peter. "Yes, go to him, go to him immediately. Take him his uniform. Fresh linen also. Comfort him. Oh, Peter, what would we do without him?" Then it seemed Clinton broke down; there was just the sound of weeping.

Walking back to the door as quietly as he could, Arnold was just about out of the room when Sir Henry spoke again. This time, however, he heard fury overriding the despair. "If André was in his protection as he proclaims so loudly, Peter, then why did he not protect him?" Arnold heard a muffled crash as Clinton delivered his own verdict. "Was André's safety so much less important than his own?"

# CHAPTER 69

October 1, 1780

*The Great House*

"*O*h, my poor girl!"
   Stepping down from the carriage, Peggy ran toward the throng of family members standing in the light rain outside the Great House, and headlong into Mrs. Shippen's arms.

"We're taking her inside," the Judge shouted to Betsey. "See what you can learn from Major Franks."

Betsey nodded to her father and waited while Major Franks helped Anne, carrying Baby Neddy, and then Melora, as each descended from the carriage. Of the three, she wasn't sure who looked the most exhausted. Anne, assuming that she would want to see her nephew, curtsied briefly and held the baby up for a perfunctory kiss before scurrying into the house. Melora, however, walked past her without uttering a word.

After telling the driver to go around to the back to unload, Betsey nervously approached Franks and held out her hand.

"Major Franks, I'm Mrs. Burd. We met at my sister's wedding. Might I ask you to step inside...so we might speak?"

"Of course. But perhaps it would be better if we talked out here. I've been in the coach the better part of these last few days."

Betsey glanced toward the house, wishing that her husband was here with her. He was so good at assessing problems. "We've read the accounts here, but what can you tell me? Was it very bad?"

Franks nodded. "It was. We feared for Mrs. Arnold's sanity. She became quite hysterical the day the General left and for two days thereafter."

Knowing how violent Peggy's disturbances could be, Betsey could well imagine the effect of this trauma on her sister. "And now?"

"She's slept for most of the past four days, which was a blessing because people have been very rude to us, very rude, since we departed West Point. Even the most basic amenities were withheld." Franks held up mud-spattered hands. "Prior to that, however, she was shown every kindness by General Washington and his staff."

As a carriage rumbled slowly down the street, Betsey wondered if the house was under observation. Her father said they should watch for that kind of thing from President Reed and his crowd. "I know she received the one letter from General Arnold authorizing her to return home. Do you know if there have been more?"

"No, I don't think so."

Betsey ran her hand through her curls. Poor dear Peggy, how would she survive this? "Is there anything else I should know about this business, Major?"

Franks thought for a moment. "Only that I'm very glad she is back with her family. She was already ill with a headache when all this began, and then to suffer as she has suffered because of that..." he stopped himself, the General was still Mrs. Burd's brother-in-law. "...the General."

Despite the dirt, Betsey took his hand. "You've been a good friend to us. Won't you please come in and rest."

"Thank you," Franks answered, a little embarrassed by her gesture, "but I believe I'll throw myself on the hospitality of my cousin. Perhaps even shop at that store of his for some fresh clothing."

"I have bad news for you, Major. Your cousin's been arrested again."

"Why?"

She blushed. "For corresponding with the enemy."

"I see," Franks said slowly; realizing the terrible timing of his cousin's arrest, the hysteria over Arnold's treachery could easily spill over. "Then there is all the more reason for me to hurry to his family. Excuse me. Please give my farewell to Mrs. Arnold and your family. I'm off to find the driver."

While Franks hurried toward the back of the house, Betsey lingered on the walk. Her beautiful, intelligent, accomplished little sister, ruined at twenty. And possibly, she thought, brushing a tear away, the rest of the family as well. What could she do? What could any of them do? As another carriage rolled very slowly onto Fourth Street, she turned and hurried into the house.

Betsey found her husband waiting for her in the foyer. "Come with me," he whispered, pulling her into the dining room. "Peggy's in the study with your father. The rest of the family's in the parlor."

"How is she?" Betsey asked, taking a seat at the table. "Major Franks says she's suffered terribly."

Neddy pulled up a chair beside her. "It was so odd. The moment we got in the house she started asking us why people were so vehemently against the General. Your father tried to explain, but it was as if she couldn't absorb what he was saying. She just sat there in a sort of stupor saying over and over that what he had done was not so wrong. That's why your father hurried her into the study. He was afraid the servants might hear."

"Do you think she believes that?" Betsey asked.

"I don't know," Neddy answered. "She is so mad for the man. But I can't tell you how dangerous it would be if she spoke like that to anyone else. You know," he paused to put his arm around her, "there are those who are sure she must have been involved with the General's plans. But there's not a shred of evidence against her."

Betsey sat up, unable to stop the tears this time. "Oh Neddy, it's so sad. If she stays here, her life..." She sighed, unable to complete the dismal picture. "But she can't go to him! And what do you think will happen to us? Evidence or no evidence, people may connect our entire family with General Arnold."

"It's true. We will have to be very, very careful."

Betsey laid her head against her husband's shoulder. "Neddy, I have to tell you something."

"Yes?"

"I was jealous. When the General was military governor here and she was so like a queen, I was jealous."

Holding his wife as closely as he could in the high backed wooden chairs, Neddy kissed her. "I think we all were."


A few hours later Betsey left Peggy's room and stopped in at her mother's bedroom just down the hall. Seated at her dressing table, Mrs. Shippen's eyes were swollen and red from an afternoon of crying. "I'm glad you're here. How is she?"

Betsey sat down on the edge of her mother's bed. "She just wants to stay in her room. She won't be joining us for dinner."

"Did she talk to you at all?"

Betsey shook her head. "Not really. She only wanted me to sit with her."

"That's the way she was with me also," Mrs. Shippen said, taking out her powder puff. "Remember when she was a little girl, she would always ask for you or me to sit with her? The only one she's ever really talked to is your father."

"What did she tell him?"

"She wanted him to agree with her about the General, that there was no treason. When he said he couldn't, she ran upstairs to her room. Oh, and she asked about Major André." Mrs. Shippen shook her head, another tear making a path across the newly dusted cheek. "Can you imagine that our girl had such evil luck as to fall in with the General and with André. When I think of all the men she could have chosen from."

Betsey stood, overcome by, as her mother had said, this evil luck. Would they ever stop crying? "I should go and find Neddy, tell Cook to set one less for dinner."

On the way down the hall, Betsey was surprised to see the door to her old room open and Melora inside. Since she and Neddy had their new house, Peggy and the General's possessions from the residence had been stored there until after the General's tour at West Point. But where Mrs. Shippen introduced order and logic to the stacks of boxes, President Reed's men introduced havoc. Storming into the house immediately after the plot was revealed, they'd thoroughly searched all of Peggy's and the General's things.

"Melora, shouldn't you be resting?"

Melora, still in her traveling clothes, turned toward Betsey. "No, ma'am."

Betsey sighed. She hadn't imagined the maid's bad humor earlier. "I'm sorry about your young man, Melora. Do you know where he is?"

"In prison, only that."

"You must be so worried. I remember how it was when my husband was captured."

"I'll manage, ma'am."

Betsey wondered if this was a preview to how the family would be treated generally in the future. She leaned against the doorframe. "Are you looking for something?"

Melora motioned to the stacks around her. "My boxes from the residence. They should be somewhere here with Miss Peggy's and the General's."

"Can I help you?"

Melora gazed briefly at Betsey and then back at the cartons. "No, ma'am."

"Well, I'll leave you to your search," Betsey said in as cheery a voice as she could muster. What could she say? What could change this? "It's good to have you back home at the Great House, Melora. It truly is. I'm sure my parents think so also." She waited, but Melora simply looked back. "Melora, I..."

"If there's nothing more, ma'am."

Betsey shook her head and backed out into the hall.


Melora waited until she heard footsteps on the stairs before closing the door and returning to the box she'd discovered just before Betsey's arrival. Though kinder, Miss Betsey lived very much in the same lofty realm as Miss Peggy. "Good to have you back home," she'd said. Could Miss Betsey really believe she thought of the Great House as her home? And, no, she definitely did not want help with her current work. Opening the carton, Melora pulled out Peggy's walnut writing box and placed it on her lap.

Jenny had told her all about President Reed's men coming, about the letters they'd found and put into the newspaper. Some of the letters showed what everyone thought, that the General had been involved in a number of illegal businesses. And one from Peggy described some ladies at a concert in a very unflattering way. Jenny didn't mention any other letters written by Peggy, probably because the men wouldn't have known where to look.

Melora slid her fingers behind the felt lining. The folded paper was just as she'd replaced it those months ago. After taking a moment to assure herself that it read exactly as she remembered, she slipped the letter into her apron pocket and quickly replaced the writing box in its container. Satisfying herself that nothing appeared amiss, she stood, closed the door behind her, and headed up to her old attic room. Judge not so that thou will not be judged. No. She would judge and she would be proud of it. Tomorrow she would find a reason to go to the market. And on that trip, somehow, she would bring the short letter in her pocket written from the British headquarters in New York to the attention of the Supreme Executive Council of Pennsylvania. The short letter from Major John André to Margaret Shippen Arnold asking if he might be of some assistance.

# CHAPTER 70

## October 2, 1780
### The Casparus Mabie Inn, Tappan, New York

With the first faint rays of sunshine transforming the world from gray to gold, Alexander Hamilton and Benjamin Tallmadge entered the prisoner's room. André, seated at a low wooden table set with pen and paper, looked up at their arrival. He forced a smile. "Gentlemen, good morning, please take a seat. I hope you'll join me for breakfast."

The two men cast quick glances at one another before Tallmadge took up a position by the window and Hamilton sat stiffly on the cot across from André. Each seemed to be waiting for the other to speak.

"Come now, gentlemen," André chided gently, "I think you have some news for me."

"We do," Hamilton said. "His Excellency told me yesterday that General Greene met with Sir Henry's envoy, General Robertson. Robertson conveyed Sir Henry's understanding of your status while you were with General Arnold and his absolute objections to the decision made in your case."

"And the outcome?"

"General Washington said nothing in this conversation altered his opinion."

Pushing the previous sketch aside, André took out a fresh sheet of paper. "When is the punishment to be carried out?"

Hamilton sighed. "At noon, Major."

André nodded, the rough scratching of his pen against the page the only sound in the tiny room. From outside they could hear the guards playing a game of cards, the innkeeper's wife scolding the laundress, and an assortment of town noises wafting in from the street.

Tallmadge looked out the window to the growing crowds around the

260 Forrest Bachner

inn. Even though he understood the inevitability of Washington's decision, the intentional destruction of a man of André's caliber was, if not against a law of man's, then surely against a law of nature. He also realized now why the Commander in Chief had so resolutely refused to meet André. He feared he might be swayed. "Is there anything we can do for you?" he asked softly.

André held the new sketch up to the light for a second before furiously filling in some detail to what looked to Tallmadge like the figure of a seated person.

"There are," André took a deep breath, "two things. Sir Henry has been so very good to me. Would one of you ask General Washington if I might write to him? It weighs very heavily on me that he might think himself responsible for what is to come."

Hamilton rose from the cot. "Of course, I'll go to him right away."

"And," André hesitated, his voice breaking, "although I'm reconciled to my fate, I would feel much lighter if I could leave this life as an officer and a gentleman. Do you understand me, Colonel?"

Hamilton nodded. André was asking to be shot, rather than the customary death for spies, hanging. But General Washington would never allow it. An exception would call the entire verdict into question. "I'll speak to His Excellency about that matter as well."

André stood and smiled as Hamilton picked up his hat and gloves to leave. "Thank you. My morning is improving already."

"Your bravery is astonishing, Major," Hamilton said from the doorway.

"It will be but a momentary pang, Colonel."

As Hamilton departed the room, he held the door for a large black man carrying a tray. Immediately, the room was filled with the mingled aromas of fresh baked bread, ham, bacon, and coffee.

"Oh, the comings and goings," André said brightly. "Breakfast again, William Lee?"

"Yes sir," Washington's servant answered, "and extra special today." Balancing the tray on one hand, he held up a corner of cloth revealing a platter of pancakes drenched in syrup. "The General said he wanted a breakfast like it was Christmas."

André gave Tallmadge a knowing look. "Your master has been very thoughtful once again, William. Please give him my thanks."

Lee placed the tray on the cot. "Your man, Peter, is outside. The General just gave him permission to visit you here."

André slapped his leg. "My god, they let him come. He must have a uniform for me." Ripping off the damning silk jacket, he added wistfully, "Would that I had never borrowed this one."

Afraid that André might be overcome again, Tallmadge crossed to the door quickly. "I shall leave you to your breakfast and your letter, Major. Please, call on me," he hesitated, his voice trailing off as he thought of the very few hours left to this man, "if I can be of any further service."

André held up a hand. "Thank you, William, you've been a welcome sight these mornings. Will you tell Peter I'll need just a moment longer?"

André waited until the servant was out of the room before addressing Tallmadge. "There is another service you can do for me."

"Anything, Major."

"When it is time, will you take my hand? I would like to see a friend at the last."

Tallmadge nodded, about to break into tears himself. "I would consider it an honor. And I agree wholeheartedly with Colonel Hamilton, you're bravery toward this event is astonishing."

"Not completely." He handed over the sketch he had been working on. The seated figure in the picture was of himself, as Tallmadge and Hamilton had found him earlier that morning: weary, haunted, alone. "I'm sure you've thought of facing death also. As we soldiers must."

But staring down at the sketch, Tallmadge knew that he had no familiarity whatsoever with the despair emanating from the portrait. "I've only considered death's possibility. Never its certainty."

Seeing Peter coming toward them, André answered quietly. "I had hoped for glory, Major Tallmadge. This certainty is all I have left."

# CHAPTER 71

## Noon, The Same Day
### The Casparus Mabie Inn, Tappan, New York

"Major, it's time."

André looked up from the letter. The two guards, Bowman and Hughes, stood at the door, both at attention, eyes fixed on some spot out the window in the blue and gold Indian summer day. So.

Lining up the scripted pages before him, he folded them in thirds, then, with great care, applied the seal. Hamilton had sent word that he would see to it that Sir Henry received the letter in good time. A great relief. The Commander in Chief must not blame himself, not for an instant. He reached for the coat lying on the bed; the uniform Peter had brought hung loosely after these past few days, but it was clean, pressed, and above all else, that of a British officer. He tugged the sleeves evenly over his lace cuffs, straightened the stock at his throat, and forcing himself to smile, glanced into the small hand mirror Peter had brought with his bundle of items. This was the face the world must see.

Without a look back he stepped from his room and down the short, dark hall to the main entrance of the inn. The door stood open. A swath of sunlight fell across the foyer. Bowman and Hughes marched onto the porch. He followed behind them.

Immediately outside, a detachment of soldiers waited, two by two, headed by a fife and drum corps. The crowds, jostling noisily for position, stretched in all directions. Not hundreds, but thousands. He motioned for his guards, holding his right arm out to Hughes, his left to Bowman. "Gentlemen, you'll allow me this honor." Bowman hesitated, seeming for a second about to say something. Instead he rubbed his right hand on his pant leg and slipped his arm through André's. Hughes, his mouth compressed into a hard straight line, carefully and deliberately hooked arms as well. Being different heights, the three men needed a step or two to synchronize their feet as they descended the steps of the inn and fell in line behind the musicians. The drum major, a smooth-faced boy not more than thirteen, lifted his stick high in the air, then thumped the drum hanging from his waist once. The corps members stepped forward. Hughes and Bowman stepped forward. He stepped forward as well.

"Will we be going far, Hughes?"

"No, sir," Hughes answered, staring ahead. "Just through town and up the hill."

André looked up at the cloudless sky. "A good day for a walk."

"If you say so, sir."

Dust and dirt rose around the procession as the crowds pressed in, walking alongside. Some seemed excited, some impatient, but most just curious, pointing him out to relatives and friends, like one might an exotic dog. He glanced down at his boots. Polished and buffed to a high shine by Peter just hours earlier, they were already covered in dust...like on every other walk...on every other day. A walk, that's all this was. And then a short stop. Shops flashed by. The smithy. The church where the trial had been held. Suddenly a voice bellowed over the din from the church tower. "Smith, we've got Smith in here. He'll be next." André looked at Bowman.

"His trial begins today. This afternoon."

He gripped his guards' arms. Smith. That so much had depended on such a man.

Fifes now joined drums, sweet and clear in the open air. Children skipped, parents shuffled lunch baskets from arm to arm, and he remembered to smile. His mother would read accounts of this day as would his sisters and brother, Sir Henry, even Honora and her father. What would be written?

He spied one of the cooks from the inn. "The music, it's very good don't you think?" The crowds closest to him stilled. "What was that?" he heard a man ask. He loosened an arm from Hughes and cupped his hand to be heard better. "I said the music is very fine today." A nervous laughter rose from the crowd.

Another man yelled, "Can you believe it, he's talking about the tune."

There was little laughter at this.

Bowman looked around at the crush of bodies, then held his face close.

"I think they're amazed, sir,... to hear you speak so at such a time."

He grinned and linked his arm back through Bowman's. "Theatrics. Pity you missed my event in Philadelphia," he winked at the guard, "and the ladies seem to like me there."

A flicker of wry amusement flickered over Bowman's face.

"Come on, Hughes, you too," he encouraged, "no long faces here."

But Hughes, the joker, marched silently, eyes still set rigidly forward.

Another familiar face appeared on the right, a guard from the church. "Good day to you," he shouted. He scanned the throng. "Good day to you all," he repeated, stepping up the pace. The crowd was noticeably quieter now.

Veering north, the procession began its ascent of a moderately steep hill leading out of the village. "Bowman, how much farther, now?"

"Just at the rise there, to the left."

He looked up toward the top of the hill. There hovering above the throngs were two uprights and a crossbar. A scaffold. "No..." he whispered. "...God, no."

"But you knew, sir," Bowman insisted. "Surely you knew."

He shook his head. "Not by these means. I detest these means."

Any hint of lightness left the faces of the three men as they climbed the short distance to the summit. There, in the clearing, the officers who had judged him guilty waited on horseback on one side of the gallows while Van Wart, Paulding, and Williams stood on the other. Peter, he noted, had been given a place just to the side of the tribunal. The crowds who had followed them up the hill spread out quickly, fan-like, about the rough wooden structure.

Accompanied by his guards, he walked slowly across the uneven field toward the officers where John Laurance sat first in line. Laurance's expression was grave. André bowed. Laurance, with his hat under one arm, bent slowly from the waist in response. With the noon sun burning through his coat, he moved down the line of Generals, bowing to each and waiting at attention as the courtesy was returned. From the corner of his eye, he saw a horse and wagon being driven under the scaffold. Soon, very soon now.

The music stopped when an officer stepped out of the crowd and into the center of the clearing. "Colonel Scammel," Bowman whispered, "the officer in charge today."

Scammel, a large man, held up a hand for quiet. "Will the prisoner please come forward." He felt a light pressure at his elbow as Hughes and Bowman backed away. He turned and gave each man a quick smile. Hughes's eyes, dark and wretched, finally, for a second, met his.

He faced Scammel. "With your permission, one last goodbye."

Scammel nodded. His face not unkind.

He searched the masses of faces clustered about him. "Major Tallmadge, could I speak with Major Tallmadge?" Behind him he heard murmuring. He turned to see the dignified form of his once captor walking slowly toward him, his face haggard, drawn. In a few strides Tallmadge had his arms about him, holding him heart to heart, as a brother would. Not his blood brother William, but a true brother. What times they could have had.

"Major..." Tallmadge began.

But he stepped back, gripping Tallmadge by the shoulder. "As I said, just a momentary pang."

Tallmadge nodded, pulled him to his chest once again, then turned and with slow steps left him standing alone. He watched until his friend was once again at the perimeter of the crowd. Just moments now. He crossed the clearing to stand beside Colonel Scammel.

"Is there anything the prisoner would like to say?"

Scammel's words sounded like lines from a play. Lines he had anticipated. He fixed his gaze on Tallmadge.

"I pray you bear witness I die a brave man."

"Would the prisoner mount the wagon."

To his right, Peter stood openly crying. The walk was over. He climbed onto the baggage cart and, waving the executioner away, reached up for the noose and pulled it tightly about his neck. Now the short stop. A breeze rustled the pines behind the scaffold, then bent the goldenrod and lavender asters dotting the clearing. Jittery with the crowds, the horse flashed its tail.

Scammel signaled the driver. Goldenrod and lavender, he'd meant to paint those colors.

A whip cracked, the terrified horse bolted forward, and John André, considered by many the most accomplished officer of the era, passed out of time.

CHAPTER 72

October 18, 1780

*Manhattan*

*W*illiam Smith opened the door to his home. "General, congratulations. The uniform looks very well on you, very well indeed."

Arnold straightened the jacket of his new uniform showing him to be a brigadier general of the Provincial Troops. "Thank you. I expect to put these clothes to good use. I can tell you, though, I still hope for my previous rank."

Smith smiled. "I'm sure time will provide that also, General. Please come with me. We'll talk in my library."

Following his host through the house, Arnold stopped to admire several pieces of furniture, china objects, and silver. One, a salver by Myer Myers particularly caught his attention. "What an exquisite work," Arnold said picking up the silver tray.

"A gift from my father for completing my legal studies. He was pleased I followed him to the Bar."

Arnold ran his fingers along the scrolled rim. "I can well imagine."

"Did you also follow your father's example, General?"

Arnold set the salver down. "Your brother, Chief Justice, is there any news of him?"

"No," Smith answered, puzzled by his guest's response but too polite to delve. "His trial continues. You can imagine our worry given the premeditated murder that we know General Washington to be capable of."

"Take heart, sir," volunteered Arnold. "I wrote to Washington myself that Mr. Smith had no knowledge of my plans. A man cannot be convicted for ignorance."

Flinching at Arnold's bravado as well as the dubiousness of his assurance, Smith held the door to the library open for his visitor to pass. While hopes for Arnold were high, so far his entry to town had not gone as expected. He didn't seem to fit. Sir Henry didn't know what to do with him, some of the senior staff balked at his inclusion, and a number of refugees in town, already desperate for money, housing, and their former lives, were complaining bitterly about the laurels, attention, and rewards heaped upon him. His new colleague was not in an easy position.

Arnold settled himself into a deep burgundy armchair and held out a handful of papers. "I've brought my notes; I'm grateful to you for helping me again. I thought our first collaboration went off very well. It should be published any day now in the papers."

"The 'Address to the Inhabitants of America,' yes," Smith smiled. "I agree." He hoped so, given the hours he'd spent incorporating Arnold's views into his own bitter attacks against the new government. Fortunately, Arnold had asked him for assistance on all his public writing. "So this next piece is to be the first salvo in the campaign for American recruits?"

"Yes," Arnold answered, "right now forty have joined my regiment. There are thousands, however, just waiting to cross over to His Majesty. I'm sure the only reason they've not already deserted is the issue of back pay." He pointed to the notes. "I've developed specific amounts for rewards and inducements for those who enlist."

"And Sir Henry approves of all this?"

"He does."

"Three guineas for every non-commissioned officer and private..." As Smith perused the numbers, he speculated on what a shock all this must have been to Sir Henry. Everyone assumed New York would be overtaken by deserters on the strength of Arnold's coming over alone. "Give me a day or so to work on this, and then we'll get together again to review the particulars. And the letter you were writing to Lord Germaine, you still want to proceed with that?"

Arnold nodded.

"You don't suppose Sir Henry will consider that you've gone over his head by corresponding directly with London?"

Arnold hesitated. "May I say something in confidence?"

"Surely, General. We Americans must sometimes confide in one another."

Arnold toyed with the chair arm. "I don't know what else to do except go directly to London. Immediately after my arrival here, I took my ideas about ending the conflict to Sir Henry and I've yet to hear back a word."

"It's André," Smith answered. "He's still mourning André."

"But André's dead! Chief Justice, he's the Commander in Chief. He must act!"

Smith wondered if Arnold had any idea that, in addition to holding him responsible for André's death, Clinton simply detested him. Sir Henry had described a meeting scarcely two weeks after the execution in which Arnold strode into his office and without a word for poor André began an aggressive defense of his claim for the full 10,000 pounds rather than the 6000 he had already received. Arnold even went so far as to say that the Commander in Chief's envoy had supported that amount, forts or no forts. Clinton was furious.

"But what can we do, General?" Smith asked. "While Sir Henry sometimes, often, moves more slowly than many of us would like, he is the Commander in Chief. I would advise you against the letter."

"But the Continental Army is broken. We should be pursuing Washington into the ground, destroying supply bases, and cutting off transportation routes. That's what Cornwallis is doing in the south. Why aren't we?"

"I don't know, General," Smith answered wearily. Lately, speaking to Sir Henry about any plans, much less about Cornwallis, was akin to swiping at a hornets nest. And speaking to him about Arnold was like stepping into the nest altogether. "You mentioned the south. What do you think of this rebel win at King's Mountain?"

Arnold shrugged. "Unfortunate, but hardly a threat. Every now and then any army gets lucky."

"Perhaps the loss will force Sir Henry's hand," Smith suggested.

"Or perhaps my regiment will. Chief Justice, I've given up a great deal by coming here. I won't stand idly by and find myself on the losing side." He stood and held out his hand. "If you'll excuse me, I should be off. I have many meetings, and an appointment to look at a house for my family."

Smith stood also. "You expect Mrs. Arnold soon?"

Arnold followed his host back to the front foyer. "Very soon, I hope. But we have an infant child, and you know how new mothers want their families about."

Smith considered the implications of what Arnold was telling him. "You're not worried for them there?"

Arnold looked puzzled.

"That General Washington might...detain them," Smith explained, handing Arnold his gloves and cane.

Arnold bowed. "They are in no danger whatsoever. Good day."

Smith watched as Arnold strode down the street, seemingly not bothered by people pausing and pointing. He was certainly a man of eagerness and energy, purpose and plan. How ironic that these enviable traits might very well work against him within the closed circle of the British officer corps he'd come to know so well. After shutting the door against the dust in the street, Smith walked over to replace the salver in its stand. If Arnold believed Lord Germaine would ever listen to an American over an Englishman, then he had much to learn about their brethren in London.

Returning to his library, Smith picked up the recruiting notes and noticed the article was provisionally titled, "Proclamation to the Officers and Soldiers of the Continental Army." They'd all so firmly believed in Arnold's popularity with the American troops, yet to form a regiment he was reduced to outright bribery. Even his own wife following him seemed in question. Studying the list of Arnold's "monetary inducements," Smith wondered uneasily about the effective price for patriotism. But, he supposed taking up his pen, surely Arnold could be relied upon to know about that.

# CHAPTER 73

October 20, 1780

_Manhattan_

*T*he tavern, smoky and dim, was located in a dark alley off the east-side docks. Downstairs, there was a bar and six small tables crammed against each other while upstairs various girls entertained throughout the day and night. A favorite haunt of enlisted men, down-and-out loyalists, and servants, it was inexpensive, shunned by officers, and reliably routine. A comfortable place for gossiping with one's comrades, perhaps taking in a fight or two, talking about people at home, or blasting the higher ups. And amidst all the talk and the foolishness, the barkeep heard every word. James Miller, story teller, singer, and confidant extraordinaire, was a very well-placed man.

As Jared approached the bar, Miller slapped him on the shoulder. "How are you, Mr. Donovan? Still enjoying His Majesty's hospitality?"

Jared sighed. At first the crew was elated at Sir Henry overturning Arnold's order. They would be paroled, not jailed. But day after day of wandering aimlessly around New York only to return to the jail at night was tearing at him. And the days he'd hear some news about Arnold or see him on the street, as he had today, were especially bad. On those days he'd sink into a depression, engulfed in his hatred of Arnold and of himself for having believed in him. How could there be a god in the world and Arnold walking around a free man? But then there was Miller.

One day on the docks, the barkeep had made it very much his business to strike up a conversation with Jared, inviting him to visit the tavern and bring his crewmates. While never saying anything specific, he'd let Jared know that he was a friend with a greater role to play in the scheme of things, that efforts were being made. Miller's hints provided the only bit of solace in the purgatory his life had become. Today he'd sent Jared a message to come here at four. And four o'clock in the afternoon it was. About the only time during the day the tavern had a lull.

"Actually, Mr. Miller, I wouldn't mind wearing out my welcome."

"You'd rather be locked in a jail than wandering the streets freely, Mr. Donovan?"

"The city's my jail, Mr. Miller."

"Well, if that's how you take things, you might want to speak with that man by the door." Miller pointed to the only other patron, a small dark man about Jared's age in the uniform of the provincial troops. "He might be able to change your mind." Miller handed Jared a tankard and added, "On the house, Mr. Donovan, and good luck."

Curious, Jared approached the soldier's table.

"May I join you?"

The man looked up. "Jared Donovan?"

"Yes."

"Then please do."

As Jared pulled up a seat, the other man took an envelope from his pocket. "This is for you." Jared recognized Melora's writing immediately. "How in God's name...?"

"Let's step back a moment," the stranger said, holding onto the envelope. "My name is John Champe. I've been sent as a deserter to join General Arnold's new regiment."

"You were sent?"

"Yes, from Tappan."

Jared struggled to understand. "To spy?"

"No," Champe grinned. "I've bent sent to take Arnold. Return him to hang in front of all those who trusted him."

Jared felt a sudden rush of energy. "I have to go along!"

"No, you're too conspicuous as a prisoner. It's what people would expect."

"Then what do you want with me?"

"Two things. First, I had to find you to give you this. That girl of yours marched right into headquarters to get help in reaching you. She knew the Commander in Chief somehow. He gave it to me himself, in case I could find you."

Jared felt a warm wave of pride and longing wash over him. "Where is she now?

Champe shrugged and pushed the envelope across the table to Jared. "Perhaps this will tell you."

Resisting the urge to tear into the letter then and there, Jared asked, "And the second thing?"

Champe put his head down closer to Jared's. "It's why I had to see you in person. I'm told you served with him for years and probably know his habits. I need to know them, too."

Jared looked over at Miller rubbing down the wooden bar. "He knows?"

Champe laughed. "Miller? He knows everything in New York!"

Much later, when the other men in the cell had finally grown quiet for the night, Jared took Melora's letter from his pocket. Pressing out the creases, he made a small cut across the wax and held the scrawled pages up to the light.

The note was very proper and formal. He supposed she was afraid it might fall into the wrong hands. The letter began by saying that she had left the Shippens: "*There are reasons, and you would agree with me. I am sure.*"

"*But mostly I am writing because you must have hope. God would not have acted, saving the forts at West Point and General Washington, if He did not intend for America to be free. And because God showed Himself so clearly for America, you should know that the country is rallying, determination growing like a great wave. The first victory has already occurred, won at a place called King's Mountain in the Carolinas.*"

Jared smiled. She was finally learning some geography.

"*So you must not be rash. We will have our lives together in that noble land I so admire. Once you are exchanged or escape, however, and whenever, you will find me, God willing, with Sarah and Mary. Until then, God bless and Godspeed. Your Melora.*"

He smoothed the paper and held it to his lips. His dear, brave girl. She'd gone back to the Highlands. It was a good decision; they would be happy there. And what news! A victory. The people rallying. Already the dark cell seemed brighter; the stars outside the grated window, closer. Suddenly, Jared found himself trembling; he understood now.

Since his father's death in a snow-bound wilderness, right through Arnold's command to row for the *Vulture*, he'd scorned God for having turned His back, for being unconcerned. Yet all that time God had just been waiting. And then, at the moment of Arnold's great betrayal, He had intervened—saving the country for people like himself and Melora, for people like his father. Humbled and wiping the tears from his face, Jared slipped out of his bunk, fell to his knees, and after praying for guidance in the months and years to come, gave thanks.

CHAPTER 74

October 23, 1780

*The Great House*

"Miss," Jenny said, knocking on Peggy's door. "Your father wants to see you in his study." Receiving no answer, Jenny knocked again. "Miss!" She hadn't time for this. In sheer frustration, she cracked open the door and was surprised to see Peggy wide awake in bed with Neddy beside her. "Miss, didn't you hear me calling you? Your father wants you."

"Tell Father I'm not feeling well."

"He thought you might say that, and I'm to tell you to come downstairs. He has something very important to talk to you about."

"What is it?"

"An article in the newspaper, ma'am."

Peggy played with the baby's fingers. "I don't want to see any newspapers." She looked down at Neddy. "They're cruel and dishonest."

Jenny sighed. With Melora's sudden disappearance there was more than enough work to go around. The washing wasn't started; Cook needed her in the kitchen. In short, her patience was wearing very thin. And now for almost a month everyone in the house had been coddling Peggy as she lay about her room, crying and "unwell." Of course they all felt dreadfully sorry for the young lady, especially since she had been taken to task in the papers for carrying on a correspondence with the English officer. But at some point everyone had to get on with the business of putting one foot in front of the other. "This one you'll want to see. It's written by your husband."

Half an hour later, Peggy sat in her father's study pouring over the reprinted copy of the General's "Address to the Inhabitants of America." Printed first by the *Royal Gazette* in New York, Arnold's explanation of his beliefs and rationale for going to the enemy was now being circulated by the colonial papers.

Perched on a ladder, in the process of converting a poetry shelf to philosophy, Judge Shippen gazed down at his daughter. As a child she delighted in helping with the shelves, holding the ladder, handing him new purchases from the desk, or playing with the figures of Greek gods and goddesses that he used as bookends. The exploits of Zeus and his court filled many a rainy afternoon. But now a very different Peggy sat in his study. At least she was finally out of her room, and more animated than he'd seen her since returning from New York. Every so often she'd look up and ask if he didn't agree with a certain point. And what could he say? No, he hadn't been enamored of the Congress in 1778, the Carlisle Commission had indeed offered everything the colonies originally wanted and more, and certainly he would prefer an alliance with Great Britain rather than with France. But as to some of the General's other statements in the address, such as his never-before-heard disagreement with the Declaration of Independence, these would have to ring very hollow in the ears of many readers, especially the men formerly under his command.

"You see, Father, I told you that the General couldn't be so wrong," Peggy said, finally folding the paper. "This letter clearly shows his concern for America; surely now the public will be convinced."

The Judge slid a new copy of Plotinus in between Plato and Plutarch. "Convinced of what, my dear?"

She looked at him as though he had three heads.

"That he isn't a traitor! That America is better allied with England! When England does finish this horrid war, Benedict will rank as one of the greatest men in the country for his foresight and action."

The Judge stood stunned, fingering a tiny crack in one of his favorite bookends, a statue of the helmeted Athena. Had nothing said by any of them in the past two weeks reached her? "Peggy, I am no clairvoyant, but you cannot believe that public opinion could turn so for the General."

"Why not? It's all true."

The Judge stepped down from the ladder, pondering his next words.

He must make her understand. "I don't want to hurt you, but what the public believes is that the General tried to sell forts and men to line his own pocket. It is one thing to take a political position, even change a political position, but to be paid for it is quite another."

"That was never his motive!"

"Perhaps not, but that's how the world sees it." Placing a stack of poetry books on a side table, the Judge sat down beside Peggy. It was time for his daughter to face reality. "If he wanted to go over to the Crown he should have simply ridden into Manhattan."

"But how would he have lived?"

"The same way all our friends in New York are living right now," the Judge answered, reaching for the sherry decanter and pouring them both a bit. "By monies taken with them or by the largesse of others."

Peggy took a sip of the sherry, unable or unwilling to reply to criticism of her husband.

"And there is that other unfortunate matter," the Judge said, deciding that he might as well say it all.

"You mean the letter from John?"

"No, although that was damaging. Some think because of the *Meschianza* and your friendship with André, that the General's relationship with the Major started there. But that's not what I meant."

"What then?"

"The execution itself. Some are saying it was the General's fault as well."

Peggy held up her hands. "Father, please don't speak of it! I lie in my bed and as hard as I try I can't make the image of John go away. You don't know how much we all liked him, and now for him to be dead, executed..." She pressed her face against the side of the chair. "How did everything go so wrong? All I ever wanted was for things to be like they used to be. All of us here, Grandfather, my uncles and aunts, the cousins, and all our friends."

The Judge thought of his brothers, nieces, nephews, business partners, and friends—everyone now so estranged, scattered, and embittered. The conflict as much a civil war as a revolution. "I know, my child. These times are not what any of us ever expected, that we would all be so divided."

"Father, I don't know what to do."

"What do you mean?"

"About the General. He's alone now in New York and you can't imagine how he suffers when we're apart. Everyone keeps telling me I must forget him...but I can't."

The Judge thought his heart might stop right then. "Peggy, I, your sisters and brother, our friends, we've all been begging President Reed and the Council not to send you away, giving them every possible assurance that you won't write or try to see him, and now you tell me you're thinking of going to him?"

Peggy took a deep breath. "I love him."

The Judge sat back and studied his daughter, another man's wife, mother to a tiny child. For all the barricades he wanted to erect around her, the time of demanding, ordering, and forbidding was past. "Then you must choose. You can choose to live without a husband and raise your child here among your family, your friends, and places that you know. Or you can go to your husband and see where fate takes you and in what society your child will be raised."

She brushed back a tear. "You actually believe people's hearts will never soften toward him, even with time?"

The Judge nodded.

Peggy gripped his hands. "Tell me? What should I do?"

He hesitated, reflecting on the other observation that could only make his daughter more upset. But with all that was swirling around them, this was not the time for subtlety. "I also believe that a man accused of treason will never be fully accepted anywhere. For his family, I have higher hopes."

His words lingered in the air while Peggy sat quietly. It wasn't until she reached for her sherry that he saw how pale she'd become, pale and shivering. "How wrong I've been, Father; how stupid."

Alarmed, the Judge stood and pulled her up into his arms, comforting her as best he could. "You can't blame yourself! You had no part."

"No, Father, I've been so wrong. So horribly wrong. You don't know!"

"Child, I do!" the Judge exclaimed, only to be silenced by a sudden defiance in her expression. Baffled, he gripped her shoulders. "What is it Peggy? What don't I know?"

As the first icy waves of comprehension washed over him, Jenny called from outside to announce luncheon. Footsteps trampled down the staircase, along the halls. While trifling in his library, the war had reached into the tranquility of the sturdy brick walls and claimed another casualty. The one he loved most in the world.

"What do I do, Father?" Peggy asked again, now frighteningly composed. "I don't know what to do."

The Judge, though terrified, spoke with caution and reserve. "I believe you should stay with us. But be aware that your future, at least in part, may rest in the hands of President Reed. And with the death of his wife, he has less tolerance than ever."

"And the other part?"

The Judge gazed up at the pantheon of Gods on the shelves above them. "Whoever decides the destinies of war I suppose."

The clock struck twelve in the foyer. The others would be waiting for them. The others who now, more than ever, required his protection. He looked into his daughter's eyes. "You can never speak of this again. Of what the General did, of his thoughts about the country, or your feelings about the General's intentions. Promise me."

Peggy nodded miserably then leaned in closer. "Do you remember one day when the British were leaving, we were in the garden, and you said we might have to find our way in this war?" She rested her head against his chest. "I tried."

# CHAPTER 75

## Judge Shippen

*I* n the end the decision whether or not to join Arnold was taken out of Peggy's hands. Reed and Matlack had their revenge. On October 27th, the Supreme Executive Council of Pennsylvania resolved, "That the said Margaret Arnold depart this state within fourteen days from the date hereof, and that she do not return again during the continuance of the present war."

The family was stunned. Our Peggy was entitled to a higher fate. My father wrote me daily offering idea after idea, but for once there was nothing he could do.

The days passed slowly. We stayed in, and no one from outside called. Friends of Peggy's, like the Chews and Franks, were frighteningly silent. From time to time she would drift into my study where we would sit, sometimes discuss a book, and sometimes not. A few times, after the others had gone to bed, I found her roaming around the house, picking up a piece of silver here, studying a portrait there. I couldn't fathom how to help her. What were her thoughts, I wondered? That she must be the most unlucky person on earth to have been singled out by Benedict Arnold? That life in New York or London would be glamorous and exciting? Was she already nostalgic for the sounds of our voices, the familiarity of our handwriting on a note? I can tell you I had no idea. But near the end she fell into a kind of stupor.

At last, the day arrived. We all rose early for one last breakfast together, Cook and Jenny joining us at Peggy's request. The baby, having no idea of the enormity of sitting in our dining room perhaps for the last time, chirped merrily through the entire sorry meal. As I was taking her to the border, Edward, Mrs. Shippen, her sisters, and Neddy kissed her goodbye indoors, out of the public view. We were all exhausted, like a family at a funeral, wounded, aimless, beyond despair.

Peggy and I made the trip in silence, holding hands. Once she tried to speak, begging, "Father, please!" I knew she wanted to explain her side, but for her own protection I stopped it immediately. "No, Peggy, you promised." She wept against *my shoulder.*

*I don't think her sorrow was for what she had done, or what Arnold had done, or even for their future. I think it was the shock of a daughter realizing that she was alone now. That no one would ever again in this world care for her, foibles and all, exactly in the same way a family does, as I did.*

*When we reached Paulus Hook, a lieutenant was there to meet us and take Peggy into New York. There was no possibility of Arnold's nearing enemy territory because of the numerous threats against his life. One kidnapping attempt had been made already. As we stood by the coach, she held onto me desperately, as I did to her. But then, with a courteous cough from the Lieutenant, she and the baby were gone.*

*While never speaking of it, her life after she left us was not an easy one. Of course, the conflict came to an end despite Arnold's contributions of burning New London and Richmond. And although initially feted, first by New York and then London, my prediction concerning traitors unfortunately proved to be accurate. The Arnolds were never completely accepted by society, neither in England, nor in Canada during their brief attempt at life within the loyalist colony at St. John. Furthermore, their financial fortunes faltered steadily after the war. Pursuing one plan after another, Arnold wandered the oceans in search of his lost mercantile and military professions. But the General's schemes, as Peggy called them, never seemed to quite work out. At his death she had the double shock of learning that the General left not only staggering debts, but an illegitimate child born during their time together, as well. Only Peggy's head for investments and thrift kept the family from sinking altogether. In time, she managed to pay off all the creditors and see her children settled in society. But all of this extracted its toll. The headaches that troubled her from youth only became more savage as the years passed, owing, she wrote, to her anxiety of mind. Then, just three years after the General's death, she succumbed to the dreaded evil, a cancer. She was only forty-four.*

*Over the course of the marriage, Peggy bore the General four sons and one daughter. And although she always referred to Arnold as the best of all husbands, I believe it was the children who sustained her. Also, for most of her married life, Peggy and I enjoyed a frequent and regular correspondence. We shared investment advice, health remedies, and wrote incessantly about the family, just as my father and I did until the day he died. At least to that degree, I never completely lost her.*

*Following the war, Peggy came home only once. The trip, however, was not a success. Very shortly after her arrival, she was ready to be gone. I think what had been lost outweighed any pleasure she might have felt at being among her old friends and family again.*

*Many times over the years I've been asked about Peggy and the treason. What did she know? What did she do? And my answer is always the same. She knew nothing. She did nothing. But of course this isn't true. Peggy, my dearest child, barely out of her teens, joined with the blackest man of our time to overthrow a country. How can a father take this in? Could she have been so political to have risked everything for her beliefs? Did the chaos of the times send her grasping for safety and security? Or perhaps, might she simply have been in love. As others live with their questions, so in turn do I.*

*The image of Peggy that lingers with me from that October Day at Paulus Hook occurred as the solemn Lieutenant led her away to the waiting coach. Pausing midway she looked back over her shoulder to wave goodbye for the last time, an exile now, frightened and bewildered. Still so very beautiful and still so very young.*

## EPILOGUE

**John André** After the war, André's mother received a pension and his brother was made a Baronet in honor of André's memory. In 1821, John André's body was exhumed and returned to England. He was buried at Westminster Abbey. The inscription on the monument to his memory, which stands in the Nave of the Abbey, reads as follows:

*SACRED to the MEMORY of MAJOR JOHN André, who raised by his merit at an early period of Life to the rank of Adjutant General of the British Forces in America, and employed in an important but hazardous Enterprise fell a Sacrifice to his Zeal for his King and Country on the 2nd of October AD 1780 Aged 29, universally Beloved and esteemed by the Army in which he served and lamented by his FOES. His gracious Sovereign KING GEORGE the Third has caused this Monument to be erected.*

**Margaret and Benedict Arnold** Peggy and Benedict were buried together with their daughter Sophia at Saint Mary's Church in the Battersea Parish
of London. The inscription above the grave records
that Arnold was the *Sometime General in the Army of
George Washington* and that *The two nations whom he
served in turn in the years of their enmity have united
in this memorial as a token of their enduring friendship.*

Benedict Arnold. Engraving by H.B. Hall, published 1879, after John Trumbull
(1756-1843). Credit: National Archives and Records Administration: 1931 –
1932 –NARA – 532921.tif.

Margaret Shippen Arnold. Margaret (Peggy) Shippen Arnold and Child. Portrait circa 1783-1789 attributed to Daniel Gardner (1750-1805). Philadelphia
History Museum at the Atwater Kent, Philadelphia. Available from: Wikimedia Commons, http://commons.wikimedia.org/wiki/File:Peggy_Shippen_
and_daughter.jpg. (accessed November 19, 2014).

**Other Arnold Family:**

**Hannah Arnold** Benedict Arnold had his sister Hannah, along with his oldest three sons, join him in St. John, New Brunswick. Hannah died August 11,
1803, and is buried in Montague, Upper Canada.

Children of Benedict Arnold and Margaret Mansfield:

**Benedict Arnold IV** Arnold IV took a commission in the British army and
was wounded while on duty in Jamaica. Refusing an amputation, he died in
1795 from gangrene.

**Richard Arnold** (1769-1847) and **Henry Arnold** (1772-1826) Both sons
farmed and entered into mercantile activity in Canada.

Children of Benedict Arnold and Peggy Shippen:

**Edward Shippen Arnold** (1780-1813) Neddy became a lieutenant of the
Sixth Bengal Cavalry, and later was Paymaster at Muttra, India. He died in
India in 1813.

**James Robertson Arnold** (1781-1854) As a colonel of the Royal Engineers, James Arnold saw duty in the West Indies and Canada. He later served as an aide to William IV and Queen Victoria, and achieved the rank of Lieutenant-General.

**Sophia Matilda Arnold Phipps** (1785-1828) After her mother's death, Sophia refused an invitation to emigrate to America and live with her Grandfather Shippen. Instead, she joined Neddy in India, married Colonel Pownall Phipps, and had five children.

**George Arnold** (1787-1828) George Arnold became a lieutenant colonel in the Second Bengal Cavalry.

**William Fitch Arnold** (1794-1846) William Arnold became a captain in the Nineteenth Royal Lancers and fought against America in the War of 1812.

Children of Benedict Arnold and Unknown:

**John Sage** All that is known of John Sage is that he was recognized in Arnold's will and like all of Arnold's other children, received land grants in Canada.

**Joseph Brant (Thayendanegea)** In 1784, the British administration in Canada awarded Brant land on the Grand River in Ontario. The Grand River Reservation of the Mohawk (now known as the Six Nations of the Grand River) was established there, settled primarily by Mohawks, but also by members of all the Six Nations in addition to other Indian Loyalists. In 1785, Brant also negotiated funds from Britain for the first Episcopal Church in Upper Canada as well as compensation for Mohawk losses from the war. At his death in 1807, his last words were: "Have pity on the poor Indians; if you can get any influence with the great, endeavor to do them all the good you can."

Joseph Brant. Portrait painted 1776. George Romney (1734-1802). National Gallery of Canada. Available from: Wikimedia Commons, https://en.wikipedia.org/wiki/Joseph_Brant#/media/File:Joseph_Brant_painting_by_George_Romney_1776.jpg. (accessed December 12, 2014).

**Aaron Burr** After the war, Aaron Burr released an account stating that while Peggy stayed with Theodosia Prevost (Burr's future wife) on the way back from West Point, she admitted to Mrs. Prevost that her hysteria at West Point had been all theatrics and that she had brought Arnold to the British side. The Shippen family responded that Burr's story was revenge relating to Peggy's rejection of his advances. Burr later served as a New York State Attorney General, senator from New York, and as the vice-president under Thomas Jefferson. In 1804, he dueled with Alexander Hamilton, killing Hamilton. In mid life he was tried for and acquitted of treason over a scheme to dominate Mexico and parts of the new Louisiana Purchase. Although he returned to a law practice in New York until his death in 1836, he was never able to escape the stigma of Hamilton's death.

Aaron Burr. Portrait painted 1802, John Vanderlyn (1775-1852). New York Historical Society. Available from: Wikimedia Commons, http://commons.wikimedia.org/wiki/File:Vanderlyn_Burr.jpg. (accessed March 28, 2015).

**Benjamin Chew** In 1790, Benjamin Chew returned to public service and was appointed President of the High Court of Errors and Appeals. He died in 1810 at 87.

**Peggy Chew** Peggy Chew married John Eager Howard in 1787 at her family's Third Street residence. George Washington attended the service. Peggy Chew later became first lady of Maryland when her husband was elected governor in 1788.

Peggy Chew. Mrs. John Eager Howard (Peggy Oswald chew) and Her Son, John Eager Howard II.. Portrait painted 1789, Charles Willson Peale, (1741-1827). The Frick Art Reference Library. Available from: Frick Digital Images Archive, item 19710 (accessed March 20, 2015).

**Sir Henry Clinton** After the war, Clinton returned to England and wrote two volumes about his campaigns in America. He became the governor of Gibraltar in 1794, and died there in 1795.

Sir Henry Clinton. Portrait painted 1777, John Smart (1741-1811). National Institute of American History and Democracy. Available from: Wikimedia Commons, http://www.artchive.com/web_gallery/J/John-Smart/General-Sir-Henry-Clinton-1730-95-c.1777.html (accessed November 18, 2014).

**David and Becky Franks** David Franks was arrested by the state of Pennsylvania in October of 1780. Later that year, both father and daughter were exiled to New York. For a time after the war David Franks lived in England, but eventually returned to America where he died of yellow fever during the epidemic of 1793. Woodford, a country estate at one time owned by David Franks, is still standing in Philadelphia's Fairmount Park and is open to the public.

Becky married Lt. Colonel Henry Johnson of the Seventeenth Foot Regiment and after the war moved to England. In 1816, Becky is said to have told a journalist that she wished she'd been a patriot.

Rebecca (Becky) Franks. Courtesy of Naomi Wood Collection at Woodford Mansion. Permission by Larry Berger, Trustee, The Naomi Wood Trust. From: The Woodford Mansion, http://www.woodfordmansion.org/images/peale.jpg (accessed March 31, 2015).

**Major David Solebury (Salisbury) Franks** On November 2, 1780, Franks was completely exonerated of any complicity in the Arnold affair by a Court of Inquiry at West Point. He was later promoted to Lieutenant Colonel. After the war he was sent by Congress to Paris with the ratification of the peace treaty. He also died of yellow fever in 1793, and, although Jewish, was taken by a friend for burial in the Christ Church graveyard in Philadelphia.

David Solebury (Salisbury) Franks. Print of miniature painted 1778 by Charles Willson Peale (1741-1827). Available from: The Miriam and Ira D. Wallach Division of Art, Prints and Photographs: Print Collection, The New York Public Library. "David Solebury Franks." New York Public Library Digital Collections. http://digitalcollections. nypl.org/items/510d47dc- 52df-a3d9-e040-e00a18064a99 (accessed March 5, 2015).

**Grace Galloway** Grace Galloway's mental state continued to decline and her travails are painfully reported in her diary. After being forced from her home, which was appropriated for the use of President Joseph Reed and his family in 1779, she lived with various friends until her death in 1782. She never reunited with her family. Though confiscated, Grace willed her property to her daughter Elizabeth. More than twenty years later after the death of Joseph Galloway, the Pennsylvania Supreme Court declared that his attainder for treason did not apply to his wife's real estate and that her property belonged to her heirs. A few months before her death, she wrote the following to her daughter: *"I am yet in Philadelphia where I have neither been permitted to live in peace, and as I never meddle with politics, I hope never to give any just reason of offense...You ask me how I live. I cannot now answer that question, but only assure you that I neither borrow nor am dependent on anybody. Nor will the state allow me one farthing... Want of health and to save your inheritance alone detains me. If by it I save my child all will be right. ..Indeed, my dear, I am not like the same person in anything but my unbounded affection for you and my solicitude for your welfare."*

Grace Galloway. Oil portrait painted about 1750 by Thomas Stokes from an original drawing. Available from: http://genius.com/4715259 (accessed November 19, 2014).

**Alexander Hamilton** Alexander Hamilton, along with James Madison and John Jay, wrote *The Federalist Papers*, served as the first Secretary of the Treasury, and was killed in a duel with Aaron Burr in 1804.

Alexander Hamilton. Painted 1806, John Trumbull (1756-1843) after Giuseppe Cerracchi (1751-1801). National Portrait Gallery, Smithsonian Institution; Gift of Henry Cabot Lodge. From: National Portrait Gallery: NPG.79.216 (accessed March 7, 2015).

**Sir William Howe** In an attempt to silence those questioning his conduct of the war in America, Sir William requested an investigation upon his return to England. The board appointed to conduct the inquiry, however, never arrived at a conclusion and disbanded. Howe later served in the war against France, was appointed the governor of Plymouth, and died there in 1814.

Sir William Howe. Mezzotint, 1777, by Richard Purcell aka Charles Corbutt (ca 1736-ca1766). Anne S.K. Brown Military History Collection, at Brown University Library. From: Brown University Library, https://repository.library.brown.edu/studio/item/bdr:227278/ (accessed March 11, 2015).

**Timothy Matlack** Served as Secretary to the Supreme Executive Council until 1782. In later years he inspected Pennsylvania's navigable waters, served as the Master of the Rolls of Pennsylvania, prothonotary of the US District Court of Philadelphia, and as a caretaker of Independence Hall.

Timothy Matlack. Painted circa 1790 by Charles Willson Peale (1741-1827). Museum of Fine Arts, Boston, A Shuman Collection-Abraham Shuman Fund. From: Museum of Fine Arts, Boston online data base, http://www.mfa.org/collections/object/timothy-matlack-35332 (accessed March 7, 2015).

**Robert Morris** Morris, known as the Financier of the American Revolution and one of the richest men in America, served as the National Superintendent of Finance from 1781 to 1784 and as a senator from 1789 to 1795. Impoverished by land speculation, he was sent to Debtor's Prison from 1798 to 1801 and died in 1806. Lemon Hill, a mansion in Philadelphia's Fairmount Park, was originally built by Morris as a farmhouse known as the 'The Hills.'

Robert Morris. Photographic print of portrait painted circa 1782 by Charles Willson Peale (1741-1827). Pennsylvania Academy of Fine Arts. Image available from US Library of Congress Prints and Photographs Division cph.3a07081.

**John Paulding, Isaac Van Wart, David Williams** Congress rewarded André's captors with gold medals and lifetime pensions. When, in 1817, the three men applied for an increase in their pensions, Benjamin Tallmadge led the effort to deny the request. Casts of the three mens' heads, made during their lives, are on display in Cooperstown, New York.

**Charles Willson Peale** Peale returned to painting after the war, although he also pursued a new interest in natural law. In addition, he designed mechanical farm equipment, founded an institution in Philadelphia for the study of natural law, and made false teeth. Today he is considered by some to be the pre-eminent painter of his generation.

Charles Willson Peale. Portrait painted circa 1768 by Benjamin West (1738 -1820). Available from: Wikimedia Commons, http://commons.wikimedia.org/wiki/File:Charles_Willson_Peale_by_Benjamin_West.jpg. (accessed March 31, 2015)

**Joseph Reed** After the death of his beloved **Hettie**, Joseph Reed finished his three-year term as President, although with flagging spirits. In 1781 he returned to his legal practice and in 1784 visited England for health reasons. He died in 1785 at age forty-four. He is buried at the Arch Street Presbyterian Church in Philadelphia.

Joseph Reed. Engraving by John Sartain (1808-1897) after Charles Willson Peale (1741-1827). The Miriam and Ira D. Wallach Division of Art, Prints and Photographs: Print Collection, The New York Public Library. "Jos. Reed, president." New York Public Library Digital Collections. http://digitalcollections.nypl.org/items/510d47df-2cef-a3d9-e040-e00a18064a99 (accessed March 13, 2015).

Esther Deberdt Reed. Portrait painted by Charles Willson Peale (1741-1827). Frick Art Reference Library. Available from: Wikimedia Commons, http://commons.wikimedia.org/wiki/File:Esther_de_Berdt_Reed_by_Charles_Peale.png (accessed March 11, 2015)

**Beverley Robinson** Like so many others, Beverley Robinson emigrated to England after the war with his wife and family. He was granted 17,000 pounds (the equivalent of $80,000 in 1840's dollars) as a partial compensation for his wife's estate in New York which had been included in the Confiscation Act of New York. He was said never to have found happiness in England, and died there in 1792.

**Edward Shippen IV** In 1784, Edward Shippen IV received a commission as justice of the peace and president of the Court of Common Pleas for Philadelphia County. In 1791 he was appointed to the Pennsylvania Supreme Court, and from 1799 until 1805, served as Chief Justice of Pennsylvania. He outlived Peggy by only two years, dying in 1806.

Edward Shippen, IV. Portrait painted 1796 by Gilbert Stuart (1755-1828). Image courtesy of the National Gallery of Art, Washington.

Other Shippen Family:

**Margaret Francis Shippen** In 1794, **Mrs. Shippen** died from a 'recurrent disorder.' In 1786, Peggy wrote to her father that she was "extremely uneasy about my beloved Mama. Her life has hitherto been marked with but few real misfortunes." However, in 1788, she wrote to Betsey that "She (Mrs. Shippen) must suffer extremely from the loss of her limbs."

Margaret Francis Shippen. Painting by Charles Willson Peale (1741-1827). Courtesy, The Winterthur Library: Joseph Downs collection of Manuscripts and Printed Ephemera.

**Betsey and Neddy Burd** continued to prosper after the war, with Neddy also managing or helping with many of the family affairs. In 1798 the couple built Ormiston, a country house not far from Mount Pleasant, the home Arnold bought for Peggy. Both houses still stand in Fairmount Park. Betsey and Neddy lived until 1828 and 1833 respectively.

**Edward** became a physician, married Elizabeth Footman in 1785, and raised a large family. He also borrowed a large sum of money from Peggy and Arnold, which was never repaid. Judge Shippen supported Edward and his family until the time of the former's death. In 1801, Judge Shippen described Edward's situation to Peggy as follows: "As to your brother, he is not possessed of a single shilling; he is indeed incapable of supporting his large family of children ...without my continued contributions. Without them he and they must indeed starve." Edward died in 1809.

**Polly** married Dr. William McIlvaine, in 1785. She died in 1831.

**Sally** married Thomas Lea in 1787, and after her husband's early death returned home to live with Judge Shippen. She declined a proposal from a gentleman with a great fortune, who was also much to her taste. Judge Shippen, in a letter to Peggy, mentioned that the suitor was encumbered with many children and that Sally "wisely foresaw evil at a distance." She lived until 1831.

Sara Shippen (Mrs. Thomas Lea). Portrait c1798 by Gibert Stuart (1755-1828.) Image courtesy of the National Gallery of Art, Washington.

**Joshua Hett Smith** Smith was found not guilty in the matter of Arnold's treason. Later, he was granted an allowance from Sir Henry Clinton and moved to England. After the war, he returned to New York and wrote a biography of John André entitled, *An Authentic Narrative of the Causes Which Led to the Death of Major André, Adjutant-General of His Majesty's Forces in North America.*

Joshua Hett Smith. Illustration from a portrait by Trumbull (1756-1843). Available from: https://archive.org/stream/crisisofrevoluti00abbauoft#page/n27/mode/2up (accessed March 13, 2015).

**William Smith** For a period of time after the war, Smith took up residency in England where he came to the attention of Sir Guy Carleton. Carleton, later known as Lord Dorchester, had Smith appointed Chief Justice of Canada. He died there in 1793.

William Smith. Portrait by unknown. From the estate of Sir Campbell Stuart (England). Available from: http://www.uelac.org/education/QuebecResource/images/c103666k_lg.jpg (accessed March 16, 2015).

**Benjamin Tallmadge.** Tallmadge served in many capacities during the Revolutionary War, including head of intelligence for Washington. Although some have suggested that he was forewarned of the André-Arnold plot, there is no known intelligence to support the idea. At the war's end, Benjamin Tallmadge moved to Litchfield, Connecticut, and became involved in commerce. He also served as a Congressman from Connecticut from 1801 to 1817. Years after the war he wrote: *"I became so deeply attached to Major André that I can remember no instance where my affections were so fully absorbed in one man. When I saw him swinging under the gibbet it seemed for a time as if I could not support it."*

Benjamin Tallmadge. Portrait c1800 by Ezra Ames (1768-1836). Available from: Wikimedia Commons, http://commons.wikimedia.org/wiki/File:Benjamin_Tallmadge_by_Ezra_Ames.JPG#/media/File:Benjamin_Tallmadge_by_Ezra_Ames.JPG (accessed March 16, 2015).

**Tench Tilghman** Following the war, Tench Tilghman married, and entered into a successful business partnership with Robert Morris. Upon his death in 1786, George Washington wrote the following to Thomas Jefferson: *"Colonel Tilghman, who was formerly of my family, died lately, and left as fair a reputation as ever belonged to a human character."*

Tench Tilghman. Etched by H.B. Hall, N.Y. 1869. The Miriam and Ira D. Wallach Division of Art, Prints and Photographs: Print Collection, The New York Public Library. "Tench Tilghman" New York Public Library Digital Collections. http://digitalcollections.nypl.org/items/510d47da-2a5e-a3d9-e040-

**Richard Varick** Varick, like David Salisbury Franks, was found 'unimpeachable' in his conduct by a court of inquiry at West Point on November 2, 1780. By direction of George Washington, he went on to organize and copy all of the papers of the Continental Army. These are now located in the Library of Congress. After the war he became recorder, speaker, and attorney general of New York, and the mayor of New York City from 1789 to 1801.

Richard Varick. Richard Varick by Unknown. Available from: Wikimedia Commons, http://commons.wikimedia. org/wiki/File:RichardVarick.jpg (accessed March 17, 2015).

**George Washington** After the war, Washington retired to Mount Vernon until he was asked to preside at the Constitutional Convention in 1787. In 1789 he was elected the first president of the United States.

George Washington. Portrait 1776 by Charles Willson Peale (1741-1827). George Washington, 1776. Oil on canvas, 44 x 38 5/16 in. (111.7 x 97.3 cm). Brooklyn Museum, Dick S. Ramsay Fund, 34.1178. Available from: http://www.brooklynmuseum.org/opencollection/objects/450/George_Washington/image/133171/image (accessed March 17, 2015).

## Author's Note and Acknowledgements

When I was in elementary school, I read a reference about poor Peggy Shippen, a lovely girl from a prominent family, who innocently and tragically married Benedict Arnold just months before his betrayal of the country during the Revolutionary War. That a lovely girl from a prominent family could have the terrible misfortune of marrying America's best known traitor greatly upset my dreamy, romantic preteen self. The memory stayed with me.

Years later when our family moved to upstate New York, I was between jobs, in search of a project, and Peggy came back to mind. I remembered that she was from New York State. Great. Perfect. I was now living in the region where she had lived, and after so many years, finally had time to look into her life. Heading over to our local library, I found Williard Sterne Randall's, *Benedict Arnold: Patriot and Traitor,* and discovered that Peggy was not from New York, but Philadelphia, and that Peggy and Benedict's story was much more fascinating than any piece of history I had ever encountered. I owe so much to Randall's book as an encyclopedic reference guide to both Peggy's and Benedict's stories. For anyone interested in Arnold, Peggy, or a long view of the American Revolutionary War, Randall's book is a gift.

In the fiction I've read about Peggy, her motives for helping Arnold range from greed, fear of losing her looks, to a tyrannical, slutty ambition. In fact, Peggy was fair and slight, with dark enigmatic eyes, and was regarded as one of the most beautiful women in America and Britain. Educated in business and the classics at home by Judge Shippen, she was also reported to be quiet and serious, as well as devoted to her father and to her sister, Elizabeth. And, along with her father, her brother, and between one fourth to one fifth of the white residents of the colonies at the time of the Revolutionary War, she was a loyalist.

I think we often tend to see the Revolution as a simple, clean war, fought and won for the right reasons. We overlook or fail to understand that it was a bloody, scary *civil* war with colonists dividing along patriot and nonpatriot lines—occurring alongside the bloody, scary rebellion of America against Britain. One of the reasons for this internal division was that an essential objective of the rebellion changed between the first Continental Congress in 1774, and July 1776, when independence was declared. As late as March 1775, one month before the battles at Lexington and Concord, Benjamin Franklin was quoted as saying to William Pitt, the Earl of Chatham, that "I've never heard in any conversation from any person drunk or sober the least expression of a wish for separation or hint that such a thing would be advantageous to America."

The origins of the rebellion, as well as the first resistance efforts, sprang from a widely supported desire for American economic autonomy along with protection of rights guaranteed in colonial charters. Understandably, then, more conservative, as well as disinterested, segments of the population had some problems when the objective turned to outright independence. For many people, protests and boycotts over trade and tax policy were one thing, whereas relinquishing membership in the British Empire for an unknown, unformed, and undefined "what" of a country was quite another. When Sir William Howe gave up his occupation of Philadelphia in June 1778, he took several thousand scared Loyalists and Quakers with him to New York. And although only two out of the 400 persons suspected of being a Loyalist in Philadelphia were executed, 121 estates were confiscated—usually without the guilt of these owners ever having been established in a court of law. With this background it seemed to me completely reasonable that Peggy's loyalism, together with a seemingly genuine love for her husband, would have been sufficient reason for her to help Arnold.

In addition to keeping Peggy's story as close to what is known of the actual history, I did the same with all the characters who were not fictional (the fictional characters being Melora, Jared, Jenny, Cook, Mary, and Sarah), as well as Judge Shippen's war reporting. The essential history is known and as I wrote above, absolutely compelling. To have changed, embellished, or ignored the way actual events occurred would have been unfair to anyone interested in the Arnolds' story, or the very complicated and layered aspects of the Revolutionary War.

In addition to the Randall biography of Arnold mentioned above, I found the following books to be of great help in understanding this fascinating history: *Angels in the Whirlwind: The Triumph of the American Revolution,* by Benson Bobrick; *The Price of Loyalty: Tory Writings of the Revolutionary Era,* by Catherine S. Crary; *Weathering the Storm: Women of the American Revolution,* by Elizabeth Evans; *The Traitor and the Spy: Benedict Arnold and John André,* by James Thomas Flexner; *Washington: The indispensable Man,* by James Thomas Flexner; *A Portrait of the Irish in America,* by William D. Griffin; *Major John André: A Gallant in Spy's Clothing,* by Robert McConnell Hatch; *Colonial Pennsylvania: A History,* by Joseph E. Illick; *With the British Army in Philadelphia: 1777-1778,* by John W. Jackson; *The Winter Soldiers,* by Richard M. Ketchum; *Portrait of an Early American Family,* by Randolph Shipley Klein; *George Washington's War: The Saga of the American Revolution,* by Robert Leckie; *Benedict Arnold Revolutionary Hero: An American Warrior Reconsidered,* by James Kirby Martin; *The Glorious Cause: The American Revolution 1764-1789,* by Robert Middlekauf; *A State Divided: Opposition in Pennsylvania to the American Revolution,* by Anne M. Ousterhout; *A Little Revenge: Benjamin Franklin and His Son,* by Williard Sterne Randall; *Joseph Reed: A Moderate in the American Revolution,* by John F. Roche; *Biographical Sketches of Loyalists of the American Revolution with an Historical Essay,* by Lorenzo Sabine; *To Serve Faithfully and Well: Labor and Indentured Servants in Pennsylvania, 1682-1800,* by Sharon V. Salinger; *Rebels and Redcoats: The American Revolution Through the Eyes of Those Who Fought it and Lived It,* by George F. Scheer and Hugh F. Rankin; *Colonists in Bondage: White Servitude and Convict Labor in America, 1607-1776,* by Abbot Emerson Smith; *Birthplace of an Army: A Study of the Valley Forge Encampment,* by John B. B. Trussel Jr; *Secret History of the American Revolution: An Account of the Conspiracy of Benedict Arnold and Numerous Others,* by Carl Van Doren; *Robert Morris-Revolutionary Financier,* by Clarence L. Ver Steeg; *Life of Margaret Shippen-Wife of Benedict Arnold,* by Lewis Burd Walker; *The History of the Jews of Philadelphia: 1517-1957,* by Edwin Wolf and Maxwell Whiteman.

I want to thank the people who helped me with the research and writing of this book. First, I want to thank the library staff at both Hartwick College and the State University of New York at Oneonta for many far-flung interlibrary loan requests as well as patient assistance with microfilm from the predigital age. Shelley Wallace, former Archivist at Hartwick, as well as the late Dr. Richard Haan, Professor Emeritus of History at Hartwick, provided valuable research assistance. Neil Ronk, Chief Guide at Christ Church in Philadelphia, spent hours patiently describing Philadelphia during the Revolutionary War and was a very welcome early enthusiast of the project. Melora Wolfe provided enormously helpful structural and editorial help on the voluminous first drafts. Ginnah Howard read several drafts, offering advice on each as well as ongoing and much needed support and encouragement. Ginnah is a friend to many writers; I count my blessings that I am one of them. Susan Brunswick, Kathryn Anderson, and Gail Henry also read and commented on various drafts. Reading drafts takes time and patience. I appreciate their generosity. I am also deeply indebted to reference librarians at the Frick Museum, New York Public Library, and the National Gallery of Art, as well as to Christopher Lewis, Media Librarian at American University in Washington,

DC, for helping me navigate the burgeoning digital access world. I also thank Larry Berger, Trustee of The Naomi Wood Trust, for permission to use the Rebecca Franks portrait in the epilogue.

Then, there are Valerie Haynes and Jane Higgins of Illume Publications. Valerie guided every aspect of the book coming into print, and Jane made it beautiful. I cannot thank them enough. Final thanks are to my husband David, a mindful observer and fine writer, who encouraged me to take a manuscript written long ago to a published form.

Any errors are, of course, my own.

Forrest Bachner
Washington, D.C.
November 2015

**About the Author**

Forrest Bachner holds a degree in history and worked as a research analyst for nearly twenty years. She lives in Washington DC and Oneonta NY with her husband.

Made in the USA
Middletown, DE
10 May 2018